Copyrighted Material

Gateway to War Copyright © 2019 by Variant Publications, Hopper Creative Group

Book design and layout copyright © 2019 by JN Chaney

This novel is a work of fiction. Names, characters, places, and incidents are either products of the author's imagination or used fictitiously. Any resemblance to actual events, locales, or persons, living, dead, or undead, is entirely coincidental.

All rights reserved

No part of this publication can be reproduced or transmitted in any form or by any means, electronic or mechanical, without permission in writing.

Version 2.0

1st Edition

GATEWAY TO WAR

BOOK 3 IN THE RUINS OF THE GALAXY SERIES

J.N. CHANEY

CHRISTOPHER HOPPER

JOIN THE RUINS TRIBE

Visit **ruinsofthegalaxy.com** today and join the tribe. Once there, you can sign up for our reader group, join our Facebook community, and find us on Twitter and Instagram.

If you'd like to email us with comments or questions, we respond to all emails sent to ruinsofthegalaxy@gmail.com, and love to hear from our readers.

See you in the Ruins!

GET A FREE BOOK

J.N. Chaney posts updates, official art, previews, and other awesome stuff on his website. You can also follow him on **Instagram**, **Facebook**, and **Twitter**.

He also created a special **Facebook group** called "JN Chaney's Renegade Readers" specifically for readers to come together and share their lives and interests, discuss the series, and speak directly to me. Please check it out and join whenever you get the chance!

For updates about new releases, as well as exclusive promotions, visit his website, jnchaney.com and sign up for the VIP mailing list. Head there now to receive a free copy of *The Other Side of Nowhere*.

https://www.subscribepage.com/organic

Get a Free Book

Enjoying the series? Help others discover the Ruins of the Galaxy series by leaving a review on Amazon.

CONTENTS

Chapter 1	1
Chapter 2	17
Chapter 3	27
Chapter 4	37
Chapter 5	47
Chapter 6	61
Chapter 7	71
Chapter 8	83
Chapter 9	93
Chapter 10	107
Chapter 11	121
Chapter 12	131
Chapter 13	147
Chapter 14	157
Chapter 15	171
Chapter 16	181
Chapter 17	191
Chapter 18	199
Chapter 19	211
Chapter 20	223
Chapter 21	235
Chapter 22	247
Chapter 23	259
Chapter 24	271
Chapter 25	281
Chapter 26	291
Chapter 27	307
Chapter 28	317
Chapter 29	331
Chapter 30	345

Chapter 31	359
Chapter 32	373
Chapter 33	383
Chapter 34	401
Chapter 35	415
Chapter 36	427
Chapter 37	443
List of Main Characters	451
Join the Ruins Tribe	461
Get a Free Book	463
About the Authors	465

1

"You do know that you're idiots for coming with me, right?" Magnus stood over Flow and Cheeks, who lay on recovery beds, both coming out of heavy sedation. "Your careers are over."

"No offense, LT," Flow said, his voice groggy, "but you messed our careers up a long time ago. Something about a move to Recon that made sure we wouldn't make rank easily."

"Pain in the ass," Cheeks added from his bed.

Sick bay on Rohoar's starship was more spacious than any on a Repub vessel, presumably to accommodate Jujari physiology. The ship had only been in subspace for a little over two hours, having left Oorajee and begun the voyage to Worru, and already Flow and Cheeks were looking a bit better. The two Recon Marines bore several sensors on their bare skin, while their bodies were covered with white blankets.

Cheeks looked over at Flow. "Guess we're just gonna have to insist on free beer for life."

Flow chuckled then winced.

Magnus liked hearing himself called "LT" again—a shortened version of his rank of Lieutenant. But to Magnus, the title was more than just a nickname. It meant he was among family. And he didn't want to put his family in harm's way any more than he already had.

"I mean it, boys." Magnus rubbed the back of his neck. "I'm really not sure you thought this one through." He muttered, "Probably shouldn't have given you the option."

"Hold up right there, LT." Flow's dark-skinned face turned hard. "You *owed* us the option."

"Damn straight, you did," Cheeks said. "Bustin' our balls on some suicide mission to protect a Luma goddess who decides to have tea with a Jujari king. Who knew *that* would blow up in our faces."

Cheeks's sarcasm wouldn't offend anyone on the team. They'd all known the op had been a mistake from the beginning, and Cheeks's appearance would attest to that, probably for the rest of his life. The right side of his face would need cellular reconstruction therapy, including a new ear. His days as a ladies' man were over until he got proper medical care, and even after that, he'd always have scarring. Then again, knowing Cheeks, he'd find a way to work the situation to his advantage.

"Listen, boys…"

"Hold up, LT." Flow struggled to prop himself up on his elbows. "We all know this stopped being about the Corps years ago. It's about brotherhood. No one gets left behind. And if someone is abandoned by the Repub, that's the same as being left behind."

"OTF, baby," Cheeks added.

Magnus ignored their comments. "If I send you both on a shuttle, you can say that I abducted you. They'll be forced to drop the charges. But as it is, you're aiding and abetting a military deserter turned fugitive. You'll most likely be tried for treason."

"That's if they catch us, baby," Cheeks said.

"Call it whatever you want, LT." Flow raised his chin. "It ain't changing my mind."

"Mine neither, LT."

Magnus sniffed then pursed his lips. These two were as good as any brothers-in-arms could ever be. He didn't deserve their respect. They'd been through a lot together and seen a lot of action. But they still didn't know about everything Magnus had done in his past. *If they knew, they wouldn't be so loyal.*

"Fine," Magnus said. "As long as we're clear."

"Crystal."

"Like a see-through dress," Cheeks added.

Magnus smiled. It was good to be reunited with them. He only wished Mouth had survived. The knowledge that the Fearsome Four no longer existed as a group put a pang in his chest that wouldn't leave anytime soon. One more Marine had been lost to the Repub's mounting indiscretion and foolhardy objectives.

"So…" Flow lowered himself back down, catching his breath. "Mind filling us in on what we've gotten ourselves mixed up in exactly?"

"Yeah," Cheeks said. "Why you got a rap sheet with the Corps all of a sudden?"

Magnus took a deep breath. "It's complicated."

Cheeks grimaced, lying back down again with a sigh. "Man, that's what all the girls say when they're done with you. You don't gotta do us like that, LT."

"I don't want to do you at all, Cheeks. No one does, last I heard."

Flow let out a laugh, then said, "He got you there, Cheeks."

Magnus smiled and reached for one of the examination stools in the corner. He sat down and rubbed the back of his neck again. "I don't even know where to start."

"How about when things went sideways in the doggy king's palace?" Flow suggested.

"When things went sideways…" The incident felt so long ago. But how many days had it been? Barely two weeks? "That's as good a place as any."

Magnus shared the harrowing tale with his men, leaving out as much as possible about Awen because… because it wasn't relevant to his men, though Cheeks, the hopeless romantic—or was he just a pervert?—would have insisted otherwise. He also left off anything that would just sound too fantastical to believe, especially the parts about Piper.

"So… you make it back to Abimbola's hideout, even more of a war hero than you already are…" Flow said. "I still don't get why the Repub wants you so bad. What—do they think you killed the senator or something?"

Magnus shrugged. "Your guess is as good as mine, Flow. But there are easier ways to take out a senator than sending a Recon Marine into an unmarked Bull Wraith, escaping with some crew, and crash landing on Oorajee. I can tell you one thing, however—something doesn't feel right about all of this."

"All of what?" Flow searched Magnus's face. "You mean the whole op on Oorajee? You think it was a setup?"

"Well, I know *we* didn't plant those explosives in the mwadim's palace, and the Tawnhack didn't either. In fact, I don't think any of the Jujari tribes did. It was too calculated, too precise. Those hyenas may be many things, but they sure as hell ain't precise."

"Who's that leave, then?" Flow asked.

Magnus shook his head. "I don't have that figured out."

"You think someone at the top is gunning for you?" Cheeks asked.

"Like I said, boys, I dunno. But if I had to place a bet, yeah, it feels like a setup."

Flow rotated his index finger in circles. "Can we go back a second? What was that about the Tawnhack and Jujari tribes? You lost me there."

Magnus recalled the conversation he'd had with Abimbola about this, suddenly realizing his Marines were still in the dark. "Not all the Jujari are the same."

"Like hell they're not!" Cheeks blurted out.

"Cheeks," Magnus said, leveling him a glare that said he meant business.

"Sorry, LT, it's just—"

"Rohoar's tribe are the Tawnhack… the largest and most revered tribe. But the ones who took you… those were the Selskrit."

"You're saying one's good and one's bad?" Flow asked. "Are you some sorta Jujari whisperer now that you got yourself a pup?"

Magnus didn't want to snap at his men, but he also didn't want the term "Jujari whisperer" to stick, nor did he want the slang term "pup" being used against Rohoar.

"I'm not saying I've got them figured out," Magnus admitted. "But I am saying that Rohoar and his kin helped save your lives. And mine, for that matter. So you can hate them all you want inside, but you sure as hell are going to be grateful on the outside. We will all show them respect and honor. Copy?"

Flow and Cheeks both nodded.

"Good." Magnus sat back down, breathing a sigh of relief. Once a nickname formed in the Recon, it was next to impossible to shut it down. Fortunately, this one had died before it started, and without much of a fight. More importantly, however, Magnus had a chance to speak his mind about

Rohoar and the Tawnhack. It was the first time he'd admitted as much to anyone besides himself. It was hard to do, but Rohoar had given him reason enough to begin to doubt his biases.

"Hey." Flow reached out for Magnus's hand and grasped it tightly around the thumb. "And about not being able to come back for us sooner... we get it. Don't worry."

Magnus squeezed back. "Thanks, Flow. I... appreciate that."

"But if you ever do it again," Cheeks added, "we're coming after you."

"I'd expect nothing less." Magnus chuckled and released Flow's hand. "Now it's your turn. How, by all the mystics, did you survive?"

Whatever life Flow had in his eyes faded as he stared past Magnus. Cheeks looked away too. That, right there, told Magnus a lot. He'd fought enough battles and lived through enough hell to know mental anguish when he saw it. Moreover, he knew Flow was understating things when he replied, "It was bad, LT. Real bad."

Cheeks nodded, and his eyes focused on some faraway place. Magnus didn't break the silence. He just waited.

When Flow didn't say anything, Magnus said, "It can wait, brothers. We have time."

Flow took a deep breath then looked up at Magnus. "No, it can't. You need to know. The blasts... they took out half the platoons."

"Half?" Magnus rocked backward. "But that's..."

"Like I said, bad. I know." Flow cleared his throat. "But that's just the beginning. Mouth was the only other operator to make it from Charlie Platoon. We looked for your body, but…" Flow looked to be fighting back some pretty raw emotions, maybe from the pain meds he was on. Magnus had never seen him like this. "Your TACNET signature was gone. We figured you'd been vaporized.

"Anyway, we rallied to Captain Wainright and managed to find several more civilians. That alone was a shock. Their Unity splick must have saved them or something…" Flow's eyes glazed over. "But they would have been better off if they'd died in the blast."

Another long silence filled sick bay. A tear left Flow's left eye and slid down his cheek. The man looked childlike.

"What happened next?"

"Jujari reinforcements came at us hard. No one really knew what was happening. Just lots of blaster fire and screams. We tried calling for evac, but the LZ on the platform was too hot. So Wainright ordered us to the secondary exfil."

"Zulu Niner," Magnus offered, referring to the mission's alternate landing zone. He hoped to reassure his friend that he'd been there too and had heard the order. "Three klicks north of the city."

Flow looked at Magnus with the hint of a smile. "That's right, LT. So you—"

"It was the last thing I heard. Tried getting there myself, but… well, you know my story."

"Right, right." Flow nodded, his gaze drifting back to the terror of his memories.

"Go on." Magnus touched the Marine's shoulder.

"We were able to hold the Jujari back. Turns out they were just as shaken as we were. Their command structure was a mess. It gave us the break we needed to get out of the building and start moving north. We kept the civilians in between us. Maybe a dozen of them when we started. At first, no one fired on us. The city was too horrified by the explosion in the mwadim's tower. We passed several Jujari who just stared skyward, oblivious to twenty-five Galactic Republic Marines and civilians walking right by them. It was surreal.

"Eventually, though, that changed. Word musta spread that we'd killed their mwadim. I mean, I'm just guessing. The way they came after us… it was… they were…"

Magnus looked from Flow to Cheeks. The men were visibly shaking. *Mystics, they've seen some horrible splick.* The mental wounds of battle had done their worst, and Magnus knew the scars would be there for years to come. *Dammit.*

"We held out as long as we could. Made it about two klicks. Then our energy mags ran out. That's when they attacked. They came at us like demons." Flow smashed his palms against his face and smeared hot tears across his skin. "Everyone fought hard, but so many… so many died. Mouth, he—" Flow choked. He turned his head away to cough. Then he swore as he tried to catch his breath.

"He didn't make it," Magnus concluded. "Copy that."

"Lost most of the civies too. Eventually, the Jujari incapacitated us. When we woke up, we were bound in a small room. They kept moving us from one place to another over the next few days, asking to speak to our generals. Always our generals. We tried to explain that we couldn't reach them, but it was no use. So they tortured us… then killed us… then brought us back to life to do it again."

Magnus blinked. "Say again?" But Flow was unresponsive. "Hey, Flow. You with me?" Magnus snapped his fingers in front of his face. "Flow!"

Flow's eyes fluttered open. "You remember all those rumors about how they bleed out their prisoners for weeks?" He was growing manic, his eyes starting to dart left and right. Magnus wondered if he should call for Valerie.

Flow reached out and grabbed Magnus's chest armor. "You remember? Well… it's true. It's all true. Only they didn't give us weeks. The 'living blood,' they call it. They bled us out in a few days then brought us back."

Magnus stared at Flow, the man's bloodshot eyes sending a wave of fear through Magnus's chest. "Easy, Flow. Come on —let's get you settled." Magnus gently pressed his sergeant's shoulders back down, but the big man resisted him.

"Hey, what are you doing to him?" Cheeks yelled.

Aww, splick. Magnus felt Flow bucking under his hands. *This isn't good.* "Cheeks, you stay where you are. Copy?"

"Who do you think you are, man? Get your hands off him!"

"Cheeks, it's me, Magnus!" Just then, Flow tried to swing

his legs off his bed. "No, buddy. No, no, no. Listen, this is Magnus. You gotta relax, pal. Hold tight."

"I said get your hands off him!" Cheeks yelled, attempting to climb off his bed.

"Cheeks! Stay where you are!"

But Cheeks kept trying to stand anyway, only to slip off his bed and collapse in a heap. His head bounced off the floor with a wet crack. He was out cold.

"Dammit!" Magnus yelled, still struggling with Flow. "Flow, listen, you gotta settle. No one's gonna hurt you. You hear me? You're safe." Despite the man's injuries and fatigue, adrenaline was giving Flow a definite advantage. His legs thrashed the covers off the bed. Magnus could barely hold onto him. The best thing he could do was to try a sleeper hold, and not even that worked.

"What in all the cosmos is going on in here?" said a voice from across sick bay. Magnus looked up to see Valerie striding in from the entrance.

"Could use some help here, Doctor Stone." Magnus was in a stymied arm lock with Flow, both men red-faced and sweating.

Valerie gave Cheeks a quick glance on the floor and then opened a cavity on the far wall. She produced a small molecular syringe, flipped it around in her hand, and jammed it against Flow's neck. The sounds of a small electrical charge emanated from the device, and within three seconds, Flow was slumped in Magnus's arms.

"Thanks," Magnus said as Valerie helped him lay Flow's unconscious body back on the bed.

"What happened?" she asked. "What'd you do?"

"I asked for their account of the last two weeks. Let's just say it wasn't great."

"Severe PTSD," she said, turning to Cheeks. She knelt beside him, checked his pulse, and examined his eyes with a penlight. "As bad as I've ever seen it."

"Me too." Magnus knelt to help her lift Cheeks back onto his bed. "He's gonna be okay, right?"

Valerie produced a small scanner and held it over his head for a few seconds. She studied the readings on the display then tucked the device back into a holster on her belt. "He'll be fine. Just one hell of a headache when he wakes." She grabbed a second syringe and administered the same injection she'd given to Flow. "Nothing some medications can't help. However, Magnus…"

He looked at her and saw the concern in her eyes.

"They're going to need time. Both of them."

"I know."

"I'm not sure you do. Whatever they've been through, it's bad. You don't get this type of reality incoherence unless you've been messed with, and they've been messed with. Like I said back on Oorajee, they've been tortured, Magnus." She paused, and he didn't know what to say. "I know you're going to want to go after the Republic leaders who've set you up. However, your guys… they're not ready to follow you there yet."

"They don't have to."

"But they're going to *want* to. I know Marines. And I'm telling you, Magnus, you can't let them. They're your brothers—I get that. I've seen this type of loyalty before." She reached out and touched his forearm. "They'd do anything for you. But this…" She looked between Cheeks and Flow. "They'll need time before they're ready to fight again, and you should be prepared."

"For what?"

"For the worst. They might never fight again. They might never even be themselves again."

Magnus lowered his head. He knew Valerie was right. The emotional and physical trauma Flow and Cheeks had been through was the worst he'd ever seen. Most guys died before it got this bad. And that was the worst of it—according to Flow and Cheeks, they *had* died.

"Flow said the Jujari killed them and then brought them back to life."

Valerie tilted her head and squinted at him. "What did you say?"

"Rumor has it that the Jujari bleed their enemies to death, siphoning off their life force or something, and then bring them back to life only to do it again. I'd never thought it was true, of course, just—you know—stories that circulated through the Corps late at night around campfires and splick. But, mystics, Flow said something about 'living blood.'"

"Living blood," Valerie repeated. "That might explain the

strange group of punctures around their kidneys and over their heart."

"You mean… like transfusion scars?"

"Something like that." She walked over to one of the black wall panels and swiped it to life. She shuffled through medical diagnostic charts, having already changed the text to Galactic common, and brought up bio scans of Sergeant Michael Deeks and Corporal Miguel Chico. "Here," she said, zooming in with her fingers to show some discolored skin tissue. Five small dots in the shape of a pentagon were positioned on each side of the lower back, over the kidneys, and another set over the heart.

She pulled the images off the wall into a holo-projection and twisted it. The patterns became three dimensional, showing five small tubes that traveled subdermally and ran to the kidneys and heart respectively like five-fingered claws.

"Holy mystics," Magnus whispered. "What is that?"

"Whatever the Jujari were doing to their blood, that's how they got to it. Based on my initial exams, the Jujari could, theoretically, use a body as a pump—"

"A pump?"

"Or more like a fuel source."

"For what?" Magnus asked.

"Your guess is as good as mine. But there's no way they could keep it up for long. The metabolic rate required to sustain such activity would be enormous. Not to mention painful."

Magnus turned from the holo-display and regarded Flow

and Cheeks. His heart was heavy for them both. For Wainwright. For the old Luma who had survived with them... and for all the people they'd lost. He wished he'd been there sooner for them and for Mouth. Maybe Magnus's MAR30 would have made a difference.

"There's nothing more you can do right now," Valerie said, placing her steady hand on his biceps. "Just let them rest and then get them somewhere safe. Away from war."

"That's the one thing I can't do." Magnus turned and put his hand over hers. "This war will consume every corner of our galaxy."

2

Magnus and Valerie walked through the empty corridors of Rohoar's ship. They'd left Flow and Cheeks to rest in sick bay and decided to head to the bridge to see how the rest of the crew was doing. The *Shining Bright Star of Mwadim Furlank over a Thousand Generations* was the rough equivalent of a Repub destroyer-class vessel. She was old, Magnus imagined, and well used. The hallways alone had enough scratch marks and hair on the floor to send a fleet of cleaning and maintenance bots into overload. But at her peak, the *Bright Star* must have been quite a ship.

In fact, most of the Jujari starships, while old, had an elegance to them that betrayed mere utilitarian war lust. Beneath the gun decks and bulbous armor were hints of beauty more reminiscent of nature than of battle. The *Bright Star*, for example, resembled a manta ray from Capriana—almost, except for the slew of turret emplacements, external torpedo racks, two backup shield-generator rectifiers, and reinforced plate armor that turned the ship into a cumbersome war hulk.

Magnus was beginning to see a theme at work in the Jujari people. Beneath their rough exterior was something of deep integrity. Though he wouldn't go as far as Awen to interpret what he saw as praiseworthy—not when they would bleed prisoners to death and back. She was crazy to overlook that. But he had to admit that there was an element of honor among the beasts, at least the Tawnhack, that he at least found... noble.

The way Rohoar had so quickly taken his son's place in honoring their debt code, for example—Magnus had never seen anything like that before. He knew plenty of Marines who would have tried anything they could to get out of the situation, and then, once committed, they'd complain until their captor was forced to release or kill them on account of their constant whining. Instead, Rohoar didn't even seem to be bothered by the drastic arrangement. Once he'd made up his mind, he didn't second-guess the decision. The closest thing Magnus could compare it to were the few times he'd seen a Marine sacrifice his or her life for others in a final act of heroism. But Rohoar's actions were not heroism—they were the equivalent of indentured servitude.

"Are you still mad at me?" Valerie asked.

Magnus slowed and looked at her. "Come again?"

"Are you still mad at me? About your bioteknia eyes."

Nothing like an assertive woman. Magnus noted—yet again—how attractive she was. But there was also sincere transparency in her question, which made her seem vulnerable, maybe even insecure.

"No." Magnus stopped and turned to face her. "I'm not mad at you."

As though his words had lifted a weight from Valerie's shoulders, she relaxed and took a deep breath. "Because I knew what it would do to your career and how much that would hurt you and then all the relationships with your Marines, and—"

"Valerie." Magnus put a hand on her shoulder. "It's okay. You made the right call."

She regarded him like a child looking for approval from her parent. "I've thought about it every minute since."

"Well… cut it out."

Valerie laughed then looked away from him. But she still seemed nervous.

"Tell me about them," Magnus said, hoping to put her at ease.

"What?"

"You gave me a brand-new toy but forgot to give me the instruction manual."

"Well, you did kind of run off to rescue your men."

Magnus smiled. "I know what I did. And your gift helped me do it."

"My gift?"

"Come on, Doc. I might not know much about implants, but these eyes aren't your off-the-shelf line, are they?"

Now it was Valerie's turn to laugh. "No, they're not." She pulled her hair back into a ponytail and tied it in a bun. "I mean, they're not the best thing on the market—we *were* on Oorajee, after all. But you'd be surprised at the kind of tech Abimbola had stockpiled." Valerie shrugged. "It was as simple as me asking him for the best he had, and then he cut me a deal."

"You're telling me *you* bought these?" He pointed at his eyes. "With your own credits?"

She smiled. "A senator gets paid pretty well."

"I can imagine."

"So it wasn't a big deal."

"It was a big deal to me." He stared into her eyes a beat longer than he wanted to. Then they both looked away. "Thank you."

"You're welcome. I figured if your military career is over, you might as well walk into your next line of work with an advantage over everyone else."

"That's… real sweet, actually." And here he'd thought the surgery had just been a hasty decision by a low-grade triage medic—the kind of doctor who had a knack for ending Marines' careers prematurely.

Valerie smiled then turned to walk away. But Magnus caught her by the arm. "Valerie, wait."

"Yes?" Her big blue eyes seemed limitless, and the smell of her hair was intoxicating. She was so close he could feel her body's warmth. How long had it been since he'd been with a woman or held someone? Out of nowhere, he felt the sudden urge to take Valerie in his arms and kiss her. Such things happened when he was tired—when his deep sense of discipline slipped. *Tighten it up, Adonis.*

"Lieutenant?"

Magnus blinked. He was holding Valerie at the elbows. "I… I just wanted to…"

Valerie leaned forward and kissed him on the lips. Her breath was hot, and she smelled like strawberries. *Strawberries! Who smelled like strawberries after spending two weeks on Oorajee?*

A senator's wife, that's who. Dammit, Adonis!

While it pained him to do so, Magnus pulled away and let go of her arms. "Valerie, we shouldn't."

"I'm sorry. I don't know what came over me."

"You're still grieving. You need time."

"No." Valerie shook her head. "That love died a long time ago."

"What do you mean?"

"The political life… is not what it's cracked up to be." Valerie gave him a look that Magnus couldn't decipher.

Is that regret or desire?

"Darin was no Marine," she added.

What does that mean?

"Anyway, you said you wanted to…?"

"Uh, yeah." Magnus had completely forgotten what he was going to ask. Her unexpected advance had caught him off guard. Then his train of thought came back to him. He shook his head. "Piper. I wanted to ask you about Piper."

Valerie's shoulders slumped ever so slightly. "She's fine. Enjoying yet another ride in a starship, this time one flown by giant 'puppy dogs.'"

Magnus smiled, feeling the awkwardness of the kiss pass. *But was it awkward? Or was it just so good that I want to do it again?* "That's kids for you." He cleared his throat. "But I mean, how *is* she?"

"Oh, you mean her abilities?"

"I was thinking something more along the lines of magic death rays, but *abilities* works." A pained look crossed her face. "Dammit, I'm sorry. I didn't mean it like that."

Valerie spread her thumb and index finger across her eyes, pushing back tears. "Marines have never been known for their bedside manner."

"Seriously, that was stupid."

"It's okay." She waved him off, collected herself with a calming breath, and closed her eyes. "I realize you and I haven't talked about this yet."

"Well, it's not like there's been a whole lot of time for it."

"That's true." She took a step back and leaned against the wall. "Piper's different. She's what the Luma call a true blood."

"The Luma?" Magnus felt blood rush to his cheeks and ears. "What's this got to do with the Luma?"

"Everything."

"You're not telling me Piper's a Luma, are you?"

Valerie laughed. "No, not at all. But she has more power in the Unity than any Luma."

Magnus froze. *What does that even mean?* "I'm lost."

"I come from a long line of Luma," Valerie confessed, placing her hands on her lower back. "Like all of my ancestors, I was bound for observances on Worru." Valerie paused and searched Magnus's face. "Sorry, *observances* is like graduate school for Luma candidates."

"I know what it is, basically. I have a friend who…" An image of Awen suddenly popped into Magnus's mind. It caught him by surprise, because he realized he missed her. *Save a woman's life, and her face haunts you forever.* He wondered if Valerie's face would do the same. "Never mind. Go on."

"Anyway, that wasn't what I wanted," she said.

"Then what did you want?"

She chuckled. "Anything other than the Order. Being a diplomat, working through everyone's problems, spending time in stuffy conference rooms and attending over-the-top dinners—that just wasn't for me. I wanted something else. Something real. Something harder."

"Harder than being a Luma?"

Her lips curled into a cute smile. "It's not all it's cracked up to be, you know."

"Wait. So you're telling me you turned down a career as a Luma to join the Republic Marines?"

Valerie nodded.

Magnus wasn't entirely surprised, of course. Looks could be deceiving. And while she might have looked more like a

Luma, the way she'd handled herself with his Z back on Oorajee and her ability to stay calm under pressure were Marine qualities. People were born with those or they weren't. There wasn't any middle ground.

Magnus ran the back of his hand across his beard. "But you just said you didn't like stuffy conference rooms and fancy dinners. Forgive me if I'm wrong here, but isn't that exactly what marrying a senator gets you?"

Valerie puffed her cheeks and exhaled. "You do stupid stuff for what you think is love. And then it gives you... well, it gives you Piper."

"That's why you got out?"

"I did two tours in Caledonia and fell in love with Darin, and then we found out I was pregnant with Piper. I wanted to stay in and serve out my time, but he insisted I get an honorable discharge. He wanted me to have Piper and said we could make a comfortable life together. His connections made getting out easy. But that didn't mean that life with him was easy." Valerie's eyes focused on something in the distance. "Part of me still wonders... you know... what might have happened if..."

"Yeah, don't go there." He wanted to be affectionate, to reassure her, but he didn't want to go back to the kiss. Well, he did, but it wouldn't have been right—not at the moment, anyway. "Second-guessing is a cruel master. It convinces us we can still change stuff in our past while it hijacks our present. Just don't."

Valerie's big blue eyes blinked at him. "Sounds like you have some experience there, Lieutenant."

"Maybe." He pulled his hand away from her. "So Piper's a savant of sorts—in the Unity, I mean."

"You could say that. She knows she's different... knows she has powers. But not to what extent."

"And you suspect she has a lot."

Valerie nodded. "That's why getting back to Worru is so important. I can't thank you enough for taking us, Magnus." It was Valerie's turn to touch him, placing a hand on his chest.

Oh man. She's gonna get you, boy. Back the skiff up.

Magnus took her hand and pulled it down, trying to be reassuring, trying not to resist her advances too noticeably. But it was noticeable, wasn't it? "It's not a problem. It seems like the best place for her... given my experiences with the Unity and all. Which isn't much. Plus, I have a friend there, and she knows the Luma master well. They'll know how to help Piper."

Valerie looked away, pulling her hands to her chest. "I'm sure they will, Magnus. I'm sure they will." Magnus sensed a measure of regret in her voice. Or maybe it was apprehension. He couldn't be sure.

"You want to get back to the bridge with me?"

"No, I think I'll go see who's in the galley. Maybe get some coffee." She rubbed her hands together and started to walk away. "Piper will be waking up soon anyway."

"Sounds good."

Valerie looked over her shoulder. "Magnus?"

"Yeah?"

"Thanks for talking."

"Not a problem. I'm here for you."

She held him with her eyes for another beat then moved away. Magnus let out a sigh as Valerie disappeared around a corner. For reasons he couldn't define—other than knowing he was still a fifteen-year-old boy on the inside—Magnus had a vision of standing back-to-back with her, blasting enemies together. It was something that belonged in a holo-comic, not in his head. So he shook the vision away almost as fast as it had appeared, and he reminded himself that her husband had died less than two weeks ago. And that she had a kid who had inadvertently committed patricide, but also saved him and his fire team—twice.

That woman is so right and so wrong for you, Adonis. Just get her to Worru and walk away.

3

PIPER COULDN'T TAKE her eyes off the giant doggy. She could hardly believe how big he was and how fluffy. All she wanted to do was pet him. And maybe play with him. But he didn't seem like the playing sort. Instead, he just liked to sit in his big captain's chair and glare at numbers on his data pad.

She'd remained by his side from the moment she was allowed on the bridge after leaving Oorajee's orbit. He ignored her mostly. Only when she tried to pet him did he pull away. But she simply couldn't help herself. His fur was far too inviting. She had to try one more time.

Piper leaned against the arm of his captain's chair, acting as casual as she knew how. Her view meandered around the bridge, and she held her corgachirp in her left hand. Meanwhile, her right hand inched up the big doggy's back until it was hovering near the base of his neck. Gently—ever so gently—she laid her hand into his thick, soft fur and began to stroke.

"Stop that!" the beast barked.

Piper recoiled, pulling her hand to her chest. This was the first time he'd spoken to her. His voice was far gruffer than she would have liked. Maybe he was a mean doggy. Or perhaps he was just having a bad day.

"I'm sorry, extra-big dog. You just look so soft."

"I'm not soft. And I'm not a dog."

"But you look like—"

"I know what I look like to you, but I'm not what you think. And I'm not for petting."

Piper raised her hand one more time.

"I'm *not* for petting, human child."

Disappointed, Piper retreated and lowered her head. "I'm sorry."

The doggy relaxed in his chair and stared at her. He had rather long teeth that protruded from beneath his flappy lips. And his eyes were big and sort of bloodshot. Maybe he hadn't gotten a good night's rest. Piper was crankiest when she slept poorly. At least, that was what her mother told her.

"So, what are you, extra-big… whatever you are?"

"I am a Jujari of the Tawnhack tribe." The beast didn't even bother looking up from his data pad when he spoke to her.

"Oh." Piper shuffled her feet. "Do all your people look like you?"

"Mostly, yes."

"Is their fur as fluffy?"

"I… don't know."

"And the same color?"

"What?" he asked.

"Do they all have spots?"

The Jujari rolled his head to glare at her with a giant eyeball. "Please stop talking, tiny human."

"You don't have to call me tiny human. My name's Piper." She extended her hand.

The Jujari looked at it for a moment while Piper waited. Finally, he accepted the handshake. Piper's eyes widened as his massive paw enveloped her forearm up to her elbow. But he was gentle, and the rough pads in his paw felt warm.

"My name is Rohoar."

"Mr. Rohoar. That's a nice name."

The Jujari pulled back ever so slightly. "You think so?"

"Sure."

"That is kind of you to say, young Piper."

"Not a problem. Can I pet you now?"

"No."

Piper sighed, lowering her head. "Okay."

"But… you can tell me about your people."

She glanced up. "My people?"

"Where do you come from? What is your home like? What kinds of food do you eat?"

Piper pulled Talisman, her corgachirp, close to her chest. This was exciting. "And afterward, maybe you can tell me about yours?"

Rohoar nodded.

"Okay, so, I come from Capriana Prime..." She paused to see if he was actually listening and not going to go back to his data pad. Adults did that a lot. Content that he was still interested, she continued. "It's mostly a water planet. But we have some really big cities on island chains. They're called atolls. They're beautiful. The cities, I mean. But the atolls are too. We have a nice house in one of the biggest skyscrapers on the main island. My daddy's a..." Piper blinked. Her heart hurt. "My daddy was a senator. But now he's... he's..."

"I already know." Rohoar placed his paw on her back.

Piper liked that. A tear leaked from her eye. She wiped it away with Talisman.

"I am sorry for your suffering, Piper."

"Thank you." The words came out small.

"I lost my father as well."

Piper looked at him, surprised. "You did?"

Rohoar nodded. "Perhaps just a few days before yours."

"A few days? Really?" More tears started to fill her eyes. This was one of the saddest things she'd ever heard of. Two people who'd both lost their daddies at the same time, riding on the same starship. She leaned in toward his chair and placed a hand on his chest. "I'm so sorry, Mr. Rohoar, sir."

"Thank you."

"How did he die?"

"In an explosion."

"My daddy's escape pod exploded too." Her lower lip quivered. "This is terrible."

Suddenly, Rohoar wrapped his whole arm around her. He drew her into an awkward hug around the chair's arm. Her heart lifted as his fluffy warmth enveloped her. He smelled a little funny, like he needed a bath, but she didn't mind. She felt some of the pain in her heart pass, melting away like snow on a sunny day. He held her there until she stopped crying.

Piper looked at her hand. It was on Rohoar's chest. She could pet him… and he wouldn't even notice. Ever so subtly, she moved her fingers in a sweeping motion.

"You're petting me again."

Piper balled her fingers into a fist. "Sorry." Rohoar let her go, so she stood up straight and wiped away the rest of her tears. Composed, she lifted her chin. "I like sorlakk."

Rohoar looked at her with a look of confusion.

"You asked me to tell you about what kind of food I like. I like sorlakk."

"What is this sorlakk?" he asked.

"You've never had raw Paglothian sorlakk?"

"No. Is it good?"

"Oh, it is!" She clapped her hands around Talisman, grateful to talk about something other than their daddies dying. "It really is! When we get back to Capriana, I'll get you some. I promise."

Rohoar opened his mouth to say something but didn't. Then he looked down at his data pad. Maybe he didn't want sorlakk after all.

"Mr. Rohoar, sir, what is your favorite food?"

He gave her what she thought was a smile, though it looked a little more like a sneer. "Slanther tripe."

"Slanther tripe? I want some!"

"It, too, is *raw*, as you say. It is the stomach of the desert lizards that come from the south of Oorajee. You must wrestle them for a day before they succumb. But when they do, and once you remove the poison sacs…" Rohoar licked his lips with a long tongue. "It is one of my tribe's greatest delicacies."

Piper winced. "Maybe I will try that when I'm older."

"That is, perhaps, a wise thought."

"So, Mr. Rohoar, what is your home like?"

"Well, like you, I have a home in a skyscraper, as you say. But it wasn't always this way."

"Did you move a lot as a kid?"

"In a manner of speaking. For centuries, my people roamed Oorajee until our numbers became too great and we began city building. But even before that, we roamed the stars, but not like your Republic does. Rather than conquest, we wanted a place to settle. To call our own."

"And you picked Oorajee."

"Our ancestors did, yes," he said.

"But why a desert planet? Do you like sand, then? It's really hot and gets in everything." When Rohoar didn't reply right away, she said, "Mr. Rohoar?"

"As it is told, our ancestors chose the desert because it was unlike our previous home. They believed that if future generations were to survive, they must endure hardships that would prevent them from falling into the comforts that killed our people—the things that weakened their minds and corrupted their spirits. The desert saved us by keeping from us the things which we could not support."

Piper blinked. "You're kinda confusing, Mr. Rohoar, sir."

He let out a long sigh. "Yes, I suppose I am."

"So, when this is all done, you will go back to Oorajee?"

"When this is done…"

"Well, I'm sure you'll be happy then, won't you?" she asked. But Rohoar just stared at the floor a few meters ahead, focused on something she couldn't see. "Will you see the rest of your family then? Do you have more family?"

Without breaking his concentration on the floor, he said, "I have a son."

"What's his name?"

The Jujari didn't reply.

"Mr. Rohoar, sir? What's his name?"

"Victorio…"

"That's a wonderful name," she said. "It sounds like 'victorious,' you know. Is he a good fighter?"

It was taking longer for Rohoar to answer her questions. Maybe he needed a nap.

"Mr. Rohoar, sir?"

"When this is done… perhaps I will see them all…"

Piper decided that Rohoar had been through a lot, just like her. She imagined that he was missing his home, too, just like her. And there was nothing she liked better when she was feeling sad than when someone rubbed her tummy. She knew she shouldn't. And he would probably yell at her again. But he did seem so sad. So Piper leaned in, laid her head on his chest, and began gently stroking his stomach. And to her delight, he didn't say a word.

MAGNUS WAS STILL SHAKING off the conversation with Valerie when the elevator slowed. A hint of her scent lingered on his cheek somewhere. It was as elusive as his feelings for her—present but impossible to pinpoint. He ran a hand over his face and blinked as the doors opened onto the bridge.

At first, Magnus panicked. He reached for his Z and trained it on the Jujari sitting in the captain's chair. *Splick! The damn Jujari's gone rabid.*

Rohoar held the lower half of Piper's corpse under his arm, gnawing on her head and torso. Magnus was five kilos of pressure away from squeezing off a blaster bolt into the back of Rohoar's head when he noticed...

There's no blood. As he stepped from the elevator, Magnus heard the faint sound of a child singing. The gentle rise and fall of the melody reminded him of a lullaby from his childhood.

What the...?

Magnus couldn't believe what he was seeing. Or hearing. The most innocent human girl Magnus had ever met was singing a lullaby to the greatest predator species in the galaxy.

They couldn't be any more different from one another. Yet the galaxy had brought them together.

Magnus sheathed his pistol and was about to clear his throat. Then he thought better of it. Rohoar had seen just as much war as Magnus had. Probably more. And Piper had endured things no nine-year-old should ever have to see. These moments—*this one right here*—were the things that healed the soul. Not fully, of course—nothing could do that—but they went a long way in helping.

For as much death as Magnus had seen, for as much as he'd delivered, he wanted to know he was also a part of giving life and allowing it to flourish. He refused to steal this moment from either Piper or Rohoar. As quietly as he'd entered, Magnus backed into the elevator and closed the doors.

4

"How soon before Sootriman is better?" Awen asked, glancing between TO-96 and Azelon, the ship's gleaming-white robot counterpart. The three of them stood on the bridge of the *Azelon Spire*, watching as the vessel commenced the docking procedures with Ki Nar Four's central platform. The volcanic planet filled the main viewing window, molten lava swirling amongst a host of charred tectonic plates twenty thousand kilometers below.

"Before Sootriman is better?" TO-96 asked. "Would you please quantify your question for accuracy's sake? *Better* is a relative term. At what level do you expect—"

"Got it, 'Six." Awen waved him off. "How soon before she's conscious and alert enough to give orders to her minions?"

"Minions?"

"Her people, her staff. Whatever."

TO-96 looked at Azelon.

"By our calculations," Azelon replied, "based on a limited understanding of humanoid physiology, we estimate Sootriman will be fully coherent in two days, six hours, forty-one minutes, and twenty-eight seconds."

"That's a pretty good understanding," Awen replied, hands on her hips. She started to pace in front of the main viewing window. "Which means I have two days of waiting around. Mystics, this is going to drive me crazy."

"Are you going to become mentally unstable?" Azelon asked, looking from Awen to TO-96.

"It is yet another turn of phrase, Azelon. An idiom, if you will. It means she expects to grow restless in anticipation of her return to the planet, Ithnor Ithelia, and the city, Itheliana, which she wants to do sooner than circumstances will permit."

"I understand," Azelon said. "Is such a lack of patience a common virtue among sentients from this universe?"

"I am afraid so."

"Hey, you two." Awen snapped her fingers. "Can you save the classroom talk for later? We have a mission to plan here."

"As you wish," TO-96 replied. "How may we assist you?"

"We're going to need to get supplies and to rally Sootriman's bodyguards. Does this ship need to have her fuel cells recharged or something?"

"No," Azelon said. "At least, not at this juncture. All systems are nominal."

"Perfect." Awen rubbed her hands together. "So we need supplies and muscle." *What I wouldn't give for a few bucketheaded Marines right about now.*

Really, Awen? Have you given up on your ideals so quickly?

Suddenly, she felt ashamed. If Magnus were here and offered to go blow up every last one of those troopers in the metaverse, she wouldn't even hesitate to take him up on it. Had vengeance taken that deep a hold on her?

But it wasn't vengeance—it was more like protection. Like keeping the rabid animal at arm's length so that others might not have to suffer. Still, the moral high ground eluded her. She was talking about taking human life. How could she live with herself if she did this? What would the Luma say?

So-Elku wouldn't have a problem.

That thought sent a shiver down her spine. *But he isn't a murderer, is he?* He was just a misguided man who wanted the stardrive… and who wished to acquire information about the Novia Minoosh and their knowledge of the Unity. That was why he'd tried to manipulate her and tracked her through the quantum tunnel. And that was why he stole the book that had been in the temple library.

Wasn't it?

More questions filled her mind, ones she didn't feel any closer to answering. Chief among them was still how So-Elku knew about the Novia in the first place. *And how did Kane know about it? No one except the mwadim ever saw what was on that stardrive, right?*

Working through the possibilities felt like trying to hold

handfuls of sand in the shallows of a tidal pool. No matter how she tried, the current whisked the granules into the sea and left her empty-handed. Worse still, however, was a lingering sense of foreboding, an imminent threat waiting for her just out of sight, lurking in the shadows. She felt the warnings, as if someone was trying to tell her to stay away. But she knew how fear could constrict the will and lead to inaction. For three months on Itheliana, fear had paralyzed her. She refused to listen to it anymore. Instead, she would forge ahead, plunging into the darkness and taking the fight to the enemy.

"If you don't mind me asking," TO-96 said with a raised hand, "is your only inquiry as to Sootriman's health about how she might assist you in your effort to return to the metaverse? Might you also be curious as to Azelon's prognosis of your friend?"

The two questions cut Awen to her core. She was beginning to wonder if some measure of metaphorical nearsightedness wasn't a significant character flaw in her. When she got focused on a task, it consumed her.

But that's the only way things get done. The alternative was cloudy judgment calls and lackluster results. Lives were on the line here—the whole galaxy was in jeopardy. And she knew in her heart that Sootriman would be fine. She'd told Ezo as much, and she wasn't about to put dishonesty on her notable list of flaws.

"Of course I care about her." Awen pulled the edges of

her jacket together and lifted her chin. "Azelon, do you expect Sootriman to make a full recovery?"

"The likelihood of Sootriman returning to full health stands at ninety-eight point seven six three percent."

"See?" Awen shot TO-96 a glare.

"You need not prove anything to me, Awen. I was already aware of the statistical likelihood of your friend's recovery."

Awen rolled her eyes. "Of course you were."

"Docking with platform KN4-31, Hangar Bay Three in ten seconds," Azelon reported, her voice reverberating in the bridge—and, presumably, throughout the rest of the ship. "Please prepare for main hull connection."

"I suggest you hang on," TO-96 said to Awen, who turned, took a seat in the captain's acceleration couch, and buckled herself in.

"Five seconds," Azelon announced. The window showed the platform's crew tube extending toward them like a blackened worm protruding from the hangar block. The *Azelon Spire* was far too massive to fit inside the bay. Instead, she would make port at the end of the gantry crane that cradled the tube.

"Three… two… one…"

Awen braced herself. The smallest nudge rocked her forward. She waited, expecting more. "Was that it?"

"That was *it*, yes," TO-96 replied.

"Docking procedure complete," Azelon reported. "You are free to move about the ship. Pending hangar access at bow deck four, section one. Awaiting permission to open doors."

"Access granted," said a voice from behind Awen. She turned to see Ezo stepping out of the elevator and onto the bridge.

"Acknowledged," Azelon said.

Awen rose from the captain's chair and moved to Ezo. "Any improvement?"

Ezo would know she was asking about Sootriman. And perhaps TO-96 would note her concern. *Now you need to prove yourself to a robot?*

"The readouts seem to be positive, though I'm no doctor." Ezo looked to Azelon. "Thank you for translating the diagnostics for me."

"My pleasure, sir. I am only sorry that I could not do it sooner. But it was not until I accessed TO-96's archives that the translation was possible. He was indispensable in that regard."

Awen noticed TO-96's eyes glowing a little brighter—more robot blushing, as if such a thing were possible. *Nothing like anthropomorphizing robots, Awen.* Maybe she needed a break from them—or from everyone. She hadn't gotten much alone time since before leaving Worru for Oorajee.

A pang of guilt filled her chest as she thought about Matteo and Master Toochu and the others who'd perished in the mwadim's palace. She wished she could go back—she'd change so much. But that was impossible. Awen thought back to Willowood's advice before the meeting with the treacherous So-Elku. "You cannot control what is done to you," the wise sage had said. "Just like you could not stop those people from dying. The only thing you get to control is your today. You choose, and the universe responds."

Oh, how she missed her mentor and hoped—to all the mystics—that Willowood was still alive. *What am I thinking? Of course she's alive! So-Elku might imprison her, but he isn't ruthless enough to kill her.* Perhaps she would use the next two days to try to reach Willowood—providing it didn't compromise her own safety... *So it's all about you?*

Sometimes her inner monologue was such a pain. Of course it wasn't *all about her*. She was doing this for the greater good. For those who did not know they needed defending yet. Whatever Admiral Kane and his associates were up to, it was evil. And it had to be stopped.

"So what's the plan?" Ezo asked Awen.

"I figure we let Sootriman stay here in sick bay. I doubt any of Ki Nar Four's medical facilities are better than Azelon's."

"Based on my initial scans of this planet's technology, I would agree," Azelon said.

Awen turned to glance at Azelon, eyebrows raised. Then to Ezo, she whispered, "I swear, she's got ears in every part of this ship."

Azelon whispered back, "If that is another metaphor for my ability to detect audio-acoustic vibrations on every one of the ship's surfaces, then yes, I have *ears* in every part of this ship."

"Great," Ezo whispered back. He smiled and returned to

a normal voice. "So we leave Sootriman in Azelon's care. Then what?"

"Well, I was hoping we could rally some of Sootriman's troops. Her bodyguard. Maybe some of those Reptalon sentries she keeps. Then they get whatever weapons they need, and we go back to Ithnor Ithelia."

"What are you, a mercenary now?"

"No." Awen shook her head. "Why is everyone having a hard time with me wanting to stop bad people from doing something evil?"

Ezo shrugged. "I don't know. I mean, you *are* a Luma, aren't you? Don't you all seek to employ 'alternative means' in accomplishing your goals? Diplomacy and splick. You know."

"Okay, first off, Luma work in teams through established diplomatic channels. My last team got blown up"—she punched her palm with a fist—"and in case you hadn't noticed, our leader betrayed the whole Order. So I'm not getting a team of Luma anytime soon. Secondly, I'm not exactly sure Admiral Kane and his troopers are going to be interested in diplomatic negotiations through moderate peace talks."

"So you're saying there *is* a place for violence…"

Awen threw her hands up. "Why is everyone so interested in my principles all of a sudden?" She looked at TO-96, who shrugged. She blew a strand of hair out of her face. "Listen, Ezo. All I know is that if we don't stop whoever those troopers are back on the Novia home world, something bad is going to happen. I don't know what they're after, but it's not good.

This isn't going to end well for anyone if we don't do something."

"Agreed." Ezo nodded. "I just want to make sure you're okay with… you know… us killing people. It's not exactly your style. Ezo's, yes. Yours? Not so much."

"I get it, and I appreciate your concern. But let me worry about my morality, and you worry about yours."

"You sure?"

"Mystics! Yes." She raised a flattened hand toward the elevator. "Can we just get on with this?"

"Sure can, Star Queen. Just remember one thing."

"And what's that?" Awen wasn't in the mood for a lecture —or for anyone else questioning her ethics.

"You do have a team."

5

WALKING through the streets of Sootriman's capital platform was just as disgusting as it had been the first time. How such a classy lady tolerated a refuse pit like this was beyond her. But she supposed that being a warlord over a rogue planet outside the Republic's domain came with certain caveats. Didn't all leadership? And Awen would be the last to question Sootriman's judgment calls, even if she didn't entirely understand them. For all Awen knew, Sootriman's citizens *wanted* their planet this way. Even illegals off the grid had rights, as Oorajee plainly demonstrated.

The smells of urine, fermented yeast, and bile mixed with odors of rusted metal and the sulfur from the planet's surface. The midday sun cast a murky green hue over the streets, which were now bustling with merchants, shoppers, and beggars. Disreputable storefronts boasting all manner of alien erotica stood side by side with seemingly decent food service and merchandising establishments—all of which sought to do honest business in this backwater world.

Ezo led TO-96 and Awen against the gyrating flow of traffic, heading toward the massive domed building in the city's center. Under full sun, Sootriman's den showed more wear than Awen remembered. Rust and oil stains crept along the surface, slowly pulling the structure down to the decaying platform's grave. Cables, poles, cranes, and wires protruded from the circular building like the bristly hairs of a Tuskavarin boar mongrel.

"Something's not right," Ezo said above the din of the crowd.

"What? Why?" Awen looked at Sootriman's den. "How can you tell?"

"There's been a fire." Ezo pointed to charring around the windows and between the metal plating. "That's not normal."

"I'm detecting residual levels of carbon monoxide, carbon dioxide, water vapor, nitrogen dioxide, hydrogen cyanide, polyethylene—"

"So it's bad, 'Six. I got it. Come on." Ezo put his shoulder down and started pushing through the crowd. Patrons swore at him as people bumped into one another and lost their grip on whatever wares they carried. Awen held on to TO-96 as he followed after Ezo, trying not to get swept away by the crush of bodies.

The trio made it through one of the larger squares before being funneled into a side street. The narrow road bent right and terminated at an intersection. Ezo pulled himself up short, narrowly missing becoming the hood ornament for a street skiff.

Even though she'd momentarily lost sight of Sootriman's den, Awen thought she could detect the sharp odor of a burnt-out fire. Ezo looked side to side and chose to go right. She and TO-96 followed him and made it to another intersection. They turned left and moved between some dilapidated apartment buildings. As they drew closer to the end of the street, Awen could see that a fire had worked its way through the structure. Soot stains marked walls, and debris littered the sidewalks below them.

"Come on," Ezo said, breaking into a run. TO-96 and Awen followed, pushing past pedestrians and dodging small skiffs. By the time Awen reached the street's end—butting up against the rounded exterior of the den—Ezo was already running toward the building's main entrance. When she and TO-96 caught him, he was staring into the blackness. The massive doors had been blown off their hinges and lay in the street.

"What happened?" Awen asked, not really expecting anyone to answer.

Ezo took a step into the entryway, examining the ceiling and walls. "Kane happened, bet you a hundred creds in Abimbola's poker chips. Careful."

TO-96 switched on two shoulder-mounted lights and helped Awen step over some rubble. They followed Ezo as he moved deeper into the tunnel. Within a dozen meters, Awen started seeing body parts of Reptalons. Hands, heads, legs. The odors of smoke and burnt flesh hung heavily in the air. She covered her nose and mouth, trying not to let her eyes linger too long on the gruesome carnage.

When the three of them reached the stairs that mounted to Sootriman's grand hall, Ezo kicked Reptalon bodies aside to make a path. Whoever had come through here—Awen agreed that it must have been Kane—had spared no one. Awen was surprised that Sootriman had failed to mention any of this during their three months together on Itheliana. Ezo seemed equally dismayed, which meant he'd been kept out of the loop too. Sootriman had never shared the details of how Kane had taken her hostage. Perhaps it was too humiliating. Or too sad. Reptalons weren't ideal friends, but Awen doubted the lizard people were the only casualties of Kane's attack.

"Great mystics…" Ezo whispered from above.

Awen didn't even want to ascend the rest of the stairs, afraid of what Ezo had found. But she knew she must. Full knowledge of what was up there would add to her motivation to stop Kane. If she really were going to betray the tenets of the Luma, she'd need to see the fruits of this enemy's labor. She'd need to know what she was up against, what Kane was capable of, and—

Awen froze on the top step, and her stomach turned. She blinked and squinted at the places where TO-96's and Ezo's lights landed. Bodies. Dozens of bodies. Maimed. Burned. Dismembered. Dried blood and ash swirled in macabre designs on the tiled floors. Slash and blaster marks scorched the pillars. Women who'd once been fanning themselves were frozen in anxious crawls away from whoever had slain them. Men who'd dashed over to defend their queen lay eviscerated on the ground. Ghastly faces filled with terror were everywhere.

Awen was about to vomit when she heard a hiss.

"Who goes there?" Ezo demanded, swinging his pistol to the far wall. TO-96 also centered his lights on the dais. "Who are you, and what are you doing here? Come out slowly!"

Awen watched in horror as a figure emerged from behind the dais. Her imagination told her it was a Reptalon carcass brought back to life—some sort of manipulation with the Unity. But to her amazement, it wasn't a trick or a walking corpse. It was a Reptalon, alive.

"Keep your hands where I can see them!" Ezo ordered. "And come down from there slowly!"

The Reptalon extended his clawed hands to his sides and began moving down the dais. But his steps were awkward, and he slipped. The lizard fell, hitting his hip on the marble steps, and then tumbled to the floor. It hissed louder, writhing in a failed attempt to get up.

"Slowly!" Ezo ordered, picking his way over the bodies between the entrance and the dais. "Don't do anything stupid!"

"Stupid," the lizard hissed. "Stupid."

"Yeah…" Ezo edged closer. "That's right. Stupid gets you shot."

"So stupid." The lizard pounded the marbled floor a scaly fist. "So, so, so stupid."

"You did all this? You betray your oaths?" Ezo asked. Awen felt like that was a pretty unnecessary thing to ask and wished she could do the questioning. But Ezo held up a hand to keep her quiet. "Hey!" Ezo jammed the toe of his boot into the Reptalon's side. "I'm talking to you, lizard brain!"

The creature rolled over on its back and hissed at Ezo. Awen had always thought that Reptalons were, by far, one of the most disturbing creatures in the galaxy. This behavior only served to confirm it.

"Saasarr is stupid!"

"Who's Saasarr, buddy?" Ezo asked. "Did he do this?"

"No, no, no." The Reptalon was distraught. He seemed to be crying, and judging from the smell of alcohol in the air, he was probably drunk too.

"Ezo," Awen whispered, raising a hand toward his arm. "I think he's a survivor."

"Gotta be sure, Star Queen. He's one of Sootriman's generals if the rank on his lapel is correct. Stand back."

She did so and watched Ezo stick his boot in the Reptalon's side again.

"Is that really necessary, Ezo?"

"You want to catch bad guys?" He glared at her over his extended arms. "Let me do my job." Ezo looked back at the Reptalon. "Who's Saasarr, and who did this?"

"Saasarr was sleeping. *Sleeeeeeping!*" The lizard rolled over and pounded the floor again, fresh blood squirting between the scales of his fists.

"Are you Saasarr?" Awen asked, unable to handle much more of this. This creature either needed to be imprisoned or sedated. And fast.

"Saasarr the stupid! Saasarr the lazy! And now she's dead, dead, dead. All because of me."

"So you did this?" As fast as lightning, Ezo placed his boot between the Reptalon's shoulder blades and pushed the barrel of his pistol against the back of its head. "You betrayed her?"

Fearing the Reptalon would answer in the affirmative, Awen clarified the question with one of her own. "Did intruders kill all these people?"

The lizard was hysterical—sobbing and writhing. "Intruders, yes! And Saasarr was nowhere to be found."

"Dammit, Awen," Ezo scolded her. "You can't offer detainees words! We needed to hear him say it."

"But he wasn't going to say it. At least not anything we wanted to hear about Kane or troopers. He wasn't even here!" She looked down at the pitiful creature and shouted over the Reptalon's grief. "Are you Saasarr?"

"Curses! Curses from the gods! I am Saasarr! Curses!" He pounded the marble with every syllable. "Intruders. It was intruders."

Ezo holstered his weapon and removed his boot from Saasarr's back. "Six, get him up."

"Right away, sir." TO-96 reached down and helped the

lizard to his feet. Saasarr struggled to stay standing, so the bot kept a hold of his arms.

"Did you get a look at the intruders?" Ezo asked.

Saasarr shook his head. "It was too late. Too late when I returned. Dead. They were all dead. And I still can't find her body. Been searching. But I've failed."

"That's because your queen is alive," Awen said.

Saasarr's eyes widened. He looked between her and Ezo. "She's alive?"

"Well, that sobered him up," Ezo said.

Saasarr acted as if he wanted to stand on his own, so TO-96 let him go. But a beat later, Saasarr was headed to the floor. The bot caught him, sparing him from another nasty fall.

"Can you get him back to the *Spire*, Ninety-Six?" Awen asked.

"And leave you two alone to search without me?"

"If this is the worst of it," Ezo said, gesturing to Saasarr, "I think we'll be just fine."

"We'll check for more survivors," Awen added. "Then we'll get back to the ship."

Ezo nodded in agreement. "If he's really one of her generals, he'll be an asset in rallying the rest of Sootriman's fighting force." Suddenly, Saasarr hurled the contents of his stomach onto the marble floor. Ezo and Awen stepped back just in time. "And get him cleaned up, would you, 'Six?"

"As you wish, sir." TO-96 hoisted Saasarr over his shoulder and began walking back toward the entrance.

"Put Saasarr down!" the lizard ordered, his speech slurred.

TO-96 could be heard reasoning with the Reptalon all the way out the door, down the steps, and into the tunnel.

"You made a good bot," Awen said.

Ezo forced a blast of air through his nostrils. "Sometimes I wonder." The two shared a smile and looked around the room as if to say, *What's next?*

"So… we keep searching?" Awen proposed.

Ezo shook his head. "Nah, I have a better idea. Follow me."

Ezo led Awen behind the dais and through a doorway that opened into a long corridor. His weapon's light revealed several doors that lined each side of the hall at evenly spaced intervals. But it was the single door at the hallway's end that Ezo seemed intent on.

He lowered his weapon and tried the lever, but it was locked. "Give me some room."

Awen stepped back as Ezo kicked the door, the metal doorjamb bending under the force. He struck it three more times before it finally gave. Ezo shined his light into what looked to be a well-appointed office complete with luxurious furniture, wall dressings, paintings, and area rugs.

"Sootriman's office?" Awen asked.

"One of them, yeah." Ezo walked around a desk in the

middle of the room and pulled out the high-backed chair. He sat, placed his pistol to the side, and spread his hands over the desk, calling up a holo-display. The first thing that hovered in front of him was a login screen. He let out a sigh.

"Something wrong?" she asked.

"Something's right. It's not biometric. Means we don't have to haul her back here." He tapped his temple for a moment. "Now, what's your password, baby?"

"Password? As in a *digital* password?"

"She always liked things old-school."

Awen was stunned. Digital passwords had been phased out decades ago in favor of quantum security. The new measures were almost unbreakable unless a person had an excellent code slicer. "We can have Ninety-Six come back if you think—"

"Nah, give me a second." Ezo cracked his knuckles and placed his fingers on the illuminated keyboard. He typed something then hit Enter. All at once, the login screen vanished, replaced by standard file architecture. "Sootriman, you're so predictable."

"You guessed it? Just like that?"

"Sure." He smiled. "It was our anniversary."

"You're serious."

"Yup." Ezo grinned from ear to ear. "She still loves me." He leaned in and began swiping through the files. "Let's see here…"

Ezo moved into a section entitled Security System and then lists of dates and cameras. Ezo tapped his temple a few more times before choosing a date and opening the data set. He chose the camera grouping marked Den and started scanning footage.

"You're pretty good at this," Awen offered. "Makes me wonder how many times you've done it."

Ezo answered absentmindedly, "Enough to know what I'm doing. Here we go."

Awen leaned in as Ezo expanded a view of the main entry tunnel. A sudden burst of light and a muffled thud grabbed her attention. The smoke cleared, and several black-clad troopers moved into the frame, led by a single bald figure in a black navy uniform.

"Kane," she whispered.

Ezo nodded, watching the footage.

The troopers shot flares that bathed the tunnel in bright light, temporarily blowing out the camera's sensors. Ezo jumped to another camera farther down the corridor. Kane pointed at several Reptalons, and the troopers responded by firing blaster bolts into the targets. Then flamethrowers appeared and bathed the walls in liquid fire, torching whatever moved along the walls.

"He's certainly methodical," Ezo said.

"He's sick."

"Agreed."

Ezo continued to switch cameras to show Kane and his troopers moving down the tunnel, dispatching Reptalons as they went. They finally entered Sootriman's inner sanctum. Awen watched in horror as Kane approached Sootriman and fired a shot at her. The large woman hardly flinched as the metal projectile missed her head by mere centimeters, biting a chunk out of her throne instead. The two continued talking until, without warning, Kane extended his weapon to one side and shot a civilian in the head.

Awen let out a short scream and looked away. "Mystics! What is wrong with him?"

"He's evil," Ezo said, still watching.

By the time Awen had forced the bile down her throat and had her eyes on the screen again, Kane was shooting more people, dispatching them as easily as someone might rid a home of unwelcomed insects on a summer evening.

Then there was a pause. Sootriman was on her feet, shouting something that the microphones could not distinguish from the screaming in the room. Kane waved his gloved hand, and a trooper shot Sootriman with a low-energy pulse, stunning her. Two more troopers ascended the dais, pulled Sootriman from her throne, and threw her down the stairs.

Awen could sense Ezo's body tensing. *No wonder Sootriman didn't say anything about this. It's horrible.* If this was hard for her to watch, it had to be brutal for Ezo. Kane knelt over Sootriman and had a discussion with her that neither Awen nor Ezo could make out. Kane nodded and stood upright. He looked at the trooper who'd shot Sootriman.

"Pause video," Ezo said. The holo-vid froze. He stared at the image, zoomed in, and pointed. "I know that one."

Awen looked from Ezo to the trooper. "You know *that* specific trooper? How? He looks like all the rest."

"No." Ezo zoomed in farther. "There, on his chest. The semigloss rank designation. And the way he's standing. I've seen him before. He was tracking us through Itheliana."

Awen froze. "You're sure?"

"Positive." Ezo took a deep breath. "Resume video."

The holo-footage played on as Kane left the den. The soldier ordered two others to haul Sootriman's body away, following Kane. Then, as if possessed by a demon, the trooper raised his weapon and began firing. The people in the room tried to scatter, screaming, but other soldiers blocked the exits. The first trooper picked people off one at a time. Head shot after head shot after head shot.

"Mystics! Turn it off, Ezo. Please."

"End video."

Awen swallowed. *This is madness. Who does that? And to what end?*

Ezo closed out the holo-display, and the room went dark again, save for the light on his weapon, which spread across the table. "That's who's waiting for us."

Awen nodded. A shiver went up her back and down her arms. "We've got to stop him."

"We will." Ezo arched out and took Awen's hand. "And —*mystics*—we must."

6

It all went back to holo-games for Squadron Commander Mauricio Longo. He'd never say that openly, of course. Comparing the risky business of actual fighter combat—where real people died—to children's games would be disrespectful. Still, his childhood memories were filled with long hours spent battling the Jujari over Oorajee. Never in a million years, however, did he think he'd get to lead a real squadron of Repub Talons into combat against the hyenas.

On the other hand, he wasn't exactly surprised by it. As he sat in his Talon's cockpit, monitoring target information and paging through the AI's proposed assault scenarios, he realized he was born for this. He was a sixth-generation pilot who stood on the shoulders of the Longo family legacy. The mere mention of his last name on any bridge, hangar deck, or ace bar elicited an attitude of reverence. Which was why he'd chosen to go by the name Ricio. If there was one thing he hated, it was being known for someone else's achievements. And the Longo family shadow was long and wide in that department.

"Viper Squadron, this is Viper One," Ricio said over TACNET. "Form up on Viper Eight, wedge formation. We are"—he double-checked the fleet roster— "position one in the holding pattern. Stand by for command attack authorization." Response pings scrolled down the side of his HUD as Ricio watched his squadron move into formation. The blue light of their engines flared across his curved window as he examined each ship in his care. Statistically, half of these ships would not survive, but he readied himself to fight as if he wouldn't lose a single one.

The FAF-28 Talon was the pride and joy of the Republic Navy, enjoying the latest developments in ion-engine technology, subspace drive-core research, advanced modular-weapons systems, and pilot-to-AI interfacing. Such additions to the Talon model had extended the short life expectancy of a pilot in combat by four minutes, or seventeen percent—a veritable lifetime as far as aces were concerned. The Talon's slender black fuselage was largest in the rear, due to its twin ion engines and dual drive cores, while the cockpit sat in the aft third with a generous wraparound duraplex window. In keeping with the ship's name, its nose tapered to a narrow point.

Even more evocative of the name, however, were the Talon's two primary wings. They raked forward from the rear with a slight backbend midway, shaped like the wings of birds of prey from any number of worlds around the galaxy. Each wing also maintained some shallow dihedral that pitched them upward. In the opposite direction, two small stabilizers protruded from the fuselage's lower aft to provide additional stabilization during atmospheric flight.

For armament, the Talon sported two primary NR330 blaster cannons nested on either side of the lower fuselage. These were complemented by secondary T-100 blaster cannons in each wing tip—lower discharge but higher frequency. And in the case of light-bomber or antiship operations, the Talon's underbelly allowed for up to four class-C torpedoes or two class-B bombs. In all, the aggressive starfighter epitomized the best the Republic had to offer, and Ricio was proud to helm one of them.

His squadron had yet to leave the protective care of Third Fleet. They circled their patron super dreadnought, the *Black Labyrinth*, awaiting orders to engage the Jujari fleet. *Fleets* was probably a better word. In the last thirty minutes, the Jujari's main contingent of vessels had been joined by two smaller battle groups made up of Sypeurlion and Dim-Telok starships.

Suspecting that this might happen, command had equipped half of Ricio's squadron for antiship strikes and the other half for standard antifighter operations. Such a load provided maximum tactical mobility. But it also meant a decrease in target specificity—meaning they'd most likely be tasked with multiple objectives instead of one or two. More objectives meant more details, and more details meant that more pilots wouldn't be coming home. But he shook that from his mind. *Not yet. Those numbers haven't been calculated yet. They're all just guesses.* We're *the ones making the decisions.*

"Viper Squadron, this is Viper One..." Ricio held the TACNET channel open as he considered what to say. It wasn't like him to be so spontaneous, but he wanted to address them before the Fleet Admiral got on the channel. The Admiral would be generic, but Ricio wanted to be specific. Statistically, he knew this would be the last time he saw half his pilots, and he didn't want them hearing trivialities. Not today.

Plus, this was a big day, one which needed someone to calm pilot nerves. This conflict had been brewing for generations... *for three hundred years,* he reminded himself. When the fleet had jumped into the system, everyone thought it would be a routine in and out. The Senate had arranged a fancy meeting with the Jujari mwadim and the Luma emissary. Everyone knew it wouldn't go anywhere. But what Ricio wasn't expecting—what no one was expecting—was war.

"I know most of you grew up dogfighting Jujari Razorbacks on the holos, and that was the closest any of us thought we'd ever get. Well, not anymore. I'm not going to lie to you —I expect this to be the fight of our lives. And I expect the Jujari to come at us hard. Looks like they've got Sypeurlion and Dim-Telok backup too. But I also expect that we'll go at them harder. The fact is, you have been fighting these bastard dogs since you were kids. You've played out this conflict a thousand times. You're the best. The Repub knows that, I know that, and you need to know that. You're going to outthink, outfly, and outfight every damn enemy you engage.

"If you get tailed, say something. You see a squadron that needs breaking up, call it out. If there's an opportunity, exploit it, but don't ever leave your wingman. And when you need new energy mags or fuel cells, don't wait for me. Fall back and reoutfit. My guess is that hangar ops will dispense with batch outfitting once the blaster bolts start flying. Get in, get out, and return to the line."

Ricio paused again, unsure of how to end his speech. He always felt awkward doing these, but he remembered how much it had meant to hear his COs genuinely rally the pilots when he was an ensign. Sure, some did a terrible job, and all the pilots rolled their eyes. But the good COs—the best ones—could make someone a better pilot and a better person. People would follow that kind of leader to hell and back. Sometimes, those speeches even made the difference between getting home and becoming space dust. And Ricio definitely wanted to get home. He'd often wondered why he stayed in the service so long after he'd gotten married and they'd had a son. Given the life expectancy of fighter pilots, Ricio had always felt it was irresponsible to keep flying. His family needed him. But they also needed the credits, and few other jobs paid out like this one—particularly in the event of his death.

Where else would I make this kind of cred?

The honest truth was, *Nowhere.*

It was more than the money, though. Privately, he didn't *want* to do anything else but fly. There was nothing like it. Flying a Talon was the closest thing to being a god that he could think of. That was precisely what the recruiter who'd come to his university had said. And damn, he'd been right. Everything about it was alluring. Even addicting. The power. The agility. The views. There was just no way he could settle for another job after this. If he couldn't fly a Talon, he didn't want to work at all. So the plan had been to fly this last mission and then call it quits. He knew it was bad luck to name your exit mission before flying it, but Lady Luck wasn't married to his wife. He was.

"A select few of you have been with me for a while now. And we've seen some action together. Caledonia. Po-Froslin. The moon base on Teslo Nine. But all of you—and I mean all of you—are the select few today. You will all be known as legends, and for those who make it home, you'll be regarded as legends in your own time. Today, we will see combat together that will be remembered for generations. You are the greatest because you made it here. And wherever we go next, we go together. We will be the masters of Oorajee. Viper victory."

Fourteen other voices flooded TACNET as one, replying, "Viper victory!"

No sooner had Ricio finished his speech than command overrode all channels and issued a fleet-wide communiqué.

"All stations, all stations," said a communications officer

over TACNET. "Red alert. This is not a drill. I repeat, red alert. Pause for the fleet admiral."

The channel pinged, and a new voice sounded, one that Ricio was not expecting to hear.

"Attention all personnel of the Republic Navy. This is Fleet Admiral Hal Brighton aboard the *Black Labyrinth*..."

Fleet Admiral Brighton? Apparently, the XO had gotten a field promotion, which was highly unusual. But then again, several odd things had been happening aboard the *Labyrinth* over the last several weeks—things that Ricio couldn't explain. Chief among them were items related to now *former* Fleet Admiral Kane. Ricio didn't have any personal contact with the man, of course, but he'd heard stories that made him extremely uneasy about the officer's ability to lead the fleet. They seemed more like something out of fantasy than reality.

Then again, Ricio had also seen plenty of strange things during his time in the navy, and sailors could weave preposterous narratives concerning just about anything that was above their pay grade. But many of the tales about Admiral Kane came from reputable sources, and *that* was what made Ricio so uneasy. These sailors weren't liars. He didn't doubt that they'd seen and heard things that rattled them.

For example, some of his contacts among the brass claimed Admiral Kane's face had changed. It started with burns across his entire head. Then his eyes changed color. Even his voice was different, they said. It was rumored that he'd been going by a different name too.

Then came the reports that he'd executed several officers on the spot for insubordination. When others asked why no one had reported the admiral, sources noted that the Senate had sanctioned his use of force. Such a claim seemed absurd to Ricio, but who was he to argue with the Galactic Republic's seat of power? Apparently, all of this surrounded the Jujari meeting. And for whatever reasons, the Senate suspected that spies were operating at the highest levels of leadership. The admiral had simply been given the authority to do what needed doing.

And then there were the rumors that Admiral Kane had gone to another universe. Some were calling it a parallel universe, others a metaverse accessed by quantum event horizons. This, of course, was the most outlandish rumor yet. But at least one or two Marines who'd been the admiral's bodyguards had supposedly leaked news about the crossing to their navy counterparts. Secrets leaked when Svoltin single malt flowed. His sources swore on the mystics' graves that the stories were true, and as far as Ricio was concerned, they might have been—but at the moment, he had a war to wage and a day to win.

"All hands, battle stations," Brighton continued. "I repeat, all hands, battle stations. We have received and confirmed classified orders from the Republic Senate to retaliate against the Jujari fleet and their allies in open naval warfare. The orders state, in no uncertain terms, that all Republic starships will and must engage any and all enemy targets without restriction in response to atrocities committed against the Galactic Republic. There will be no quarter. The enemy's retreat or destruction is the only acceptable outcome."

Holy mystics, this is happening. Ricio could hardly believe what he was hearing.

The fleet admiral continued, "Targets have been selected in order of priority and delivered to each fleet for dissemination. Redundancies have been attached to each order set should any element fail. Each fleet is commanded to execute orders with haste, and all fighter and bomber squadrons have been cleared for combat. Command attack authorization level alpha. I repeat, this is an alpha-level command attack authorization. Fleet Admiral out."

The channel closed, and Ricio sat in his cockpit, feeling the low hum of his Talon's drive cores in his seat. His hands were tight on the controls, and he could hear the thump of his heart in his ears. He knew his squadron wouldn't have been scrambled unless the threat was real, but hearing the admiral's voice made it all the more so. This was it.

The next voice that came over TACNET was that of Captain David Seaman, commander of the *Labyrinth's* two Talon squadrons, Viper and Raptor, and the head of SFC—strategic fighter command. While it didn't have the squadron capacity of the Carrier-class ships, the *Labyrinth* was the only Goliath-class Super Dreadnought in third fleet capable of hosting thirty fighters. It was also the command ship, so Captain Seaman, and therefore Ricio, would take point on all fighter squadron activity for third fleet.

"Viper and Raptor squadrons, your commanders have

received your target coordinates in order of priority and are feeding them to your Talons' AIs now."

Ricio already had the order packets ready to disseminate and punched Transmit at the captain's word. His HUD displayed near-instantaneous receipt confirmation to all fourteen fighters.

"Stay on target, and happy hunting," Seaman replied. "You are cleared to engage the enemy." The captain closed out the channel, and Ricio resumed control of his comms.

Whether from fear or excitement, his hands trembled as he gave the final command and loosed his fighters. "You heard him, Vipers. Let's get dirty."

And just like that, the void's most significant killing force was unleashed upon the Jujari.

7

"We've been granted permission to send a shuttle to Docking Bay One," Rohoar said, looking up from the captain's chair's built-in data pad.

Magnus spun around from the main viewing window, where a blue-and-green image of Worru loomed. "Come again?"

Abimbola turned from Magnus and eyed Rohoar too.

The Jujari shrugged. "Did I say something unclear?"

"You were clear," Magnus replied, stepping toward Rohoar. "It's just that you said Docking Bay One."

Rohoar double-checked the display. "That is correct, scrumruk graulap." Rohoar had given Magnus that Jujari name back on Oorajee—it roughly translated as *little hairless warrior*. But given Rohoar's humiliating step away from national leadership, the former Marine let it slide. It was, in fact, fast becoming a term of endearment—at least, that was how Magnus interpreted it. Doing so helped it feel less like an insult.

Rohoar repeated the information. "Docking Bay One. I don't see the problem."

"No one ever gets Docking Bay One," Abimbola said. "Not on any Repub planet I know of."

"Exactly," Magnus replied. "It's saved for galactic dignitaries."

"And you are not a galactic dignitary?" Rohoar asked.

Magnus shook his head. "Not even close, buddy. At least not in the way that gets you a premium parking spot."

"Unless you count being an outlaw as one of the requisites." Abimbola grinned. "In which case, you get the best spot, buckethead."

Magnus smiled at the jab then stroked his beard, lost in thought. "I don't think it has anything to do with me, actually. I think it has everything to do with you."

Rohoar recoiled. "Me? What for?"

"Think about it. A Jujari starship—following a diplomatic ambush and a newly begun war with the Republic—jumps into orbit over Worru and requests docking permission for a shuttle."

"That'll get you a spot up front for sure," Abimbola said.

Magnus pursed his lips and nodded in agreement. "Seems a few people might be very interested in our arrival. Abimbola, can you summon the crew to the bridge?"

"All of them?"

Magnus smiled. "All of them."

Magnus, Abimbola, and Rohoar sat in silence as the elevator doors opened in succession, delivering a new batch of riders to the bridge with each cycle. Dutch, Haney, Gilder, and Nolan saluted Magnus and stepped to the side. To his surprise, they'd refused transport to the Republic fleet when they were on Oorajee and opted to remain with him—something that would get them court-martialed upon their return.

Magnus tried to argue their decision, but Dutch, speaking for all of them, had respectfully declined his pleas. "We've come this far with you," she'd said back in Abimbola's headquarters. "We're not leaving your side now." As with Flow and Cheeks, the move was most likely career ending unless Magnus could help them fabricate some sort of story when all this was over.

Next came Rix, Simone, and Silk, the three most notable Marauders who'd fought with Magnus in his efforts to rescue the Marine hostages in the Western Heights. Apparently, Cyril, the code slicer and bomb tech, had wanted to come, too, but Abimbola said he was in no shape to fly. The three Marauders insisted Abimbola take them with him, and after several minutes of deliberation, the warlord relented.

"You're not getting paid for this, though," he said. "You're doing this on your own." They'd agreed, and only then did Abimbola let them on Rohoar's shuttle.

And then there was Titus, the stranded Marauder Magnus had helped save under the gate in the Western Heights. According to Abimbola, the man had insisted he be taken along, as he owed Magnus a life debt. Magnus had last seen Titus sprinting away from his skiff—one overrun with Selskrit. The guy had been cool, calm, and collected, even in the face of certain death.

When Magnus overheard Titus's conversation with Abimbola, he stepped in. "Let him come."

Abimbola raised an eyebrow. "You sure about that? Because you do know that if you keep collecting warriors like this, we're going to run out of food."

Magnus laughed. Feeding troops was a very real and often overlooked priority for any commander, and supply-chain management was far down on Magnus's list of skill sets. "Believe me, Bimby. I know." He patted the giant Miblimbian on the biceps. "But that's why I have you."

Last on the bridge were Valerie and Piper. All eyes watched them as they exited the elevator—one the epitome of elegance despite her cargo pants and tactical shirt, the other the picture of youthful innocence as she clutched her ratty stuffed corgachirp. Piper also held a new holo-pad that she'd acquired from Rohoar. The two had developed quite the bond over the last several hours, which had surprised everyone. Rohoar and Piper truly represented the opposite ends of the species spectrum.

"All right, listen up, people," Magnus said with his arms folded. Abimbola stood beside him, while Rohoar stayed in his captain's chair. "We've been given the green light to dock a shuttle on Worru. But something tells me we may get more than we bargained for."

"How so?" Valerie asked, her hands folded over Piper's chest in a protective posture.

"Let's just say that I don't think the Luma were expecting a Jujari destroyer-class starship to jump into the system."

"Are you expecting resistance?" Dutch asked.

"No. But I also don't want to go in without a plan, which is why you're all here."

"So what's the plan, LT?"

Rohoar's shuttle arrived at Docking Bay One without incident. There had been no orbital escort and no more communication with the traffic control tower than was to be expected. For all intents and purposes—besides the strange permission to arrive at Docking Bay *One*—this was a routine shuttle arrival. Still, something felt off.

"You okay there, buckethead?" Abimbola asked.

The two of them stood behind Rohoar as the Jujari piloted the shuttle to the landing pad. Surprisingly, Rohoar was a natural with the helm and, when asked, insisted that he came from "generations of starfaring Tawnhack." Magnus doubted the statement's validity, as the Jujari seemed like anything but starfarers. Yet their old ships, despite being rough around the edges, appeared to bear out at least some of Rohoar's claims.

"Hey, buckethead. You good?" Abimbola repeated.

"Just on guard." Magnus realized he was squeezing the back of Rohoar's chair tightly enough to leave indentation marks when he let go.

"What's the worst that can happen?" Abimbola asked. "They're Luma peacemongers, right?"

Magnus chuckled. "That's exactly what I've called them."

"Seems we agree, then." Abimbola jabbed Magnus in the ribs.

"Still, the last time I underestimated one of them, she saved my life."

"Twice, if I'm not mistaken. Once in the street, and once in my jail."

Magnus turned to the giant. "Yeah… that's right."

"But who's counting?"

Magnus touched his in-ear comm, which Abimbola had supplied. "Team One, you ready?"

"Ready to check myself for fleas after riding with that Jujari," Simone replied from the aft cargo bay.

"I am on the comms network too," Rohoar said, powering down the drive core with a few taps on the dashboard.

"Good. Then you'll know to get yourself a flea bath later tonight."

"We have a job to do, people," Abimbola said. "Just follow the plan."

"Understood," Simone replied. "Team One is good to go."

"Team Two?" Magnus asked.

"Team Two, standing by," Dutch replied.

"Good. Nolan, what's your twenty?"

"Sorry, Lieutenant. I'm in the head, belowdecks, sir."

Magnus rolled his eyes.

"Hey." Abimbola nudged Magnus again. "When you have to go, you have to go."

"Copy that."

Over comms for all to hear, a zipper closed, followed by the distinct forced-air vacuum of a toilet flushing. Water splashed in a sink as a man's tenor whistle filled ten seconds. Finally, a door slid audibly open, and Nolan stepped out of the head and into the cargo bay.

"Hey, Nolan," Dutch said. "Your comm channel is wide open."

There was a pause. Magnus heard several people giggle in the background, including Piper.

"My bad," Nolan said, and his comm went silent.

"We're all gonna die," Magnus said to no one in particular.

Abimbola placed a large black hand on Magnus's shoulder. "Yeah, but we'll have fun doing it."

Just then, Nolan's head appeared as he climbed the alternating-tread staircase into the bridge. "Here, Lieutenant."

"Nice of you to join us."

"Are you going to whistle a tune for us too, pilot?" Abimbola asked.

"Very funny."

"Okay, Nolan, you have the helm."

The warrant officer nodded and swapped out with Rohoar. "She'll stay warm, Lieutenant."

"That's what I like to hear." He looked out the front window and then gave the camera monitors a quick glance. Magnus noted the presence of a boarding party waiting behind the hangar bay's blast-wall window. He counted several Luma and twice as many Worruvian guards. "Keep the stabilizing thrusters firing for a few more seconds, Nolan. I don't want anyone approaching the ship until Simone's team is clear."

"Copy that, sir."

Magnus tapped his comm. "Simone, you're clear to move."

"On it."

A dashboard indicator illuminated, presumably for the starboard door opening—Magnus couldn't read Jujarian any more than he could speak it. He watched an exterior camera feed of Simone, Rix, Silk, and Titus making a dash to a cluster of freight containers on the opposite side of the ship from the blast wall. "You sure you know how to operate this thing even though it's in Jujari, Nolan?"

The pilot nodded. "She's laid out a lot like the Sparrow, actually. I don't anticipate a problem."

Magnus patted him on the shoulder. "Good man." To Abimbola and Rohoar, he said, "Let's do this."

MAGNUS AND ABIMBOLA escorted Rohoar down the cargo-bay ramp and onto the tarmac, where a dozen nervous-looking Luma waited to receive them. He found himself looking for Awen's face, but she wasn't among them. Instead, all he saw was a tightly bunched cluster of robed mystics who'd probably never seen a Jujari in real life. He wondered how long it had been since Worru had hosted one of the notorious warriors. *Maybe never.*

The tension was amplified, however, by another two dozen armed Worruvian guards behind the Luma—which was why Magnus and Abimbola both openly carried blasters. Magnus held his MAR30 in low ready position, while Abimbola rested a bulky M101 double-barrel blaster cannon on his shoulder. The Miblimbian also wore his sheathed bowie knife on one thigh and his holstered BFT6 Tigress on the other.

Must be a damn fine sight striding out of this shuttle, Magnus mused.

For his part, Rohoar went weaponless—in other words, he didn't have a blaster. But Magnus had seen Jujari maws and paws in action and knew that the former mwadim could handle himself anywhere in the galaxy just the way he was. Instead of carrying a weapon, the Jujari had found a ceremonial robe on the *Bright Star* and secured it around his neck.

The long crimson cape gave him a royal air that was surprisingly dignified.

"Is that a traditional thing the mwadims wear?" Magnus had asked before they left the shuttle.

"No." Rohoar had held the fabric up. "It's a bath towel I found in a locker."

Magnus gave a slight smile as the three of them walked up to the lead Luma on the tarmac.

"Greetings in the name of our great Master So-Elku and the elders," said a diminutive man in maroon-and-black robes. He bowed, never taking his eyes off Rohoar, and spread his arms out. "The Order of the Luma welcomes you in peace. I am Elder Neevis."

"Rohoar is Tawnhack, mwadim of the Jujari," Rohoar replied, placing a fist on his chest. He had reverted to speaking of himself in third person, once again embodying his role as the mwadim.

Magnus wondered—not for the first time—if the Jujari leader had given up his throne to take up his son's obligation to serve Magnus. *Is it permanent? How long is Rohoar hanging around, anyway?* They'd had to leave Oorajee so quickly that there hadn't been time to discuss any of these details.

"It is an honor to make your acquaintance, Mwadim Rohoar of the Tawnhack," Neevis said, mimicking Rohoar's posture with a hand to his chest. "I will be your chaperone for the duration of your stay. If you need anything, please know I am at your disposal."

"Rohoar accepts."

Neevis bowed again. This time, his eyes darted to the shuttle's cargo bay. "Is there anyone else on your shuttle whom you wish to bring with you?"

That was a strange question. Magnus didn't like this guy, and it wasn't just because of his beady eyes and spiked hair.

"No," Rohoar said. "Rohoar is all."

The elder's eyes darted between the shuttle and Rohoar for a few seconds. "Very well." Neevis straightened his back and smoothed his robes. "As for your escorts, their weapons are not needed here on Worru."

"They will keep their weapons," Rohoar replied.

"Ah, yes... but you see—"

"Neevis's guards have weapons."

The elder showed hints of having his feathers ruffled—a twitch in his eyes, a curling of his lip—but composed himself. "They do, and that is for all of our protection."

"That is for Neevis's protection. And these two"—Rohoar gestured at Magnus and Abimbola—"are for Rohoar's. Rohoar knows how the Luma fear the Jujari."

"I beg your pardon? Mwadim Rohoar, we—"

"And Rohoar understands. You look delicious to Rohoar."

"Excuse me?" Neevis placed a hand on his chest as a look of shock flooded his face.

"Rohoar knows the perfect sauce for Neevis too."

"Pushing it," Magnus said under his breath, knowing that the hyena's large ears could hear him just fine.

"Mwadim Rohoar..." The elder bit his lip. "I want to assure you that—"

"Rohoar is kidding, Neevis!" The Jujari barked in laughter. Magnus looked at Abimbola. The Miblimbian shrugged and started to laugh, as did Magnus. All three of them guffawed as the elder nervously tucked his hands into his sleeves.

When the laughter died down, the elder asked, "May I escort you to Elder's Hall in the Grand Arielina? You will most certainly wish to have an audience with Master So-Elku, I presume."

"That's a yes," Magnus whispered.

Rohoar bared his teeth. "This is what Rohoar wishes, Neevis. Yes."

The elder gave a fake smile, blinking repeatedly. "As you wish. This way."

8

Ricio had the initial mission objectives displayed on his HUD. Distances and coordinates updated in real time as his squadron approached the Jujari armada. Oosafar filled his window to the right, adorned with twin moons, Tlamook and Hormook. Dead ahead, the enemy had gathered their ships in a cone formation pointed at the Republic Navy.

Ricio's AI displayed the first target, designated as Tango One, a Pride-class battleship. At least, that was how the Repub's target classification system noted it. The starship only resembled a battleship in its size. Where a Pride-class's monohull had elegant lines that raked back from a pointed prow, the Jujari vessel was blunt faced and modular. Its blocky sections were linked together by massive gantries and structural cylinders. If a Repub battleship looked sleek and lethal, its Jujari counterpart felt muscular and menacing. In fact, this was the general comparison Ricio made for every other ship type in the enemy's fleet.

"First mission objective uploaded," Ricio said over naval TACNET. "Looks like we drew a battleship, Vipers." Ricio manually locked the enemy ship's vector into his navigation system. The AI would do the same, but there were some things Ricio liked to do himself.

Suggested flight paths and attack vectors filled Ricio's HUD. Tango One was the farthest ship to the right of the enemy battle group, toward Oosafar. Apparently, SFC had decided to nip at the enemy's heels before assaulting the head. It was the most conservative approach, at least initially.

While working inward from the fringes might keep casualties to a per-minute minimum, those minutes eventually would add up, becoming hours and days. Sometimes, it was just better to be aggressive right out of the gate and get it over with—even if it meant heavy losses—than to fight the emotionally numbing and physically exhausting battle of attrition. Ricio hoped that command had some surprises up their sleeve. Otherwise, this was going to be a very long day—added to an already long deployment. He missed home.

Ricio held two fingers to his lips, kissed them, and placed his fingertips on a pair of printed pictures wedged under his ship's main diagnostic display. One image was of his beloved Marguerite, taken while they were on their honeymoon on Triber-Westfall. The other was of his son when he'd graduated from the mock-pilot school for children. Philando had only been five, but he'd puffed his chest out like he was a grown man, proud of the badge pinned to his child-sized uniform. He would make a great pilot one day—Ricio was sure of it. *I just hope I live to see it.*

Warning indicators flashed on his HUD as three pairs of enemy Razorbacks circled Tango One, apparently anticipating Ricio's attack vector.

"Viper Two through Seven, prepare to engage hostile fighters bearing two two nine mark four eight."

Six confirmation icons went green, followed by Viper Two saying, "Copy that, commander."

"Viper Eight through Fifteen, you're Charlie Team. You've got the battleship. I want your first volley focused on their engines, as most of their power will already be diverted to their forward shields. Let's get her dead in space before slitting her throat."

"Understood, sir," Viper Eight said.

"And watch those turrets," Ricio added. The Jujari's version of the quad-barrel auto turret was notoriously efficient. But they did have one weakness. "Keep your speed up and stay lateral. No head-on assaults until they're taken out."

"Roger that."

Ricio watched as the top half of his squadron increased their speed and headed toward the back of the enemy formation. Other than a few stray blaster shots, the fighters were left alone—the armada's main guns were too busy firing on their Repub counterparts, leaving the fighters to fend for themselves. Ricio wished the starships well then said, "Viper Two through Seven, on me." He peeled off from his current vector, three pairs of Talons in tow.

The Pride-class battleship grew larger with each second as Ricio accelerated to attack speed. His AI acquired targets and disseminated them to the other six fighters, automatically prioritizing them by pilot. Ricio's display showed the Razorbacks preparing for the engagement, too, their underbelly thruster-fins unfurling to form two weaponized wings near the bow. The ship's dingy-bronze main body was arched and ridged like a dog's back and had two engines on either side of its boxy stern.

Unlike the Repub, the Jujari tactic was to move in triplets. The first trio of Razorbacks rolled right, toward the battleship's stern. Viper Five, Six, and Seven—Bravo Team—would have an even ship-to-ship dogfight. Meanwhile, Ricio's sensors locked on the left-most trio. The other two Razorbacks were handed to the rest of what his AI marked as Alpha Team: Viper Two and Three, with Four picking up any slack.

Ricio's AI tracked the three Razorbacks as they rolled over the battleship's bow. "Watch those turbo turrets," he reminded everyone. As if prompted by his words, the turrets erupted in automatic fire. A blistering barrage of blue blast bolts filled the void directly behind Ricio's fighters, trailing them by less than ten meters. *Way too close*, Ricio noted.

Meanwhile, the Razorbacks circled around Ricio's flank, executed an about-face with a half roll, and opened fire with their blaster cannons. The simple maneuver had been called an Alcion for so long that no one even knew where it had gotten its name.

"They're trying to pin us against the battleship," Viper Two exclaimed over Alpha Team's closed channel. His ship's shield absorbed several glancing blows on the port side.

The enemy's maneuver was simple and had been performed quickly—both things that Ricio admired. "Full thrusters!" He shoved the throttle lever forward and felt his Talon suck him into the seat. He had yet to fire a shot, and already, the Jujari had the upper hand. Ricio had been overconfident and underestimated the enemy. It was a noob mistake—one he wouldn't make again.

As soon as Ricio and Alpha Team were clear of the turbo turrets, he initiated a Paraguutian Cobra maneuver: a quick flip along the Talon's horizontal axis while the craft was still traveling forward. The maneuver was named after the desert reptile on Paraguu that flipped over on a pursuing enemy. The lizard acted like it was wounded, only to launch a surprise attack with sharp teeth and venom sacs. Nasty suckers.

The fighter maneuver brought his weapons to bear on the trailing Razorbacks. The other six Talons followed his lead, flipping on the enemy. They traveled backward just as fast as they had been moving forward.

As soon as Ricio had target lock, he squeezed the main trigger on his flight yoke. Twin streams of red blaster fire erupted from the NR330 cannons nested inside the fuselage. The force vibrated his cockpit. The first volley reduced the shields, while the second tore into the cockpit, no doubt killing the hyena-like pilot. Ricio watched as the lead ship exploded in a short-lived fireball that was swallowed by hard vacuum. He'd gotten lucky—very lucky.

"Scratch one," Ricio said.

He watched as the next Razorback lost its shield, compliments of Viper Three and Four, but not before spraying them with a barrage of return fire. The two ships attempted to dodge the incoming blaster bolts and broke off in a lethal game of chase. Viper Four's shield was below fifty percent—the Talon was flying slower than his wingman too. Viper Three, meanwhile, acquired a lock on the Razorback and fired a torpedo. The missile followed the retreating craft and went straight through the arched fuselage, hitting the midbody drive core. The explosion was massive, forcing Ricio's helmet visor to dim against the bright light.

The third enemy ship took heavy fire across its port side, reducing its shield. Ricio joined Viper Two in the attack, barely missing a heavy blanket of enemy fire. Ricio rolled right while Viper Two rolled left, allowing the enemy fighter to split between them. Rico executed another Paraguutian, still maintaining momentum from his original trajectory away from the battleship. As soon as he had a target lock, he squeezed his trigger. Blaster fire from both his Talon and Viper Two's tore off the enemy's port wing and chewed up the fuselage with such force that the Razorback went whirling into an uncontrolled spin. Though it was not as satisfying as an explosion, the ship and pilot were lost to the void.

"Good shooting, Alpha Team," Ricio said. "Status, Viper Four."

"Starboard engine at twenty percent, sir. One of those hits sent a power surge through my shields."

"Understood." Ricio swiped a glance over Viper Four's icon in his HUD, soloing it for direct communication. "Get back to the *Labyrinth* for repair."

"Copy that, sir."

Ricio immediately pulled up Bravo Team's progress on his HUD. The remaining three Razorbacks had been dispatched. But so had one of his Talons.

"Bravo Team, report," Ricio said over general comms.

"We've lost Viper Six," Viper Five said.

Ricio felt the all-too-familiar dread in the pit of his stomach. His underestimation of the Jujari had just cost him a pilot—and in the opening salvo too. He stretched his fingers in his leather gloves and then grabbed the controls again. "Provide cover for Charlie Team. Let's take out those turrets."

Ricio pitched his Talon forward again then brought the vessel around to bear on the Jujari battleship. He maintained speed, targeting the two turbo turrets near the stern. He could also see Charlie Company beginning their second pass on the battleship's engines. Apparently, the first pass hadn't completely taken them all out, which meant the battleship's captain would be diverting power to the aft shields, making Viper Squadron's job all the harder.

"Sooner rather than later," Ricio said to Alpha and Bravo Teams. He couldn't risk losing another fighter this early, and getting too close to the Jujari battleship would all but ensure casualties.

Ricio's AI notified him of target lock, and he squeezed off a single torpedo on the aft-most turret. Out his cockpit window, the rocket-propelled missile streaked its way across the horizon's black canvas, bypassed the energy shields, and found its mark on the battleship's port side. The turrets had been on fighter overwatch—too busy with the Talons to pick up the torpedo. Several plumes of orange flame and debris bubbled out from the side and then dissipated as the explosion's fuel was spent.

Ricio bared his teeth in a triumphant sneer. "Just like that, Vipers. Keep it coming."

He felt confident that the battleship's turrets would be switched out of fighter-overwatch mode and begin tracking all targets indiscriminately. It would make sending any more torpedoes troublesome, but it didn't matter. His squadron had a hole for shield penetration.

"Port side, aft section." Ricio's finger tapped the air in his HUD, marking the spot on the enemy's hull. "All ships in position, open fire!"

His Talons focused their blaster fire on the charred hole. For the first few seconds of their assault, blaster fire struck the energy shields, like large stones thrown into a purple sea, and rippled out in all directions. Ricio was getting close enough that he could actually see the waves along the transparent field. But the shield was weakening.

"Come on!" Ricio pulled his second trigger, activating the

wingtip-mounted T-100 blasters. "Activate secondary weapons systems!" Those fighters flying beside Ricio opened up with their wingtip weapons too.

Faster than Ricio had expected, a hole opened up in the shields. The next blaster bolts sailed through and drilled the side of the battleship. Ricio watched with excitement as the Talon's combined firepower cut deep into the enemy ship, causing mini explosions all around the wound. He even noticed secondary and tertiary explosions emanating from the top and bottom of the hull deeper in. Suddenly, the aft shields disappeared.

"Take out the engines! All remaining ships, focus fire on the breach, and take out the aft turrets!"

Like fire wasps swarming a wounded Boresian taursar, Ricio's Talons dove on the ship, widening the burning hole on the hull's port side with every shot. Then they pulled up and skimmed the surface, flying danger close. Talons strafed the turbo turrets, taking out one at a time, before pulling up on the starboard side of the ship, only to circle back for more.

By the time Ricio had finished his second pass, Charlie Team reported that the engines had been destroyed. Likewise, all aft turrets were out of commission, and the battleship was falling away from the rest of the fleet. In another few minutes, the Jujari vessel would be pulled into Oosafar's gravity well and meet its end—either as a fireball in the skies or a relic in the dunes.

"Viper Squadron, fall back," Ricio said, a smile creeping

along his face. "And stay clear of the forward turrets. She may be mortally wounded, but she'll still try to pull you down."

Confirmation indicators lit up his HUD. Ricio banked away from the battleship and waited for his squadron to fall in. They'd been lucky that the enemy fleet hadn't sent more Razorbacks. That meant the Jujari were playing things conservatively too.

He pulled up the next order set. His eyes widened as he scanned the brief. Apparently, CFS *did* have a surprise up their sleeve. Ricio studied the position of the Carrier-class dreadnought identified in his navigation computer. "Great mystics…" he said under his breath.

Taking down a carrier would mean rendering the enemy fleet's fighters incapable of refueling and resupplying in orbit—instead, the fighters would be forced to do so on Oorajee's surface. But like Repub ship-positioning doctrine, the Jujari carriers were heavily guarded and covered in the center of the fleet. Ricio wasn't sure if they could pull this off.

"If you need more energy mags, torpedoes, or fuel cells, now's the time," Ricio said over TACNET. "Because we're going after a carrier."

9

"To what do we owe the great pleasure of hosting such an esteemed guest?" So-Elku said, spreading his arms toward Rohoar, almost as if he meant to embrace the Jujari but then thought better of it.

Smart guy, Magnus thought. The Luma elders and Worruvian guards stood in a semicircle behind So-Elku, all facing Magnus and his two friends.

"Master So-Elku," Neevis said, stepping in between the Luma master and the Jujarian mwadim, "may I present—"

"Nonsense! I know who this is. The whole galaxy knows who this is, Neevis. It is *me* you should be presenting to *him*."

"Master?"

There was a momentary pause as Neevis looked from So-Elku to Rohoar and back again. His brow was furrowed in a nervous expression.

"Well?" So-Elku spun his finger in circles, insisting that Neevis turn to face Rohoar. "Go on, then."

"May... may I present—"

"Louder! More confidently."

"May I present to your mwadimship the head of the Order of the Luma, Master So-Elku."

Magnus winced as Neevis bowed. The man looked as if he might fall over or throw up. Maybe both. But the entire thing was just a charade on So-Elku's behalf. Only a complete idiot would be unable to spot the Luma master's insincerity. Magnus actually felt bad for Rohoar—but only for a second. He guessed that the Jujari sensed So-Elku's guile. And more than that, Magnus knew Rohoar could take care of himself just fine. He'd sooner shred the Luma to pieces than suffer the man's flattery for much longer. Magnus liked to think that it was only for the sake of Piper's safety that Rohoar had not already devoured the man.

That would be something to watch. Magnus stifled a grin.

"Mwadim Rohoar, what brings you to our humble planet?" So-Elku asked, hands clasped in an overly earnest gesture. Magnus looked around the ornately appointed room, the domed ceiling, and the lush garden beyond. *Humble, my ass.* Though the trees in the garden would make for some ideal cover...

"Rohoar is here to ascertain whether or not the Luma may assist the Jujari in finding safety for her tribes against the Republic."

"What?" The Luma master pulled his head back in

surprise. If So-Elku wanted Rohoar to repeat himself, however, he'd be sorely disappointed. In his short time among the Jujari, Magnus had observed that they hated repeating themselves.

When Rohoar didn't respond, So-Elku interlaced his fingers and frowned. "This is because of the Republic assault on your ships, isn't it? We've heard rumors."

"It is because of the Republic waging war on our people," Rohoar corrected.

"Quite so, quite so…" So-Elku pursed his lips, taking his time to respond. "And where would you suggest we help move an entire planet's worth of inhabitants? That is, surely, no small feat. I'm doubtful it can even be accomplished."

"The Luma assisted the Caledonian relocation, as they did the Septarians during the Diamond War."

So-Elku raised an eyebrow. "Well, those were very small relocations, which—"

"And the Luma relocated the populaces of three planets in the binary star system of Pel-Ell in less than two months common. Six other planets, three of whose populations are at least thirty percent larger than Oorajee's, also saw relocations within the last two years in the Feddamallarin system."

Rohoar had clearly done his homework. The Jujari weren't as dumb as they looked. And if So-Elku's momentary flash of astonishment was any indicator, he realized that.

"Clearly, the great Jujari mwadim knows a considerable amount about our peacekeeping efforts. Such knowledge must've come with practiced study and attention to detail…"

Magnus could already hear the slick-talking politicking of a well-oiled statesman. It made him sick. If Rohoar *had* been serious about needing help—which he wasn't—such an interaction would have been not only disheartening but downright demeaning as well. Magnus wondered how many other similar conversations had taken place with species in need.

"And as such," So-Elku continued, "you obviously know that our resources are spread thin due to the Kiltar revolt in the Onyx system, which has also displaced billions of Lepeedu on two planets and six moons. Even if we wanted to help you—which, I assure you, we do—there is simply no way we could for at least another six months." The Luma master placed his hands together in prayerful entreaty. "I'm so very sorry, Mwadim."

Rohoar opened his mouth to speak, but So-Elku cut him off. "The most I can offer, at the moment, is sanctuary for you and your crew until such time that we can devise a new strategy, one that preserves the lives of as many of your people as possible against the Republic's *war* on your planet. It is a terrible, *terrible* thing they are waging. Terrible."

"My crew is few," Rohoar replied, "and we will return to my ship."

"So soon? Would you not at least stay for a meal? Dinner after vespers, perhaps?"

While Rohoar considered the proposition—one Magnus knew the Jujari would turn down—a peculiar thing happened. Somewhere inside Magnus's mind, a voice spoke to him. It was as clear as if someone stood twenty centimeters away, yet as he looked around, he could see no one standing that close. *Leave now, Magnus*, the voice said.

So-Elku glanced at Magnus as if noticing something. "Is everything all right there, soldier?"

Magnus concealed his emotions with the help of years of military discipline. He was about to reply when Rohoar said, "Do not address my Marauders."

So-Elku snapped back to Rohoar, cleared his throat, and reoffered the invitation to dinner.

You must leave now and get to Ki Nar Four, said the voice, growing more assertive. It belonged to a woman. Older but strong. *You all need one another.*

Mystics, I'm going crazy, Magnus thought. This was his mind's way of telling him that he needed to slow down, to rest. He hadn't had a vacation since…

You're not going crazy, Magnus.

Wasn't a voice in his head telling him that he wasn't going crazy proof that he was, in fact, going crazy? This wasn't good. The only problem was that the voice was far too real to be ignored.

Magnus, we don't have time for this, she continued. *I already told you, you're not going crazy. My name is Willowood, and I'm a friend of Awen's.*

Splick. This was for real. *So are you another Luma or something? Hijacking my head?*

I am a Luma, yes, and I haven't hijacked anything. I'm merely communicating with you in a way that So-Elku can't detect.

Magnus stared down at the Luma master. *He's bad, isn't he?*

Quite. As I said, you must leave right away. It isn't safe for any of you. But more importantly, Awen needs you on Ki Nar Four. And Piper needs her.

Piper?

Yes. Awen will understand when she meets her. You need to leave immediately. I will do my best to keep So-Elku from following your ship once you leave the system, but it won't last long. And Ki Nar Four will be on his list of places to check, so whatever you do from there, you must do it quickly.

Magnus watched Rohoar and So-Elku speaking but didn't hear their words—he was far too consumed with the conversation happening inside his mind. *And what about you? Where are you right now?*

There was a moment's hesitation before Willowood answered, *My present state doesn't concern you. Now, go. The clock is ticking, and So-Elku wishes to detain you, if not kill you.*

Kill us?

Magnus waited for Willowood to reply, but no answer came. He suddenly felt as if he had a winning hand in a high-stakes game of Antaran Backdraw. Blood threatened to rush to his face, adrenaline making his hands want to shake. But such gambling tells would tip So-Elku off in an instant. He already seemed to suspect something. *Hold it together, Adonis.*

"And how about the rest of your crew? Surely, they are famished," So-Elku continued. "Especially that little one."

"Little one?" Magnus asked, stepping forward.

So-Elku glared at Magnus. "Why, yes. Our sensors show there is a child on board."

"No, they don't."

"I beg your pardon?"

"That shuttle has Jujari cloaking tech. No scanners can penetrate it, including yours, Luma."

"What I meant to say was—"

"You said what you meant to say. We're done here."

Magnus made to turn around, but something held his feet to the marble floor. He looked down. "What the hell?"

"Whoa!" Abimbola exclaimed. "What's happening?" The giant's feet were fixed to the floor as well—and Rohoar's too. The Jujari let out a deep growl. Things were going sideways a lot faster than Magnus had anticipated.

"I will take the child and her mother," So-Elku said calmly. "The rest of you may leave as you came."

"Not happening." Magnus tried to raise his MAR30, but nothing happened. It felt as though his brain had just been disconnected from his arms.

"Ah-ah-ah, Marine," So-Elku said, adding a repeated *tsk* with a waving finger. "Don't you know it's against the law to fire on Luma?" So-Elku walked closer to him, examining him from head to toe. "You do look awfully familiar to me, though. I'm sure I've seen you before. Hanging around with this one—" So-Elku tipped his head toward Abimbola. "And I do mean *hanging* around."

Does he mean the jail on Oorajee? How is that even possible?

"Though I was told all the loose ends on Oorajee had been tied up." So-Elku tapped his chin. "Apparently not. But no matter. I'll take care of what Moldark couldn't."

"Moldark?" Magnus asked. "Who's Moldark?"

"I'd tell you, but you won't live long enough for it to matter."

Live long enough? "What's that supposed to mean?"

So-Elku winced. "You know, for such a highly regarded Marine—I'm sorry, *ex*-Marine—you sure are thick headed. But what was I thinking—aren't all Repub troopers that way?"

"You're gonna kill us, then? Seriously?"

"No, no, no. I'm not. But they will." So-Elku gestured toward the guards behind him. "People don't realize that killing is such a messy affair, and it conflicts with so many of my principles. But it's a necessary affair nonetheless and often the only way to bring lasting peace. Wouldn't you agree, trooper?"

Magnus had to do something—and fast. *The guy's crazy. And how is Awen even friends with him?* None of it made sense.

So-Elku strode to within a few centimeters of Magnus's face. Magnus felt helpless. The only thing he could move was…

His mouth.

Magnus looked into So-Elku's eyes. "Simone, take the shot."

So-Elku blinked as he registered the order. Before he could say anything, a dazzling shower of magenta lightning bolts exploded around him as Simone's sniper bolt slammed into a force field. While the round failed to hit So-Elku's body, it did send him sprawling onto the floor beside Magnus.

Magnus felt his limbs return to his control. He was free, as were Abimbola and Rohoar.

"Fall back!" Magnus ordered, lowering his MAR30 on So-Elku and firing point-blank. Another explosion of magenta electrical tendrils lit up the room. The moment his weapon discharged, Magnus's bioteknia eyes flashed. The hexagonal tactical overlay filled his vision and populated it with vector indicators, target information, and bio stats—too much to consider. All Magnus really wanted to know was if he'd hit So-Elku.

To his astonishment, however, the MAR30's high-frequency burst—at less than a meter away—did little more than push So-Elku across the floor toward the entrance. Only a starship's shields had enough power to hold off a barrage like that! Still, if it meant keeping the man out of play, that was fine by him.

"Stay down!" he yelled at the Luma. Then to the rest of the team, he gave an order on comms. "Back to the ship, on the double!"

"Stay where you are!" demanded the lead guard, blaster trained on Rohoar. The man took one step too close to the Jujari.

"Bad idea, buddy," Magnus said.

In a furious flash of fur, Rohoar chomped the man's arm in two. The blaster—hand still wrapped around the handle—clattered to the floor before the guard could even scream. Rohoar lunged at the next nearest guard and swiped a claw across his neck. The man clutched his throat as blood and air hissed from between his fingers.

Abimbola sent another guard flying back five meters, shooting him point-blank at the end of his M101. The weapon whined as it recharged, ready for another double-barrel wide-displacement discharge, which Abimbola then dispensed with a deafening *krah-boom*. A third guard surprised Abimbola on his flank and managed to strike him in the hip with a blaster bolt. Abimbola buckled only slightly. In one swift motion, he drew his bowie knife, threw it backhanded into two full rotations, and buried the blade in the man's chest.

Just then, Magnus noticed a Luma elder lowering his head and closing his eyes. *That can't be good*, Magnus thought, deeply suspicious of whatever witchcraft these demented mystics used. He had seen Awen do some crazy splick for good. He didn't want to stick around to find out what these Luma could do for evil.

Magnus didn't want to kill the old man. *You really gonna fire on a Luma elder?* None of this felt right. But this was about survival—he'd ask questions later.

Magnus matched his MAR30's sights with his eye's targeting reticle, squeezed the trigger, and felt the weapon kick in his hands. He sent a three-round burst into the Luma's center mass. The man rocked back then looked down at the smoking hole in his chest. The sage tried to scream, but there were few organs left for that purpose. He slumped to the floor, as did the guard directly behind him.

Gateway to War

A warning indicator flashed in Magnus's vision. He ducked just in time to avoid return fire meant for his chest. His thumb toggled his MAR30 to wide displacement, and he aimed at the cluster of Luma and guards, double-checking that Abimbola and Rohoar were behind him. When he squeezed the trigger, a wave of blue light leaped from the blaster's rectangular barrel and swept across the room with a subsonic vibration. Anyone in the wave's path was knocked backward, many of them dead before they hit the floor.

"Let's go!" As Magnus turned to run toward the exit, he saw So-Elku struggling to his feet. The Luma master waved his hand weakly, and the doors slammed shut. "You've got to be kidding me."

Just then, a volley of enemy blaster fire erupted from behind Magnus. He turned to see Abimbola take out two guards with one shot, sparks exploding from the bodies and landing on some of the pillows strewn about the room. Several caught fire and began giving off smoke. Magnus was about to help Abimbola dispatch the remaining guards when a series of sniper rounds dropped no fewer than four of the enemy. He saw the muzzle flashes from the garden beyond.

The guards turned and started shooting into the garden, but Magnus could tell by their random weapon fire that they had no idea where the snipers' hides were any more than Magnus did. Content that Simone and her fire team had their rear, Magnus ran for the exit. Rohoar was right beside him, and Abimbola sounded like he was in tow. So-Elku was almost to his feet, about three meters from the doors, when Magnus heard the Ready chime of his MAR30. It was charged for another wide-displacement shot.

"I thought I told you to stay down!" Magnus fired and watched the blue wave fling So-Elku backward. A shock wave of magenta static spread along the wall as So-Elku's body slammed against it.

Abimbola reached the doors first and started pulling. Magnus joined him. But when he looked for Rohoar, he spotted the Jujari racing toward So-Elku, claws outstretched. Magnus thought to tell him to stop, but he knew it would be useless. Plus, if anyone had a chance of breaking through whatever mystical powers kept the Luma master safe, it was Rohoar. The Jujari slashed at So-Elku's face. The Luma screamed as more magenta energy danced into the air. Suddenly, Rohoar was sent to his back and slid several meters.

"Just leave him!" Magnus yelled, backing down the steps while laying some covering fire for Rohoar. His energy mag was below five percent. "We gotta get out of here!"

No sooner had he said those words than a new wave of guards entered Elder's Hall from a side corridor. The target counter in Magnus's vision started skyrocketing. Rohoar was on his feet again and running out the doors after Magnus and Abimbola.

"You still there, Simone?" Magnus asked over comms.

"I am, but all these security guards are starting to put a crimp on my vacation."

"Anything you can do to take care of them?"

"I think Rix and Titus have a little something cooked up."

"Good. Send it. Then you need to get back to the ship."
"Copy that."
Magnus addressed his pilot. "Nolan?"
"Go ahead, Lieutenant."
"We're coming in hot."
"That's fine, sir."
Fine? "Why's that fine, Nolan?"
"Because we have plenty of heat here at the moment too."
Dammit.

10

Magnus, Rohoar, and Abimbola were charging down the pillar-lined hallway leading out of the Grand Arielina when a massive explosion resounded from Elder's Hall some fifty meters behind them. The shock wave caused Magnus to miss a step, but he recovered before going all the way down. His ears rang, and his vision blurred momentarily. Then he cast a quick glance over his shoulder to see bodies and debris tumbling down the steps.

"Guess Rix and Titus cooked up something real tasty," Magnus shouted over comms more loudly than he intended.

"Sure did," Simone said. "Though I doubt they'll be able to hear for a few days."

"They won't be the only ones. What's your position?"

"Silk and I are halfway to the hangar. Rix and Titus put that explosive on a five-second timer—"

"Three-second!" Rix interrupted.

"Rix! Are you all green back there?" Magnus asked.

"Copy that. Titus and I are rounding the building exterior in sixty."

Magnus was already out of breath, and they weren't even out of the building yet. Was he really this out of shape? "Listen, primary exfil is a no-go. I repeat, do not proceed to the hangar bay. Nolan, you copy?"

"Still loud and clear, Lieutenant."

Magnus couldn't tell if the sound of blaster fire was behind Nolan on comms or behind himself. "Head to secondary exfil."

"Secondary exfil confirmed. On my way."

"Everyone else, listen up—"

Just then, blaster bolts sparked across the floor and slammed into the pillar beside Magnus's head. He swore and ducked behind the massive stone column. Abimbola and Rohoar dove for cover on the other side of the hallway.

Magnus took a deep breath and peeked around his cover. About twenty new enemies filed out of the smoke-filled room. The surviving guards were clearly shell-shocked, but that didn't make their blaster fire any less lethal. He swung the barrel up and around the column. His eyes presented several targeting options. He chose the closest one, listed at forty yards away. All Magnus had to do was think about zooming in, and his eyes expanded his sight picture. He squeezed the trigger and sent a bolt into a guard's head. The body fell while a Confirm icon flashed in Magnus's vision. He rolled back to cover and took another steadying breath.

"Simone, can you set up overwatch outside the main building?"

"Can do, buckethead."

"Good. Seems like we stirred up a nest of fire wasps in here." Magnus spun back out and took out two more guards. Abimbola wasn't having as much luck with the M101, so the Miblimbian unsnapped his Tigress and raised it with one hand. The weapon's loud *boom, boom, boom* report sent Magnus's ears ringing even worse. But he knew that every round meant one more enemy combatant they didn't have to deal with.

"Copy, buckethead," Simone said. "Silk and I will take up flanking positions and cover your retreat. And if Rix and Titus would hurry the hell up, you might get some ground support when you pop out too."

"We'll take all the help we can get." Magnus sent another three blaster rounds downrange. His eyes notified him that his current magazine was at less than two percent. He scolded himself for letting it get that low. *Noob.* Magnus ejected the energy mag and reached for another one on his hip. The new mag was inserted before the spent one had stopped clattering along the marble floor. He racked a charge and selected wide displacement, setting the draw threshold to maximum. This shot would drain the mag. But it would also clear their retreat. Hopefully.

"Get ready to run, boys!" Magnus yelled to Abimbola and

Rohoar. Then he pivoted into the hallway and sent the energy wave tearing down the hall like an electrified garrote wire. The narrow line of energy lanced against each column like the taloned finger of a fire-breathing monster. Charred gashes smoked in the aftermath as the shot collided with people at the far end, and several guards met their end—bodies halved and heads severed. It was a gruesome scene and one Magnus did not relish. His sole objective was getting out of the danger area and to Nolan's LZ.

"Run!" Magnus yelled. Abimbola and Rohoar took off down the hallway, beating hard toward the light of day. Magnus followed, turning every few steps to make sure they weren't being followed. His eyes counted down the meters to the threshold's exterior steps. Then he heard shouts and saw more Luma and guards move between the columns behind them. His eyes glitched, unable to process the numbers without an extended look.

Splick! How many reinforcements do these peacemongers keep on hand?

Magnus followed Rohoar into broad daylight, and they bounded down the steps, along with Abimbola, three at a time. Magnus looked up when he heard the whine of Rohoar's shuttle. Nolan was inbound.

"There!" Magnus pointed to a low wall with slender light posts. "Set a defensive perimeter!"

"Will do, buckethead," Abimbola replied.

"Rix? Titus? What in splick's name is taking you so long?"

"Here!" Rix yelled, waving from around the left side of the building.

"Get over here, and double up on Abimbola and Rohoar!"

"Copy."

Magnus was down the steps, sucking air hard. He slid through the dirt and leaned his back against the low wall just as blaster fire skipped off its top. "Simone?"

"Already got you covered, buckethead."

Magnus searched the surrounding buildings on the opposite side of the large lawn some three hundred meters away.

"You're not gonna see us," she said, "so don't bother looking. We see you, and that's all you need to know, Marauder."

He smiled. "Copy that."

Marauder. Magnus still hadn't gotten used to the new team designation—he might never. But he found it endearing, especially in a firefight. It meant that he belonged somewhere and was part of a team, even if it wasn't the one he'd started out with. He reminded himself to thank Simone later. The small comment meant more to him than she knew.

"Simone, wait for my signal. Can't risk losing you and Silk early. Everyone else, stay covered, and protect the shuttle."

Nolan descended to the lawn. The green grass lay flat under the ship's thrusters. Even the tree limbs on the lawn's distant perimeter rustled violently. Magnus shielded his head as small pebbles pelted his body.

Unlike the many noobs Magnus had worked with, Nolan never actually touched down. He hovered the shuttle less than a meter off the deck, keeping her completely stationary under heavy fire. *The kid's a damn pro.*

More Luma and guards burst out of the entrance like a flood, pouring down the exterior stairs, blasters blazing. Magnus reloaded his last energy mag and took down one combatant after another. The enemy-rich environment made target acquisition easy for his eyes. He could have taken a pray-and-spray approach and still maintained a ninety-percent effective fire rate. Targeting reticles vanished as soon as the victims' bodies wavered. *Target eliminated*, the results read over and over.

Bolts of light crisscrossed the front steps in blues and reds as sparks showered Magnus and his men. More and more blaster fire landed on the shuttle, but Nolan held her steady. *Like a splick-flying rock.* There were good pilots, and there were great pilots. And then there was Nolan.

Fortunately, Rohoar's light armored transport had a robust shield generator—certainly better than any Republic LATs. That defense might be the only reason anyone got out of this alive. Round after round burst upon the shuttle's shield and exploded into a blossom of orange light. The constant *pings* and *smacks* were mind-numbing. Magnus was sure the shield would give way at any second. But it didn't. Somehow, it held. Now all he had to do was get everyone on board.

A new type of blaster bolt suddenly appeared in the air, smacking up against the shuttle's hull. It was magenta, like the sparks that had danced around So-Elku. Magnus chanced a glance around the wall, thinking he'd see the Luma master.

Instead, however, several Luma extended their hands, firing a strange form of energy from their palms.

What the hell?

Each burst of magenta energy swelled around the Luma's hand before discharging. The men and women who fired on the shuttle braced their feet against the blasts, rocking back, then summoning new orbs of energy as soon as the last were spent.

"Overwatch!" Magnus yelled. "We need that covering fire!"

"Inbound," Simone said.

She'd barely finished the word when the fast report of twin MS900 sniper blasters cracked through the air. The sound echoed off the buildings, masking the location of Simone and Silk. The high-speed blaster rounds were even too fast to trace with the naked eye. But Magnus knew the two women were securely positioned across the lawn in the far buildings.

As soon as the enemy noticed the change in assault vectors, a few of them called out, "Sniper!" While some of the Luma scattered from the steps, others lowered their heads and formed blockades against the incoming sniper fire.

"What are they doing?" Titus asked over comms.

"More Luma magic," Abimbola replied. "Dark arts, if you ask me."

"Doesn't matter," Magnus said. "The guards have broken off. Everyone, load up!"

Simone and Silk had bought the window of opportunity

that Magnus needed. He backed away from the wall in a crouch, still picking off guards as he made his way toward the lowering cargo-bay ramp. Rix and Titus were first inside, followed by Rohoar and then Abimbola. Each man sent extra rounds toward the stairs, eager to take out one more of the enemy before Nolan peeled away.

The MS900s continued to lay down suppressive fire, pinning the blaster-wielding guards behind half walls, lampposts, benches, or what he guessed was a Luma's Unity-generated shield. Magnus grieved over how many people he'd killed. This wasn't a sanctioned Repub mission, nor was Worru some hostile planet in the hands of a ruthless warlord. Or was it? The whole idea of using his stock-in-trade against the Luma just seemed… well, wrong. But there was more going on than he realized, and coming here had obviously been a bad idea. He had to get Valerie and Piper to safety. Then he'd ask questions.

With a final burst of full auto, Magnus covered his retreat then pounded up the ramp. "Go, go, go!"

He'd barely given the order when Nolan tipped the shuttle's nose down and pegged the thrusters. Magnus grabbed the handhold and watched as blue sky filled the bay's opening.

"Silk's to the west," Simone said over comms. "Second building in from the street, rooftop. I'll be on the east side of the street, first building."

"Copy that," Nolan replied, pushing the ship toward Silk's position.

Magnus scanned for enemies as Nolan slowed to a hover

about twenty meters above the ground. He spun the shuttle to face the Grand Arielina so the ramp touched down on the building's front edge. Magnus spotted Silk making a run for him.

"Come on!" Magnus yelled.

Blaster fire and orb energy filled the air around the shuttle. Silk ducked, but Nolan held the shuttle steady. The shields would hold. All she needed to do was get there. Since Nolan had the nose of the shuttle pointed toward the enemy, Magnus couldn't have returned fire even if he'd wanted to.

"Does anyone have eyes on those blasters?" Magnus yelled. He extended a hand toward Silk, who was running like a professional sprinter, legs and arms pumping.

"I see 'em," Simone said, and several sniper shots ripped off in quick succession. "Scratched three."

Damn, she is good.

"I've got Silk!" Magnus pulled her into the cargo bay.

"Copy that." Nolan shoved away from the building.

Silk paced the bay with her hands over her head, breathing heavily. "That was close. Good flying, ace," she said up the ladder to the cockpit.

"Thanks, but we ain't out of the weeds yet. Hang on." Nolan rolled the shuttle to the right, slewing across the street, and then righted the ship. He placed the ramp down exactly as he'd done on Silk's building.

Magnus spotted Simone beside a ventilation shaft. "It's now or never," he said.

"Copy." Simone stood, slung her weapon over her shoulder, and sprinted toward Magnus. His eyes displayed the closing gap in meters, counting down from 21.6.

"Incoming!" someone shouted over comms.

"Hold on," Nolan yelled, his voice straining as he jerked the controls. It was the loudest Magnus had heard him speak. The shuttle lurched, nose moving up and to the left. Magnus tumbled down the ramp but caught himself just before rolling into open sky. A smoke trail appeared below his legs as a rocket ripped through the air.

Shuttle-wide alarms sounded moments too late as Magnus watched the rocket make a wide two-hundred-meter turn. "It's coming back around!" Just then, he noticed Simone throwing herself down and pulling up her MC900. *Is she attempting a shot?*

Magnus's eyes instantly calculated the time to impact, Simone's distance and angle relative to the rocket's trajectory, and the statistical likelihood of her success. It wasn't good.

He found himself holding his breath as the window of opportunity closed, and he realized they had no backup plan. Nolan couldn't see the rocket, no one else had a weapon trained on it, and the shield wouldn't stand against the ordnance. Magnus thought he could attempt the shot too, and he tried to pull himself back up the ramp, but even if he succeeded, there wouldn't be time to unsling his MAR30.

Simone had to make this. Magnus looked down and saw the woman fire. The muzzle's shock wave scattered dust and debris across the rooftop. The blaster bolt streaked across the sky and collided with the rocket, detonating it into a flash of orange-and-white light. The explosion pained his eardrums and pelted the shuttle with shrapnel. One red-hot piece sliced into Magnus's head, and another stabbed his hand. He let go of the ramp in a cry of agony. His stomach lurched as his body left the shuttle.

"Gotcha!" Abimbola grabbed Magnus by the wrist and hauled him up. Magnus flopped onto the deck, blood streaming down the side of his head.

"Damn, Bimby!" Magnus said.

"You can thank me later."

"We get one more shot at this," Nolan yelled over comms. "Make a run for it, Simone!"

"Copy that!"

Even from his place on the floor, Magnus could see Simone stand and start running for the edge of the building again. Nolan backed the shuttle toward the roof's edge as more blaster fire filled the air just above Simone's head. But Magnus's eyes told him she was on track to make it—trajectory and velocity looked good. She was going to make it.

The shuttle lurched forward. Nolan swore as a sizable gap appeared between the ramp and the building's roof. The blaster fire was the densest it had been, ringing off the hull incessantly. Magnus's eyes recalculated Simone's numbers. The ship was too high and the gap was too wide.

"Jump!" Abimbola yelled. He extended his arm, hand spread wide.

Simone took three more strides and leaped, then she sailed through the air, blaster fire and orb energy crisscrossing all around her. She flew forward, both hands outstretched. Abimbola grabbed one, but Simone wasn't far enough over the ramp. Her body dropped, yanking Abimbola down—but the giant kept his grip on the shuttle.

Magnus heard a heavy *thud* as Simone's body slapped the underside of the ramp then rebounded off it. Her momentum was too high, and the force ripped her hand from Abimbola's grip. Simone flew away from the shuttle.

Abimbola roared, and Magnus watched in horror as Simone's body flipped end over end. Several blaster rounds struck her, erupting into sprays of orange sparks before her body broke against the sidewalk. Magnus felt helpless—a feeling he'd had a thousand times before. This was one more scene, one more memory that he'd replay at night before going to bed. *Same as all the others.* For a moment, no one said anything. Only the whine of the engines and the pelting blaster fire filled the open comms channel.

"We have her?" Nolan asked in desperation.

"No," Abimbola replied.

"What? I can't—"

"No!" The giant turned away from the ramp.

"Get us out of here, Nolan," Magnus said. "Head due west twenty klicks. Stay low to avoid the anti-air defenses. Then get us back to the *Bright Star*."

There was a pause as Nolan pushed the ship forward. "Copy that, Lieutenant."

Nolan managed to keep the shuttle out of Plumeria's city-wide planetary defense network, making orbit within ten minutes. No one spoke as the crew recovered from the firefight. Valerie attended to Magnus first, administering laser sutures to his head and hand then wrapping both wounds with gauze. When she cleared him, he climbed up to the bridge and took a seat beside Nolan. It was another minute before either of them spoke.

"I'm sorry, Lieutenant."

Magnus shook his head. "Wasn't your fault, Nolan."

Nolan licked his lips. "It was, though. I thought I saw…" Nolan lowered his head and squeezed his eyes shut. Tears streamed down his reddening cheeks. "I thought it was another rocket. But…"

"You tried to dodge it."

Nolan nodded, biting his lip and pulling snot away from under his nose. "It wasn't. It was just some idiot guard with a big blaster." Nolan pounded the dashboard with a fist. "A *blaster*."

"You made the call you thought was best, Nolan."

"Did I?" He glared at Magnus. "I don't know that. 'Cause if I'd waited a half second more, I would have realized what it was… I wouldn't have moved the ship, and she'd be—"

"Nolan."

"She'd still—"

"Nolan, listen."

"She'd still be here!"

Magnus grabbed the back of the man's neck and got right

in his face. "Now, you listen to me, sailor. What you did is what any of us would have done in the same scenario. Only we couldn't have done half of what you did back there. Getting the rest of us off the deck? The way you caught Silk? You're a damn professional, Nolan. A damn professional, you hear me? So don't you tell me what you would have done differently, because then you'd have to do all of it different, and none of us would be here. You hear me right now?"

Nolan nodded.

Magnus leaned his head up against Nolan's, and their hot tears dropped together onto the cockpit floor. "There is nothing I'd ask you to do differently. *Nothing.*"

"Copy that, Lieutenant."

"What'd you say, Nolan?"

"Copy that, sir."

Magnus let the pilot go. "That's what I thought." Magnus coughed twice then wiped the tears from his eyes. "Best damn shuttle pilot I've ever seen. I'm proud of you."

"Thank you, sir."

"You're welcome. Now, get us back to the ship. We have a new mission."

"Right away, sir."

11

By the time Awen and Ezo returned to the *Spire*, Saasarr was sober and clean, no small thanks to TO-96. The bot had carried the lizard to sick bay, given him a shower, seen to his wounds, and provided him a potent head-clearing agent. Then Saasarr saw Sootriman lying across the room.

"And that's where he's been ever since," TO-96 said with a wave of his hand.

Awen and Ezo looked at the reptilian humanoid kneeling reverently beside Sootriman's suspended body. "Thanks, 'Six," Ezo said, patting the bot on the shoulder. "We've got it from here."

"Are you sure that you would not like me to *hang around*, as it were?"

"Negative, buddy. You can head back to the bridge with Azelon. She's better company for you, I'm sure."

TO-96 froze. He looked at Awen then back at Ezo. "Right away, sir. And thank you, sir. You are most kind, sir."

"You… feeling okay, 'Six?"

"Indeed, sir. I will be on my way now. To see Azelon. On the bridge."

Ezo stepped aside, as if the bot didn't have enough room to walk past them already. "Okay, then. See you later, wire brain." TO-96 walked by and exited sick bay. "That was weird," Ezo said.

Awen chuckled. "I didn't think it was possible, but he *does* seem smitten with her."

Ezo nodded.

"But… I mean, that's impossible, right?" Awen asked.

"Yeah, totally," Ezo said, though he didn't sound so sure. He turned and walked toward Sootriman and Saasarr, but before he could speak to them, Awen placed a hand on his arm.

"Let me," she said and moved past Ezo. "Saasarr?"

The Reptalon didn't so much as move. His head remained bowed, hands on the ground, legs curled beneath him. Awen moved closer and knelt as well.

"Saasarr, thank you for coming to see your queen."

"Is she… is she going to live?" As soon as the lizard finished the question, his yellow eye appeared behind a wrinkle in his skin, glaring at her.

"Yes, the ship's AI says she should make a full recovery. She just needs rest, which is what she's getting now."

Saasarr's eye closed. His nostrils flared, and he released a slow breath. "How was she injured?"

"We were on…" Awen wasn't sure if this was the right time to broach the subject of quantum physics and the existence of the multiverse. "On another planet, being pursued by enemies. She took a blaster round to the back."

"Who shot her?"

"It was the same people who killed everyone in Sootriman's lair and took her hostage."

Saasarr uttered something under his breath. Awen guessed it was an expletive or some sort of dark oath. Then he turned toward her and opened his eyes. His tongue flicked the air and darted between razor-sharp teeth. "Saasarr will find them, and then Saasarr will destroy them. Saasarr swears this before the gods."

The finality of the lizard's dedication had a strange effect on Awen. On the one hand, she felt buoyed by the warrior's resolve. This Reptalon was not a creature she'd ever want to cross in a dark alley—or even a well-lit alley. His entire demeanor epitomized violence, much like the Jujari. So having him on their side was exactly what she'd hoped for. Saasarr's allegiance to the cause ensured that they were one step closer to eliminating the threat posed on Itheliana.

On the other hand, the Reptalon spoke with such brutal clarity that Awen found herself doubting her own. Was premeditated murder really the course they had to embark on? Perhaps the enemy could be reasoned with. That was, after all, the premise that she'd dedicated her life to. Oath swearing like Saasarr's had all but ensured the genocide of sentient species the galaxy over.

But Awen knew there was no stopping the lizard now. She imagined that he took his vows toward Sootriman very seriously. And considering the holo-footage she'd seen in Sootriman's office—the brutality, the indiscriminate savagery—she knew the troopers in Itheliana had to be stopped. No amount of discussion would get them to back down. Constructive dialogue required the mutual respect and a genuine willingness to at least try to see things from the other party's perspective.

When Awen thought back to the holo-footage, to how she'd been stalked in the streets of Ithnor Ithelia, even to how Sootriman had been bound and lowered by Kane, she realized—not for the first time—that she was not dealing with a sane enemy. She was dealing with monsters. So she needed monsters as well.

"Well... okay, then." Awen glanced back at Ezo, who seemed pleased by the Reptalon's words. "But you're going to need help, Saasarr. That's why we've come here."

"What do you mean?"

"These people are not alone, and we have come to solicit aid from Sootriman's personal guard."

Saasarr looked away from her and lowered his head again. "They are all dead."

"Dead? But what about the rest of the Reptalons? And the humans we saw by her throne? Surely, there must be more than those who were killed in her den?"

Saasarr hissed. "Dead. Do not make Saasarr repeat himself."

This couldn't be true. There had to be more than just him—there just *had* to be. "Then she must have a police force in the city... a small army... *something*."

"Saasarr's queen is not an oppressive tyrant, human. Who do you take us for—bloodthirsty mongrels?"

The thought had crossed my mind, she wanted to say but thought better of it. "There's no one else you can think of, then, Saasarr?"

The lizard flicked his tongue in the air several times. "No, human. Saasarr is all you have."

Disappointment filled Awen's chest like a physical weight, threatening to pull her to the ground. As vicious as Saasarr was, he wouldn't be enough. She didn't need to be a military tactician to know that. She'd barely made it off the planet alive, and that was with a highly modified bot with missiles! And Ezo, of course—he counted for something.

No, what Awen needed, what they all needed, was a highly trained group of warriors equal to the task. Like Republic troopers still loyal to preserving peace... and to maintaining sanity. What she needed was Magnus.

"Thank you for your pledge of protection," Awen said finally.

"No." Saasarr flared his nostrils. "It is a vow of vengeance. There is a difference."

Awen paused, aware that she was about to say something she'd never said before. "Then... thank you for your vow of vengeance." The lizard hissed and lowered his head beneath the plane of Sootriman's bed once again.

Awen rose to her feet and left Saasarr to his watch. She gave Ezo a disappointed smirk and shrugged. "What now?"

"I'm not sure," Ezo replied, keeping his voice low. He glanced over Awen's shoulder. "I mean, that guy's a badass, but not even he can take on those troopers by himself."

"My thoughts exactly. We need an alternate plan."

"I say we camp out here for the remaining two days that Azelon said it will take for Sootriman to recover. Maybe she knows something we don't. She's got to have other connections."

"Two days…" Awen rolled the number around in her mind. "Isn't that, like, forty days in the metaverse?"

Ezo shrugged. "Sounds about right."

"Imagine… imagine what they could do…"

"None of that is certain, Star Queen. Don't go psyching yourself out before we've even begun."

"So you don't think they're uncovering some new technology—something they can use to their advantage—even as we speak?"

"I don't know what I think right now. But I do know hypotheticals can kill you faster than reality sometimes. So just take a deep breath, and we'll figure this out." Ezo looked across at Sootriman. "Right now, she needs to get better before we do anything. That's a hard stop we can't get around. We also know we have a friend in the lizard there. That's more than we had before."

"But still not enough."

"How is it that Ezo is suddenly the optimist here?" Ezo's raised voice drew Saasarr's ire. "Sorry." He gave a thumbs-up to the Reptalon. "Keep guarding. You're doing great." Back to Awen, he whispered, "Listen, we've got this. The universe has a way of working things out. Just have a little… you know…"

"A little faith?"

"Your words, not mine, Star Queen."

AWEN FIGURED the only thing that would distract her enough from her incessant worrying was being on the bridge with TO-96 and Azelon. She found the two bots staring through the main window, looking out over Ki Nar Four's volcanic surface some twenty thousand kilometers below. In a strange way, the view was beautiful, she had to admit. And having two metal-and-composite humanoid bodies side by side, looking out at it, seemed fitting.

Awen stepped onto the bridge and cleared her throat. She assumed the two bots already knew she was there. Still, it seemed like the right thing to do.

TO-96 and Azelon turned at the same time.

"Hello, Awen. And how is Sootriman?" TO-96 asked cordially. Again, Awen felt this was a formality, as he surely knew how the woman was doing in far more detail than Awen could.

"Fine. Resting."

TO-96 nodded. "And the Reptalon?"

"He won't leave her side. He seems deeply concerned for her well-being."

"He should be."

Awen cocked her head. "What's that supposed to mean?"

TO-96 hesitated. He looked at Azelon then back to Awen. "Ah, I now understand that you are not *in the loop*, as it were."

"No, I guess I'm not. And for the record, you're getting better at using figures of speech, no matter what Ezo says."

TO-96 placed a hand on his chest in such a human gesture that Awen almost forgot he was a bot. "Why, thank you, Awen."

"Now, what loop am I out of?"

TO-96 raised a finger as if to make a point but then seemed to think better of it. "I believe this is information for Sootriman to share."

"Whoa, Ninety-Six. You can't go leading a girl on like that."

"Like what?"

"You can't just say, 'I know a huge secret,' and then turn around and say, 'Never mind, I can't tell you.'"

"But I thought better of my intended course as I considered other factors that played into the dynamics of human interaction." The bot tilted his head. "I am confused. In considering what is best for one human, I inadvertently did not do what is best for another human. Your species is extremely complicated."

"Welcome to being human, Ninety-Six."

"Yes. How arduous…"

"You don't know the half of it."

"Awen," Azelon said, "I am detecting a starship that has just jumped out of subspace." The bot turned to the main window, where several new transparent layers of information superimposed themselves on one another.

"Here? Now?"

"Yes to both questions." Azelon moved her head around the window as if scanning and analyzing. Then a new image appeared, a massive starship filling up the screen. "The vessel is currently three hundred thousand kilometers away. Do you recognize it?"

It took Awen a second to respond. She couldn't believe her eyes. "Yes… yes I do. It's a Jujari destroyer."

"I can confirm Awen's assessment," TO-96 added.

"Is it hailing the planet?" Awen asked.

"Negative," Azelon replied. "It is only emitting its ship name on a repeated algorithm."

"Its ship name?" Awen asked. "What… what's its ship name, then?"

Azelon hesitated. "I am sorry. I think there is a problem with my translation protocol. I will need a moment. Forgive me, Awen." Azelon twitched. "No. I was wrong. Everything is working properly, and I cannot detect any issues with my translation protocol."

"What's the ship's name, Azelon?"

"*Naked Monkey Butt.*"

12

"Magnus, is that you?" Awen said over the holo-transmission.

Seeing Awen's face again was... disarming. He was back on the streets of Oosafar, helping her flee from the mwadim's palace. Then he was in Abimbola's jail, watching her bargain for his life. Then he was on the skiff to meet that smuggler—Enzo or something—and his overly familiar bot. There had been that long talk on board the ship... and then she was gone.

He and Awen had spent hardly any time together. But the time they had spent had been memorable. Intense, and memorable. But not more so than any other op in which he'd rescued someone. He'd rescued Valerie, after all, and she was...

What?

Splick. This was getting complicated. Still, Awen was different. The way she'd talked during their one-on-one conversation aboard Enzo's ship... before the nav bot had asked Magnus to touch his missiles. *Crazy robot.*

Awen was different because... *because she's the total opposite of everything you stand for, Adonis.* He seemed to have an inclination toward opposites.

"Put us through," Magnus said.

"As you wish, scrumruk," Rohoar replied.

Awen's face lit up with a smile when the transmission connected. "Magnus. It *is* you."

"Hey, Awen. Good to see you again."

"You too." She laughed. "Nice ship designation."

"I figured that would get your attention if you were out here."

"Like nothing else could."

There was an awkward pause as both of them smiled. Magnus felt the eyes of everyone on the bridge fixed on him. Including Valerie. But what did he care?

"How did you know where to find us?" Awen asked.

"Well, that's a fascinating question. We're coming from Worru."

Awen's eyes lit up, just as Magnus thought they might. "Why in all the cosmos were you on Worru?"

"I should probably explain that in person."

"Right. Okay, we're sending our coordinates now. TO-96 confirms that there's an open docking bay adjacent to ours."

"Roger that. See you soon."

She hesitated. "Yeah. See you soon. *Azelon Spire* out."

"*NMB* out."

UPON THEIR ARRIVAL at the docking platform, Awen had insisted that Magnus and his crew come aboard her ship—something about it being more spacious than his. And by the looks of it from their docking approach, she wasn't kidding. Magnus had never seen anything like it. Its iridescent hull was shaped like some sort of megalithic sea creature. Everyone on the bridge looked at it slack-jawed.

"What system is *that* from?" Titus asked.

"None I've ever seen." Abimbola ran a hand over his jaw. "Where'd that Luma go get a ship like that, buckethead?"

"I have no idea." Magnus turned to Rohoar. "Can you pull up anything else on that ship? Maybe some sort of Repub top-secret firewall?"

Rohoar stared ahead as if he hadn't heard Magnus at all. The Jujari was clearly impressed.

"Hey, Rohoar." Magnus snapped his fingers.

"I'm sorry, scrumruk. What did you request?"

"Any additional metadata on that ship."

"No," Rohoar replied without looking at his data pad. "There's nothing more on it."

"Strange." Magnus studied Rohoar a second more. The hyena was really taken with the ship. Magnus turned to Titus.

"How many life signs are we detecting? I want to make sure we're not walking into a trap."

"Our scans are unable to penetrate the hull, Magnus," Titus replied from the sensors console.

"Definitely smells top secret to me," Abimbola said. "But she's too damn pretty to be a Repub bucket of bolts."

"Hey." Magnus shot a look his way. "We're not the ones building rickety old contraptions in the desert."

Abimbola shrugged. "Have to work with what you've got."

"Isn't that the truth." Magnus gestured toward the rest of Abimbola's crew. "I want everyone armed and stacked behind me in stages, in case there are any problems. Rohoar, you stay with the ship and keep her ready to book if we pop smoke."

"Pop smoke, scrumruk?"

"Emergency retreat," Abimbola said.

Rohoar raised his head. "I think Magnus will be needing me."

"Oh? And why's that?" Magnus asked.

"Anyone else can run this ship. Titus, for example." Rohoar pointed to the Marauder. "It's so simple even he can do it."

"Hey," the man protested.

"But only I can protect Abimbola's buckethead scrumruk."

Magnus made to protest, but the Jujari really seemed to want to come along. Plus, he had a point—that was, assuming

Titus could actually fly this ship. But it was true that no one was fiercer in battle than a Jujari.

"Okay, you can come. But make sure Titus knows what he's doing. The rest of you, I want you locked and loaded in three. Valerie, I want you and Piper in your quarters."

Fortunately, Valerie nodded and led Piper toward the bridge's elevator.

"Let's move, people."

WHEN THE BLADES of *NMB*'s port hatch spiraled open, Awen stood there, eyes wide. Magnus kind of figured that four Marine and navy troopers, three Marauders, and a former Jujari mwadim pointing weapons at her would be overwhelming—which was the point. Based on her genuine surprise, however, Magnus decided there wasn't anything to worry about.

Awen said, "There's no threat here. Promise."

"Lower 'em," he said over his shoulder, dropping his hand. "We're clear."

"You came ready for a firefight, I see," Awen said.

"Didn't want to take any chances."

"Shoot first, ask questions later. Am I right?"

Magnus raised an eyebrow. "You're learning."

In a poorly coordinated attempt to greet one another, Magnus leaned in for a side hug while Awen extended her hand. Magnus adjusted, extending his hand, but Awen leaned in for the hug. The result was an awkward collision that left Magnus leaning over his gun and Awen's cheekbone pressed against his chest plate. They patted one another on the back and then pulled away.

"Good to see you," Magnus said.

"Yeah, you too." Awen smoothed her clothes with two hands. "Who're your friends?"

"Right. This is Rohoar."

The Jujari lowered his head and exposed his neck toward her. "It is an honor to meet the Luma emissary of my people once again."

Awen's eyes lit up. "Thank... thank you, Rohoar. It's an honor to meet you too."

In a whisper, Magnus asked, "You okay?"

"They don't speak to women, remember?"

Magnus *did* remember, thinking back to when he'd escorted her through the mwadim's palace. "People change," was all he could think to say. He straightened himself. "And I think you remember Abimbola."

Awen stepped forward to shake the Miblimbian's large hand. "Yes, quite. It's good to see you again, Abimbola."

"And you, Madame dau Lothlinium."

"And here you have Rix and Silk, two of Abimbola's Marauders."

They waved at Awen.

"And finally, four of the Repub's finest: Marine Corporal Aubrey Dutch, Private First Class Tony Haney, Private First

Class Waldorph Gilder, and Navy Chief Warrant Officer Shane Nolan."

"Pleased to meet you all," Awen replied with a wave. "And thank you for coming. Please, come aboard."

Magnus turned to Rohoar. "Would you please go get the others?"

"Right away, scrumruk."

"Thank you."

THE EXTERIOR of Awen's starship should have given it away. But it wasn't until Magnus was standing on the bridge and met Azelon that he realized the vessel was from some advanced alien species. The Repub was still centuries away from anything this complex, and to his knowledge, nothing like it existed in any other part of the galaxy.

"Pretty impressive, right?" Awen turned around in the middle of the bridge.

"I'd say."

The rest of the crew seemed dumbstruck too. The gleaming surfaces, soft blue-and-white lighting, sleek black controls—all of it was almost *transcendent*. That was the best word Magnus could think of. But he wasn't even sure if that was right. He was a Marine, not a poet.

"Where did you say this ship was from?"

"I didn't."

Magnus continued to look around, head on a swivel. "Right."

The slender white robot spoke up again. "This ship hails from—"

"Let's save that for later, Azelon," Awen said.

"Understood, Awen."

The bridge's elevator doors opened. Magnus instinctively raised his MAR30 but not all the way. A man in his late twenties—most likely a Nimprith, judging from his narrow eyes and olive skin—stepped from the elevator, accompanied by the modified nav bot. The last time Magnus had seen this pair, he'd asked Enzo to stay behind on Worru and protect Awen. Based on Magnus's experiences on the Luma home world, he guessed Enzo had done a stand-up job.

They approached Magnus's team, hands extended.

"Enzo," Magnus said, taking his hand.

"Eeezo," the man replied.

"Right. Good to see you again."

"You too."

"And you're TT-96 or something," Magnus said, shaking the bot's hand.

"TO-96, sir. Pleased to meet you once again."

"Pleasure's mine." Magnus leaned in and nodded toward Awen. "I can see you did as I asked—back on Worru, I mean. Thanks."

"She got herself into some trouble similar to what I'm guessing you found. You were right to ask us to stay behind."

"Good to know my gut's still got it."

Ezo turned to Abimbola. "It seems you just can't escape these two, now, can you, Abimbola?" He gestured toward Magnus and Awen.

"Seems that way," Abimbola said, flipping a poker chip. "The gods have weighted the odds, and when that happens, well…"

"Somehow, I don't think the gods have anything to do with this, Miblimbian. But to each his own." Ezo nodded at the other Marauders. "Rix, Silk, good to see you." They nodded in reply.

"Right," Magnus said. "And this is the rest of my crew, with three more on the way." Magnus made the introductions with Dutch, Haney, Gilder, and Nolan.

"We've got two more in sick bay," Awen added. "We'll introduce you later."

"Sounds good," Ezo replied.

"So, what's this all about, Magnus?" Awen asked.

"Well, I'm hoping you can fill in a few blanks yourself."

"Oh?"

"But it might take a while, and we don't have that much time." Magnus looked around, noticing there weren't going to be enough seats for everyone. "Got somewhere we can sit?"

"Right this way, Magnus," Azelon said, gesturing toward the elevator.

"Dutch, I want you and the others to stay put here on the bridge. Bimby and I need to debrief my friends."

"Understood, LT."

"When the others get here, send Rohoar and the ladies

my way." He turned to Azelon. "How will the rest of my crew know where to go?"

"That will be taken care of, Magnus. There is no need to worry."

"Good." He looked back at Dutch and the rest of his ragtag crew. "You need anything, reach me over comms."

"Copy that."

MAGNUS AND ABIMBOLA sat down in heavily padded white chairs finished with tan leather as Awen and Ezo joined them. The oversized seats were scattered throughout a mess hall that looked more like a hotel's grand parlor than it did a starship's dining facility. The closest ship Magnus could compare this to was Valerie's—yet for all its luxury, Valerie's still paled in comparison.

Round orbs of light hung from the curved ceiling, suspended in midair. Embroidered purple banners—which seemed more like war pennants than wall dressings—hung on the walls. And the white tables were spotless, as if they'd never been used. In fact, it felt as though this entire ship had never been used. Which was strange, as Magnus had the most peculiar feeling that this vessel was older than any other in the galaxy.

"Would any of you like something warm to drink?" Azelon inquired, and everyone's hands went up. For the first time in a long time, the notion of drinking something for comfort—beyond the mere practical purposes of staying alive—stirred in his belly. But they needed to get this conversation started and to share information. Decisions needed to be made.

Still, a cup of coffee would be perfect right now. "Do you have anything like coffee?" Magnus asked.

"I am unfamiliar with this *coffee*. However, I am capable of formulating anything with a molecular pattern so long as I have the proper parameters."

"I have no idea what the parameters for coffee are, so maybe something that's—"

"I believe I can be of assistance here, sir," TO-96 interrupted. The bot turned toward Azelon. "Please reference my file marked Human, Dietary Protocols, Liquids."

Azelon paused then said, "I have it. Thank you, TO-96."

"So… you're gonna make me coffee, then?"

"Affirmative. Anyone else?"

"So you said you came from Worru?" Awen asked, reclining in one of the chairs, hands on her lap. Magnus couldn't get used to Awen not being in her Luma robes. Seeing her in a mix of street clothes and an oversized captain's jacket was… nice.

"Yeah. But, if you don't mind, can we jump to where you got this ship?" The rest of Magnus's crew nodded, some verbally agreeing.

Awen took a deep breath and leaned forward, elbows on her knees. "I opened the stardrive."

"You opened the stardrive?" Magnus couldn't hide his excitement. "No way."

"Yes way. And it was awesome."

Magnus waited for her to go on, but she didn't. She just sat there, smiling.

"Mystics, Awen! Are you gonna tell me or what?"

"Eh. I don't think you'd be that interested."

"So help me, Awen…"

"Okay, okay!" She raised her palms, a huge smile across her face. "It gave us coordinates to a quantum tunnel."

"A quantum… tunnel?"

"And it led us to the Novia Minoosh."

"The Novia who?" Magnus hung on her every word as she went on to explain the discovery. He could feel his eyes growing wider and wider. Had they not actually been sitting on an alien starship from a different universe—*What'd she call it? Metaspace?*—he wouldn't have believed a single word. It was all far too fantastical. But here they were, and he could no more deny the ship beneath his feet than he could the blaster in his hands.

Ezo and TO-96 nodded as Awen shared about coming to Ki Nar Four to change ships and meeting Sootriman. She described their jump to the other universe, and she spoke of a habitable planet and an ancient abandoned city. Then she shared about being attacked by a Republic admiral as well as by So-Elku.

"Did you say *Kane?*" Magnus asked. "As in Admiral Wendell Kane?"

"I don't know his first name. Fifties, bald, creepy looking. Wears a pinky ring?"

Magnus nodded slowly. This piece of news rattled him the most. He knew Kane. Not personally, of course, but by reputation. Who didn't? The man was considered one of the navy's greatest commanders, though Magnus thought better of the adjective—*most ruthless* was more appropriate. Admiral Kane had gained a reputation among the Navy and the Marines for accepting the deployments that no one else wanted to take. As a result, he employed tactics that didn't exactly comply with Repub standard operating procedures or the Intergalactic Code of Ethics.

No one outside of the military knew of these breaches, of course, and everyone in power seemed to dismiss his behavior, figuring that if Kane was ready to accept the danger that no one else wanted to face, they were willing to overlook methods that no one else would be allowed to use. It was rumored that if Kane had ever failed, the Repub would have disavowed his actions and thrown him under the proverbial skiff.

Instead, Kane became a legend. He'd led Third Fleet into the initial hellhole of Caledonia, taking chances no one thought he should. But his ballsy efforts had made the first Marine landings possible. Without him, Magnus's entire battalion would have been blown out of the sky before ever touching down.

At the Battle of Po-Froslin, Kane had sacrificed several of

his battle cruisers and one destroyer in a wild attempt to drive straight through the enemy fleet's formation. While thousands of his own sailors died, no one could deny that Kane had turned what would have been a months-long conflict into three days of fighting. Second Fleet came in to clean up the pieces, but Third received all the medals.

And then there was the moon base on Teslo Nine. Kane's group of ships had endured a week of heavy bombardment from the planet-based artillery, all while bobbing and weaving behind the moon like a boxer staying just out of reach of an opponent. His constant vigilance had allowed Marine landings on the moon base, which then gave the Republic access to the planet. The Senate never said a word about his strikes against the artillery—strikes that resulted in untold civilian deaths. Kane had won. And since the end justified the means, the means had been overshadowed by the end.

According to Awen, Kane seemed to have access to whatever this quantum-tunnel technology was, and that worried Magnus. And if *Azelon Spire* was representative of what Awen had discovered from this Novia Minoosh species—and Kane was willing to try to kill for it—the galaxy was in trouble. Awen went on to describe the troopers who'd assaulted her—black-clad Marines in what Magnus guessed was modified Mark VII armor with three white stripes on their shoulders. He froze. The pieces of a complicated puzzle were coming together.

Magnus had long suspected that the three-striped troopers were rogue Repub operatives, but no one had ever been able to say for sure. Nor was anyone certain who directed these troopers. Some claimed it was a secret session of the senate, operating off the books. Others feared the troopers were a clandestine division of the Marines.

His thoughts turned toward the Bull Wraith that had captured the Stones' ship. Then he thought of the one-sided assault on the Jujari fleet that Brigadier General Lovell had alluded to with Rohoar. He considered the assault Awen had described. It was Kane… all of it had been Admiral Kane this whole time.

He's gone rogue.

No. Magnus corrected himself. *He's gone mad.*

Magnus was spellbound as he listened to the rest of Awen's story—about her three months on the planet and the discovery of the quantum-tunnel generator. The time dilation between the two universes was also a head spinner, but he knew that advanced quantum physics involved some crazy splick well above his pay grade.

The news that a second contingent of Kane's men had returned to the Novia's planet was unsettling, to say the least. All Magnus could figure was that they were after some of the alien tech. *'Cause that's what I would want.* And Novia tech in Kane's hands spelled trouble for both universes. He had a strange feeling that it wouldn't be long before he was fighting battles on several fronts. *Splick, aren't you doing that already, Adonis?*

When Awen seemed like she was done giving the short version of her story, Magnus checked the time displayed in the corner of his bioteknia eyes. Piper would be arriving at any minute, and he needed to fill Awen in on the little girl before she arrived. To save time, he skipped most of the action surrounding the rescue of his men and focused on Piper... on her powers... and just how much she freaked Magnus out.

13

Piper held her mother's hand on one side and Rohoar's on the other as they walked through the shiny new starship. Her mama had insisted that holding one hand—*hers*—was enough. But Piper wanted to hold the big dog's too. So she passed her corgachirp to her mother, saying, "Here, Mama. Can you please hold Talisman?"

As soon as her mother had taken the stuffed animal, Piper reached out and grabbed Rohoar's finger. The Jujari recoiled at first, though Piper hadn't meant to startle him. But once he saw it was her, he relaxed and then let her hold on.

The three of them walked down the corridor. Mr. Titus had been ordered to the bridge by someone in his earpiece. Piper looked over her shoulder to make sure the Marauder knew where he was going. "If you get lost, just come back and find us, Mr. Titus."

The man smiled at her. "Thank you, Piper. I will."

Piper, her mother, and Rohoar continued walking for several minutes. They listened to a woman give them instructions over the ship's speakers. "Continue to follow the illuminated path." Piper bet it was some kind of fancy AI. She'd never seen a ship this unusual before, and it just *had* to have a fancy AI.

Piper marveled at the bright-blue dots they'd been following. Each dot appeared along the white floor then disappeared when she stepped on it. Piper tried to watch several of them fade by removing her foot as soon as she put it down, but the action only made her stumble.

"Piper, keep your head up," her mother said, tugging on her hand.

"Yes, Mama."

"Continue forward ten meters," the woman's voice said from somewhere overhead. "Then turn left."

Maybe they were close to wherever they were going. Piper hoped she would get to explore the ship more. And meet new people. *Meeting new people is the best.*

"Please turn left."

A set of doors slid open. Piper looked into a big room filled with tables and chairs. The crew from her ship sat near the middle while two robots served warm drinks. Piper wanted a drink, and she wanted to talk to the robots too. They looked *very* interesting.

No sooner had she stepped through the doorway than everyone turned to look at her. As she got closer, Piper noticed two new people—a woman with pointy ears and purple eyes and a man with narrow eyes and a long coat.

"Hi," she said to the purple-eyed woman. "My name's Piper."

The woman extended her hand, and Piper shook it. "Hi, Piper. My name's Awen."

"You're really pretty."

Awen placed a hand on her chest. "Why, thank you. You're lovely too."

"Thanks." She turned to the man. "What's your name?"

"My name's Idris Ezo. But you can just call me Ezo."

"Okay. Are those your bots?"

Ezo followed her outstretched finger toward the two robots serving drinks. "One of them is, yes. Would you like to meet him?"

"Oh, yes please." Piper absolutely loved robots, and these two looked like they'd be her favorite. She was sure of it.

"Hey, 'Six. Need you over here."

"Right away, sir."

The gray-plated bot walked toward her, and Piper's eyes widened as she tried to take him in. His eyes glowed a vibrant white behind a translucent face shield. He had rockets on one forearm and a blaster on the other.

"What do they call you?" Piper asked.

"I am TO-96. At your service."

The bot bowed to her, and she couldn't help but giggle. "You are very nice."

TO-96 glanced up, tilting his head. "Nice? That is kind of you to say."

"Who made you?"

"I am a navigation robot originally manufactured by Advanced Galactic Solutions but modified by Idris Ezo."

"I'm Piper," she said, extending her hand. "I'm just a human, made by humans."

"I am very pleased to make your acquaintance, Piper." The bot shook her hand gently. He was so cool.

"How many star systems have you been to?"

"Piper," her mother said. "That's enough."

"Can I meet the other robot?"

Her mama sighed. "Yes, but quickly. You'll have time to ask them plenty of questions later."

Piper walked up to the slender white robot and extended her hand. "Hi, I'm Piper."

Instead of grasping Piper's hand, the robot mimicked her posture, thrusting her right arm into the air with her hand extended. "Hi, I'm Azelon."

Piper laughed, covering her mouth to keep the noise down. To her surprise, the bot covered its mouth too and giggled—which made Piper laugh even more.

Then the bot stopped and asked TO-96, "How am I doing with the human greeting ceremony?"

"I believe it needs some work," TO-96 said.

Then Azelon looked at Piper. "Forgive me. I haven't met many humans before."

"That's okay. I've never ever seen a bot like you before.

So… I think that kinda makes us even."

"How are we 'even'?"

Suddenly, Piper felt her mother's hand on her shoulder. "Piper, sweetie, you need to—"

"Hey, you're the ship's voice," Piper exclaimed. "Which means you're a girl bot."

"Darling…" Her mother sounded cross.

"Why, yes, that was my voice," Azelon replied. "And I am modeled after the feminine archetype."

"Your voice is wonderful. Good job."

The bot tilted her head. "Thank you."

"Piper, let's leave the bot alone. You'll have plenty of time to speak with her later."

"Okay, Mama."

Her mother turned her around while some of the troopers brought over chairs. Piper hopped into one right next to Awen. Her legs dangled over the side. It was a really big chair. She looked over at her mother, who sat on the other side of her, and then at Rohoar, who seemed to fit the chair just right. The room had grown quiet.

"What was everyone talking about before?" Piper asked

"Actually, we were talking about you," Awen replied.

"Me?"

Awen nodded. "Magnus was telling us all about your daring escape from the black ship, your journey across the desert, and your last several days on Oorajee."

"Did he tell you that my daddy died?"

Awen's eyes fluttered for a moment, like she was going to

cry. "Yes, Piper. He did tell us. We are so very sorry to hear about his passing."

"Thank you." She lowered her head. "I've been very sad about it. Mama has too."

"I imagine so."

Piper wiped her nose on her sleeve. Her eyes were watering again. "Where do you come from, Miss Awen?"

"Me? Oh, I come from a planet called Elonia. But now I reside on Worru... at least... I used to."

Piper reached out and touched Awen's hand. She didn't mean to. It just... happened. As soon as her palm touched Awen's skin, it was as if Piper could see inside of Awen's soul —as if she were dreaming that she could see the world as Awen saw it. But it wasn't just Awen's present that Piper could see. It was her past too. Everything was there in a flash.

Piper saw Awen as a child and the faces of her mother and father. She was in school with Awen as a teenager, being picked on by her peers. Then she saw Awen at a beautiful-looking school with hundreds of other students, all dressed in lovely robes. They were training to serve different worlds and species. And they knew how to move inside of...

"You're a Luma," Piper said.

"Wha... What did you say?"

"You went to observances when you were seventeen. But your parents didn't want you to. You decided to anyway because you wanted to help people. You were upset that your parents didn't agree with you. I'm sorry for your pain."

Awen pulled her hand away and clutched it against her chest. The room went very still.

"I'm sorry," Piper said. "Did I say something wrong?"

Awen shook her head. "No, Piper. But… how did you know all that?"

"Know all what?"

"All those things about me?"

"I felt them. When I touched you."

Awen looked concerned. Not *mad* concerned, just *regular* concerned—like she didn't understand what Piper had said. The pretty lady with the pointy ears and purple eyes looked at Piper's mother. "How long?"

"Since she was very small."

"And does she…?"

"A little, yes."

Then Awen did something very odd. She slipped down from her chair and knelt in front of Piper, holding Piper's hands in her own. "I think there is an important reason why you and I have met, Piper."

"Well, that's good. I don't have many friends, so I like making new ones."

Awen smiled. "Yes, we will be friends. But I think we will be more than that."

"What is more than friends?"

"Piper, you are very special," Awen explained. "But sometimes being very special also means we are very different."

"From others?"

"Yes, from others."

"Like you felt on Elonia in school?"

"Exactly like that, yes." Awen brushed a strand of hair behind her ear. "The way I got over those feelings was by being with others like me. When I was with them, I didn't feel different. Instead, I felt like I belonged."

"Are you saying that you're like me?"

"Yes. Yes I am."

Piper took a deep breath. "That makes me happy."

"It makes me happy too. It also means that I would like to teach you some things about your abilities."

"My powers?"

"Your powers, yes. I would like to teach you more about them. Would that be all right?"

Piper looked at her mother, who nodded.

"Okay. I'd like that a lot. Thanks, Miss Awen."

"You're welcome. It's truly my pleasure. Piper, you are a marvel and a wonder."

That was exactly what her mama always said about her.

"What did you say?" Piper's mom asked Awen.

"I… just said that it's my pleasure to be her teacher." Awen glanced at Magnus then back at Valerie. "I thought you just indicated that was acceptable."

"No, no, not that," Valerie replied. "The last thing—what you just called Piper."

"A marvel and a wonder?" Awen dismissed the phrase with a wave. "It's just an expression—something my master called me. I thought it was fitting for Piper, too, seeing as how she'll be my first—"

"Your master… on Worru?"

Awen nodded.

"Who was your master?" Valerie asked.

"Elder Willowood. Why, do you know her?"

Valerie nodded. "Felicity Willowood is my mother."

14

Awen stared at Valerie, suddenly aware of the woman's likeness to Willowood. How was it even possible that she would meet the daughter of her mentor on a Novia starship in the middle of the Omodon quadrant? The odds were… *beyond comprehension*. There was no other explanation than that the Unity had brought them all together.

"That's who was speaking to me in Worru," Magnus said to Valerie.

"Excuse me?" Valerie asked.

"The person who told me to come here. She called herself Willowood."

"You were with my mother?"

"No, no. She was in my head."

"In your head?"

"Telepathy," Awen said.

"I know what it is," Valerie said curtly, not even bothering to look at Awen. "What did she say to you? Did she say where she was?"

Awen got the feeling that Valerie hadn't seen her mother in a long time. Now that Awen thought about it, Willowood *had* mentioned that she'd had a child what felt like "a lifetime ago." She hardly talked about it, so Awen had dismissed it. Apparently, "a lifetime ago" had referred to *Valerie's lifetime*. Awen would never have guessed that Willowood's daughter was only a few years older than she was.

"No," Magnus replied. "She just said that we needed to get off Worru fast and that Awen and Piper needed one another."

"She did, did she?" Valerie asked.

"That's what she said, yup."

Valerie gave Awen a stern glare. "Piper needs Awen…"

What in all the mystics is this *about?* Awen held Valerie's stare without blinking. "Is there something I can help you with, Valerie?"

The woman's attention snapped back to Magnus. "And why didn't you tell me this before we came here to Ki Nar Four?"

"Honestly? Because I didn't think anyone would believe me. Splick, I hardly believe it myself. Plus, it's not like I knew who this Willowood person was. Is. Whatever."

"Well, next time a voice starts talking to you in your head, you should share it with your crew. Or at least with your doctor."

"Doctor?" Awen's eyes darted between the two of them. There was an awkward pause in the conversation. Finally, Valerie sighed, scratched an eyebrow, and then sat back in her chair. "I'm sorry. I'm… this is…"

"Hey," Magnus said, reaching across for her hand. "It's okay, Valerie. Everyone's under a ton of stress. And it sounds like you just found out that your mother is—I don't know, alive, maybe? Like it's news to you or something?"

"It's news to me, yes."

"Then we get it. Cut yourself some slack."

Valerie's shoulders relaxed. The woman was wound tight. And it was Magnus who was helping her unwind. As in, Valerie trusted him… maybe even liked him.

Suddenly, it was Awen's turn to tense up. Magnus was staring at Valerie an overly long time. So Awen straightened her back and looked at Piper, trying to get her mind off whatever corgachirp trail her thoughts were headed down. Speaking of corgachirps, Piper had a very nice stuffed one in her hands.

"I like your corgachirp," Awen said, trying to change directions.

"Thank you, Miss Awen. His name's Talisman."

"Where'd you get him?"

"He was a gift. From my… my…"

"From her grandmother," Valerie said softly. "When she was just a baby."

"So," Piper said, wrinkling her nose, "does this mean that

Awen's master is my grandmother?" She clutched Talisman and stared into the stuffed animal's eyes.

Valerie placed a hand on Piper's head and began to stroke it. "Yes, darling. That's what this means."

As Valerie sat there, running her hand over her daughter's blond hair, a heavy silence fell over the mess hall. The entire conversation over the last twenty minutes—from Magnus's daring rescue on Oorajee to his betrayal by the Republic and even Awen's account of their three-month stay in an alternate universe and her own escape from a hit team—had all been incredibly surreal.

"We have to go back for her," Valerie said at last.

Magnus sat up straight. "What?"

"We have to go back for my mother. If she's in trouble, then we have to help her."

Magnus cleared his throat. "Valerie, I'm not sure how much you caught of what happened back there, but we're outmanned and outgunned. There's no way we're walking into that again with any hope of survival let alone mission success."

"I must agree with Magnus," Abimbola said, speaking up for the first time since they'd sat down. "The Luma are far more prepared for battle than I would have ever suspected. These are not the Luma the galaxy has come to know and trust."

Awen understood Abimbola's sentiment. Before her encounter with So-Elku after the ambush, the Luma Master had been the epitome of dignity and integrity. But with him trying to strip her of the stardrive, combined with Magnus's account of the incident on Worru, he was no longer the man she'd once known. That the Luma master and the Elder Guard would try to stop Magnus with force—would try to kill him and his team—was simply the next step in his evolution toward becoming… whatever it was he was turning into.

If Willowood was still alive, she needed rescuing, as did any other Luma still loyal to the Order. Given that Willowood was able to communicate with Magnus telepathically, Awen guessed her mentor was somewhere close to Elder's Hall—presumably in an underground jail of some sort. And given that possibility, there would be others with her—Awen was sure of it—who could amplify Willowood's abilities to reach Magnus.

But freeing Willowood and the other Luma wasn't the only problem they faced. There was still the issue of Kane's reconnaissance team that had stalked Awen on Itheliana. Magnus's theories about Kane and his team of rogue Marines made as much sense as anything else. Whatever the operatives had been sent to do, it couldn't be good. There was the very real possibility that Kane would gain access to the same discoveries that Awen had made. And now that So-Elku had a book from the temple library—something she needed to check with Azelon about—who knew what sort of power he was wielding? Kane's forces had to be stopped as much as So-Elku's.

Lastly, and most importantly, there was the issue of Piper. Based on what Magnus had told Awen about the little girl's abilities and what Awen had just witnessed herself, Piper needed help. Fast. In fact, Awen was amazed that the little girl hadn't killed anyone else yet. It was as if someone had managed to keep her powers tempered. *Or something*, Awen thought, looking at the stuffed corgachirp in Piper's hands. Valerie *had* said it was a gift from Willowood when Piper was a baby.

Awen sent her soul into the Unity and was instantly aware of the bright aura surrounding Piper. As she'd suspected, the little girl was the epitome of a true blood. Every cell in her body seemed to resonate in perfect harmony with the Unity, shimmering like a star's surface. She was almost too brilliant to look at. *Almost*. For as much as Piper's soul radiated, there was something else holding the explosive power at bay, like a dam resisting the waters of a mountain lake.

There, stuffed in Piper's arms, was a dampener. Awen didn't know how, and she couldn't have replicated it if she'd wanted to, but the stuffed animal was acting as some sort of ethereal governor. So strong was the effect, and so bright was Piper's soul, that Awen wondered what would happen if the child was ever more than a few meters from the item. Even with the corgachirp in her escape pod on the Bull Wraith, the little girl had unwittingly killed her father. No wonder the toy had been named Talisman.

Piper's powers were... well, they were greater than anything Awen had ever seen before. In fact, Awen doubted she'd be able to teach Piper how to control her abilities. The task would take time, especially considering how young the girl was. And it would take ingenuity. Awen would have to come up with new ways to keep Piper from hurting anyone while she trained—Talisman wouldn't be enough. But once she was taught, she would… *what?*

Awen tried to fathom just how strong someone with Piper's natural giftedness would be when fully equipped in the Unity. Piper was—more than anyone Awen had ever met— the quintessential true blood, a being born to be one with the Unity. There was no telling what she'd be capable of when her training was complete.

Why the universe had chosen this moment, of all times, to gift someone like Piper to the cosmos was another question worth answering. If Kane and So-Elku's combined evils were as great as Awen suspected, then perhaps it was no doubt that someone like Piper had come along.

Awen looked at the girl with a mix of sorrow and wonder —sorrow because it seemed that no one had told her the truth about her father's death, and wonder because… *Piper, you may just be the answer the galaxy is hoping for.*

"I know what we need to do," Awen said.

Everyone turned to face her. A plan was forming in her mind, emerging like a sunrise on a foggy morning.

"Say again?" Magnus asked.

"I know what we need to do. But I'm not exactly sure how to do it, though I have a hunch."

"Well, Star Queen," Ezo said, "I think it's safe to say that we're all ears."

"I am not all ears," Rohoar protested. "I am Jujari, with

only two ears. Do not include me in your frivolous descriptions."

"It's an expression." Ezo rolled his eyes. "If it's not bots, it's Jujari. Somebody's gotta train 'em."

Awen cleared her throat to regain everyone's attention. "The way I see it, we have three important objectives." She looked around and saw all eyes fixed on her. Magnus, Abimbola, Rohoar, Valerie, Piper, Ezo, and even the two bots were intent on whatever she was about to say. Good, she thought. 'Cause this is gonna need all of us to pull off. "First, we know that Willowood and her contingent of Luma need to be rescued on Worru." She held up one finger. "Second, Kane's operatives on Itheliana must not be allowed to leave the planet with anything they find." She raised a second finger. "And Piper…" Awen hesitated. "Piper needs to go to school for her powers."

"Is it going to be a boring school?" Piper asked. "I hate boring schools."

"Piper," Valerie said, shushing her with a finger on her lips.

"No," Awen replied. "I don't think it will be boring in the least."

"And you plan to do all this how?" Abimbola said.

Awen pushed some loose strands of hair behind her ears. "Well, that's where Azelon comes in."

Everyone looked at the gleaming white bot. Suddenly self-aware, the bot placed two hands on her chest. "Me? Why, certainly. How may I be of assistance, Awen?"

"The way I see it," Awen explained to the group, "time, not force, is our greatest obstacle. Abimbola, you have enough Marauders to create a sizable fighting force if we need one. Magnus, you have enough experience to train just about anyone in the art of war, as does Rohoar. And Rohoar, you have an entire fleet if we ever needed one. But time is what we really lack. It takes time to mobilize resistance. It takes time to plot strategies. And it will take time for me to train Piper. So what's the one way we can buy time?"

"By going back to metaspace," Ezo concluded.

"Exactly."

"The time dilation," Magnus said. "You want to take us all back through the quantum tunnel and set up shop on Ithelinelli?"

"Itheliana," Awen corrected.

"We can leverage the time dilation and square away whatever we need to," Ezo said. "It's brilliant, Star Queen. You can train Piper, we can raise up a fighting force of some kind, and then by the time we get back here…"

"Only a few days will have passed if we spend another three months over there," Awen concluded. "So-Elku and Kane won't even know we've left the protoverse."

"Okay, a few questions," Abimbola said. "First, where are we getting more soldiers from?"

"Right," Awen said. "So, I haven't figured all of this out yet, obviously. But that's where you all come in. I don't think we need that many more hands. At least not yet."

"What do you mean?" Magnus asked.

"Well, the operatives that assaulted us in the Novia's capital city, Ithnor Ithelia, numbered maybe about... I don't know. What would you say, Ezo?"

"Ask 'Six. He's the one who got the count."

"I counted twenty-four operatives using Repub tactics," TO-96 replied.

Awen pinched her lower lip. That was more than she remembered. Magnus wouldn't like those odds.

"No way," Magnus said, confirming her worries. "Twenty-four former recon Marines in full kit? We'll need reinforcements for sure."

"Okay, so we pick up some Marauders and Jujari from Oorajee, then Azelon gets us back to metaspace." Awen looked at Abimbola and Rohoar. "Problems so far?"

"Several of my Marauders would be willing to come—I am sure of that," Abimbola said.

Rohoar nodded. "I also believe that I could secure a few of the Tawnhack—if it is what my oath bearer wishes."

"Oath bearer?" Magnus said in surprise.

Apparently, that was a new term to Magnus. Awen still found the entire arrangement quite entertaining. The elite Repub warrior, sworn to slaughter Jujari, was now bound in covenant to one Jujari unto death. Awen wondered if Magnus even knew that part of the arrangement. Probably not—he most certainly wouldn't have agreed to that. *We'll keep it a surprise.*

Rohoar ignored Magnus's comment and continued speaking. "We could take the *Shining Bright Star of Mwadim Furlank over a Thousand Generations* back to Oosafar and collect the needed reinforcements while you go on ahead to found a village."

"Found a village?" Magnus chuckled.

"That would give us a good start," Abimbola said.

"Azelon," Awen said, "we'll need a place to train on Itheliana without being detected."

"I'm sorry, Awen," said the bot, "but I do not think that is the wisest course of action."

Awen was taken aback. "Why not?"

"Depending on what this enemy reconnaissance team is excavating, the planet will not be safe for any of you until it is cleared of all hostile threats. Additionally, So-Elku has stolen the codex, which means he is also aware of the temple and its significance, even if at the most fundamental level."

So it was true. So-Elku *had* stolen a book—the *temple codex*, whatever that was.

"Well, there goes that piece," Ezo said.

"Not entirely, sir," TO-96 said. "It seems that the Novia's star system is host to another habitable world that can easily accommodate our specific needs."

"TO-96 is correct," Azelon said. "The likelihood of detection by the enemy stands at 3.4711 percent. Less, so long as they do not find a way to leave Itheliana's surface within the allotted time frame."

"Let me see if I get this straight," Magnus said to Awen, resting his elbows on his knees. "Rohoar and Abimbola return to Oorajee to rally a few more hands while the rest of us set up camp on one of TO-96's other planets. Then Azelon jumps back to this side of the quantum tunnel to pick up Rohoar, Bimby, and whoever else they've collected. From there, I help coordinate interdisciplinary battle readiness while you work with Piper. Then, when the time comes, we stage an assault on the Novia's home world to take out the rogue operatives. When that's done, we head back to Worru to put an end to So-Elku and rescue Willowood and any other Luma." Magnus seemed out of breath and slightly exasperated. "Does that about sum it up?"

"Well, when you say it like that, it does seem a little outlandish." Awen wasn't sure whether something was wrong with Magnus or if he was just tired, but his skepticism caught her off guard. This wasn't the man she remembered. Then again, what did she actually know about the Marine? She scolded herself, realizing that she'd probably spent more time fantasizing about him than actually being with him. But wasn't this the trooper who'd just risked his life in an impossible attempt to save hostages held deep in Selskrit territory?

Cut him some slack, Awen. The guy's probably frayed on all sides. You would be too.

"But... yeah," Awen resumed. "That's the long and short of it."

"I like it," the giant Miblimbian said.

"You do?" Magnus asked, sounding bewildered.

"So do I, scrumruk," Rohoar said.

Magnus snapped his head to the Jujari. "Okay, but we have no idea what kind of resources we're going to have at our disposal. Plus, I have no idea how long it will be before we're ready to take on a highly trained group of rogue operatives, let alone confident enough to face the numbers we saw on Worru. Not to mention the fact that they have all their *supernatural splick* that, frankly, scares me to death."

"Yeah," Awen said, "but so do we." Her eyes rested on Piper. The little girl was holding her corgachirp, eagerly looking at everyone's faces.

"Are we done talking now?" Piper asked. "I'm bored."

"Trust me," Awen said, ignoring the little girl's comment. "When Piper and I are done, I'm not sure it will matter what the enemy throws at us."

Magnus stared at Awen for a second then appeared to study Piper. Each member of the group exchanged glances and nods.

Is this actually happening? Awen pushed another strand of hair behind her ear.

"I'm in," Valerie said.

"Me too," Piper said. "As long as we can eat first."

"Well…" Abimbola flipped his poker chip, checked the result, then looked up. "I'm in."

"Ezo is in," Ezo said.

"And Rohoar. Rohoar is in as far as he can be and then even more after that."

"I would like to report, for whatever it is worth, that I, too, am *in*, as it were," TO-96 said. "Perhaps not as deeply as Rohoar but as far as a modified navigation bot can go."

"And I am more than happy to accommodate you in

whatever way you need," Azelon said. "It seems to the Novia Minoosh that your mission is worthy and, if you have searched your own souls and found yourself worthy, that your hearts are thus pure."

"That was… very eloquent," Awen said to Azelon. "Thank you."

"You are most welcome, Awen."

Awen stared at the bot for a moment longer. Something about that phrase was very familiar. She'd heard it before, or something close to it. It felt noble. And old. She noticed Rohoar staring at the bot too.

"Eh—what the hell," Magnus said, breaking Awen's train of thought. "I'm in too. If we're gonna pick a fight, might as well do it with you people."

Awen clapped her hands. "Magnus, I almost forgot. I have another member for your team."

"What d'you got, Awen?"

"I have a Reptalon."

Magnus blanched. "A Reptalon?"

"A Reptalon?" Rohoar repeated. Suddenly, the Jujari rattled off a stream of curses in his mother tongue as his hackles stood up.

Awen had forgotten about… *that*.

15

Ricio led Viper Squadron on a steep attack vector, diving on the Jujari carrier from above and behind. So far, the starship's turrets hadn't picked up his Talons, as they were too busy fending off multiple attacks from other squadrons that covered Ricio's approach. His orders were to take out the carrier's engines and communications array. Two additional squadrons were tasked with taking out the ship's defenses while three more squadrons engaged the Razorbacks that poured out of the carrier's sides, fresh from their most recent rearming. It was a risky assault this early in the confrontation, but the reward was too good for command to pass up.

"Bravo Team, once you're inside the shields, I want all antiship munitions targeting those engines," Ricio said over comms. "Don't hold anything back. We only get one shot at this. Alpha Team, on me. We'll make a run down the spine for that commutations array. Take out any turrets you can reach as we go, but don't deviate from my flight path."

Ricio's HUD lit up with green confirmation icons. He pushed his throttle forward, squeezing even more speed out of his Talon. The Jujari carrier's aft was coming up fast. "Prepare for shield penetration."

Ricio looked down onto the ship's bridge, knowing his pilots would be flattened across it if he didn't time this maneuver just right. Likewise, if they pulled up too soon, they wouldn't be close enough to the deck, ensuring that the turrets would quickly eviscerate them.

A thin film of blue shimmered ahead. It was the shield's visible barrier and the point of no return for Ricio's squadron. These shields couldn't stop physical ordinance, but they'd prevent all energy weapons.

"Ten seconds to shield penetration," Ricio noted. His Talon was at max throttle, barreling toward the carrier's stern. The blocky-looking command module sat atop the superstructure like a mountain of metal freight containers. If he did this correctly, Alpha Team would make the enemy's bridge crew piss themselves with a danger-close flyby, while Bravo would lay waste to the carrier's exposed engines.

"Five seconds." As soon as they broke the barrier, the Jujari ship's sensors would alert the turret's targeting system. They'd have fewer than three seconds to conceal themselves along the carrier's upper deck.

"Three... two... one..."

Ricio's ship slipped through the blue membrane, as did

the rest of Viper Squadron, hurtling toward the bridge. He could already see the turrets turning from their current targets farther toward the bow and preparing to fire on him.

"Alpha Team, pull up on my mark!" Ricio said, his voice raised. "Bravo, you've got the engines!"

His AI's vector path analyzer sent him a warning notice, indicating where his Talon was deviating from its precalculated trajectory. One line on the HUD represented the mathematically optimum course, accounting for Repub SOPs—standard operating procedures—and FAF-28 Talon spec tolerances. The other indicated his current flight path. The AI did not like that the two trajectories weren't lining up, and it told him so with an emergency klaxon and the words *IMPACT WARNING* flashing in red letters. But Ricio knew his ship, and he knew that the turrets would pick them off if he followed the ship's AI.

As soon as he felt the AI attempt to take control, Ricio said, "Disable automatic override. Command override Lima Tango Niner."

"Automatic override disabled," a synthesized voice replied.

The bridge was so close that Ricio could make out Jujari faces looking up at him through their topside observation windows. In the nanoseconds that elapsed, he imagined what the hyenas must be thinking as they watched a squadron of Repub Talons fly close enough to spit on. This was going to be close.

"Mark!" Ricio yelled. He pulled back on his control yoke. The force buried him in his seat, making his harness straps go limp. Even with the inertia dampeners, Ricio grunted against the mounting g-forces as all the blood in his head rushed to his feet. The edges of his vision started to fade, forcing him to grunt even louder. *Stay awake, Ricio! Stay focused!*

His Talon pulled up with meters to spare, narrowly missing the bridge's main command window as his fighter continued toward the deck below. He was pretty sure he saw some Jujari duck.

The warning klaxon in his cockpit continued to blare, signaling his imminent demise. But Ricio trusted the ship's thrusters and knew what she could take. He knew what his body could take too. Even though he wasn't as young as he once was, he'd been diligent in meeting all physical training requirements even if his seniority permitted him to skimp on the reporting side. It paid off in times like this.

Ricio continued to pull back on his controls. The Talon's frame groaned while the inertia dampeners attempted to protect his body from the high-g maneuver. The carrier's main deck raced up to meet him. A less talented pilot would have panicked, but Ricio trusted his instincts. He leveled out just before grazing a flat section of the carrier's upper deck. Any contact at that speed would have vaporized him, but Ricio hadn't survived this long by accident. He looked in the rear-facing holo-screen camera feed, identifying the remaining ships of Alpha Team. They'd stayed tight on his tail. *Hot damn!*

He stabilized the fighter from the near miss and looked at his targeting monitor. His AI illuminated turrets down the spine of the main deck, followed by the communications relay about two kilometers ahead. His squadron would be at the target in seconds.

"Take out what you can, Vipers!" Ricio ordered.

He fired a volley of blaster bolts at the nearest turret to starboard. The weapon had just finished its rotation—coming away from firing on Talons toward the bow—when Ricio's bolts struck the joint where the unit connected to the deck. The turret popped off the carrier like a bottle top. Small electrical fires flared and then fizzled out.

More Talon blaster fire hammered down the carrier's deck, pounding its way into turrets. The units exploded in dazzling displays of sparks and short-lived plumes of fire and smoke. A few turrets got some shots off, but the blaster rounds went high, glancing off the very tops of the Talons' shields.

Ricio bobbed and weaved, flowing around protrusions in the carrier's bulwark as smoothly as he might cloud surf back on Capriana. The feeling was exhilarating, and for a moment, he almost forgot he was in battle. *Almost.*

"Comms array ahead!" Ricio yelled, his voice somewhere between ecstatic and unnerved. His HUD sent quadruple reticles overlapping on the target, each blinking when it had a lock. "Open fire!"

Ricio squeezed off a steady stream of fire and watched as the red blaster bolts sailed in slow motion toward their target. They connected in a fireworks display that lit up his entire front window. Orange sparks shone like a star's face, flooding his cockpit with light. Ricio rolled left, lowered his throttle, and peeled away. He looked to confirm target elimination on his HUD, but to his astonishment, his AI reported that the array was still intact. In fact, it hadn't taken any damage at all.

"I need visual damage assessment," Ricio said, hoping one of the Talons toward the back might have eyes on what had happened.

"Negative result," Viper Seven said. "It's got a shield of some sort."

"Dammit," Ricio said over comms, letting his emotions get the best of him. It was unprofessional, but he didn't care. His team's primary target was *fortified*.

Ricio continued his wide left turn, flying across the top of the starship from bow to stern, the bridge looming ahead like an ominous mountain peak arrayed in storm clouds and lightning bolts… or in their case, debris and blaster fire.

"Bravo Team, how are those engines coming?" Ricio asked.

"Viper One, this is Viper Eight. We have disrupted fifteen percent of the starboard engine configuration. However, they seem to be protected by their own energy-displacement field. Only torpedoes are proving effective."

"Understood, Viper Eight. All fighters, let's use up our torpedoes on these targets. Blaster seems ineffective. Alpha Team, as soon as we take another pass on this comms array, link up with Bravo Team and use your remaining ordnance on the engines."

Ricio steered back along the deck, vectoring toward the command bridge. He'd need all this distance and then some to obtain torpedo lock on the comms array with so many obstructions. The alternative would be to pop up above the carrier's irregular surface and get a clear shot at the array, but doing so would expose them to the turrets—and enemy fighters. So far, they hadn't drawn any Razorbacks, but he feared that was a temporary respite.

"Circle up at the bridge's base," Ricio ordered Alpha Team over comms. "I want us stacked up in a line on this next approach. Acquire lock, but do not fire until the previous Talon's torpedoes have detonated. Fire if the target remains. We need to conserve as many missiles as possible for when we rejoin Bravo Team."

Confirmation icons lit up his HUD.

Ricio took point as he came about in the bridge's shadow. Small antennas, pipes, and hatch panels were so close to his port window that he could almost reach out and touch them. His wings skimmed the carrier's surface, threatening to catch the slightest rise and cartwheel the Talon into a somersault. But Ricio was an expert pilot and knew what he was doing.

His fighter's nose came around and lined up on comms array for a second time. He still had all three of his torpedoes, and he planned to fire only one. Not only did he suspect that one was all he needed, but it was also the most conservative approach if he wanted to optimize shot-per-fighter ratios when engaging the engines.

A flick of his eyes armed the centermost torpedo under his Talon's belly, activating its target-acquisition sensors. A torpedo-target reticule appeared in his window. The ship's AI placed it on the comms array, instantly comparing the Talon's relative position with the target coordinates. Ricio watched as the distance-to-target value rapidly decreased. He swerved to avoid a small tower then bobbed back the other way to miss a domed protrusion of some sort.

"Fire," his AI's smooth voice said.

But Ricio held his trigger finger. He wanted to be closer. He pushed his throttle lever forward and heard the drive cores whine. The force pressed him back in his seat.

"Fire," the AI repeated.

Still, Ricio held his trigger. Enemy turret fire whizzed meters over his head, brilliant blue-and-green light reflecting off his cockpit's rounded window. *Just a little bit closer*, he told himself.

"Optimum engagement window closing," the AI said. Ricio squeezed the trigger and let the torpedo loose. The missile streaked across the carrier's deck. Ricio rolled to the left again, cut throttle, and pulled back, sending his Talon into a tight turn. Though he was blind to the impact, the torpedo's explosion peppered his Talon's shields with debris and sent a shudder through the fuselage, jarring Ricio against his restraints.

So I was a little close.

Then, over comms he heard, "Target eliminated!" It was Viper Six. "All fighters, hold torpedoes. Target eliminated."

That was easier than he thought it would be. Apparently, the Jujari hadn't planned on anything but enemy blaster fire making attempts on their communications system—turrets could pick off torpedoes kilometers away. But a torpedo fired danger close along their deck? *Yeah, didn't plan on that, did ya?*

"Alpha Team, join Bravo Team on engine assault."

His fighters confirmed and peeled off. Ricio backtracked along the deck for the second time then pulled up and over the bridge—but not before sending a volley of blaster fire into the command structure. It wouldn't do a tremendous amount of damage, but it might shake them up a bit.

Ricio flew out into empty space, seeing Bravo Team set up for another pass on the engines. Already, Viper Five and Seven were joining them, lending their unspent torpedoes to the attack. The carrier had slowed, pulling away from the main group. Ricio had no sooner lined up to join Bravo Team than he noticed something unusual—far to the rear of the armada was a single Jujari destroyer. While every other ship in the system was engaged in open battle, this one was…

What is it doing? Ricio grew curious enough that after he'd fired his remaining two torpedoes and engaged a defending Razorback in a short dogfight, he peeled away from the main conflict to investigate.

The destroyer hung in low orbit, engines at idle. Ricio couldn't be sure, but he thought he detected vapor trails farther down in Oorajee's atmosphere—evidence of recent shuttle activity. He initiated a sensor sweep, and sure enough, his AI indicated a Jujari shuttle landing on the surface far below.

Ricio selected SFC with a flick of his eyes over his HUD.

"Command," he said over a private channel, hailing Captain Seaman. "This is Viper One."

"We read you, Viper One," Seaman said. "Go ahead."

"I'm looking at a destroyer-class starship on the far side of Oorajee behind the armada, ship designation *Shining Bright Star of Mwadim Furlank over a Thousand Generations*. Are you able to confirm?"

There was a momentary pause as Captain Seaman reviewed Ricio's sensor data. "Confirmed, Viper One. That ship was reported as having already left the system. You are cleared to investigate at your discretion."

"Copy, Command. Viper One, out."

"Command, out."

Ricio reviewed the damage assessment on the carrier and saw that the vessel's engines were below fifty percent and falling. This massive starship would be crippled within a half hour. "Mission accomplished," he muttered to himself. It was time for the next one. The Jujari destroyer was about fifteen minutes out. Ricio rolled to starboard and headed toward the stray vessel. "Viper Squadron, on me."

16

Abimbola had barely been on the ground ten minutes when Rohoar pinged him over comms.

"Abimbola," came the Jujari's raspy voice.

"Go ahead."

"I will not go ahead. I will remain standing still."

Abimbola winced. He tended to forget the Jujari's propensity for all things literal. "Speak, Tawnhack."

Abimbola knew that forthright behavior would seem insolent by human standards, but for Miblimbians and Jujari alike, it was close to normal. Maybe that was why he liked being around the beasts—in some strange way, they reminded him of his home, Limbia Centrella. *Perhaps, when this is all over, I will go to you again, Centrella.*

But now was not the time to reminisce. Now was the time to gather resources. To train. To prepare for battle.

"Sensors are detecting an incoming squadron of enemy fighters."

"Enemy fighters? You mean, Repub Talons?"

"Yes. Repub Talons."

Horhish. This wasn't good. He and Rohoar had hoped to make it in and out of the system undetected. When he'd flipped for the odds, he'd gotten tail side on his poker chip—a bad omen. He'd shrugged it off. But he knew better than to ignore bad omens. He should have guessed that something would go wrong.

"How far out?"

"We have ten minutes to get back to the ship."

"Well, I've got a dozen Marauders who are willing to come with us. The rest want to stay, and I can't say I blame them. My explanation wasn't exactly *sane*."

"I have eight."

"Okay, then. That makes an even twenty. I think we can do some damage with that number."

"We can also kill a lot of enemies."

Abimbola grinned. "Yes, and that."

"I will be at your location with the shuttle in…" It sounded like Rohoar was tapping a screen with a nail-tipped finger. "Three minutes."

"We'll be ready."

THE TRIP into orbit was relatively uneventful, save for the

jeering remarks made between species. The shuttle stank of wet fur and body odor.

Abimbola stood behind Rohoar as the former mwadim prepared to enter the *Bright Sun's* docking bay. In the distance, he noticed a dozen or so bright spots converging toward them—the attack fighters. Behind them, nearly hidden by the planet's horizon, were the combined Republic and Jujari fleets, engaged in full-out war.

"How long before they're in weapons range?" Abimbola asked Rohoar.

"Ninety seconds."

Abimbola gauged the distance to the docking bay. They'd be secure in another minute, he figured. "We're gonna be cutting this close."

Rohoar winced. "I do not plan on cutting anything or doing so closely."

"I mean, we're not going to have a lot of time to jump."

"You are correct—we won't. My warriors will take up battle stations."

"How can we back you up?"

"Back me up? Into what?"

Abimbola cursed under his breath. "Where can my Marauders help you?"

"Will not our ship's systems be too complex for your people to understand?"

"Eh, you learn a thing or two about Jujari tech when you spend a few years on Oorajee."

Rohoar grunted. *Was that satisfaction?* Abimbola couldn't be sure.

"Do you have anyone who can monitor sensors?" Rohoar asked. "I could also use a second person at the helm if you have a good pilot. And any engineers for systems support."

"Sure. Need more help with defenses?"

Rohoar licked his chops with a long tongue then counted on his fingers. "I will have two more vacancies in turrets."

"Consider those needs met."

"Good, good," Rohoar said, adjusting the shuttle to line up with the docking bay's shimmering force field.

Abimbola climbed down the ladder into the cargo bay. "Listen up, Marauders. We've got enemy fighters inbound. FAF-28 Talons. Rohoar has places for his Tawnhack..." The hyenas let out growls, leaving Abimbola to wonder if he'd misspoken. "And he has two more positions for turrets and one for sensors. Zoll, Bliss, I want you taking orders from Rohoar. Robillard, you're on sensors."

"But I want to put blaster bolts downrange, Boss," Robillard said.

"Trust me, if we make it through this, you'll have plenty of opportunities to shoot all the horhish you like. I need you calling out targets."

"Copy."

"Berouth, I want you backing up Rohoar at the helm. See if you can't speed up the jump calculations."

"If it's all in Jujari, it might make it tough. I'm a little rusty."

"I think I can help with that," Cyril said with a raised hand.

"Good," Abimbola said. "Do it."

"Dozer, Nubs, I want you on systems."

"Understood," they said together.

"And Cyril?"

"Yes, sir?" said the young man in his squeaky voice.

"It's good to see you in one piece."

"Thank you, sir."

"After you help Berouth with the translation, I want you looking for any way to hack their systems—comms, nav, weapons. If there's a weakness to exploit, I want you slicing it."

"Right away, sir."

"The rest of you, look to double up on each position and fill in if anything happens." His Marauders nodded, looking at each other and at their Jujari counterparts. They hadn't even left the system, and already they were about to have more action than any of them had bargained for.

THE TALONS CAME at them from all sides. Robillard was designating and redesignating targets faster than Abimbola could keep count. Over the comms, he sounded like a spastic traffic control operator on a capital planet.

"Damn, these Repubs are fast," Robillard exclaimed.

"Just keep calling 'em out," Abimbola replied.

The enemy fighters landed blow after blow on the *Bright Sun's* shields. Abimbola lost his hold on the bridge's handrail several times as the destroyer shuddered under the impacts.

"Dozer? Nubs?" Abimbola tapped his earpiece to check in with his gunners.

"We're here, Boss," Dozer said. "But damn if these Jujari can shoot! Giving us a run for our creds."

"Good. Just don't let them have all the fun."

"We won't," Nubs said. "These Talons keep trying to get inside our shields."

"Keep 'em out, Marauders."

"The Jujari seem to be doing that just fine," Dozer replied.

"Good." Off comms, Abimbola looked at Berouth, who sat hunched over a side command console, tapping furiously. "How we doing on those jump coordinates?"

"Almost there. Cyril's translation script has most of the hard stuff worked out but not everything. Jujari math is… special."

"Ask me questions," Rohoar added from the captain's chair. He constantly adjusted the course to account for the enemy's pursuit, rolling the massive destroyer as if it were a starfighter. "I can translate for you."

"You just focus on keeping those fighters out of reach," Berouth replied.

"They are too far away to reach already."

Berouth made to respond, but Abimbola waved him off. "Stick to the jump. I need to know as soon as we're ready."

"Almost there…"

More incoming fire rocked the ship, and Abimbola grabbed the railing.

"Hey, Boss!" Cyril said from a console across the bridge.

"What?"

"Think I've got something I can exploit."

"Whatever it is, do it fast."

Ricio's squadron was having an unusually hard time breaking through this destroyer's defenses. Whoever was captaining the vessel had put the turrets on manual—at least, that was what Ricio guessed. While there was nothing faster than an AI, manual operators—good ones, at least—were more intuitive. And these Jujari knew what they were doing. Ricio's fighters were only ever able to get so close before being repelled.

"Damn, they're good," Viper Two said.

"Just stay after them," Ricio replied. "We'll find a weak spot."

"Sir," Viper Three said, "I'm detecting a drive-core surge. They're preparing to jump to subspace."

"Can you clone their jump coordinates?"

"I'm attempting to do so."

"Get me those coordinates." Ricio scanned his sensor data and noticed a variation in the shield-generator pattern on the destroyer's starboard side. "There! Starboard side, near the aft section." It wasn't much, but there was enough oscillation in the energy field that there might be some structural incoherence. Ricio lined up on it himself, but Viper Five was already closer.

"I see it," Viper Five said. "Targeting now."

"Fire at will!"

Rico watched and waited for Viper Five to fire on the weak spot. But nothing happened.

"Viper Five, SITREP!" Ricio watched as Viper Five peeled away. He decided to take the shot himself. With target lock confirmed, Ricio squeezed his trigger.

Suddenly, music blared over comms. It was an old show tune from Ricio's parents' generation, campy and obnoxiously happy.

"What the hell?" Ricio said.

"Where is that coming from?" Viper Five asked.

Ricio looked at his HUD, noting that his cannons had failed to fire. He was still on course, heading toward the shield anomaly. He squeezed the trigger again. The song changed, and a thrashing mega-metal song threatened to blow out his eardrums.

"What's happening?" Viper Five asked.

"We've been hacked," Ricio replied. It pained him to say it, but whoever was aboard that ship was good. *Damn good.* He gritted his teeth. "Viper Squadron, fall back."

Suddenly, coordinates appeared in his HUD.

"Viper Three," Ricio said, "are those what I think they are?"

"Yes, sir. And just in time too."

Viper Three had no sooner spoken than the Jujari destroyer streaked forward in a blurry smear across the void. Then she was gone, blinked out of existence.

"We've lost them, sir," said Viper Five.

"No, we haven't." Ricio looked again at the coordinates glowing on his screen. "We know right where they're going."

"Command, this is Viper One."

"We read you, Viper One," Captain Seaman said. "Looks like they slipped through your fingers, Commander Longo."

Ricio didn't like the insinuation. "We're not completely empty-handed, sir."

"What do you have for me, then?"

Ricio sent the coordinates with a flick of his eyes. "A jump destination."

Silence filled TACNET as Ricio waited for the captain to review the data. He knew Seaman would be interested. If a Jujari destroyer was jumping away from a major galactic conflict—no, *the* galactic conflict—it meant something important was happening. What, exactly, Ricio hadn't the slightest idea. It was undoubtedly above his pay grade. But he knew it was big.

Ricio tried piecing together the clues. Granted, he was no investigator, but he did have a curious mind. The ship's random appearance in low orbit, the shuttle from the surface, and a code slicer who had just hacked a Republic firewall in less than sixty seconds—this was high-level splick.

Finally, Captain Seaman's voice broke through the silence over TACNET. "Good work, Commander. It seems you brought us something of value after all."

"Honored to serve," Ricio replied. "What are our next orders?"

There was another pause. "You are wanted back on the *Black Labyrinth* for refueling and debriefing."

Ricio balked. "But, Captain, we just—"

"Those are your orders, Commander Longo."

"Understood." Ricio brought up the *Labyrinth's* coordinates and set a course. "Viper Squadron on our way."

"Good. And hurry." Seaman's voice had softened. "It seems your little discovery has some of the brass very interested."

I knew it. Ricio shook his fist in the air. While he hadn't gotten the kill, perhaps he'd gotten something worth much more.

"See you shortly, Viper One."

"Viper One, out."

"Command, out."

17

Piper missed Rohoar even though he'd only been gone for a few hours. She'd asked her mother if she could go with him to Oorajee. She thought it would be wonderful to see his home and try his food. But her mother told her that going with Rohoar was too dangerous. Rohoar would be okay, as he wasn't afraid of anything. Piper figured that was because of how big and strong he was.

Magnus wasn't afraid of anything either. He was big and strong like Rohoar but in different ways. Less furry ways. Piper had many dreams of Magnus rescuing her too. He always saved her when the city was destroyed. Every time, he walked out of the rubble and took her by the hand. Of course, the dreams felt far more real than just ideas. Her mother had instructed her to call them *dreams*, saying that calling them anything else might scare people. But Piper didn't see why.

Piper felt safe when she was near Magnus the same way she felt safe when she was near Abimbola, the biggest man she'd ever seen—as tall as a building. And just as strong. When they'd met, all Piper could do was stare at Abimbola's beautifully dark skin. She wished hers were that beautiful. Between these three important people in her life—Rohoar, Magnus, and Abimbola—Piper had nothing to be afraid of. She didn't see the difference between staying on the ship with Magnus or going to Oorajee with Rohoar and Abimbola. In the end, she'd be safe, and they'd all head to the metaverse together.

Piper had made herself comfortable on the ship's bridge, cozying up beside a smooth staircase with Talisman and three pillows that one of Abimbola's Marauders had offered her. She refused to stay in her quarters, arguing that if she couldn't go with Rohoar and Abimbola, she at least deserved to remain on the bridge near Magnus. The adults nodded the way grown-ups did and let her stay.

Piper studied Azelon. The way she interfaced with the ship's controls was remarkable. Azelon was definitely the most beautiful robot Piper had ever seen. The robot and the ship were linked together, her mother explained, being "one and the same." Piper didn't think it was weird that a ship and a robot could be the same thing. In fact, she wondered why more ships didn't do that. Especially since Azelon was so pretty. Which was why she guessed TO-96 liked her so much.

Azelon stood before the big bridge window, moving the floating holo-displays around the room. Her white body was beginning to glow a soft blue. She was also moving the holo-screens around faster. Bright lights and colored lines linked them together. She was amazing to watch. TO-96 looked at Azelon too. He seemed enamored with her every movement. Perhaps they would fall in love and get married. Piper would like to attend that wedding.

When Azelon announced that they were ready to jump into metaspace, Piper gripped Talisman in excitement.

"Are you okay?" Awen appeared over Piper's shoulder and placed a hand on her arm.

"I'm so excited, Miss Awen! I've never been to another universe before."

Awen laughed a little. "Well, you have every reason to be excited. I don't know many other people who've been to another universe either."

"Is it wonderful?"

"Yes, Piper. It's very wonderful."

Of all the new people Piper had met, Awen was her favorite. While Piper couldn't articulate it, she was drawn to something deep inside Awen—an inner beauty that was magical, as if Awen had summoned it from some far-off place in a fairytale and then hidden it inside her soul. Piper wanted to know what that beauty was, where it came from, and how she could have some of it too. It made Awen kind and understanding. But it also made her strong.

Awen's inner strength seemed to make her more powerful

than all other people Piper had ever known. And Piper hoped Awen would teach her about how to be different and still be powerful. Adults always told Piper that she was special. But she started to realize that *special* was really just a nicer way of saying *different*. And being different meant she had to change schools, houses, and friends. Piper was tired of being different.

That was, until she met Awen just a few hours before. Awen was different. And beautiful. And strong. Piper wanted to be like Awen. Maybe then she would be strong enough to force the pain from inside her heart. Piper suspected that her mother was lying to her about how her dad had died. The energy in her had done things before. It had danced on the ceiling. It had turned out the lights. And even though her mother had said that her last ten holo-pads had bad batteries, Piper suspected it was the power inside her body that had damaged them. The same energy that had hurt her father.

No. It didn't damage him. It killed him.

"So you're going to teach me?" Piper asked Awen.

The woman furrowed her brow, like she'd been concerned with the question. Or maybe she just didn't understand it.

"You're going to teach me, right?" Piper repeated. "When we get to the metaverse, I mean. How to use the energy inside me and be like you?"

"I'm going to try my very best, Piper, yes. Is that okay with you?"

Piper nodded, squeezing Talisman. "I don't want to hurt anyone else."

"Wait… what did you say?"

Piper looked up. She'd said something she wasn't supposed to. Being in trouble was the worst.

"Attention, all hands," Azelon announced, her voice sounding much louder than it usually did, filling every part of the bridge and maybe even the rest of the ship. "Prepare for metaverse transition in ten seconds."

Piper clapped her hands. Azelon's body was glowing brighter, and the holo-screens were forming a long line between the robot and the main window. "This is it, isn't it?"

"Yes, Piper. But hold on…" Awen stepped down from the upper landing and sat on the floor beside her. "What's this about hurting other people?"

"Nothing."

Piper didn't want to be in trouble with Awen. She shouldn't have said that thing about hurting people. Would Awen tell her mother?

"Five seconds," Azelon announced. The bot's blue body was getting too bright to look at.

"Piper, how many people have you hurt?" Awen shook her head. "I'm sorry, I didn't mean it like that."

"Three…" Azelon said.

"Piper?"

"Two…"

"Piper?"

"One…"

Azelon pulled her hands in by her sides. All the holo-screens rushed toward her as if flying into her chest. One by one, they disappeared until there was a very bright flash—

And then darkness. Everything was still. Piper expected some loud sound or vibration or feeling. But there was nothing. Suddenly she noticed a star in the big window. It was purple, like Awen's eyes. Then there was another and another. As Piper's vision adjusted to the darkness, more and more stars began to appear, connected by a pink cloud. It looked like a giant batch of cotton candy with thousands of purple stars stuck in the sticky strands of sugar.

"Are we in metaspace?" Piper stood up and walked to Azelon. "Are we in the metaverse, Miss Azelon?"

The bot turned to face her. "Yes, Piper. We have arrived in my universe of origin. Welcome."

"I'm so happy to be here!"

"And I am *happy* that you are here."

"Once the bad guys are off your planet, do you think you could show me around?"

"Show you around?"

"You know, show me where you come from, where you live, all that sort of thing."

"I come from manufacturing bay two hundred and thirty-nine, and I exist in this ship. I am unsure what else there is to show you that is of interest, Piper."

TO-96 stepped forward. His servos whined as he knelt until his head was at Piper's level. "I am quite sure that Azelon will be able to facilitate a tour of Ithnor Ithelia such that your questions will be answered to your liking, young Piper."

Azelon turned to TO-96. "Was my answer insufficient?"

"Yes," TO-96 replied. "Humans have an interesting way of submitting data queries at times. But once you get used to it, I anticipate you will find it endearing, as I have."

"Ah. I look forward to learning more about their behavior."

"Be warned." TO-96 stood to face her. "It is not always an easy task. It is, however, a rewarding one."

"Duly noted."

"You're both funny," Piper said. "I think you make a good couple."

TO-96 turned to Piper while Azelon tilted her head. "I do not understand this designation," Azelon said.

TO-96's eyes flashed once. "It means…"

"It means you should get married," Piper stated. "Are you gonna get married?"

"Piper," Valerie said, having just entered the bridge behind the little girl. "Leave those poor bots alone."

"Yes, Mama."

"Come, let's get you settled in our quarters. I want you rested before we make landfall."

Piper rushed to her mother and took her proffered hand. Then she looked back at Awen and smiled. "I can't wait to start, Miss Awen."

Awen waved. "Me too."

Piper thought her new teacher seemed sad. Or maybe scared. Either way, it didn't matter. Learning from Awen would be fun. *Everything will be just fine. Awen will see.*

18

Does Piper suspect she killed her father? The question plagued Awen so heavily that she hardly cared that she'd returned to the metaverse. She sat at the sensor's station on the bridge, chin in her hands, watching as the Novia Minoosh's planet came into view in the main window. The lush green-and-blue world loomed against the star-strewn background. Awen barely noticed. She wanted to take Piper aside and find out everything the little girl knew. She wanted to ask her about her powers... about the things she'd seen. And about what had happened to her father.

Awen suddenly realized that maybe Piper's father hadn't been the only person the little girl had harmed. *What if there are others?* Memories from Awen's own childhood on Elonia stirred in her mind. She'd found her own abilities challenging to manage at times. *And mine weren't anything like Piper's. No one's are.* The poor thing was probably terrified. Awen remembered how scared she'd felt the first time one of her classmates winced at what Awen had done. It was a horrible feeling. *And I never killed anyone.* Piper was probably scared more than she let on, which meant Awen needed to get her team settled on this new planet, and fast.

"So where are we headed, Azelon?" Awen asked.

"The third planet from the system's main star," Azelon replied. "It is named Nieth Tearness in honor of the planet's original settlers."

Awen snapped her eyes toward the bot. "Wait. They weren't Novia Minoosh?" She looked at TO-96. "You mean to tell me there are more species in this system?"

TO-96 raised a hand. "I am sorry, Awen. No, they were indeed Novia Minoosh. What Azelon means to say is that the name refers to their particular calling—their *profession*, if you will—rather than to their species."

"TO-96 is correct," Azelon said. "Please forgive me."

"Don't worry about it." Awen placed a hand on her chest. "Almost gave me a heart attack there. I'm not sure I can handle the discovery of a second species right now."

"There are many more than two, whenever you are ready, Awen," Azelon said.

"Many more? What's *many more?*" Awen's head swam at that thought, but she regretted posing the question. She had far more important things to worry about than playing emissary in a new universe—a conclusion she could hardly believe she was accepting. "Wait. You know what? Never mind. I don't want to know. At least, not right now, anyway."

"As you wish," TO-96 replied with a bow of his head. Azelon had raised her finger as if to expound on her point, but TO-96 waved her off. "Awen is not in the *headspace* to *deal with it* right now."

"I do not understand anything you just said," Azelon replied.

"Save the data for later dissemination."

"Very well."

"And in the meantime," Awen said, "what can you tell me about this new planet?"

The elevator doors slid open in a smooth *whoosh*. Awen turned to see Magnus step onto the bridge.

"Hey," he said with a wave.

Awen waved back. "How's Sootriman?"

"Everything looks good. Another day and a half before she's conscious. At least, that's what the ship's med systems seem to show."

"You are correct, Magnus," Azelon said.

Magnus put a hand on the back of his neck. "I'm not sure I'll ever get used to you, Azelon."

"Used to me?"

"They are not used to a ship being self-aware and fully integrated into all client systems," TO-96 explained.

"Yeah, that," Magnus said. "Just a little weird. Anyway,

Sootriman's good, and the Reptalon has been escorted to his quarters on the *other* side of the ship."

"Great. Thanks." Awen had kicked herself for not remembering the bad blood between the Jujari and the Reptalons. Inviting one onto the ship had been a mistake. But then again, it was Rohoar who'd arrived second. It wasn't Awen's fault—it was just the way things had unfolded. She could no more tell Saasarr to turn back from avenging Sootriman's would-be killer than she could ask Rohoar to stop serving Magnus and Magnus to stop protecting Piper. It seemed they were all caught up in this together, and she had to make do. "When Rohoar gets back, we're going to—"

"Need to figure something else out, I know," Magnus replied. "We will. In the meantime, Saasarr is enjoying some kind of strange meal that the replicators produced for him."

"That is optuna trunkfish from Orran Five," TO-96 said. "Or at least, Azelon's best approximation based upon my limited data set. It is a delicacy among Reptalons."

"Well, apparently he really likes it," Magnus said. "Ezo and I were worried that nothing would pull him away from his vigil at Sootriman's side. But that awful stuff did the trick."

"Awful, sir?" TO-96 asked.

"Splick, yes." Magnus waved his hand in front of his face as if warding off a foul odor. "Stuff is heinous. Like sticking your face inside a dead body."

Awen raised her eyebrows. "And you know that because…?"

"It just is, okay?"

"Whatever you say, Marine." Awen chuckled as Magnus came to stand beside her.

"So what do we got here?" he asked.

"Heading to the new planet," Awen said.

"It is called Nieth Tearness," Azelon explained. "And no, they are not a new species."

"What's not a new species?" Magnus asked, looking to Awen for help.

"Never mind." She laughed. "Keep going, Azelon."

"As you wish." A picture-perfect representation of a planet appeared in a hexagonal holo-screen just in front of Awen and Magnus. Like Ithnor Ithelia, this new planet contained green and blue, indicating lush continents and vast oceans. But Nieth Tearness had less landmass and far more water than the first planet. "As you can see," Azelon continued, "eighty-nine percent of the planet's surface is covered in water."

"That's even more than Capriana," Magnus said.

Awen nodded. "So I guess that means that the population was fairly low." No sooner had she said it than she scolded herself. *Determining population by landmass? What if they could breathe underwater too?* For as long as she'd lived on the alien planet—even surviving on one of their old ships—she still knew next to nothing about the Novia's physiology.

"Affirmative," Azelon replied. "Nieth Tearness served as a sister planet whose population was dependent on Ithnor Ithelia for the majority of their basic needs."

"And you still think this is a good place for us to set up camp?" Magnus asked no one in particular.

Azelon looked at Awen and then TO-96. When no one else replied, she said, "Affirmative. Even with the additional occupants your crewmates propose to bring from Oorajee, your dietary and energy needs will place a fractional demand on the planet's resources. Furthermore, given your proposed combat preparations, you will not have any additional time to cultivate the necessary crops and energy supply while still adhering to a conservative timeline. Therefore, the majority of your nutritional requirements will be met by my replicators. Likewise, your energy needs will be met by a temporary battery-node array."

"Sounds like we'll be living in the lap of luxury, then," Magnus said. "When do we get there?"

"Approximately fifty-eight minutes, Magnus," TO-96 replied. "Now that we are in-system, we will make a short subspace jump to just outside the planet's gravity well, then we will advance under normal ion engines to low orbit."

"Speaking of time," Awen said, "how long has it been?"

"That is an incomplete question," Azelon said.

"Do you mean how much time has elapsed since we last left?" TO-96 asked.

"Yeah, exactly." Awen stood and moved close to Magnus.

"Our most recent duration in the protoverse—"

"That's our universe," Awen said to Magnus.

"—was roughly eighteen hours. Following what I have

discerned to be a twenty-to-one time-dilation ratio, that correlates to fifteen days local time."

"Damn," Magnus said. "You mean to tell me even though you just left here less than a day ago, fifteen days have gone by already? Out here, I mean?"

"That's correct, sir," TO-96 said.

"Wait, so…" Magnus looked at Awen. "If you were gone from our universe for a couple of days, that means…" He seemed to be attempting the math in his head.

"Don't hurt yourself there, trooper."

"I can handle this."

"I didn't say you couldn't. Just take your time."

Magnus waved her off. "Was that like three months or something?"

"Well done, sir," said TO-96.

"See?" Magnus said to Awen. "I can still do the math."

"And aren't you just so proud of yourself."

"Ninety-plus days… that's a long time," Magnus said. "What'd you do with yourself?"

Awen felt her eyes glass over. The memories of her time in the city came back as if they'd happened only moments ago. She remembered exploring the temple library while the others searched the city. She'd been afraid of going back inside the Unity, haunted by the dark presence that possessed Admiral Kane's soul. She had bitter conversations with Ezo and cost her friends a lot of time by not facing her fears sooner. Eventually, however, she consented to exploring the temple library from inside the Unity. And what a day that had been—little more than eighteen hours ago by one timetable and *fifteen days* by another.

"We did plenty," Awen said. "That's for another day. Azelon, tell me—are you picking up anything from Itheliana? From the intruders there, I mean?"

Azelon nodded. "Yes. The Novia's continued presence in the city is a part of my consciousness, though the information they provide is often sporadic or incomplete. Is there something I can answer specifically?"

"Sure. I mean, have they... I don't know... discovered anything they shouldn't have? Or damaged something? Or taken something they shouldn't have touched?" The more Awen spoke, the more she realized how vague her questions were. *What are you asking, Awen?*

"If you mean, has the military force that pursued you in the city found anything of value that might serve an ulterior purpose to do others harm, then no, at least not from what the Novia can ascertain."

Awen let out a sigh. "Well, that's good news."

"However, it does seem that the contingent of intruders—as you call them—"

"They're a former recon team," Magnus interrupted with a raised hand. "Former Repub Marines—traitors and murderers. But let's just call them what they are."

Azelon nodded then amended her description. "The enemy's reconnaissance team is spending an inordinate amount of time near several points of interest that the Novia find distressing."

Awen's heart tightened. "What do you mean *distressing*?"

"The Novia note significant energy expenditures near two collections of material reservoirs."

"Material… like rare metals or fuels or something?"

"They are far more complex than that," Azelon said, "but yes."

"That can't be good," Magnus said.

"The Novia do not think you should be overly concerned, however," Azelon continued. "The enemy's team is not close to discovering a method of entry to these reservoirs, which are heavily fortified."

"I wouldn't count on that," Magnus replied. "They're trained to blow splick up. It's part of their tradecraft."

"The Novia are reasonably sure you have nothing to fear," Azelon countered. "I calculate that there is less than a 5 percent chance they will penetrate the city's defensive measures."

"I concur with her findings, Awen," TO-96 said. "The potential is negligible."

Their reassurances didn't lower Awen's sense of urgency. These Paragon troopers needed to be stopped and quickly. Whatever it was they were after couldn't be good.

"Where do you recommend we set up base camp?" Magnus asked.

"Here." Azelon pointed to an island that expanded to meet her fingertip. It lay just below the planet's equatorial line and was shaped like a triangle with rounded corners. "This is the largest island, Ni No. I believe the founding city's ruins will best accommodate the list you provided, Awen."

"What list?" Magnus asked. "You gave her a list?"

"I did, yes. Basic things. Safe shelter, adequate space for training, varied terrain, inspiring views."

"Inspiring views?"

"Do you have a problem with that?"

"We're training for battle, not a vacation in the Venetian system."

"And what I'm about to lead Piper through is going to be harder than you can possibly imagine, so a meditative environment will go a long way in easing her anxiety."

"Whatever floats your starship, Awen. Just maybe think about consulting me next time. If we're gonna be a team, we gotta think like one."

"I figured you could train anywhere."

"And I didn't figure you'd need picturesque vistas."

Awen pursed her lips in thought. "Fair enough." Magnus had a point. And she did like the idea of being a team. With him. That felt good. How often had she wished he'd been with her on Ithnor Ithelia? How often had she wanted to ask him what to do next or wished he would blow something up that she couldn't—like the troopers?

But something bothered her about what Magnus had just said—the way he'd referred to her as a *Luma*. Was she still a Luma? From the first moment she'd learned what the Order of the Luma was, when she was a child, she'd wanted to be one. She'd learned about them at school, keeping the reading assignments a secret from her parents after they told her the Order was rubbish. That was the only time in her life that her parents said they didn't mind if she failed the unit test on a subject. But she'd achieved a perfect score on the exam and even opted to take electives on the Order for further study.

But after what she'd seen So-Elku do—and after what he'd done to Willowood, Magnus, and the others—she wasn't sure. This wasn't the Luma—at least, not *her* Luma. This was something else. She felt sick to her stomach and wanted to get as far away from the Order as possible, to renounce her oaths and reject the title she'd worked so hard to obtain. *If manipulating and killing for your own purposes is what being a Luma is about, then I want nothing to do with it.*

And what were So-Elku's purposes, anyway? She wasn't sure. But after meeting Piper, Awen was at least convinced that it had something to do with the little girl… and something to do with the codex he'd stolen from the temple library. What those things had in common, she had no idea.

It was hard to reconcile So-Elku's behavior with the man she'd believed he was. The betrayal was deep, like a blade slowly piercing her heart, twisting in small painful fits that made her want to weep. She'd trusted him, revered him. His office epitomized everything the Luma stood for. His very title of master meant he fully embodied the Order's ethos. If he'd failed, if he'd fallen, were the Order's ideals to be questioned too? *Surely, the desire to fight for the best interests of a species is noble, isn't it? But why, then, did that produce such horrible fruit? How could I —or any of us—have missed this?*

She didn't want to be a Luma anymore. Not with So-Elku muddying the waters. Surely, there was still good in the Order—she wasn't so naive as to think that the whole thing had rotted away. But she hated the sound of the name. *That* was what bothered her. When Magnus had called her a Luma, she'd resented it. And she wanted to get herself as far away from it as possible.

19

THE SHUTTLE RIDE to Nieth Tearness's surface had been uneventful for Magnus. It was nice, he admitted, not to be chased or shot at or preparing to fast-rope into a hot landing zone. Instead, for once, he just enjoyed the view. He glanced over at Awen, who likewise seemed to be enjoying the view. Her purple eyes were even more intense under the sun's otherworldly light. Magnus found himself staring at her. He jerked away and looked out the shuttle's cockpit window.

The ocean stretched out from east to west, north and south, dotted with islands of various sizes. The system's violet-hued star cast the land in deep green, the islands lying in stark contrast to the purple-blue oceans. It was, he had to admit, a beautiful sight. Maybe the Elonian wasn't that far off in her need for stunning views. Still, they had a job to do, and Magnus was eager to get started.

Ezo had agreed to stay behind to look after Sootriman, Saasarr, Valerie, Piper, and the bots while Magnus and Awen took everyone else planetside to get settled. Nolan piloted the shuttle to land in a large clearing in the center of the ruined city. Even though Azelon had assured them that the planet's inhabitants had long abandoned their residences, Magnus still tasked his Marines and Marauders with setting up a perimeter as soon as the skids touched down.

The remains of large stone buildings lay to each side of an open hexagon. The ruins had been reclaimed by the forest long before, covered in a myriad of mosses, grasses, vines, and—where there was enough soil—trees. Still, Magnus could make out windows, doorways, and balconies in the buildings. His troops cleared the closest structures as best they could, but the only signs of life Magnus could see were various types of local wildlife—birds, some form of monkey, and ground animals that darted into burrows mined between stone blocks.

"It's abandoned, LT," Dutch said over comms.

"Copy. Let's get the lay of the land then set up base camp."

"Roger that."

After Magnus conferred with Awen back on the ship, she stepped onto the grass-covered stones behind the shuttle and stretched her arms. "Smells good."

"Ocean air smells familiar," he said. "Just not sure I can get used to the purple-light thing."

"You will. It grows on you."

"I'll take your word for it. Where do you want to set up base camp?"

"Well, it's a team decision. What do you think?"

"Well, we'll want optimum visibility of all terrain but the least amount of exposure."

"Which means what?" Awen turned to look at the hexagon's perimeter. "Something like that?" She pointed to a small rise behind the north side's main body of buildings. It had several trees near the summit but seemed relatively free of obstructions. It also had a cluster of buildings that might serve as suitable housing so long as they were accessible and in relatively good repair.

"Something like that, yes."

"Lieutenant," came a voice in Magnus's ear.

"Is that you, Ninety-Six?"

"It is indeed, sir. Well done…"

Awen, hearing the voice too, rolled her hand in circles, prompting Magnus to keep the bot talking.

"Auditory pattern matching can often be a challenging skill for a biologic to master," TO-96 added.

"Got it, Ninety-Six. Did you want to contribute something to our base-camp choice?"

"Ah, yes. That is precisely why I was transmitting to you—a contribution."

When TO-96 didn't make any additional comment, Magnus asked, "And what is that contribution?"

"Ah, yes. After hearing your limited specifications, Azelon and I have denoted three possible locations for your base camp. You should see those in your eyes now. Of course, should you provide more data for us to consider, we could expand or contract our search results as desired."

"Did you—" Magnus blinked several times. His bioteknia eyes flickered as data streamed down the right side, populating his vision with vector indicators, waypoints, and intercept distances. "Did you just hack my eyes?"

"*Hack* seems to be a fairly aggressive word, Lieutenant. I prefer to say—"

"Just call me Magnus."

"As you wish, *Magnus*."

"Keep going."

"Ah, yes. I prefer to say that we deduced your new eyes' operating protocols and have expedited the transmission of valuable data in the most efficient way possible."

"So you hacked me."

"Cyril likes to use the word *sliced*, Magnus."

"Cyril?" Magnus spun around to where Cyril stood near a ruined building on the east side of the hexagon. Since everyone was on the same comms channel, the young code slicer had obviously heard this entire conversation. As Magnus locked eyes with him, Cyril waved with two fingers.

"Betrayed by a code slicer," Magnus said. "Someday they'll rule the galaxy."

"I just offered them a few suggestions," Cyril said.

"Like I said, betrayed." Magnus gave the kid a smirk and a slight shake of his head then turned back to Awen, who looked slightly confused.

"Hacked your eyes?" she said.

Magnus shook his head and gave her a dismissive wave of his hand. Trying to change gears, he said, "Seems we have a few possibilities to check out, but yours is top on the list, Awen."

"Okay... but I still don't—"

"I said it's nothing."

She shrugged. "Lead the way."

AFTER EXPLORING the two secondary options, Magnus and Awen ended back at the first site, the hill behind the northern end of the hexagon. It offered a good view of the ruined city as well as the oceans far below. The island's triangular shape rose sharply out of the sea, some of its sides being sheer cliff faces instead of steep slopes. So high was their observation post that they could even see other islands on the horizon, appearing as hazy bumps in the humid air.

Magnus and Awen explored what they decided would be their new base camp, wading through knee-high grasses and stepping along ruined walls. The air would have been painfully hot were it not for the constant breeze rising up from the ocean. Magnus wondered if the climate was always this comfortable.

"I feel like this was some sort of spiritual center." Awen was speaking off comms, calling over her shoulder at him from inside one of the main building's doorways.

"Yeah? Why's that?"

"It feels very austere. And the rooms are spacious with high windows."

Magnus leaped down from a boulder he'd climbed and walked across what he thought was the town's square. He joined her in a doorway that led to an open room. It could hold maybe thirty or forty people and seemed to have evenly spaced windows in—yet again—a hexagon pattern.

Awen walked over to one of the walls and pulled some vines from the surface. She was curious—that was for sure. Magnus wanted to warn her that the vines might be poisonous or carnivorous, but she'd acted too quickly. Where he was cautious and strategic, she seemed more intuitive and adventurous. *Just the type to get herself killed on an op.*

"Look," she said, pointing to marking on the walls. "It's some sort of decorative script."

"Looks like squirrel scratch to me."

"No, no, it's not." She moved to another wall and pulled the vines away. He was sure she would have to visit sick bay before the day was out. "Look, it's too detailed to be meaningless. It's saying something."

"Whatever you say, Luma."

Awen turned on him with a look in her eyes reminiscent of a boot-camp drill instructor. "Don't call me that, please."

Magnus froze. *Splick, now what'd you do, Adonis?* "What'd I say?"

"Don't call me *Luma*."

"But… isn't that—"

"No, it's not what I am. Not anymore at least. And maybe not ever again." She returned to the wall and let the vines fall back into place. "Just don't call me that anymore."

"Copy."

Awen walked to the far side of the room. There was a wide window about chest height that looked over the north coast. She rested her elbows on it and stared at the ocean, the waves shimmering in the purplish-white sunlight all the way to the horizon.

Say something, Adonis. Magnus walked through bits of stone and clumps of grass to stand beside Awen, mindful of how still she was. He'd never been one to think he understood the opposite sex. Hell, all of his relationships had ended pretty badly. Especially his marriage to Dani. He never knew what to say to her or how much to tell her. But in this particular moment—here with Awen—he actually felt that he knew what to say, like he knew what she was going through.

"I'm not a Marine anymore," he said, his voice just above a whisper, almost lost in the sound of the wind.

Awen turned to face him. "What'd you say?"

Magnus cleared his throat. "I'm not a Marine anymore."

"That's a little melodramatic, isn't it? At least, it's presumptuous. You'll get your name cleared. We'll figure all this out."

"No," Magnus said, shaking his head. "It's not even about that." He tapped a finger just beside his right eye. "These... they're not real anymore."

"I... don't understand."

"That orbital strike that we survived on Oorajee blinded me. Abimbola had some bioteknia eyes that Valerie gave me. Surgery went well, apparently."

"So... those aren't your real eyes anymore?"

He sighed. "Nope."

"Okay. So you have prosthetic eyes, what's the big deal?"

"They're a no-go in the Corps. Too easy to hack. Human biology may be old-fashioned, but it's pretty hard to take over in battle. Tech like this is cool, but it makes you a liability. I'm out."

"You're saying you've been discharged?"

"Well, not officially, but... yeah. And even if I could clear my name, there's no way they'd be interested in moving a finger once they found out I was no longer a viable asset. So, like I said, I'm not a Marine anymore."

"But don't you guys have that saying? 'Once a Marine, always a Marine'?"

Magnus stared at her long enough that Awen eventually looked away. He didn't mean to make her uncomfortable, but he didn't have the energy to explain a Marine slogan that tore his heart in two.

Awen played with a few strands of grass that had grown between cracks in the stone sill. "You're trying to comfort me —is that it? Shared experiences, similar emotions?"

Magnus examined the windowsill. "Something like that. Why? Is it working?"

"No." Awen hesitated. "Maybe."

Magnus caught her smiling at the blades of grass. Something about the way her lips curled made him want to… *Splick*. He felt like he was in tertiary school again. He hadn't felt anything toward a woman since Dani, then suddenly, Awen shows up on a mission gone sideways, and Valerie appears on a broken-down shuttle in the middle of nowhere. *What is the deal?*

Magnus was tired. He desperately needed rest. He needed a break from plotting and strategizing and trying to stay ten moves ahead of his enemies. Hell, he wasn't even sure if he was one move ahead at this point—he hardly knew what his side was doing, let alone what the enemy was up to. Still, coming here felt right. And being with Awen again was…

What is it, Adonis?

Good. It *felt* good. Like being with an old friend.

Even though you've known her for fewer than three weeks?

Combat forged strange bonds. And no matter what happened next, Magnus knew he was connected to Awen in ways he wouldn't be able to describe. So he wouldn't try. He would just be in the moment.

"Listen, I get feeling betrayed." Magnus leaned against the stone ledge, looking out to the ocean. "And I get feeling disenfranchised, like you've been left behind or abandoned. Like the thing you joined isn't what it once was. But you know what's kept me going?"

Awen shook her head. Magnus thought he saw a tear slide down one side of her face.

"My next mission. This one, I mean. I've got a new unit." He suppressed a chuckle. "Crazy as they are, and diverse as they are, I'm responsible for them now in some strange way. Humans, Jujari, a Miblimbian, a bunch of Marauders, bots, a little girl—"

"And me." Awen looked at him, fighting back the tears that filled both eyes. "Don't forget me."

"Couldn't if I tried." He smiled at her as she held the floodwaters back. "When everything goes sideways, Awen, I've got you."

"Thank you," she mouthed.

The two of them rested against the ledge, watching the light grow long across the water. "We're something new, you know," Magnus said. "Something different. I doubt there's any going back for either of us. So whatever *this* is, we gotta figure it out together. We make the best of what we have—we make it work. We train who we've got, and we get the job done. When it's all over, if we survive it, then we can worry about putting things back together. But until then, we do this. We become who we need to be right now, and we stick together. That's how we endure, that's how we fight, that's how we win."

Awen didn't say anything, but Magnus noticed her nodding out of the corner of his eye. His monologue had drained whatever energy reserves he had left. He felt spent. The loss of identity, the several near-death experiences, the energy needed to formulate a plan—it had all caught up with him.

Finally, Magnus lowered his head, feeling his body's weight slump between his shoulders. Just as he did that, he felt

Awen lean against him. Then her head rested on his shoulder armor. He thought that if he moved a muscle, she might jerk away, startled like some shy woodland creature. So he didn't. He wanted the moment to last, fearing it might never happen again.

20

Nearly two days had passed before Piper was allowed to take the shuttle down to Nieth Tearness. She'd begged her mother to let her go at least a hundred times, but no matter how much she pleaded, Valerie didn't budge. So Piper took to badgering TO-96 and Azelon instead. At least *they* didn't ignore her but always offered some status update on Magnus and Awen's progress, complete with pictures and "percentages of completion."

When TO-96 had finally given the all-clear to Piper, she raced through the starship to find her mother. Valerie was in sick bay, as she always was, attending to Sootriman's recovery. And for the first time, when Piper entered the medical unit, Sootriman was awake. Ezo stood on one side of her while Saasarr stood on the other.

"Well, hello there," Sootriman said in a smooth voice. "You must be Piper."

"And you're Sootriman." Piper froze, wide-eyed. Sootriman was quite possibly the biggest lady she'd ever seen. Beautiful. Powerful. "You look amazing."

Sootriman laughed. "Thank you, Piper. You look lovely yourself."

"Thanks." Piper extended a hand and walked toward Sootriman. "Pleased to meet you."

Sootriman reached down from her bed and took Piper's hand. "And you."

"You've been asleep for a while. Are you feeling better?"

"I am. Thank you for asking."

"Everyone seemed very concerned for you and your recovery," Piper said. "I think you must be very important."

"No more than others."

"Then maybe everyone just likes you. I can see why."

Sootriman placed a hand on her chest and looked across the room at Valerie. "You have quite a wonderful girl here."

"Thank you," Valerie said. "Piper is special."

"No more than others," Piper replied. The adults laughed at that, but Piper didn't see why it was funny. She turned to Sootriman. "Are you going to come down with us? To the planet's surface, I mean? TO-96 and Azelon say Magnus and Awen are ready to have everyone else come down."

"Magnus?" Sootriman looked at Ezo. "Who's *everyone else?*"

"There's a lot to explain." Ezo looked at Piper. "I'm sure we'll be down once Sootriman is feeling more rested."

"But she's been asleep for *days*. I would be *so* rested right now if I were her. I'd be sick of resting, I think. It would be time to go outside and do something fun."

"Okay, dear," Valerie said, placing her hands on Piper's shoulders and escorting her toward the door. "Let's leave Sootriman alone."

"And head to the surface?"

Valerie turned toward Sootriman.

"Got it covered," Ezo said then proceeded to thank Valerie for all her help. "You get our little cadet to her new teacher. We'll be down to join you in a day or two."

"You're sure?"

"From what I hear," Sootriman said, "your care has been amazing. I think he can handle it from here." She placed a hand on Ezo's arm. "Just go be with your daughter."

"Okay. We'll see you planetside, then."

"Bye, Sootriman," Piper said with an emphatic wave. "See you soon!"

As the shuttle descended toward the landing zone—a small clearing outside the central hexagon—Piper's heart raced. Base camp looked so exciting! Slate-blue tents with yellow markings were arranged in a pattern to one side of the hexagon, while the other side had several large tents and two open areas with strange-looking furniture in them. Portable light poles were spaced evenly throughout the camp, and Piper even thought she saw a place for a campfire with chairs around it.

Beyond the camp, bordering it on all sides, looked to be the ruins of an old town. The buildings were half hidden by vines and trees and grass, but she could still make out their shapes despite the forest's attempts to swallow them up. Some buildings stood atop a small knoll to the town's northern end. These buildings looked the most interesting to Piper. Then, several hundred meters past the edge of town, in all directions, the island dropped away toward the ocean far below. She couldn't *wait* to explore this place! It looked so magical.

"Prepare for contact," Nolan said from his seat behind the shuttle's controls. "In three… two… one…"

Piper felt the shuttle lurch as it landed in the field beneath them.

"Touchdown," Nolan said.

Piper clapped her hands then squeezed Talisman. She slid down the ladder into the cargo bay and ran toward the ramp. Her boots tapped out a rhythm as she waited for Dutch to open the door.

"I wonder if someone's excited," Dutch said.

"I am, Miss Dutch, I really am!"

"Huh. That's funny, because I really couldn't tell." Dutch smiled and pressed a large button on the hull's side. A mechanism whined as a slit of light appeared near the ceiling then grew wider with each second that passed.

"Piper, wait for me," her mother said. Piper glanced back at Valerie but only for a second—she was compelled to catch her first glimpse of this new world. She couldn't miss a thing.

The tops of distant trees appeared, then the outline of some buildings, and then people's heads. She saw Awen and Magnus and the rest of the Marines and Marauders who'd come down to help set up.

"Hello!" Piper said. Before the ramp was even all the way extended, she was bounding toward Awen.

"Piper," her mother yelled.

"It's okay," Awen said, laughing as Piper approached her. At the last second, the ramp hit the ground and caused Piper to stumble. She would have hit the metal floor had Awen not scooped her up. "Gotcha."

"Piper, you have to be more careful!" Valerie said as she trotted out of the shuttle.

"Thanks, Miss Awen," Piper said, grinning at the Luma.

"No problem. But listen to your mother, okay?"

"Okay."

"It's good to have you both here," Magnus said. "Can we show you around?"

"Please," Valerie said. "Lead the way."

Magnus and Awen took them into the barracks section. This was the first part Piper had noticed when they were landing.

"Each tent can hold four people," Magnus explained. "They were built for Novia Minoosh, who were bigger than us, so originally, these were two-person tents. For you, however"—Magnus winked at Piper— "we've got one just for you and your mom."

"Thanks, Mr. Lieutenant Magnus, sir!"

"You can just call me Magnus."

"Okay, Mr. Lieutenant Magnus, sir," Piper replied with a wide smile.

"That's gonna be a hard habit to break, I think," Awen said to him.

Magnus smiled. "Anyway, yours is right here in the center." He led them toward a blue tent in the middle of the cluster and pulled back the main flap. Piper peered inside to see a very spacious interior complete with two beds, ceiling lights, a storage pod, and a utility pod.

"And what's that pod?"

"Your own bathroom. It holds a shower and a toilet."

"That way you don't have to share with any of the smelly troopers," Awen added, thumbing in Magnus's direction.

Piper giggled. "They're not so bad. As long as they don't fart." That comment made everyone laugh. Piper liked when adults laughed.

"Would you like to get settled?" Magnus asked, looking from Piper to Valerie.

"Nope," Piper said. "We want to see *everything*."

"Piper..." her mother scolded. "Maybe it's best that we—"

"Please, Mama? I really want to see everything."

"Very well." Valerie looked at Magnus. "Let's *see everything*."

Magnus winked at Piper and led the way out of the sleeping tents and toward the open areas. "Over here, we have two sparring arenas," he said, gesturing to large pens made of metal stations and wire. Piper noticed large panels that looked like holo-projectors on top of tall poles. "These are mostly for the troopers, but you might be in here once in a while, too, Piper."

"What's sparting?"

"Sparring," Valerie corrected. "It's a way of practicing fighting people without actually hurting anyone."

"Oh. So I'm going to learn how to fight people?"

The adults got quiet. No one seemed to want to answer her. It was weird, like they were confused by her question. But Piper didn't think her question was confusing at all.

"Yes," Awen said at last. "You're going to learn how to fight bad guys."

"Cool."

"But not at first."

"That's okay. Just as long as I don't have to wait too long."

"And over here," Magnus said, shifting directions and indicating each large tent with the flat of his hand, "we have the mess hall, the shower facility for the rest of us, the armory, and the enclosed combat-simulation environment, or ECSE."

"What is an ECSE?" Piper asked.

"It's an acronym for what Magnus just said." Awen explained what an acronym was. "And one thing you'll learn about troopers is that they'll never miss an opportunity to make an acronym out of something."

"Okay," Piper said then turned to Magnus. "TYMLMS."

Magnus glanced at Awen and Valerie then back at Piper. "What'd you say?"

"I said, TYMLMS."

"I think she made you an acronym," Awen whispered. Piper nodded.

"And what's it stand for?" Magnus asked.

"Thank you, Mr. Lieutenant Magnus, sir."

All the adults laughed again, but Magnus seemed to like it the most. "Nice one, Piper."

"Thank you."

"I think she has you figured out there, Magnus," Awen said.

"Seems she does," he replied.

"If you don't mind," Valerie said, stepping close to Magnus, "the Novia Minoosh... they didn't have Repub tech for all this, right? I mean, there's no way they called that big tent an ECSE, did they?"

"No. I gave specs, and then they supplied us with what tech they had on board. As it turned out, they had plenty of ideas on how to improve my designs too. The results are pretty cool"—he winked at Piper— "if you ask me."

"Can we see? Can we?"

"Of course, Piper. This way."

Magnus led the group to the last of the large tents, which someone had marked with a temporary sign that read ECSE. He placed his hand on a scanner built into the tent's sturdy exterior wall, and the gray metal doors slid apart.

"After you," he said, ushering Piper and Valerie toward the opening.

Piper stepped inside to find herself swallowed by a dark room. Even with the light from outside, the space felt ominous and black. It got even worse, however, when everyone had finished filing in and the doors closed. She let out a small yelp as the blackness enveloped her.

"Computer," Magnus said, "begin simulation alpha zero one."

"Acknowledged," a quiet feminine voice said.

Like a sunrise growing in the morning sky, the air above Piper's head began to glow. It was subtle at first, almost indiscernible. But within a few moments, soft purple light filled the sky overhead. As it did, Piper could make out the ruined buildings around the hexagon as well as the other tents in the camp. Within a few more seconds, the base camp was as clear as it had been a minute before when they were outside.

"I don't understand," Piper said, turning to see Magnus and Awen standing with the rest of the Marines and Marauders. She looked at her mother, who seemed completely enamored with their surroundings. "Where'd the tent go?"

"It feels like it disappeared, doesn't it?" Magnus said.

Piper nodded.

"But it didn't. We're still inside it."

"I am?"

"Watch." Magnus pulled a pistol from his hip, one she'd never seen before. It looked very unusual—sleek and white, like something Azelon would use. Magnus pointed it at one of the stone buildings on the edge of the hexagon and pulled the trigger. A dazzling blast of blue light leaped from the gun and struck the building with so much force that it exploded into a shower of stones and fire.

Piper covered her ears and winced. She felt the heat of the explosion wash over her face. Magnus suddenly turned in the opposite direction and fired at the closest large tent—the armory. He squeezed the trigger again, and another blaster bolt tore a hole right through the canopy, leaving a singed orange outline and a trail of smoke.

"Mr. Lieutenant Magnus, sir," Piper yelled with her ears still covered. "I don't think you're treating everything respectfully. Someone's going to get mad."

"Normally, you'd be right." Magnus holstered the gun and helped pull Piper's hands away from her ears. "But watch this. Computer, reset simulation alpha zero one."

"Acknowledged."

To Piper's utter amazement, the hole in the tent rematerialized as if it had never been there. She turned around to see stones and fire moving backward, like a holo-movie playing in reverse. The fire was sucked into the rocks just as the stones reorganized themselves in their moss-covered form.

"Whoa…"

"Yeah, whoa is right," Magnus replied.

"Can I try? I want to blow something up!"

Magnus laughed. "Soon enough. But first, Awen has something for you."

"Like a present?"

"Like a present, yes," Awen answered. "Come on."

"Computer," Magnus said, "end simulation."

"Acknowledged."

The light in the sky faded away, as did the rest of base camp, until all that remained was a single pinprick of light that spread across the tent's entrance.

Awen walked back through the group and headed for the door. She placed her hand on the scanner, and the sections slid apart, revealing base camp just as Piper had seen it moments before.

"Can this project other places too?" Piper asked Magnus as they followed Awen.

"Anything you can imagine."

"Anything?"

"If you can imagine it, this place can create it."

"That's incredible," Valerie said.

Magnus nodded. "Agreed. It's the best visual-replication tech I've ever seen. Blows anything we have out of the water. And then some."

"I'd say," Valerie said. "And... that pistol..."

Piper looked up and saw Magnus give a *really big* smile. "Yeah... wait until you see the other toys the Novia made."

Piper's mom looked happy. *Really* happy. "I can't wait," Valerie said.

21

Once everyone was out of the ESCE, Awen took Piper's hand and led her to the hexagon's northern edge. She felt Piper turn and look behind them. Following Awen's quick instructions, only Valerie came with them—everyone else was disappearing back into the camp.

"Where are we going?" Piper asked.

"To my favorite place on the island," Awen replied.

"Is it up there? On that hill?"

"It is."

"And you said there's a present for me?" Piper hugged the stuffed corgachirp so hard Awen thought the head was going to pop off.

"Yup," Awen said, squeezing Piper's hand gently. "It's pretty special." She could tell the little girl was excited by how big her eyes were. "Just a little farther."

Awen led Piper and Valerie down a grass-covered street bordered by several old buildings. The structures loomed overhead like sleeping giants beneath green blankets. The three of them passed empty windows and dilapidated door frames as the street began to slope upward. Awen felt the muscles in her legs strain as the path rose. Piper padded along beside her without any signs of stress, while Valerie's labored breathing matched Awen's.

"Are we there yet?" Piper asked.

"Not yet, little one," Awen replied.

"How much farther?"

"Another hundred meters or so."

"Okay."

As the street began to level out, the view opened ahead to the small clearing that Awen and Magnus had discovered a few days before. Awen led Piper under the old gate that separated this space from the rest of the town. As they stepped beneath it, a soothing sensation flooded Awen's senses. She'd noticed it when they first arrived but had been too overwhelmed from the journey to think much about it…

Who am I kidding? Really, she'd been too preoccupied with being alone with Magnus to think much about anything else. Awen had decided the sensation had just been her emotions playing with her. Only when she returned to the clearing later by herself did she realize there was something strange about the temple's atomic composition. Something had been done to it in the Unity. When she stepped into her second sight, she saw it—a bed of vibrant orange energy underlying every stone, step, and structure. It held this space like a giant hand palming a collection of gems.

She didn't know the full purpose of the energy, but one aspect of its presence was that she could slip in and out of the Unity with the mere whisper of a fleeting thought. So effortless was her first attempt to see with her second sight that she startled herself. The idea had barely entered her mind and—just like that—she'd crossed over.

This knoll was a thin place where the veil between the natural realm and the Unity was more like a clear silk curtain than heavy fabric. Instead of trying to shove the barrier aside like a heavy suitcase, Awen simply sighed, and she was over the threshold. Whatever this place had been, the Novia had made sure that those fluent in the Unity would have the easiest time accessing it. That made it sacred, safe, and the best place to train Piper. Awen was beginning to wonder if Azelon had known precisely what she was doing by recommending this planet and not Ithnor Ithelia.

"Look," Piper yelled.

Before the women could protest, Piper let go of Awen's finger and bolted toward the center of the clearing. A single short tree stood at an odd angle over two large boulders. The tree's full branches shadowed the moss-covered rocks, creating a patchwork of purple-hued sunlight against the greenery. Surrounding the tree and the rocks were a shallow bowl and a knee-high stone wall. Awen felt sure this had been a fountain of some kind. The remains of an arch lay in the bowl, as if it had once been a bridge between the clearing and the pedestal where the tree and boulders rested.

Piper climbed over the half wall, raced down and up the bowl, and clambered up the nearest boulder. The poor kid had been cooped up inside starships and hideouts for so long—it probably felt terrific to stretch her legs and play. This was the closest thing to a playground she'd probably seen in weeks—maybe longer.

"Mama! Look at me!" Piper said, dropping Talisman and grabbing hold of a low-lying tree limb. The old bow didn't so much as shudder under the girl's small weight.

"Piper!" Valerie yelled, brushing past Awen and racing toward the little girl.

But Piper was oblivious, kicking her legs and giggling. Valerie jumped over the half wall and ran down the smooth basin. And then Awen noticed that Valerie wasn't running toward Piper so much as she was running toward Talisman, the stuffed corgachirp.

As Valerie neared, the animal tumbled off the boulder, falling farther away from Piper. It landed among some rubble below the boulders and rolled down the far side of the basin. Meanwhile, Piper was pulling herself higher into the tree, legs wrapped around a second branch.

"Piper!" Valerie yelled again, reaching for the corgachirp, though the girl was lost in play, giggling to herself as she climbed. "Piper… Talisman! You dropped him!"

Awen's heart stopped as Piper's hand slipped off a branch. The girl realized the mistake a moment too late, unable to recover from the fatal error. A small peal of terror broke the otherwise gentle mood of the clearing as Awen dashed forward. But neither she nor Valerie would be able to save Piper from her fall.

Awen's heart sank as if she were watching the event in slow motion. She actually thought of entering the Unity and catching the little girl. She could probably do it under different circumstances. But Piper's small body was careening toward the basin at least five meters below. There wasn't time.

Valerie screamed, outstretched hand grasping for her daughter, who was too far away.

Mystics, save her!

Piper's body hit the grass-covered stone bowl with a loud *crack*. The sound wasn't what shocked Awen—it was the blast of energy that knocked her off her feet, sent her backward, and slammed her into the ground some six meters toward the gate.

Awen's head throbbed. She already felt a lump forming on the back of her skull. She opened her eyes to see the purple-blue sky of a new day stretching above her, seabirds riding the ocean winds.

Awen blinked several times and tried to prop herself up, gasping for breath. The fall had knocked the wind out of her. Then she looked across at the tree and the boulders. Some of the moss and grass around Piper's point of impact had been raked back, as if someone with a garden tool had ripped away weeds. Clods of dirt and chunks of rock lay in all directions for a dozen meters. Awen couldn't see Piper, but she could see

Valerie. Like Awen, the woman was struggling to raise herself on her elbows and blinking toward the basin.

"Piper?" Valerie asked, weakly at first. She repeated her daughter's name as she got to her knees.

Awen was finally able to stand and started walking and then jogging toward Piper. She feared the worst. Whatever had just happened was the result of her carelessness. She shouldn't have let Piper climb the tree or allowed the girl to move so far away from her stuffed animal. *Mystics, this is all my fault!*

"Piper!" Valerie's voice broke as she scrambled over the stones.

"I'm right here, Mama," a soft voice said. "I'm okay."

Relief washed over Awen, so much so that she nearly collapsed. She couldn't see the little girl, but her voice sounded cheerful. As Awen and Valerie converged on the ancient fountain, Awen noticed a deep recess in the basin. It looked like an impact crater from a meteor strike. Reaching up from inside and clutching at the crumbling edge was a tiny hand.

"Hold on, baby!" Valerie yelled. Blood trickled from the woman's temple. Valerie looked up at Awen then back at the crater.

The two women lay on their bellies with the arms extended down into the crater. The stone debris dug painfully into Awen's ribs as she and Valerie reached for Piper, who—strangely enough—looked as if nothing had happened to her.

Destruction surrounded her, but Piper was completely unharmed.

"Are you okay?" Valerie asked, grabbing Piper's right hand while Awen grabbed her left.

"Of course, Mama. I already told you so."

"I know… it's just that—"

"I'm okay. Promise."

Awen helped pull Piper to the surface and fell on her rear end.

"Are you okay, Miss Awen?" Piper asked. "You look like you're bleeding. You too, Mama."

Valerie reached up and touched her temple then looked at the blood on her fingertips. "It's nothing, baby."

"I hurt you, didn't I?"

"No, no, no!" From on her knees, Valerie clutched Piper around the waist and held the little girl's head against her shoulder. "I just hit my head, that's all. It wasn't you."

"That's not entirely true," Awen said.

Valerie's eyes snapped open. She glared at Awen with a look of rage and fear. But Piper's expression concerned Awen the most. The little girl seemed confused… yet hopeful.

"Awen, please don't speak," Valerie said.

"No, Mama. I want to hear her."

"Baby, no. She doesn't—"

"What do you mean, Miss Awen?"

"I mean, you did do this." Awen pointed to the crater. "You did push your mother and me back. You didn't mean to

—we know that. But the powers you have… they're strong enough to hurt people."

"Like my daddy."

"No!" Valerie held a hand at Awen. "Stop! No more of this!"

"Yes, Piper. Like your father."

"No! It's too much!" Valerie's voice shook in fury as hot tears streamed down her cheeks. "Don't listen to her, baby. She doesn't know. She wasn't there."

"She does know, Mama. And so do I."

Valerie froze then held Piper away from her to look her in the eye. "What?"

"I know I killed Daddy."

The sound of a child saying such words was perhaps the worst thing Awen had ever heard. She had no experience to compare it to and hoped to all the mystics she'd never have to listen to it again. The worst part was knowing that the pain tearing through her heart was a fraction of that in Valerie's. And Piper's.

"You… what?" Valerie's eyes darted around as if in terror, and her hands squeezed Piper's arms as if pumping air bladders. The woman took short breaths, blinking like she might pass out.

Awen was at her side in an instant, holding Valerie upright. "I've got you," Awen said, and Valerie looked at her, but her eyes were glassy and forlorn. "Valerie? Stay with us."

Valerie's emotion burst outward as if someone had released the pressure valve on a dam. Her body crumpled, hands still holding Piper's arms. Deep wails poured from her mouth, racing past bared teeth and lips pulled back in agony. Amid the spasm-riddled pleas that issued from the woman's tortured soul, the only word Awen could make out was, "Why?"

Tears streamed down Valerie's beet-red face. She shook, reaching for Awen to help keep her upright. But soon, Valerie was in a fetal position, crumpled on the ground like a child. To Awen's amazement, Piper wrapped Valerie in a motherly embrace, laying her head on the woman's back. Awen kept a hand on Valerie, too, gently rubbing her shoulders and head.

The three of them remained hidden in the shade of the tree, Valerie's sobs mixing with the sounds around them. Birds cried far above, the ocean breeze rustled the leaves, and warm air moved among the boulders and bodies, carrying the sorrow away one beat at a time. Awen couldn't imagine how much pain Valerie felt. It was bad enough to lose a life mate, but to have it happen at the hands of one's own child—and then to hear that child accept responsibility—must have been... *devastating* didn't begin to describe it.

Awen wasn't sure how long they huddled there before Valerie stopped weeping. The sun had crept across the sky, beginning its sweep of the afternoon. When at last the woman sat up, Piper was right there, eager to embrace her and brush away her tears with her small hands. Awen, too, wanted to console the woman, who looked longingly into both her and Piper's eyes.

"Thank you," Valerie said barely above a whisper. She

turned to Piper. "I'm so sorry you've had to live through this, my love."

"It's okay, Mama."

"No, it's not. Your father and I wanted a normal life for you. One far away from…"

"From my powers?" Piper asked. But Valerie said nothing.

At once, Awen understood the problem. Admitting that the Stones wanted to keep Piper from her powers would inadvertently cast the little girl and her abilities in a negative light, while not doing so would just avoid the truth, which was ethically wrong.

Amazingly, it was Piper who resolved the situation. "I know I'm not like everyone else," she said, looking her mother square in the face. "I've always known, I think. I thought everyone had what I had. But when I realized that you and Daddy were doing things to hide me or keep me from learning more about what made me the way I was, I realized I was different. It was everyone else who was normal."

"Piper, that's not—"

"But I liked being different, Mama. I knew there must be a reason I was the way I was. I was just hoping that… I don't know…"

"What, baby?"

"That you'd—you know—explain it to me one day."

Fresh tears welled up in Valerie's swollen, bloodshot eyes. "I'm so sorry," she whispered, grabbing Piper behind the head and pulling their foreheads together. "I never meant for it to be like this."

"I know, Mama. I know."

"I'm so sorry…"

"It's okay. We can't fix what's broken. But we can clean it up and make something new."

Valerie let out a small laugh. Awen guessed the words were a common saying, maybe one Valerie had used more than once.

"Yes, we can," Valerie replied, pulling away and wiping her cheeks.

"That's why the universe has brought me Awen, I think," Piper added. "To teach me. If Grandma can't be here…" Piper turned to Awen, a broad smile spreading across her face. "Then Awen can fill in."

A surge of pride flooded Awen's chest. She highly doubted she'd ever be the woman that Willowood was, but to be compared to her, especially by this marvelous child, was an honor beyond measure. "I'll certainly try," Awen said. "I will do my best—I promise you that. Both of you."

Valerie took Awen's hand. "Thank you, Awen."

"It's an honor, Valerie."

Valerie squeezed Awen's hand, rolled her lips inward as if to fight back another wave of emotion, and then rubbed her cheek against her shoulder.

"We're gonna get through this," Awen said. "Together. Piper, you, and me. We have a job to do. We're gonna answer some of those questions the galaxy is asking of us. And the ones we can't solve? They'll work themselves out. We just need to keep moving forward one step at a time."

"Sounds good to me," Piper said. "And, Mama?"

"Yes, love?"

"No more secrets, okay?"

Valerie let out something between a laugh and a yelp—joy and sorrow all wrapped in one. "No more secrets." Awen stood up and gave the two of them some space while they embraced.

When they finally pulled apart, Piper said, "So, do I get my surprise now?"

Awen smiled, brushing a strand of hair behind her ear. "You bet, Piper. It's in there." Awen pointed toward the main building that she and Magnus had found two days prior. Azelon had said the building was a temple for an ancient sect of Novia committed to purposes not unlike Awen's. "Let's go check it out."

22

Piper took Awen's hand, setting off for the largest building on the far side of the plaza. Valerie reached down and took Piper's other hand as they neared the entrance. Piper didn't know what to expect, but her heart raced with anticipation. Whatever Awen had prepared for her, Piper was sure it was beautiful.

Piper tilted her head as the three of them crossed the threshold, straining to look up at the ceiling. The building's interior was stained black and covered in beautiful gold lines. The markings formed designs that stretched across the walls, ceiling, and pillars. Piper noticed spiraling circles, crisscrossing X patterns, and waves that almost looked like they were flowing across the walls. Inside each shape, Piper saw small letters in some sort of language that she couldn't understand. Narrow windows were evenly spaced between columns, and a wider one on the far side of the room looked out on the ocean that stretched to the horizon.

But for all the room's beauty, what made Piper freeze in place was the thing that sat in the middle of it—some sort of body suit draped across a stone slab. It was made of smooth white body panels held together with blue fabric underneath. Translucent tubelike channels ran around the joints and formed a round outline in the center of the chest as well as a circle in the front of the pelvis. Next to it sat a helmet made of the same white material, complete with a darkened visor.

"What... what is that?" Piper asked, releasing the women's hands. The suit looked like it was exactly her size. "Is it for me?"

"It is. But first..." Awen knelt and touched the stuffed animal in Piper's hand.

"What're you doing?"

"May I have him?"

"You want Talisman?" Piper pulled the stuffed corgachirp to her chest. She'd had the animal since... forever. Her mother had told her to never let Talisman out of her sight. Ever. So the creature had been her constant companion, going everywhere she went, even to the bathroom. Kids in school had laughed at her for it. Some had even taken Talisman away and played catch with him. That was when Piper had first noticed that she was powerful—*dangerous* even. She hadn't meant to shock them. But she had. They'd dropped Talisman and stepped away from Piper, calling her all sorts of bad names.

"I don't want to keep him," Awen said. "I just want your mom to watch over him. So you can look at your present."

"But what about…?" Piper looked to her mother. "What about how he protects me? I don't need him?"

Valerie smiled and shook her head ever so slightly.

"The truth is," Awen said, turning Talisman around to look in his eyes, "we always need a good friend. And I think Talisman has been an excellent friend to you, don't you?"

Piper nodded.

"But you won't need him in the way you once did. Not anymore."

"What do you mean?"

Awen handed Talisman to Valerie and gestured toward the suit on the stone slab. Piper felt a gentle nudge forward. "Go ahead," Awen said. "Check it out."

Piper walked to the stone slab as if approaching something holy. The suit looked absolutely amazing. She reached a hand out towards it but froze.

"You sure it's really for me?" Piper asked, looking over her shoulder. "I won't get in trouble if I touch it?"

"No," Awen said with a chuckle. "You won't get in trouble."

Maybe Awen didn't know her mother very well. Piper looked at Valerie just to be sure it was okay. When her mother nodded, Piper turned back to the suit and touched the smooth plates. They weren't cold, and they weren't warm either. But they seemed strong, made of some sort of plastic or metal—Piper couldn't be sure. As for the fabric, it was woven together, made of interlaced materials that felt very tough. Piper grabbed the suit and picked it up. It was light and smelled brand new.

"It's the coolest," she said. "It's the coolest thing I've ever seen. But what's it for?"

"This is your Novia Unity suit." Awen walked around the stone slab and picked up the helmet. "It's something Azelon and I came up with."

"A Unity power suit? You designed it?"

Awen nodded. "Yup. And it's going to help you harness all of that energy that's flowing inside of you."

Piper suddenly felt embarrassed. She lowered the suit, rubbing the fabric.

"What's wrong, baby?" Valerie asked.

"You mean... this suit will help me not to hurt anyone?"

Awen cleared her throat. "That's right, Piper. This suit is designed to help you control everything inside you. Talisman, here, helped suppress your powers. But this suit will help you manage them. To use them in amazing ways."

"So I can use them for good?"

"Exactly."

"And you're going to teach me how?" Piper asked.

"I am going to do my very best, yes."

Piper examined the suit, holding it reverently between her hands. It was beautiful—a truly magnificent gift—and probably very expensive. Even though her parents were wealthy, they always made a point of making sure Piper was appreciative of even the smallest gift. Gratitude, they'd always said, was the archenemy of bad attitudes. But Piper had no problem feeling appreciative about this present. It made her feel so important that she almost cried at how incredible it felt. A real-life Luma emissary and an alien robot from another universe had made it just for her.

"Thank you," Piper whispered. She felt warm tears fill her eyes. "I love it." The surge of emotion flooded her chest and then moved down her arms, past her hands, and into the suit. As if someone had flipped a power switch, the translucent channels in the suit illuminated with a vibrant blue glow.

"What's happening?" Piper held the suit up, ready to let go if it caught on fire or something.

"It's normal." Awen knelt next to Piper again and touched the suit's chest. "You see here?"

Piper nodded, jaw open.

"That's the Unity link. It illuminates when it feels a strong connection with a user. That's you. And all these"—she pointed to various glowing lines around the joints and along the limbs—"are the channel battens. They help spread your energy out, allowing you to harness it—to use it—in wonderful ways."

"So... *I'm* doing this?"

Awen smiled. "You sure are, Piper. You sure are."

"But I didn't do anything."

"You don't have to. You are special just by being you."

"Okay. Can I try it on?"

"I thought you'd never ask."

Awen had left the room, saying she'd be back in a few minutes. In the meantime, Valerie helped Piper into her new Unity power suit once her regular clothes were off and lying folded on the stone slab. The suit fit like it had been tailor-made for her body. It was like wearing a second skin, and it felt amazing.

"How do I look?" Piper asked her mother.

"Like a star," Valerie replied.

"You really think so, Mama?" Piper turned from side to side, looking at her torso, legs, and arms. The channel battens glowed the same as before, while the Unity link on her chest and the glowing circle at her waist cast the room in a soft blue hue.

"Yes, I really think so, my love," Valerie replied. "You are absolutely radiant."

"Looking good," said a voice from the entrance.

Piper spun around to see Awen standing in the doorway… in her own Unity power suit. For once, Piper couldn't think of what to say. Awen's suit resembled Piper's in almost every way, only it was bigger. That, and the helmet Awen held in one arm made room for her pointy Elonian ears. Awen made the glowing skin tight suit look *really* impressive.

"You are… I mean, you look *magnificent*!"

"Thanks, Piper." Awen had her hands on her hips and leaned to one side. "You look pretty magnificent yourself."

"Yeah, but not like you."

"You'll get there," Valerie said softly. "Someday soon. But..." Valerie eyed Awen from head to toe. "You do look sensational, Awen."

Awen's face turned a little red. "Thanks," she said, looking away. Then she caught Piper's eye. "Why don't we give these things a try? What do you say?"

Piper's heart leaped. She couldn't *wait* to see what this suit allowed her to do. "Can I, Mama? Please, can I?"

"Of course, my love." Valerie looked at Awen. "Shall I leave you two alone?"

"That would be best, yes."

"Sounds good." Valerie took a knee beside Piper and held up Talisman. "I'm going to take him with me, okay? He'll be waiting for you back in the tent."

Piper didn't want to let Talisman go. But she did want to know how this fantastic suit worked, and she knew she couldn't do that if she kept her corgachirp. "I'll see you back in the tent." She touched Talisman's nose as she always did. Then she looked at her mother. "And I'll see you then too." Piper touched her mother's nose too and gave her a kiss on the cheek. "Thank you, Mama," she said in her ear.

"You're welcome. But you have more people to thank than just me."

"I know. But you're first."

Valerie held her in a long embrace. Piper felt her mother's hair sweep across her face. She loved the smell of it. She wanted to be like her mother in every way. But now she also wanted to be like Awen. Piper suddenly wondered if Awen's hair smelled this good.

"Have fun, baby."

"I will, Mama."

Piper sat on one of the two boulders under the tree in the middle of the plaza. Her legs were crossed in front of her while her helmet sat a meter below on the ground near the tree trunk. Awen sat on one of the other boulders, legs crossed and hands on her knees, palms up. Piper copied Awen's hand posture and tried to sit up as straight as she could.

"This is your first lesson," Awen said.

"Cool."

"Shhh."

"Sorry."

"When I am speaking, you are not," Awen said.

"Okay."

"Shhh."

Piper wanted to apologize but thought Awen might get upset.

"When I want you to speak, I will ask you a direct question or give you a command. If you understand, just nod."

Piper nodded quickly.

"If you have a question, you may raise one finger, like this." Awen lifted her right index finger. "Do you understand?"

Piper nodded.

"Good. Now, your most important job is observation. Do you understand what the word *observation* means?"

Piper froze. Her eyes darted left and right. She wanted to speak but wasn't sure if that was allowed. Finally, feeling as though she might burst, she asked, "That was a question, right?"

"It was. You may answer."

"Observations are things I make with my eyes and ears and stuff."

"Correct. But you have more than just your five senses. Do you know what your five senses are?"

"That's a question I can answer?"

"Yes." Awen smiled. "These are all questions you can answer."

"Okay, good. My five senses are sight, sound, smell, taste, and touch."

"Very good. But you have five more."

"Five more?"

"Shhh."

Piper pulled her lips into her mouth.

"In the Unity, your senses work the same way, giving you another five. But in the Unity, you will feel things more dramatically than you do in the natural realm. Things will seem more vibrant. Sounds are clearer, smells are more distinct, and you can see farther than you've ever imagined."

Piper couldn't *wait* to go inside the Unity. It sounded even more amazing than real life.

"Are you ready?"

Piper nodded a lot.

"From this point forward, I offer myself to you as your faithful guide. If you accept, I will serve you, lead you, teach you, and equip you to the best of my abilities. Where I fail you, I ask for your forgiveness, and where I disappoint you, I ask for your understanding. I will always seek to honor your interests above my own and meet your needs as I am able.

"I will ever be at your disposal, and—should the opportunity present itself—I will freely offer my life in defense of yours. My firm hope is that you will take what you can from me and advance further and faster than I could ever hope to. I pledge you everything I have without jealousy in your success or envy of your reputation. This is my solemn oath to you if you accept me as your teacher."

Piper blinked. She had never heard anything so convincing in her whole life. *Did Awen practice saying this?* Maybe this was a Luma thing—she wasn't sure. All Piper knew was that Awen's speech was really important and that she was supposed to say something in reply. But it needed to sound equally important.

Piper took a deep breath then said, "I will always hope and try to listen to you and do the best in all the things that you tell me about honor… and observation with important things. And I won't disappoint you. I mean, but I probably will, so I can't promise that. But I don't mean to, honest. And to serve you and use my inside voice and my listening skills. And I'll try not to get upset. But sometimes I get overtired and hungry. And more things like that. And faster and far. And I want your success too. That's my oath."

To Piper's relief, Awen seemed really happy. It looked like she was trying not to laugh. Piper had tried to be sincere. Maybe she'd made a mistake with her speech.

"Did I say something wrong?"

Awen shook her head, holding a fist to her mouth and making a funny face. "No, Piper. It was perfect."

"Oh, okay. Good."

"So you'll be my student?"

"Yeah, of course."

"Then, from now on, you will call me teacher."

"Okay, teacher Awen."

"Shhh."

Piper's eyes got wide. *This is hard work!*

"And I will call you student."

Piper nodded.

"Now, take my hands."

Piper reached across the gap between the boulders and took Awen's hands.

"Ready?" Awen asked.

"Uh-huh."

"Good. Here we go."

23

THE THING that caught Awen off guard the most was just how much she was coming to love this little girl. Piper was unlike any other child Awen had ever met. She was sincere yet playful. Powerful yet naive. Precocious yet fragile. And above all, the child was endearing. Her return pledge of fidelity had been too sweet for words. It was hard not to adore her.

The suit seemed to be working as intended. Awen hadn't even taken Piper into the Unity yet, and already, the girl's suit was glowing. That was unexpected. Awen thought the suit would only glow when Piper had learned to maintain a link with the Unity while still being conscious in the natural realm. At least, that was what Azelon had assured her. Instead, the suit had powered on moments after the little girl had touched it. Apparently, Piper was more powerful than Awen had guessed.

As they held hands across the boulders and prepared to begin, Awen took a deep breath, remembering the first time she'd made the leap into her second sight. The serendipity of Awen doing with Piper what Piper's grandmother had done with Awen was not lost on her. But despite the joy of the moment, Awen wished Willowood was here instead of her. Shouldn't she be taking her own granddaughter into the Luma legacy?

She had almost decided against the whole endeavor, but Valerie had changed her mind. Awen had gone up to the *Spire* and was continuing power-suit preparations, two days prior, when Valerie caught her in a corridor outside the engineering research lab.

"I need you to do this," Valerie said.

"Whoa. Hello, Valerie," Awen said in surprise. "You need me to do what?"

"To train Piper. I need you to train her like you're planning to do." She paused. "I know about the suits too."

"You do?" Awen said. *How did she know?*

"Yeah, Azelon told me. Listen…" Valerie stepped closer to Awen. "I'm sorry about earlier."

"Earlier?"

"You know, when we were all talking, when you came up with the plan. I was…" Valerie touched her temple, seeming to search for the right words. "I was upset that you and my mother had… that you both were…"

"That she was my teacher?"

Valerie nodded. "Yeah."

"And that she's not here now to train Piper herself?"

"That too."

"Honestly, Valerie, I get why you're upset, but neither of those things is in your control."

"I know. And that's why I'm apologizing. Mom was lucky to have an apprentice like you. And you are lucky to have a student like Piper. I get it. But that's not everything. It's just…" Valerie let out a long sigh.

Awen thought of interrupting her but felt like she'd already been a little too direct. Valerie needed the time to explain herself, so Awen let her search for the right words even though it was taking a while.

"It's just that I always wanted to be a Luma too," Valerie confessed at last.

That was *not* what Awen was expecting to hear. She tilted her head. "So why didn't you?"

Did Valerie and her mother have a fight? Maybe they'd had a difference of opinion over a career path, much as Awen had with her own parents. Or maybe…

"Wait a second," Awen said, piecing the story together on her own. "Do you mean to tell me that you didn't inherit *any* of your mother's blood abilities?"

Valerie shook her head. For some reason, in that fleeting moment of brutal honesty, Awen thought Valerie looked like a small child. Like Piper.

"I inherited my dad's blood," Valerie said softly.

"You didn't get anything at all?"

Valerie shook her head, a despondent and distant look in her eyes.

Awen couldn't believe it. Willowood was one of the most potent Luma she'd ever known—one of the most powerful elders in the council. The very idea that her daughter wouldn't inherit any true-blood abilities was… well, it was possible, admittedly, but highly improbable. Even more shocking was the fact that the latent powers in Valerie's line expressed themselves so demonstratively in her daughter. Perhaps in jumping a generation, Piper's abilities had been magnified.

Awen suddenly felt her jealousy of Valerie begin to fade. Where before she'd been envious of the woman's beauty, status, and—if she was being honest—attention from Magnus, she felt those triggers begging to lessen. They didn't disappear entirely, of course. But it seemed that Valerie had *wanted* to be a Luma—that she'd dreamed of it—and the fact that she couldn't gave Awen something that Valerie would never have. Surely, if Willowood had been Awen's birth mother, she'd want to be a Luma too. *Mystics*, Willowood was like a surrogate mother for Awen, and she *still* wanted to be like her—a Luma of high regard. But without any true-blood traces in Valerie's DNA, there was no hope of her ever being selected for observances no matter how well respected her mother was. There was no cheating biology.

"I'm so sorry, Valerie."

"Don't be. I've had a good life—lived my own adventures, made my own way in the galaxy. Now it seems Piper got what

I didn't, and I need you to do for her what my mother can't... and what I can't."

"I will do my best." Awen placed a hand on Valerie's shoulder. "I promise."

"I know. And she's counting on you whether she knows it or not. She needs you."

"And we need her."

Valerie nodded, staring off into the distance again. "Yeah. We do."

THE FIRST THING that Awen noticed when she pulled Piper into the Unity was just how bright the child was. So bright, in fact, that Awen had to raise a barrier between them. Piper wouldn't be able to see it—at least Awen didn't *think* she would—but it would bring some relief to Awen's second sight.

"Can you hear me?" Awen asked.

"Yup," Piper replied. "I can totally hear you! Wow, this place is totally awesome!"

"You don't need to shout, Piper."

"Sorry."

"It's okay. And yes, it is totally awesome, but I need you to do your best to abide by the rules. Only talk when I ask you something or give you a command. Understand?"

"I understand. Sorry, teacher Awen."

"Just teacher."

"Sorry, teacher."

"It's okay. Now, I want you to tell me what you see."

"I see you. You're glowing. Your eyes look amazing."

"What else do you see? Look around."

Piper blinked, and her eyes settled on the two boulders. "I see the rocks we're sitting on."

"Good. What do you notice about them?"

"It's like… they're vibrating, maybe?"

"Very good. That's exactly right."

"I think they're moving together. At the same time. Maybe like a song or something. Sysnser… sysnsergist… gistic…"

"Synergistic."

Piper repeated the word.

"It is. Well done," Awen said. Piper was more perceptive than she'd expected. Already, the girl was able to notice the synergy in matter. *Exceptional*, Awen thought.

"You can see them, but can you also hear them?"

"Yes." Piper nodded.

Then the girl did something that caught Awen entirely off guard. Piper reached down and touched the boulder beneath her. As soon as she did so, the rock's vibrations changed. Instead of moving in the same pattern as Awen's boulder, Piper's rock began to move in harmony. The two rocks started producing complementary notes. She was altering the boulder's frequency! And it sounded *beautiful*.

"Piper, what are you doing?"

"I'm sorry." As soon as Piper pulled her hand into her lap, the boulder shuddered and snapped back to its previous state.

"What did you just do?"

"I'm so sorry, teacher. I didn't mean to—"

"No, no." Awen waved her off. "It's okay. But... how did you do that? I mean, how did you know how to do that?"

Piper shrugged. "I'm not sure. I just wanted them to sing together but not the same note. Sometimes that's boring."

"Yes," Awen said with a chuckle, "sometimes it is boring. So, what did you think about them?"

"I don't know. I guess I just pictured them. In my head maybe? Or in my heart? Then I saw the note I wanted my rock to sing instead of the one it was singing."

"So you touched it."

"Uh-huh. And I asked it to sing my note instead."

"Amazing," Awen whispered to herself.

"Would you like me to do it again?"

"Only speak when I ask you, remember?"

"Oops." Piper covered her mouth with her hand.

Awen knew she should take Piper out of the Unity and let her rest and talk about what she'd just experienced. But Awen had never seen someone do what Piper had done—not during the first time on the other side of the veil. Piper didn't look tired. She could handle more—Awen just knew it.

"What else can you see, Piper?"

The girl looked at the tree beside them and followed it skyward. "I see the tree."

"And can you see its branches?"

"Yes."

"How about its leaves?" Awen asked.

"Uh-huh."

"And what about the flowers between the leaves?"

Piper didn't say anything right away. Awen looked to where the girl was staring. She seemed fixated on a particular branch and a specific flower. This was good.

"Piper? Can you see a flower?"

"Yes, teacher."

"What does it smell like?"

"It smells like… paladial lavender."

"Good."

All of a sudden, Awen's head filled with the smell of paladial lavender. In fact, it was so strong that she could taste it. Awen jerked at the overpowering scent. She hadn't been focused on the flowers overhead—she'd been focused on what Piper was experiencing. But somehow, Piper had brought the smell down to her. In fact, Piper had summoned the scent from all the flowers.

The energy swirled around the boulders and weaved between Piper and Awen in a fine pink mist. More amazingly, the flowers continued to produce their ethereal scent long after they should have. Something like a blossom had only so much pollen in it. But what Piper was doing—at least so far as Awen could figure out—was causing the flowers to produce more and more energy, as if she was summoning them beyond their capacity.

"Piper… what are you doing?"

"They smell so lovely, don't they?"

"Yes, they do. However, you must answer my question."

"Oh, I just wanted to smell them more."

"So you made them create more scent?" Awen asked.

"Oh, no. I asked them if I could have more. Mama says I like smells maybe a little too much."

Again, Piper was doing things that only advanced students were able to do. Awen was beside herself. *How is this possible?*

"How are you feeling, Piper?"

"Fine, teacher."

"You're not... tired or anything?"

"Tired?" Piper giggled. "Of course not."

Awen raised her eyebrows. Such feats would have drained the resources of any first-year student on Worru. They really needed to go back into the natural realm again. *Right, Awen?* But the girl seemed like she was just getting started, and her powers were... outstanding!

"Would you like to keep exploring?" Awen asked her.

"Yes, please!"

"I want you to close your second sight."

"And open my natural eyes?"

"No. I don't want you to see anything."

"Ah, I understand." Piper shut her eyes so that wrinkles formed across the bridge of her nose. "Ready."

"What can you feel?"

"Feel?"

"Yes. Against your body here in the Unity. Anything?"

Piper paused, turning her head. "The air. It's warm."

"Good."

"And it's coming from over there—" She pointed to the southwest.

"Yes, very good."

"And I can feel..."

"Go on," Awen said.

"I can feel layers... many layers."

This was good. Since all atmospheres were made up of molecular layers, each pressing against the next, Piper's ability to sense such a composition meant that—

"There are so many, teacher... too many."

"*Too* many?"

"I can feel them all." Anxiety was beginning to rise in Piper's voice.

"All?" Awen asked.

"I feel—I feel all the layers."

This concerned Awen. Piper shouldn't be feeling *all* the layers of the atmosphere, just those immediately around her. "You mean, just the air around you."

"No," Piper said, her voice frantic. "From far away. From... *everywhere.*"

"I just want you focused on the layers around you, Piper. Where are you going?"

Awen noticed the Unity link in Piper's chest beginning to glow more brightly. The battens also absorbed more energy, working to dissipate the buildup. If Piper was really feeling *all* of the molecular energy of the atmosphere, that was not good. It would overload her senses... and her brain.

"Go ahead and open your eyes, Piper."

"I can feel the vibrations..."

"Piper."

"From the other side of the planet…"

"Piper, open your eyes!"

The girl squeezed Awen's hands until it was painful. "But it's too much. I can't… I don't know where to look. I… I…"

"Piper! Open your eyes now!"

"Oh, Miss Awen! I feel so lost!"

That's it, Awen told herself. At once, she let go of Piper's hands and severed their connection to the Unity. Piper gasped, clutching the boulder beneath her. Awen steadied the girl's shoulders.

"Look at me," Awen demanded.

Piper was delirious, her eyes flicking around in all directions. She was crying but without tears or sound.

Awen slid over onto Piper's boulder and put her arms around the girl. "I've got you, Piper. I've got you."

Piper inhaled in ragged gasps, sucking air as if she'd just surfaced from too long a time underwater.

"I've got you. Breathe. Just breathe."

When Piper finally did make a sound, it was the wail of a small child who'd just broken something in her body. Awen cringed, flooded with a sense of guilt so deep it threatened to make her cry too. And cry she did.

The exercise had been too much for Piper. Awen should have stopped the lesson after the boulders. But she wanted to see what else the girl was capable of. She'd been selfish. They were not one lesson in, and already, Awen had hurt her student.

"I'm so sorry, Piper." Awen gently rocked the girl. "I'm so, so sorry. I will never do that again. I won't let that harm come to you like that again," she said, though deep inside, Awen felt she was making a promise she couldn't keep.

But Piper's abilities weren't the only thing in play here. Awen felt as if this island—this temple—*wanted* Piper to explore her powers and was calling her. Awen couldn't be sure, but something had aided Piper. In fact, now that she thought about it, Piper's suit should have kept an overload like that from happening—that was the whole reason for the power suit that Awen and Azelon had designed.

Azelon. Awen needed to speak with Azelon right away. Something was going on here that needed explaining. She felt it in her bones. Before Awen took Piper back into the Unity, she needed to know what Azelon was not telling her. She needed to know *everything.*

But until then, she had a soul to console. So she sat on the boulder, weeping with Piper into the late afternoon. She watched the sun sink slowly toward the horizon while the seabirds called out high overhead. It wasn't until after dark that Awen carried a sleeping Piper back to her tent and explained everything to her mother. When she was through, Awen roused Nolan from his sleep and ordered him to take her back to the *Spire.* She had a robot to interrogate.

24

"What in all the mystics happened down there?" Awen demanded.

Azelon stood on the bridge as if Awen had asked her about the weather forecast or how to reach the nearest bathroom on the ship. "Could you please provide additional information?"

"No," Awen shouted. "You know exactly what I'm talking about, and your sensors monitored the whole thing!" She knew she was letting her emotions get the best of her. But this AI knew more than she was letting on. "I thought you said the power suits we designed would keep Piper from hurting herself, and she almost lost her mind!"

"I do believe that Awen is upset with you, Azelon," TO-96 offered.

"Upset?" Awen asked, striding up to the nav bot. "Oh,

this is not upset. This is *way* past upset, Ninety-Six. This is *I'm going to feed your body to the incinerator and rip your motherboard out of the ship*. You read me?"

"Loud and clear, Awen." TO-96 turned to Azelon. "I do believe you are what humanoids call *in trouble*."

Azelon looked between TO-96 and Awen several times before asking Awen, "How may I be of assistance?"

"For starters, I want to know everything there is to know about whatever is going on in the Unity on that island."

"I'm afraid that such a task may exceed your life span, Awen."

"Then expedite the process with the most pertinent data."

"Acknowledged. The island of Ni No was an early settlement of the protectorate sect, the one ordained by the Novia Minoosh's core council to both shield the Novia populace and attack those who might do them harm."

"You already told me all that. I want to know *how* they did what they did, Azelon."

"With regard to…?"

"With regard to their powers in the Unity."

"Acknowledged. Thank you for clarifying. Each member of the Gladio Umbra—"

"The what?" Awen asked.

"The Gladio Umbra—loosely translated as *sword shadow*—were individually selected from the Novia's priestly sect on account of their devotion, vigilance, and fluidity."

"Fluidity? Explain that."

"Fluidity: the candidate must demonstrate interleaving

proficiency within the levels of the Unity, far exceeding that of—"

"Whoa, whoa. Hold on." Awen waved her hands in the air. "Go back. *Levels of the Unity?* You're saying there's more to the Unity than the Unity?"

Azelon tilted her head. "Of course, Awen. There are three, to be exact."

Awen felt light-headed. This was news to her. "Why didn't I know about this?"

"It is clearly stated in the codex."

"The codex?" She was having trouble keeping up.

"The primary source book of the ancients, kept until recently in the temple library in Itheliana."

"You mean... the book that So-Elku stole?"

"If you are referring to the human who departed the system bearing the codex, then yes—So-Elku."

Awen put one hand on her hip and ran the other one over her face. "I can't believe this."

"I can provide holo-footage of the event if you like."

"Mystics, no. That's not what I meant."

"It is another figure of speech," TO-96 said to Azelon.

"Acknowledged."

This was big. *Really big.* Whatever the Novia had discovered meant that there was more to the universe—the *universes*—than anyone had ever known. *Mystics, this is confusing.* Awen's head hurt. She needed to sit down. And she needed a stiff drink.

"May I offer an observation, Awen?" TO-96 asked.

"At this point, anything that helps clarify this mess would be greatly appreciated."

"Understood. It seems that both you and Piper were operating within a vacuum within the Unity."

"A what?"

"Granted, I am new to all this discussion of the Unity. My presence within Novia's singularity is, without a doubt, the most fascinating element of my existence to date."

"Less personal commentary please, Ninety-Six."

"Ah, quite right. My apologies, Awen. My hypothesis is as follows. The environment that the Gladio Umbra cultivated was accustomed to operators who navigated the multiple realms of the Unity at once. Two new operators—you and Piper—who were only used to navigating in one realm would, therefore, be drawn to the others. This follows the fundamental law of physics that postulates that atmosphere always seeks to fill a vacuum. My scenario seems all the more applicable when an operator of immense power is introduced into the vacuum. The greater the atmosphere, the greater the vacuum—"

"The greater the force," Awen finished. "Which is why Piper was so easily pulled deeper into her experience in the Unity."

"Precisely."

"I can corroborate TO-96's hypothesis," Azelon said. "It is rational and holds up to my own analysis."

"Thank you, Azelon," TO-96 said with what sounded like genuine gratitude in his voice.

"You are most welcome, TO-96."

"You flatter me—"

"Get a room!" Awen shouted. Then she froze, cupping her hand over her mouth. "Mystics, I'm so sorry. That was highly inappropriate of me." She needed sleep. And time to think.

TO-96 blinked several times. "Awen, if you are referring to biological reproductive copulation and the colloquial behavior of securing a paid space for said activity, might I remind you that Azelon and I—"

"Are robots. I know, I know." She pinched the bridge of her nose, squinting against a growing headache. "Like I said, sorry. I'm tired, I'm upset, and I've got to figure out how to teach a little girl to control her abilities in not one, not two, but *three* ethereal realms of the cosmos in *two* different universes before she hurts herself or someone else."

"Would summary teachings of the Gladio Umbra help?" Azelon asked.

Awen released her nose and looked up. "Wait. What?"

"Would summary teachings of—"

"I heard what you said. I mean, you have that?"

"Of course, Awen. Shall I compile an archive based upon the most pertinent aspects of the ancients' teachings with specific regard to your training of Piper?"

"Mystics, yes!"

"Acknowledged." Azelon paused for a second then said, "A tiered document has been delivered to the ship's data system, accessible from any terminal, filed under 'Gladio Umbra, a Brief History,' accessible by your voice command."

"Azelon, I take back every bad thing I ever said about you."

"How many *bad things* did you say about me? And will they compromise my system?"

"Apparently not, because you bots are still annoying, but I can't seem to get along without you."

"I believe that was a compliment, though I am having trouble parsing the implicit speech." Azelon looked at TO-96.

"It is a vexing and often deeply taxing endeavor," TO-96 replied. "But a rewarding one nonetheless, I assure you."

AWEN SAT ALONE in her quarters with her feet propped up on her desk—one towel wrapped around her torso, another around her drying hair. Despite the *Spire* being a warship, the Novia's larger physiology meant that each crew cabin was more spacious than anything she'd ever been used to. The extra room was a welcome change that she took full advantage of.

Awen had treated herself to a hot shower. The running water helped clear her head, especially after the day's events. *Which were what, exactly?*

Mind-blowing, that's what.

Piper's abilities were more than Awen could have imagined, amplified further by the forces explained by TO-96's vacuum theory. Together, they'd made for an out-of-control free fall into the Unity that had almost killed Piper. It probably would have killed Awen and most everyone else on the island had the energy gone nova.

Awen took a sip of that strong drink she'd requested. TO-96 made sure the replicator created something as close to Gundonium bratch as possible. It stung going down, but it worked like a charm on her headache. She swirled the golden liquid in the glass before downing the remainder in a final swig.

"Computer, access file name Gladio Umbra, a Brief History."

"Accessed. Request confirmation name required."

"Awen dau Lothlinium."

"Receipt confirmed. File transferred."

A small blue icon glowed twenty centimeters above the desk. The symbol was a circle, open on the bottom, with a pointed arrow touching the inside top. It rotated steadily as the word *Open* hovered beneath it. Awen removed her feet from the table and adjusted the towel holding up her wet hair.

"Here goes nothing." She touched the floating symbol.

Glowing holo-pages appeared in a thick stack, extending to the wall and fading into infinity. She could see from the first page that the documents had been translated into Galactic common.

"Thanks, Ninety-Six." She pulled up the first page, adjusting it to suit her desired reading preferences.

The Gladio Umbra had indeed been an elite sect of the

Novia, selected on account of their abilities—both natural and acquired. But according to this account, they'd also been misfits of one sort or another. It seemed that their organizational priorities had clashed with those of the Novia's ruling body. Awen had realized long ago that the politics of any civilization were as complicated to the native species as they were to outsiders. The Novia Minoosh were no exception.

The Novia had plenty of enemies in their day, and successfully fending off assaults, both foreign and domestic, had become a priority. But to achieve an adequate level of proficiency, the Gladio Umbra needed their own space for *advancement*—or as one translation termed it, *meditation*. It seemed that the distractions of everyday Novia life prevented them from doing their job defending the populace at large.

Thus, it was eventually decided that the Gladio Umbra would leave Ithnor Ithelia and take up residence on the less-desirable planet of Nieth Tearness. Here, they would be free to pursue all means necessary to ensure the survival of their people, providing both a *shadow* to keep the Novia hidden from the enemy's sight and a *sword* to dispatch any hostile force that decided the Novia was too enticing a prize to pass up.

From within their sanctum on Ni No, the Gladio Umbra discovered that there were indeed two more levels to the Unity. This fact sent Awen on a study binge that made her lose all sense of time. Within the Unity, the most general realm, lay the Foundation—the fundamental plane that defined the origin of all things. As implied by its name, this plane appeared as a broad valley far below everything that Awen had ever explored. Immediately, she wanted nothing more than to see it.

Below the Foundation was yet another realm—something the Gladio Umbra called the Nexus. It was the Unity's root network, which served all things that grew from the Foundation, sort of like an underground root structure for a vast forest. Apparently, the accumulated power of the Nexus was so strong that only the greatest Gladio Umbra were able to move within it. Anyone daring to stretch into its reaches for too long without adequate training risked absorption into the network and would be lost forever.

The co-planetary existence between the Novia's general populace and Gladio Umbra worked well for a few hundred years. But as time went on, the Gladio Umbra became both revered and scorned by the Novia. *Something they have in common with the Luma,* Awen thought. On one side, the protectors of the populace were honored for their courage in the face of danger and violence of action. On the other, their adherence to time-honored traditions felt antiquated, especially when the Gladio Umbra became critical of the Novia. At first, their criticisms were held in confidence, shared only as warnings. But as the Novia slipped further away from their founding ideals, the Gladio Umbra's warnings turned into prophetic chastisements. The Novia populace had no stomach for the forceful admonishments, and they distanced themselves from the monastic order altogether.

When the Gladio Umbra were no longer interested in

preserving what the Novia Minoosh had become, and the Novia Minoosh no longer required the Gladio Umbra's antiquated means of protection, the two groups parted ways. To Awen's amazement, the disagreements became so strong that the Gladio Umbra eventually boarded ships and left the star system altogether.

"Never to be heard from again," Awen read aloud. She sat back and pulled her towel up a little higher over her chest. "So that's how you were abandoned." Her thoughts drifted to the small island of Ni No.

Awen would have loved to see the Gladio Umbra in their prime. Aside from wondering what they looked like—a significant omission that seemed to permeate all of Azelon's files on the Novia Minoosh—Awen imagined that there were many rhetorical similarities between them and the Luma. *Except that the Gladio Umbra didn't turn on one another,* Awen reminded herself. Still, they had in common the sacred call to protect civilization against evil. *Until Luma forgot it, that is.*

Awen let her eyes linger on the words *Gladio Umbra.* Perhaps it was time for the order to be resurrected.

25

"Are you ready?" Awen asked Piper. They sat on the boulders together, now on their seventh day of training. The morning sun was burning off the dew while a stiff breeze blew in from the ocean.

"I think so." Piper shook her head. "Yes. Yes, I'm ready, teacher."

Awen winced at the word *teacher*. The word had started to annoy her over the past days. It wasn't a bad word so much as it was connected to something that she didn't much care for anymore—the Luma. She'd learned new words in the last week that she thought of using with Piper instead of the Luma's terms.

"Good, doma," Awen said, introducing the Gladio Umbra's word for *apprentice* for the first time.

Piper cocked her head. "What'd you call me?"

"Doma," Awen replied. "It's an old word... a word that the Gladio Umbra used for someone just like you."

"Doma," Piper repeated. "I like it."

"As do I."

"Do I have a new word for you?"

Awen raised her eyebrows. She hadn't really thought about that, but *yes*, there was a word for Awen's position. "Shydoh. You may call me shydoh."

"That sounds pretty. I like it. *Shydoh.*"

Hearing Piper say the ancient word made the hair on the back of Awen's neck stand up. Awen realized that these weren't just words—they were something stronger. *Could they even be weapons?* Maybe *that* was why she'd been so unprepared for what had happened to Piper on the first training day. Awen had taken Piper into the Unity expecting to be a Luma, planning to use the unseen realm for peace. But there was another aspect to the Unity that she never would have thought to explore. *Power.*

Awen had been far more cautious since the near-fatal events of that first day. She'd been reckless to try to make such hasty advancements with Piper. Her enthusiasm and curiosity had gotten in the way of her judgment, and she'd nearly lost Piper over it. *Not anymore*, she'd thought. *Never again.*

Every night after parting ways with Piper, Awen walked back to the temple and took out her data pad. She pored over the documents that Azelon provided on the Gladio Umbra, often forgetting to eat, drink, or sleep for hours at a time. Awen soon realized that she couldn't take Piper to places in the Unity that she hadn't been to herself. So the more Awen read, the more she delighted in exploring the Unity's deeper realms and learning about the Gladio Umbra and their ways.

Still in her power suit, Awen would lay the data pad aside—sitting in the middle of the floor with her legs folded beneath her—and slip into the Unity. Unlike Piper's suit, which served to curb the girl's powerful surges, Awen's suit acted as an amplifier, giving new strength to her abilities in the Unity. Awen burned through the midnight hours, exploring the Unity's Foundation and then—like a miner digging for treasure—diving into what the Gladio Umbra called the Nexus.

But whenever Awen's thoughts turned toward So-Elku, she shivered to think what he might be doing with his version of the newfound knowledge. Azelon had informed Awen that the book So-Elku had stolen contained information about the Foundation and the Nexus. Cursory as the codex explanations were, Awen knew that the Master Luma was powerful and resourceful—he would be working on exploring the same realms as Awen. That scared her. It also motivated her to move Piper along as fast as possible without harming her. If So-Elku knew about Piper and her powers, he would want the little girl for his own purposes and corrupt her even as a child. As soon as Piper's presence was felt in the Unity—and perhaps So-Elku had already sensed her—Awen guessed he would stop at nothing to capture the girl. Awen would do everything she could to train and protect Piper.

"You ready, doma?"

"Sure am, shydoh."

Awen squeezed Piper's hands, and the two slipped into the Unity.

"Today, I want to take you somewhere new," Awen said.

"New?"

Awen could hear the excitement in Piper's voice as the two of them floated high above the island. They were at least a thousand meters from the ocean's surface, watching the world from within their second sight. Everything shimmered with ever-unfolding layers. The seabirds left long trails of glowing particles behind them, flitting about in the wind. The rays of the sun sparkled in slender shafts that stretched to infinity. And the ocean hummed like the low notes of a stringed instrument, creating harmonies that could be heard all the way out in space.

"I want to take you to the Foundation," Awen said. "It is something I have only just started to discover myself. And beyond that, the Nexus."

"Is it safe?" Piper asked.

"Index finger."

"Sorry." Piper raised her finger.

"Yes, doma?" Awen asked.

"Is it safe for us to go there?"

"No, it is not safe. Nothing in the Unity is. But neither is anything in the natural realm. All of life is fragile. The sooner you accept that, the sooner you will treat everything like it's sacred."

Piper seemed to consider Awen's words.

"Do you still want to go?"

Piper raised her chin. "I do."

"Good. You can let go with your left hand," Awen said, releasing her grip. "But hold tight with your right."

Piper nodded.

"Whatever you do, don't let go."

Piper nodded again, her eyes growing wide.

"Here we go…"

AWEN AND PIPER dove toward the ocean like a pair of silvershore falcons hunting for fish. Awen felt her hair flail against the back of her power suit, whipped by the wind. The noise in her ears rose to a roar as she and Piper streaked through the morning sky and plummeted the remaining distance to the ocean's surface.

Piper gave out a scream as the deep-purple water raced up to meet them. Then, in an explosion of sound and color, the two mystics penetrated the surface and plunged into the ocean. They raced through the depths, their speed increasing with every fathom they covered. Finally, the pair shot from the bottom of the translucent ocean into open air—into another realm.

From horizon to horizon, Awen reviewed the mountainous woodland expanse she'd visited before. The vista was breathtaking, one rivaled by nothing else she'd ever seen in the natural realm.

"It's beautiful…" Piper said in a respectful tone that felt much older than her nine years of age allowed.

"Yes," Awen said. "It certainly is."

Piper extended an index finger.

"Yes, doma?"

"What is this place?"

"It is the Foundation of the Unity. The beginning of created things."

"I like it," Piper said.

"As do I, doma. As do I." Awen paused, and then pointed to the woodland floor far below them. "And beneath the forest you'll find the Nexus."

To the general observer, the ground looked impenetrable, as old as time itself and just as unchangeable. It was, in fact, nearly so—even for something in the Unity. The first two visits Awen had made to this location resulted in unsuccessful attempts to pass through the grass in the meadows. So complete were her failures that she wondered if the Gladio Umbra's findings of the Foundation and the Nexus weren't either hyperbole—which she doubted—or merely outdated, as if the Foundation had solidified over a millennium of lying dormant. It was only by sheer determination that Awen had finally succeeded in passing through the great barrier and into the Nexus.

Piper held up her finger again, and Awen inclined her

head for the girl to speak. "Can we go down? Into the Nexus?"

"Not today," Awen said. "Next time."

Piper scrunched her nose in disappointment.

That's good. At least she's not bored. But then again, how could she be in a place such as this? It was, Awen surmised, the most beautiful place in the *universes*.

"AWEN, ARE YOU THERE?" TO-96 said from the earpiece lying beside Awen on the boulder. As soon as she opened her eyes, she and Piper were in their natural minds, sitting atop the boulders.

"Whoa," Piper said, blinking wildly. "That's so cool."

Awen nodded in agreement and reached for the comms device. She placed it in her ear. "Go ahead, Ninety-Six."

"I thought you might like to know that Rohoar and Abimbola have returned."

"Wonderful," Awen replied. "Thank you, Ninety-Six." Just then, Awen remembered something that she'd been meaning to ask the bot for some time. "While I've got you, Ninety-Six, I have a question."

"How may I be of service?"

Awen extended her legs and slipped off the boulder. It felt good to walk. She looked up at Piper. "You can run around if you want. Just not too far."

Piper nodded, slid down the rock, and then bolted away.

"I'm afraid I don't understand," TO-96 said. "You would like me to run around the ship? And what, precisely, is 'too far'?"

"Not you, Ninety-Six," Awen said with a laugh. "I was speaking to Piper."

"Ah. My apologies."

Awen stretched her back, arching under the warm sun. "Okay, so, listen. We've been talking about the Novia Minoosh now for almost three months."

"That is almost accurate, yes."

"But in all this time, neither you nor Azelon has told me what they looked like. I mean, I can't recall ever seeing a single holo-image, painting, cave drawing—nothing. We never found a trace of them in Itheliana, and now that I think of it, neither of you bots has included a description in any conversation or data dump."

There was a long pause after Awen finished speaking… long enough that she became incredibly suspicious. Something *was* going on here. And worse, she felt a fool for not putting this together sooner. With all the data that Azelon had on the Novia Minoosh, wasn't it absurd—*obscene* even—for there not to be a single image of the most advanced civilization Awen had ever heard of? Either the Novia didn't *want* to be known in their biological form, or…

Or someone's keeping it from me.

"Ninety-Six?"

"Yes?"

"You're being awfully quiet."

"More than usual, yes."

"And?"

"And what, miss?"

"Well? Why haven't any of us seen what the Novia Minoosh looked like? What haven't you told me?"

"Because, Awen, I do not believe that is my story to tell."

Story? Awen put her hands on her hips. "Then whose is it?"

26

Magnus felt confident that everything was in place at base camp to receive the remaining team members coming in from Oorajee. TO-96 expected them back any day but said his calculations weren't entirely accurate. Once they arrived, Magnus would give them a day to rest, and then they'd begin training. Magnus knew they had a lot of ground to cover in a short amount of time.

Aside from needing more lessons on how to program in the ESCE's creation architecture—and how to use holo-projected hard light without killing anyone—what Magnus really required now was weapons. Lots of weapons.

He'd already seen what Azelon could do with the ship's onboard three-dimensional printers. They were, by far, the most advanced versions of the tech Magnus had ever seen. When he was setting up base camp, if Azelon didn't have some supply that Magnus needed in the ship's manifest, she printed it—easy as that. The printers were able to work in any medium at any scale because, she claimed, the Novia's printers worked at an atomic level—something unheard-of by Repub standards.

Magnus still didn't know what Kane was after, but he decided that Azelon's 3-D printers could revolutionize any fighting force's capacity to wage war on its enemies. Hell, Azelon didn't even need raw materials for her printers—the tech was fed an infinite amount of atomic particles from the Unity. As long as the link remained established, the printers could work around the clock, producing literally anything Magnus could think up, given enough time—*and* providing that the matter was stable. Volatile or highly unstable compounds, for example, needed special printers with containment fields.

To Magnus's chagrin, Azelon didn't have any of *those* style printers aboard the *Spire*. Apparently, the risks were too high to keep such a printer on a starship. Instead, they were saved for highly protected ground-based facilities. *So no nuclear or binary bombs, Adonis,* Magnus reminded himself. In the end, however, he didn't see that as a problem, since he could still manufacture grenades and heavy weapons that used stable chemical reactions to detonate.

Magnus stood with his arms crossed inside the engineering lab's control room on deck six, section three. He looked through a full window into a room nearly twelve meters high and twice as wide and deep. The floor had a pristine mirror finish that reflected the soft glow of blue lights in the ceiling and walls. Long multijointed arms sprouted from each of the room's four corners, terminating in a cluster of tools Magnus couldn't even begin to name. The arms were folded and still as if waiting for his input commands.

"Good morning, Magnus," the computer's voice said. Well, it was Azelon's voice, but he still had a hard time with the fact that Azelon could speak to him both from her physical body and through the ship's communications system at the same time.

"Morning, Azelon."

"What would you like to create today?"

Magnus massaged one hand with his thumb, smiling. He always felt a peculiar delight coming into the engineering lab. To have almost complete unfettered creative control was… well, it was intoxicating. But today was especially exciting. He felt like a kid—he was so happy he could skip around the room.

"Today, I need weapons, and I need armor."

"Requests acknowledged." After a minute, Azelon asked, "Shall we start with a base platform?"

"Why don't we, yes."

"Novian or protoverse?"

Magnus paused. For whatever reason, he hadn't even considered that the Novia Minoosh had weaponry. Which was stupid, he realized. Of course they did. They must have had enemies like everyone else. But as interested as he was in seeing the aliens' tech, Magnus also understood that the weapons needed to work in *his* universe too. Meaning, it was necessary to service and refit them with tools he'd have access to anywhere in the Republic. They'd also need to be compatible with standard-issue Republic energy magazines.

Still, his curiosity got the best of him.

"Let's see what you've got, Azie."

"Azie?"

"Yeah," Magnus replied with a smirk. "I figure if we're gonna keep working together like this, you need a nickname. Everyone gets a nickname."

"But you don't have a nickname for Awen."

Magnus felt his face get warm. "She doesn't need a nickname."

"Why not? You said that everyone—"

"I know what I said. Just stick to the point. Your nickname is Azie, and we're building weapons and armor today."

"What's your nickname, sir?"

"Magnus."

"But you said—"

"Dammit, Azie. I know what I said. Focus."

"Understood." The lights faded, and the print room went black. Suddenly, a row of what Magnus could only describe as highly advanced firearms appeared in a long line, about twenty across, projected in translucent blue light. The weapons hovered side by side with names, descriptions, and specifications listed beneath them. It was like being at a fancy weapons bazaar on some back-world planet.

"What am I looking at?" Magnus asked.

"This is bank one of the Novian assault-blaster catalog."

"Bank one?"

"Affirmative."

"How many *banks* of assault blasters do you have?" Magnus asked.

"Please define a period."

"Define a what?"

"Period: a specific time frame denoted by exact years or distinguishable features relating to cultural advancements or—"

"Got it. How about all periods," Magnus said.

"For Novian assault blasters for all periods, I have one hundred eighty-six banks."

Twenty times one hundred eighty-six... Magnus couldn't do the exact math in his head, but he knew it was at least a couple thousand. "And, Azie, how many weapons categories do you have?"

"I currently have records for fifteen categories and twenty-nine subcategories for handheld military-grade ordnance. This does not include handheld explosives, missiles, or quantum weaponry."

Magnus let out a whistle. Maybe *this* was what Kane was looking for. For the first time since boarding her, Magnus realized Azelon wasn't just a starship—she was a war-manufacturing machine. Whoever the Novia Minoosh were, and whatever they were known for in this galaxy, Magnus knew one thing about them—they were bona fide badasses.

Whether they used all this tech to harm other species

remained to be seen. For all he knew, they'd been a peaceful civilization with a hefty armory acquired over thousands of years. But Magnus shuddered to think what Kane would do with something like this. In fact, he got chills just imagining what the Republic would do with even *half* this. *Nothing good*, he realized. *Nothing good at all.*

"Okay, then," Magnus said, massaging his other hand. "We gotta narrow this down somehow, Azie."

"Understood, sir. Perhaps you can assist me by outlining your objectives or desired outcomes."

"Fair enough. At the end of the day, I want to walk away with one assault blaster and one sidearm for each warrior I'm going to train. Powerful and simple yet versatile enough to engage a wide array of enemy combatants in different armor configurations." He thought for a second, rolling some ideas around. "They need to have interchangeable energy magazines, and ideally, they need to be able to use mags from the protoverse as well. Likewise, I need to be able to maintain them using tools from my galaxy should they need calibration or repair."

"Anything else, sir?"

"Yeah. I'll need two different sizes, I think. One for Jujari physiology and another for human."

"That will not be a problem."

"'Cause you just happen to have all our measurements in your system too?" Magnus said.

"Sir, I scanned and stored your measurements within nanoseconds of you boarding me for the first time."

"Now you're just talking dirty, Azie."

"I beg your pardon, sir?"

"Never mind."

"Is there anything else you would like, sir?"

"Sure is. We have these grenades, back in the protoverse, called VODs. Stands for variable—"

"Variable-output detonator. I see it here in TO-96's archives. Yes, I understand the device in its entirety. Would you like to manufacture some of these?"

Magnus thought about it for a second. "Sure, but... you think you could spice them up a bit? Maybe make them—I don't know—Novia style? 'Cause by the looks of those assault blasters, it seems to me like the Novia had some pretty sweet splick at their disposal."

"Sweet splick, sir?"

"Eh, never mind the expletives. Just, can you modify them?"

"Of course, sir," Azelon said.

"Sweet."

"Anything else? Or shall we proceed?"

"We're gonna need some armor too. But let's start with the firearms. Copy?"

"Affirmative."

The weapons in the print room disappeared. Magnus watched for something else to replace them, eager to see what Azelon might come up with, and she didn't disappoint. Three new weapons appeared, each with its specs listed beneath it.

"Please consider the following," Azelon said. "Note that I

have translated all item names and specifications into Galactic common. Since many of the acronyms and terms are proprietary to the Novia Minoosh, I suspect a fair amount of mistranslation to be present. However, I have attempted to adopt your nomenclature standards wherever possible so as to make the logic and memorization of each device more conducive to your species."

"Roger that, Azie. Waddya got here?"

"First is the DS1479-91A." A stocky rectangular weapon expanded to fill about half the room. Magnus was shocked at just how big the projected weapon was—easily eight meters wide. He chuckled. *Azelon sure knows how to put on a show.*

"The DS1479-91A—lightweight and extremely portable—was developed as an all-purpose assault blaster for a wide range of deployment scenarios. It features a lattice-work stock, bio-linked operational access, dual inline mag ports, multidirectional sighting, and ultra-high-speed energy delivery."

"Ultra what?"

"Ultra-high-speed energy delivery. The DS1479-91A is capable of delivering one megajoule of energy in point-zero-two-second pulse intervals."

"I'm embarrassed to say that you completely lost me," Magnus said, holding up a hand.

"My apologies, sir. Perhaps a better way to say it—to put it in your terms—is that the DS1479-91A delivers ten times the energy of your MAR30 at a rate of three thousand blaster rounds per second."

Magnus felt his jaw fall open. If any such weapon ever existed in the Marine arsenal, there was no telling what kind of hell the Republic could unleash. He wouldn't entrust this sort of firepower to them. *Splick,* he hardly trusted himself with it. However, he also knew the type of enemy he was up against, so he'd take every advantage he could get.

"Would you care for a demonstration, sir?" Azelon asked.

"A demo? Of this? Now?"

"Affirmative."

"Knock yourself out, Azie."

There was a momentary pause. "I believe that means that I should proceed with a virtual demonstration?"

Magnus snickered. "Yup, that's what it means."

"Acknowledged."

All text disappeared, and the DS1479-91A shrank to human size and appeared in the hands of a trooper who looked precisely like Magnus—same patchwork of Marauder armor, same beard, but all in translucent-blue outlines. Virtual Magnus loaded two energy magazines into the receiver, pressed what real Magnus assumed was a charge button on the side, and then tucked the firearm's stock into his shoulder. With his feet shoulder width apart and in line with his target, virtual Magnus brought the DS1479-91A up and sighted in on something off-screen. The view rotated so that real Magnus looked downrange with virtual Magnus, eyeing three targets, each one hundred meters apart.

In a flash of light, virtual Magnus fired the weapon. A withering spray of blaster bolts erupted from the barrel, blowing the first target apart and spreading its remnants downrange.

Magnus—real Magnus—giggled like a schoolboy. He hadn't been this giddy since… since his captain had handed him his first MAR30 on a demo day. This weapon was unlike anything Magnus had ever seen. Hell, it was unlike anything he'd ever imagined!

Virtual Magnus adjusted and fired on the second target, laying waste to it as effortlessly as the first. The third he dispatched with equal efficiency.

Magnus let out a "Woot!" and pumped his fist in the air.

The simulation vanished, and Azelon asked, "Does this meet your expectations?"

"Meet my expectations?" Magnus said without any attempt to hide his enthusiasm. "Hell, yes, it does!"

"Would you like to see the other platforms?"

"Are they better than this one?"

"I am unable to quantify the term *better*, sir. Could you—"

"Can they do more damage in less time?" Magnus asked.

"No."

"Then we have our base platform."

"Very good, sir. I am pleased, as the DS1479-91A was my first choice as well."

"Glad to know we're on the same page. So, what mods can we make?"

"Mods, sir?" Azelon asked.

"Modifications. For instance, it needs to be maglock adaptive, and we're going to need to make the magazine receivers compatible with standard Repub issue."

"I can utilize TO-96's findings on these topics?"

"Absolutely. And I want to make sure there is a variable-output function for single-round, three-round burst, and full-auto modes. Mystics, these new recruits will unload a full magazine before the firefight even starts if we don't."

"Acknowledged," Azelon said.

"Also, is there a way to borrow some functionality from the MAR30?"

"What features specifically, sir?"

Magnus thought through the question and decided that the MAR30's distortion function was unnecessary, given that the Novia weapon's energy output could decimate just about any solid structure he could think of. "I was thinking some version of the wide-displacement function. A single pulse, variable frequency. Take out several targets at once in an outnumbered scenario."

Azelon paused, presumably processing Magnus's requests. Finally, she said, "If we utilize the DS1479-91A's multidirectional sighting feature and its gimbaled barrel to command the trajectory of individual blaster rounds, we can achieve a similar effect without unduly draining energy-magazine capacity."

"I have no idea what you just said, but if you're good with it, so am I."

"Would you like a demonstration?"

Magnus smiled and gave a short chuckle. "Azie, for the

record, you never need to ask me if I want a demo. The answer will always be yes."

"Acknowledged, sir. Demonstration initiating."

Virtual Magnus appeared once again, looking downrange. This time, a dozen smaller targets were spread across the firing range at different heights and distances.

"The onboard computer will need time to calculate the precise location of each target," Azelon explained. "But we can make that time adjustable by reducing potential accuracy."

"I like it."

"In a perfect scenario with at least two seconds of calculation allowance, twelve targets will be eliminated as follows…"

Virtual Magnus squeezed the trigger. Two seconds passed before the weapons spit out a staccato burst of twelve rounds. To real Magnus's amazement—and probably virtual Magnus's too, he concluded—each round struck its own target, blasting an eight-centimeter hole clear through it.

"Damn, Azie," Magnus said, letting out another whistle.

"Does this meet your satisfaction, sir?"

"It meets my satisfaction and then some."

"The only thing I must warn you about is that this function will only be available to operators with a Novia biotech interface, or NBTI."

"A biotech interface?"

"Correct, sir. The calculations required for this operation place high demands on both the AI and operator. I will need several days to properly integrate each user into the Novia Defense Architecture."

"The NDA."

"Affirmative."

"Damn, you like your acronyms almost as much as the Marines do."

"I am unable to verify that claim. However, I will take your word for it, sir. Shall I proceed in manufacturing a prototype for you?"

"Sounds good. Only, there are two more things we need to talk about."

"What's that?" Azelon asked.

"What color is the body?"

"That is an excellent question, sir. The receiver is covered in a glossy-white telecolos emulation compound, while the stock and barrel tip are what you would call matte gray."

"Go back," Magnus replied. "Tele-*whatever* emulation compound? What's that?"

"It's a material that emulates visual information and projects it within the average spectral range of most sentient life forms in the metaverse."

"So… you're saying it can change color."

"Among other things, yes."

"Patterns?"

"Yes. Material synthesis, environmental cloning—anything within the visible light spectrum."

"This just keeps getting better and better." He could think of several applications for such tech—most notably, armor.

"What is your second point of discussion, sir?"

"The name. There's no way we're saying DS14-whatever in the field. That may have worked for the Novia Minoosh, but that's not gonna work for us. So I'm thinking of something else."

"What do you propose?"

Magnus scratched under chin, then said, "What about something simple, like the NOV1."

"NOV for Novia, plus the first integer of your numbering system." Azelon paused. "It is acceptable to the Novia."

"Hold up—the *Novia?*"

Magnus had forgotten that when he was talking with Azelon, he was conversing with the entire Novia singularity in some form or another. But that also begged another question that had been scratching at the back of his head since Awen first filled him in on their initial findings. If the Novia were a peace-loving species that sought to see the unity of all things —*blah, blah, blah*—why were they suddenly all right with him using their 3-D printers to manufacture advanced weapons for an assault force? The answer, Magnus feared, was that Kane's men were getting closer to some resource or invention that the Novia Minoosh didn't want them having access to.

"Yes, sir. As I said, the Novia approve of your proposed name as well as your suggested modifications. Pending the results of your team training, the weapons significantly increase your likelihood of mission success."

Magnus thought to ask for the actual percentages but then thought better of it. If they were low, that would only serve to dishearten him. At the moment, he was on a high unlike any he'd been on in a while. It was best to stay there and take Azelon's statement as a compliment.

"Please let them know I'm thankful for their help," Magnus said.

"And they are grateful for yours."

"Good deal."

"Now, sir, what would you like to make next?"

"Azie, I thought you'd never ask."

27

"Rohoar!" Piper shouted from across base camp in the hexagonal plaza. She ran toward the Jujari with outstretched arms, outfitted in her glowing power suit. "I'm so happy to see you!"

"As am I happy to see you," Rohoar replied, kneeling to embrace Piper in his furry arms. They felt warm and soft, just like last time.

"I missed you."

"Thank you."

"And did you miss me?" Piper inquired.

"I'm afraid there was no time to miss anything."

Piper pulled away from Rohoar and tilted her head at him. He glanced at Awen, who stood to one side. Awen had a curious look on her face, like she was trying to communicate with Rohoar inside his head. She could do that sort of thing really well.

"I mean," Rohoar said, "yes, I missed you, Piper. I had a lot of time to miss you. I believe that is all I did while I was away from you. All I did was miss you until I could not miss you anymore."

"Overdoing it," Awen said with a tight smile.

Rohoar's eyes darted around. That made her giggle. She hugged him again. He still smelled like he needed a bath.

"Well," Piper said, "I didn't have too much time to miss you either. Miss Awen—I mean, my shydoh—has been keeping me *very* busy. Super busy, even."

"Your what?" Rohoar asked, his ears perking up.

"My shydoh. It's an old word she learned from the Gladio Umbra. It means teacher."

"Does it?" Rohoar asked, looking to Awen. "How interesting."

"Do you like my suit?" *That* got his attention back, she noticed.

"I do see you are wearing a strange suit to cover your nakedness."

"That's inappropriate!" Piper lowered her voice to a whisper. "That's what my mother says when I use that word."

"Jujari don't need such suits. We have fur."

"But this is a special suit."

"Special in what way?"

"It lets me do amazing things," Piper replied.

"Like what?"

"Um, like this. Watch."

"*Piper*," Awen said cautiously. "Careful."

"I won't do anything fancy, shydoh. Promise."

"I'm watching you," Awen said, hands on her hips.

Piper whispered to Rohoar, "She doesn't want me to get hurt, that's all. But watch!"

She stepped away from Rohoar, lowered her head, and closed her eyes. Then she stretched out her hand and held it palm up. Suddenly, a tiny purple flower appeared, growing from her skin as if it had been soil.

When Piper opened her eyes, she could tell by the look on Rohoar's face that he was amazed. He sniffed at the flower, pulled back, inhaled, and released a giant sneeze.

Piper winced but didn't move, still holding the flower toward him.

"It's real," Rohoar said, sounding full of wonder. "I wish to grow a flower from my hand too. Can you teach me?"

"Maybe someday. But I think you'll need a power suit, and I doubt Awen has one in your size."

"I definitely don't," Awen said. "At least not yet."

Rohoar reminded Piper so much of Talisman it hurt. Come to think of it, she'd seen about as much of her stuffed corgachirp as she'd seen of Rohoar in the last week. But where she was content to keep Talisman stored in her tent, she did not want Rohoar stored anywhere. Now that he was on Nieth Tearness with everyone else, she hoped to see him every day.

"So how was your trip?" Piper asked her fluffy friend.

"My trip?" He looked at his feet.

"No..." She giggled. "Your voyage, I mean. What did you do?"

"First, we turned the ship on a heading toward Oorajee. Then we powered up the main drive core. Then we entered coordinates for Oorajee. Then we made the jump subspace and activated the modulator. Then—"

"Maybe you can summarize," Awen suggested.

"Summarize?"

"The basic high points of the trip... the most memorable aspects."

"Ah," Rohoar said. "We recruited eight Jujari and twelve Marauders for our mission. We also narrowly missed certain death at the hands of a squadron of Republic Talons."

"Republic Talons?" Piper asked. *That doesn't make sense.* "Why would Republic starfighters want to hurt you? That isn't right. I'm sure it was just a mismanderstand—a misderstanding—a mis—"

"Misunderstanding," Awen said.

"Yeah, a misunderstanding."

"It may have been," Rohoar replied. "But the important part is that we returned safely here."

"To me!"

"Yes, to you, Piper. And I am grateful for that."

"Meee too." She hugged him again, unable to hold herself back.

"Can I show you around?" Piper turned to Awen. "Can I show him around, shydoh?"

"As you wish, doma." Awen checked the time on a small data pad built into the wrist of her suit. "Class resumes in twenty-four minutes, so you have until then."

"Thank you, shydoh." She took hold of Rohoar's index finger and pulled him forward. "Come on! This way!"

PIPER LED Rohoar through the buildings that climbed toward the knoll where the training ground was. The street heading up the hill had been cleared by Magnus and his team. The old stones were free of grass and dirt, as were many of the buildings. It was beginning to feel like an actual town—an old one but a special one nonetheless.

Rohoar seemed to be fascinated with the buildings. He paused several times to examine the stonework, even tracing some of the carved lines with a fingernail. Piper was glad that he liked Ni No so much. That was one more thing they had in common.

Once they reached the end of the street, Awen ran ahead and dashed under the gate. "This is my tree!" she said, pointing to the middle of the open plaza. "And these are the rocks Awen and I sit on for meditation. We just repaired the fountain and filled it with water again. Isn't it beautiful?"

Rohoar just stared at the sight, unable to move past the gate.

"Rohoar, come on." Piper motioned him with both hands. "Isn't it beautiful?"

"It most certainly is." His voice was much softer than she'd expected it to be. Wasn't he excited?

Not content with how slowly he was moving, Piper ran back to him and took his finger. She pulled, urging him to step farther into the plaza. "Come on. I still have more to show you."

"The tree," Rohoar said, pointing to the branches. "It's blossoming."

"Yeah. I love the flowers. And they smell so good too."

The petals were yellow and white. *Perfect summertime colors*, Piper thought.

"You're probably tall enough to smell them without a boost, you know," Piper continued.

"Indeed," he said. "I can smell them from here."

"Oh, right! You can smell really good, can't you?"

Rohoar nodded, not taking his eyes off the tree.

"Come on, this way." Piper pulled Rohoar toward the temple at the top of the plaza. She couldn't wait for him to see it—and the view of the ocean. But the fluffy Jujari was moving so slowly. Maybe he was tired from his trip. Sure enough, the closer they got to the temple, the slower Rohoar walked. Then he stopped altogether. Piper was jerked backward by his sudden stop in momentum.

"Mr. Rohoar, sir?" She looked up at him. His eyes were locked on the temple. "What's... what's wrong?"

"I... this place is..."

"It's beautiful, right?"

Rohoar nodded almost imperceptibly.

"Come on. Wait until you see the inside." She pulled and pulled, finally getting the big doggy to budge. He was so heavy. She'd hate to have to carry him if he decided to stop walking.

As they stepped over the threshold, Piper looked up to see Rohoar's head slip below the stone doorframe. He was the perfect size for it. And he really seemed to like this place, maybe even as much as she did. His hand slid away from hers as he walked among the columns. He touched the stone walls with trembling hands, tracing the lines, feeling the script.

"Can you read that, Mr. Rohoar sir?"

He shook his head. "No." The way he examined everything was so... what was that word Awen had used? *Reverent.*

"My shydoh—that's Awen—she says TO-96 is planning to come to translate it as soon as he has some free time."

"I would like to know what it says."

"Right? Me too!"

"And this is where Awen placed my power suit the first day I found it." Piper pointed to the stone slab in the middle of the room. "When I came in, I didn't even notice it at first, but then—"

Rohoar brushed by Piper and seemed to stumble as he neared the granite table. Then Piper watched in curious fascination as Rohoar did something extremely unusual, at least to her. He fell on his knees and leaned on the slab. Then he lowered his head, tilted his neck slightly to the side, and rested his forehead and muzzle in small divots on the slab. It was as if the smooth indentions had been carved out just for his head.

Rohoar mumbled something so low that it felt like a growl, but Piper could still make out distinct syllables. It was almost like he was chanting. The batten channels on Piper's suit began to glow. She looked at her arms and chest. *Is he making that happen?*

"Mr. Rohoar, sir?" Piper took a hesitant step toward him. "Are you okay?"

Rohoar's mumbling grew louder. Suddenly, Piper noticed more light filling the room. It was coming from the lines on the walls. The columns started glowing too. Wherever there were lines and script in the temple, light emerged, as if the carved markings were electrified with brilliant yellow.

"Rohoar?" Piper asked, spinning slowly around the room. "Are you seeing this?"

Still, the Jujari was preoccupied with his prayers. His voice was snarling. If Piper hadn't felt safe with the doggy, she might have been scared. But clearly, this place meant something to him—which didn't make any sense. He was a Jujari, from Oorajee not Ni No. There was no way for him to know about this place. Was there?

At last, Rohoar's voice began to fade, his snarl turning to a low roar and then a soft mumble. Finally, he was still. The glowing subsided, both in the temple etchings and on Piper's suit.

The sound of waves crashing on the shore far below came in through the window. Sea birds shrieked in the distance, and the warm breeze whistled softly through the temple. Piper didn't dare move. Something marvelous had happened—something extraordinary. She had to tell Awen and her mother.

"Rohoar?" asked a sudden voice from the temple entrance. It startled Piper. She turned to see Awen leaning against the doorframe.

"Shydoh! You need to—"

"Hush, doma."

"Yes, shydoh."

"Rohoar?" Awen asked again. "Are you all right?"

Rohoar lifted his head off the stone slab and nodded. He slowly pressed himself off the table, took a deep breath, and turned to face Awen.

"This place is what you've been looking for, isn't it?"

Rohoar nodded. "Yes. For generations."

"I... I don't understand." Piper looked between Awen and Rohoar. "What do you mean? This is kinda confusing."

"I think we'd better let Rohoar tell his story," Awen said. "Don't you think so, *Jujari*?"

28

Rohoar sat quietly in a chair beside a campfire within base camp. Everyone had rearranged chairs to form a loose semi-circle around the fire. They were all bathed in the fire's bright light. The other eight Jujari Rohoar had brought with him sat closest, while the Marines and Marauders filled out the remaining seats. Valerie, Sootriman, Ezo, Azelon, and TO-96 had also arrived from the *Spire* for the special meeting. The only person not present was Saasarr, as Magnus and Awen still hadn't figured out a suitable way for the Reptalon to be around any Jujari. Piper sat on her mother's lap, but Awen could tell the little girl just wanted to be with Rohoar.

"You've got to give him some space right now," Valerie said. Piper looked at Awen, presumably for confirmation.

"She's right," Awen said. "You can spend more time with him tomorrow, I imagine."

Rohoar cleared his throat, silencing the room. He had the most captive audience Awen had ever seen. "Every mwadim inherits the legacy of our people, passed from one mwadim to the next. In it, there are a great many secrets, things that are known to mwadims and no others. What I share with you today, I do so breaking my solemn vow. However, it seems to me that we are in a unique situation, one that justifies the betrayal of my promise to my people. For in fact, it seems I have returned to our origins among the stars after all. I wasn't certain, thus my silence. But I am certain now. The legends were not merely made-up fantasies shared with our offspring to put them to sleep. It seems the legends are true after all. And I, Rohoar of the Tawnhack, have lived to see it. My only hope is that I will survive long enough to tell of it and restore that which we have lost.

"It has long been told that our ancestors were birthed among the nebula, traveling through the void as wayward starfarers, ever searching for a land to call our own…"

Awen moved her lips in time with Rohoar as he recited the ancient manuscripts of his people—manuscripts she'd memorized during her first few years of observances. She'd become enthralled with Jujari culture and took to learning everything she could about their history. However, she'd never heard a real Jujari recite the ancient texts like this. It almost made her feel like she was back in school—as if all the fighting and horror had never been, and she was with her data pads and archives, poring over them until the early hours of the morning.

"When at last our ancestors came upon a desert planet," Rohoar said, "they named it Oosafar—*Gift of the Gods*. They were given the nomadic life and instructed to keep the lands cleansed of all things impure, lest a seed of corruption impregnate itself in the tribes and bring them to ruin just as it did with those who'd gone before us. When the Jujari tribes became too great in number, we began city building. However, our nomadic mandate still reigned, so we could not live within any walled room. Therefore, white fabric enclosed every private space, even the skyscraper's peaks, where the pack leaders and mwadims lived."

Rohoar paused to take a deep breath. His massive shoulders rose and fell as he studied his warriors. Then he looked to Awen. She was surprised by his sudden attention on her and felt small under his commanding gaze. *Is he going to ask me a question or demand something of me? Why the long stare?*

"What our people have never known, however, is the story of the mwadims, of the protectors of our people. The history was deemed so sad that it would break the heart and crush the soul were it ever known. Thus, it was kept solely by those whom the gods had chosen as carriers—as stewards of the histories—and hidden from the tribes for fear that it would bring the packs to ruin. The true story of our people would be all but forgotten were it not for the lineage of the mwadims and the stardrives that they pass to their successors."

Awen's heart rate spiked as she heard Rohoar mention the device. Her face flushed, and beads of sweat formed on her brow.

"Our ancestors were indeed starfarers, but not always. We left the land of our forebears—a different world from Oorajee—because we were unable to see eye to eye, tribe to tribe. Where once we were esteemed protectors, we soon became enemies. We were unwanted by the pack, deemed unfit to serve and resistant to the winds of change that blew across our people.

"We were once the chosen Gladio Umbra, sworn protectors of our brothers and sisters—we were once Novia Minoosh." Rohoar looked at his kinsmen, staring each of them in the eye. The room was utterly still for almost a minute before he continued. "What we did not expect, however, was that we would be called to protect our people from themselves. The larger pack's lust for power, for oneness, for the singularity of the consciousness was something the Gladio Umbra chieftains regarded as a threat. Their warnings to the pack were met with resistance—so strong that eventually, our ancestors decided to leave. But not before bitter words and hostile vows were exchanged. In the end, our ancestors decided it would be better to distance themselves from their kin than risk the pain of watching them trade their sentient individuality for a life of supposed immortality.

"It was from this very place—this planet—that my forebears departed the system in search of a new home. They boarded their starships, taking only what they could carry, and buried the shame of their people's choices. They set their eyes to a new horizon, never to return again. So severe was the separation that they created a new tongue and committed themselves to a lifestyle of austerity such that they would never be tempted by the lusts that had doomed their kin.

"Thus, they endeavored to travel as far away as they could, choosing to leave the star system indefinitely. For hundreds of years, they wandered, stopping in systems that provided safe haven and nourishment but never finding a new home. But no matter how far they voyaged, they only ever encountered memories of their former society, as the reach of the great Novia Minoosh had spread throughout the galaxy.

"With their souls torn asunder, our ancestors finally decided to use a quantum tunnel to leave their universe behind altogether. It was then that they found Oorajee, embracing its hostile environment as the penance that would keep them from falling prey to the comforts that had swallowed their ancestors."

Rohoar went silent, his words haunting Awen, as they surely haunted everyone who heard them. Even Rohoar's warriors seemed awestruck by what he'd shared. His claim that this was a closely guarded narrative was evidently quite true.

"For hundreds of years, our people spread across Oorajee, building alliances with outcast species in our part of the galaxy—with those who seemed similarly averse to the trappings that unbridled technology offered. We remained content on our planet. But without knowing it, we also had paid a high price for our separation.

"When people run from a fight, they invariably discover a stronger one within. So strict had our ancestors been—so hostile to the temptations they thought would corrupt them—that they embodied a visceral resistance to anything outside of their beliefs. It produced in us violence—toward others and toward ourselves—that went far deeper than we could have imagined. We were, in fact, lost without our larger tribe. The ages had created a hostility born from sorrow and separation that only one thing could heal."

"Reuniting with your people," Awen said, more to herself than anyone else.

But Rohoar had heard her. "That's correct," he replied. Again, he stared at her, taking a deep breath. "That's why Mwadim Rawmut chose you, Awen."

"Me?" Awen gasped. She placed both hands against her chest, eyes wide. "Whatever do you mean?" But she felt she already knew the answer—or at least felt the start of it forming.

"Rawmut the Great had tired of fighting—had tired of seeing the tribes turn upon one another in endless confrontation. He also tired of Oorajee and longed to see our homeland. So he began planning to do something that no other mwadim had dared to do before him."

"Reconcile," Awen said.

Rohoar nodded. "He wanted to reunite with our ancestors. To make things right. He thought that perhaps, after so many thousands of years, the old offenses would be forgotten and new relationships could be forged."

"Then why not make it happen yourselves?" Awen asked. "I still don't understand how I fit into all this."

"Rawmut feared that the Jujari could not be trusted with an encounter with the Novia Minoosh—with our ancestors. We were not the same as those we left behind. Long ages spent roaming the cosmos and living in the sand had made us hard. Ruthless. Rawmut feared that a reunion would result in bloodshed. And I believe he was right. So he formed a plan with three of his closest advisors, myself as one of them."

"And what was this plan?" Awen asked, now on the edge of her seat. This was it. This was what she'd been waiting for, at long last.

"Your reputation preceded you, Awen of the Luma."

Awen winced at the use of the term.

"It was believed you were a true advocate for the Jujari," Rohoar continued. "A kithrill—a true friend. And it was believed that if anyone could figure out a way to reunite our peoples, it would be you."

"I still don't understand," Awen said. "Why not just ask me? I would have—"

Rohoar waved her off. "And what would have happened when the Republic discovered a Luma ship entering our star system without Senate approval?"

"But there are ways—"

"There are spies, Awen of the Luma. You may be a gifted emissary, but I do not suppose you are also skilled in espionage."

Awen frowned, her head tilted. She wasn't sure if Rohoar's remark was a compliment or an insult. Still, she mulled the scenario over in her head, trying to find the angle.

"So… Rawmut asked for a meeting with the Republic *and* the Luma to discuss a peace accord."

Rohoar nodded.

Suddenly, the truth of it all was coming to bear on Awen. Such a meeting was brash, brazen, and ballsy—typical Jujari. But if anyone could pull it off, it was the Jujari. "Rawmut had no intention of making peace with the Republic, did he?"

"And once again, your skills of perception are equal to your reputation."

"He went through all of that just to… hand me the stardrive?"

Rohoar inclined his head.

So it wasn't some incoherent act of a dying mwadim. It was intentional. He was going to hand me that stardrive all along.

"And he expected me to… what? Figure out where your people came from and arrange a meeting? That seems outlandish!"

Rohoar waited as Awen's exclamation died. When he had her full attention again, he said, "But it worked, did it not?"

Awen froze. *What?* "I… I don't…"

"I am Rohoar, former mwadim of the Jujari, son of the Tawnhack, and I now rest on the land of my ancestors—all thanks to one Awen dau Lothlinium."

Awen blinked several times, trying to connect the dots. *How can any of this be good?* There had been so much bloodshed, so much loss. And even more, the Novia Minoosh were extinct—at least in terms of being a physical species. She doubted Rohoar would thank her once he found out they were a glorified computer program. *How is any of this justifiable? How is any of it right?*

Worse still, she had the feeling that she'd been taken advantage of—flattering though it was—as if she'd been duped into doing the Jujari's bidding. *And all for what? So they could have a family reunion around a meat pile and howl at the moon?*

But isn't that your job? Awen argued. *Mystics,* she hated fighting with herself.

"Rohoar, this entire proposition—if it's true—"

"It's true," he insisted.

"This proposition is hard to accept. It has been… so costly."

"Imagine the pain we have felt at losing the connection with our ancestors."

She couldn't argue that. Still, so many lives had been lost. Surely there was another way. "The explosion," she said. "What about the explosion?"

"Yeah," Magnus said, speaking up for the first time. "I'd like to know about that too."

"I'm afraid I have less to tell there."

Magnus sat up straight. That was his posture that said, *I'm pissed, and I want answers now!* But before he could speak, Rohoar continued.

"Suffice to say, we do not believe the ambush was the result of any Republic meddling nor any act of the Luma. Nor was it Jujari retaliation."

"Who do you suspect, then?" Magnus asked.

"Admiral Kane," Awen offered before anyone else could say anything. "That's who Rawmut warned me about."

"Could you elaborate, please?" Rohoar asked.

Awen sat back, letting the chair cradle her body. Everything was coming together for the first time in a long time. She felt overwhelmed by all the information, by all the loose ends coming together. But it was good. She'd needed this—needed to move forward.

"As he was dying…" Her thoughts went back to his bloodied body on the dais. She felt him press the stardrive into her hand. Her ears rang. And then there was a sting in her thumb. The needle. "He told me not to let *him* have it. I don't see how he would have expected me to keep anything from a Jujari—he would have saved that for one of his own. And he knew I would not know the ways of the military, so this was no soldier he was warning me about. It had to be someone I could face myself, someone who would be coming after me now that I possessed what *he* wanted."

"And he's been chasing you all along," Magnus added.

"Yes." Awen turned back to Rohoar. "So how did he know? How did Kane come to Rawmut?"

"That I do not know," Rohoar replied. "My suspicions are that one of the other counselors betrayed Rawmut and sold the information for their own personal gain."

"Do you have proof of this?" Magnus asked. "Anything we can track?"

Rohoar shook his head. "I'm sorry. But this is only my foostrath speaking."

"Your footstrap?" Magnus asked.

"Foostrath, *foosrath*," Rohoar stressed.

"Foostrath means *gut*," Awen said. "Intuition."

"Copy that."

"All I can tell you is that Kane came to Rawmut and offered him anything he wanted for the stardrive. But Rawmut refused. Kane became enraged, and our mwadim had to have the man removed forcibly." Rohoar paused, considering something. He raised his jowls in a sneer. "There was something not right about that man. Something that I saw in the Unity about him which did not settle well."

"So you saw it too?" Awen asked, shocked. Not only had someone else seen the evil in Kane that she had seen, but—*hold on*—Rohoar had some sort of abilities in the Unity too. *That's why the temple glowed when he chanted in it with Piper. Of course!* Awen's mind went wild with thoughts, connecting the Gladio Umbra to the Unity to the Jujari and now back to Rohoar. She had more questions than could fill an entire data pad if given enough time.

"I saw great darkness in him, yes. And so did Rawmut. Somehow, that being tracked Rawmut down. Tracked *us* down. It longed for the stardrive because it longed for—"

"The Novia Minoosh," Magnus suggested. "Splick. What the hell are we talking about here, people? Are you saying that there's some ancient species that has a vendetta against the Jujari's ancestors or some splick?"

No one answered right away. Finally, Awen said, "I'm not

sure any of us can draw any real conclusions right now. This is… well, it's a lot. Let's just sit on it, shall we?"

"I'm uncertain how sitting on *this* will help us determine viable paths forward, Awen," Rohoar said.

"Sorry," Awen replied, rubbing her hand over her face. She was tired and needed some fresh air. "It's just an expression that means we need time to think all this through. Sort it out, you know?"

"Ah, very well. I do understand. I'm sure my own kinsmen and kinswomen have their own questions for me."

"On that point," Awen said, "have you spoken to Azelon about all this? And, if not, why didn't she bring it up from the moment she saw you?"

"Those are fair questions, and ones I assume only Azelon can answer. I suspect that she—that all the Novia—were waiting for me to return home first… to figure this out for myself. Without knowing that we Jujari carried on the legends of our ancestors, would Azelon not fear that such news might be too much for a stranger to bear?"

"I guess I hadn't thought about that," Awen replied. "But you do plan on speaking to her, correct?"

Rohoar nodded. "I do, yes. Eagerly so. And yet… also fearfully. Perhaps when all this fighting is done."

Awen wanted to insist that Rohaor take a shuttle up to the *Spire* this moment. But she understood his position, probably more than most. Pride, honor, and respect were values that the Juajri and—she assumed—the Novia took very seriously.

"Mwadim Rohoar," TO-96 said, raising his hand. "I have a question."

"It's just Rohoar," replied the Jujari. "Now my son is the mwadim."

"Ah, I understand. I have a question about time."

"You are a bot. Don't you already know the time?"

"Forgive me. Not the time of the day. This is more a matter of personal inquiry. You mentioned roaming the metaverse for several hundred years and then being on Oorajee for another several hundred years. However, given the time dilation that we discovered—that is, an algorithmic time discrepancy between our two universes—even three hundred years in the protoverse would represent more than six thousand years here. And you've spent at least that long, if not more, on Oorajee. Yet my sensors do not indicate that much degradation among the ruins of Itheliana or here on Ni No."

"I must acquire a bot like you, TO-96." Rohoar turned to Ezo. "If you would like to part with him…"

"He's not for sale." Ezo added in a whisper, "As much as I'd like to sell him at times."

"I heard that, sir."

"To answer your question, you are right in discerning the time dilation between our worlds. While it has been several centuries since we last measured it, I can tell you that it is not static."

"I beg your pardon?" TO-96 asked.

"It is not static. It is dynamic. In fact, by our calculations, it is accelerating more every day."

"So you're saying it has an exponent?" Ezo asked. "The time dilation is growing wider?"

"Yes," said Rohoar. "So your readings are probably accurate, nav bot. We have been away from our people for a little over two thousand years. But if the current time-dilation ratio is used, the total elapsed duration would appear to be more than ten thousand years."

Magnus whistled. "That's a long time."

"Which means," Ezo said, "if we're not careful, we could end up living an entire lifetime in a matter of minutes."

"That is correct, sir," TO-96 said.

"Which means the clock is ticking," Magnus said. "And we don't have time to waste."

29

THIS WAS, by far, the most diverse team Magnus had ever trained. It was one thing to take a group of humans from different planets and get them to work together. *Splick*, just getting people from the same planet to operate as a cohesive unit was stressful enough. But to have multiple species with differing languages and various levels of combat training, all attempting to achieve the same objective, was downright *infuriating*.

"Cease fire, cease fire!' Magnus yelled. "Computer, end simulation."

"Acknowledged."

The open field and metal targets faded away to reveal a room of flat gray panels seamlessly joined from floor to ceiling. A few panels remained on, filling the ECSE with blue-tinted light. The room was full of Jujari, humans, and whatever else the rest of Abimbola's Marauders were. Some of them cursed, while others examined their weapons as if the fake blasters had misfired. *They hadn't.*

"Bliss, you just shot what's-his-face in the back."

"Saladin," snarled a Jujari. "And I'm female."

Magnus winced. "And you—" he snapped his fingers, trying to remember another Jujari name.

"Longchomps."

"Longchops, you just killed—" Magnus snapped his fingers again. *Mystics, memorizing everyone's names is a pain in the ass.*

"Robillard, sir," said the Marauder who'd been shot. "But people just shorten it to Robi."

"You just killed Robi, Longchips."

"And I don't appreciate that," Robi added. "Really puts a damper on my day."

"He stepped in my way," Longchomps protested.

"You shot him *three* times," Magnus said without emotion.

The Jujari's eyebrow lifted.

"Yeah, that's right. *Three.* And you, Cheese?"

"Czyz."

"You've gotta wait to bite the targets."

"But, but—"

"No buts. You were already struck four times before you got to the closest one. In real combat, you'd have been dead. You wouldn't be biting anything but dirt. Shoot first, chase down, and *then* bite. We work *with* what you can do, not in spite of it."

"Maybe if these blasters were real, he wouldn't have to bite anything," Bettger insisted. She was one of the few human women on the team, and Magnus could already tell she was going to be a handful.

"You don't get real blasters until you can master these—*as one*," Magnus said, placing extra emphasis on the last two words.

"And what *real* blasters are we getting?" a Marauder named Shorty asked. "Some old extras you've scrounged together?"

Magnus thought about the weapons he and Azelon had designed. But not even those beauties could shrug off the sour mood he was speeding toward, thanks to these dimwitted noobs. The way they were headed, Magnus didn't want to share any of his new toys with them.

"If you don't know how to work together as a team first, it doesn't matter what weapons I give you. Understand?"

The team responded with a series of nods and grunts. The truth was, these recruits would all have plenty of time to work with the new weapons once Azie had them ready in a few weeks. With any luck, Magnus would get several months to whip these troops into an effective team. In his experience, it took a year to build a cohesive combat unit. It could be done in less—they'd just suffer more friendly losses. Even six months would be better than nothing. But at their current rate, Magnus feared they'd need a year. *And somehow*, he thought, *I don't think I'm going to get anywhere close to that.*

Suddenly, a sliver of bright light appeared from one side of the hall. A figure stepped through from the outside. When the door slid shut again, Magnus saw Awen. He smiled at her and gave a small wave, asking her to stay where she was. "Everyone, stand down. Take a ten-minute break. Hydrate, stretch, then we'll rerun this one until we get it right."

The team piled through the exit beside Awen and into the afternoon light.

"How's it going?" Awen asked, sounding tentative.

"We're all gonna die."

"That bad, huh?"

Magnus shook his head. "No, not *that* bad, but bad enough. They don't need advanced tactics and warfare—they need boot camp."

"How's that?"

"None of them are working from the same base level. They're all at different places, and most never having had basic combat training before. The Jujari want to maul everything they see, the Marauders are reckless and unorganized, and my Marines are too cautious. It's like trying to herd cats."

"So... we're all gonna die."

Magnus laughed, running a hand over his face. "I need a drink."

"It's five o'clock somewhere," Awen replied. The two of them shared a look and then fell silent. "So? What's next?"

"I've got to slow things down. Get them working from

some common baseline. The problem is, we don't have time for that. You can't rush this sort of thing. And there are so many intangibles, like personality chemistry and experience. I've worked with various teams before, but nothing this extreme. Without a whole lotta time, I just don't know how we're going to take on a unit like Kane's in Itheliana. They're pros. No mercy. One shot, one kill, repeat."

"You'll find a way," Awen said. "I believe in you."

"I'm not sure belief is enough."

"Well, someone once told me that we train who we've got, find their strengths, and cover down on their weaknesses, and we get the job done. Isn't that right?"

She was using his own call to action against him. *Damn, she's good.* "Something like that," he said.

"So, do it."

"Huh?"

"Cover down on their weaknesses. A herd of cats is nothing I'd want to cross. Maybe instead of getting individuals to work together like you would in one of your special-units teams, you look at each group as its own team. That way, you don't have to worry about individual personalities— you just have to manage groups who already are used to one another."

Magnus looked at Awen, considering what she'd just laid out. He could hardly believe it, but she had a point. In fact, it was a *great* point.

Why didn't I think of that?

"What," she said after a few seconds. "What'd I say?"

"You're a damn genius, lady, that's what."

"Really?" Color filled her cheeks.

Magnus liked when she got embarrassed—he knew it didn't often happen with a woman like her. "How about you?"

"With Piper?"

Magnus nodded.

"It's going well. Very well, I'd say."

"That's good to hear."

Awen got a far-off look in her eyes. "It's like she was born to live inside the Unity. Like the natural world is an inconvenience."

"An inconvenience?"

Awen waved him off. "Maybe that's too strong a word. I just mean she seems like she is more *capable* when it comes to operating in the Unity." Awen looked to be considering her next words carefully. "You ever heard of a savant?"

"A what?"

"Guess not. It's a person who is so gifted in one particular area that they have deficiencies in others. Like people who are really good at advanced physics or politics but—"

"But have no social life whatsoever."

"Exactly."

"I knew a few of those." Magnus eyed Awen.

She paused. "Hey, I have a social life!"

"Really?"

"Totally."

"When was the last time you went out on a date?"

Awen frowned, her mouth opening and closing like a fish's. "That's none of your business," she finally said.

"Like I said, no social life. You're a savant."

"Anyway," Awen said, "Piper will be the most powerful operator in the Unity that I've ever seen."

"That's high praise coming from you."

"Well, it's true. She's a true blood, a natural. It's almost like all the power that Willowood had—the power that was supposed to go to Valerie—skipped a generation and went to Piper, but it was three times as much."

"Like Piper got Willowood's, Valerie's, and then her own dose of Unity-power juice?"

"Juice?"

"Fuel, giftedness… whatever."

"Yeah," Awen said. "Something like that."

"So I take it that's not how this stuff normally works… like, passing on traits from one generation to the next. I'm guessing Valerie being skipped and Piper getting a double or triple dose is unusual."

Awen nodded slowly. "Very. I've never heard of it happening before. In fact, I don't even know how it's possible. The only explanation I can think of is that Valerie is hiding her gifts."

Magnus shook his head. "And I doubt that very much."

"How so?"

"We've been through enough together that if she had any Unity juice, she'd have used it already."

"Maybe she has, and you're just not aware."

"Nah," Magnus said. "Being around you and Piper has taught me a few things about people who dabble in the Unity, and Valerie ain't like you at all."

Awen seemed taken aback. Magnus couldn't tell if she was upset or flattered. Either way, he liked when she was caught off guard. Just like when she was embarrassed, her nose twitched. It was... *adorable.*

Pull it together, Adonis. You've still got a job to do.

He wondered when that job would be over. When—if ever—was he going to be able to settle down and have a *normal* life? Somehow, deep down, he doubted there was an end point. There was always a job to do, ever "one more mission." And the way things were going at the moment, he wondered if he would come home from these next two missions—wherever *home* ended up being. If he lived through the assault on Ithnor Ithelia against Kane's operatives, he still had to survive the attack on the Luma, and then clear his name before the Republic hunted him down for treason.

Listen to yourself, man! What Marine talks about survival?

Marines only spoke of victory, of winning against all the odds. But he felt himself... getting soft, perhaps, or tired. Or maybe it was that he still felt lost—disenfranchised from the Corps—from his unit.

"What's wrong?" Awen asked.

"Huh?"

"You look upset. What's wrong?"

"Nothing."

Awen scoffed. "Listen, you don't have to answer if you don't want to, but don't lie to me."

"I'm not lying..." She was staring straight at him.

Dammit. Magnus hated trying to explain what he was feeling, but this woman had a way of pulling it out of him. "You're annoying, you know that?"

"What? Why?"

"Because you are." Magnus folded his arms. "What did you call the Novia who lived here again? The Gladio..."

"Gladio Umbra. Why?"

"It's what we should call you."

"Call who? Me and Piper?"

"Yeah. Maybe it's what we should call all of us."

"Why would you say that?" Awen asked with a peculiar smile. It was almost as if... she'd been thinking the same thing.

"Well, I'm not a Marine anymore, and you're not a Luma. If that's the case, then what are we? We need to call ourselves something, don't we?"

Awen crossed her arms and stared at him.

"We might as well not reinvent the wheel," he continued. "And it seems like we have enough Jujari around to make it legitimate."

Awen opened her mouth then closed it without saying anything.

"Now it's your turn," Magnus said. "Spill your guts."

"I'd be lying if I said I hadn't thought about it already.

Truth be told, I like the idea. But I'm not sure it's our call to make."

"You mean… Rohoar needs to decide?"

Awen nodded. "I feel like we'd be intruding. How would you like it if some alien up and decided they wanted to be a Marine without going through any initiation or training—without passing any sort of test or rite of passage?"

"Point taken."

"I'm up for it," she said. "Really, I am. But let's ask him first, shall we?"

"Agreed." They shared another long silence before Magnus asked, "So, what do you make of all that?"

"Of Rohoar's history lesson?"

Magnus grunted in assent. It had been twenty-four hours since the former mwadim dished on his people's ancient history, blowing everyone's mind in the room—including his own people's, it seemed. This was the first time Magnus had been alone with Awen since, so he wanted to take the opportunity to debrief her.

"Well, it certainly is fascinating."

"Ha!" Magnus barked. "That's an understatement if I ever heard one."

"Well, it is, isn't it?" She put her fists on her hips.

"It's more like universe shattering if you ask me, but *fascinating* works if you want to undersell it." The two of them shared a smile. "So, you believe him?"

"Yeah," she replied. "You?"

"I'm not sure how I couldn't. I mean, I'm not gonna

argue with their ancient history. And he clearly seems to know what he's doing here. Piper already mentioned that the temple lit up when he knelt at the stone table."

"It was pretty amazing to see. When I walked in on it... well, I was blown away."

"Was it *fascinating*?" he asked. Awen hauled off and punched him in the arm, and he rubbed it in mock pain. "Ouch! Easy!"

"If it is all true," Awen said, "it means we have a lot to catch up on. Everything as we know it is about to change. I mean, it already is changing." She brushed a hair behind her ear. That was adorable too. She really did have cute pointy ears. "Once the galaxy finds out about quantum dimensions, the tunnels, the Novia, and the Jujari, it's going to be... I mean, it's the greatest discovery anyone's ever made beyond subspace travel."

"And you made it," Magnus said, hoping to remind her of the role she'd played in all this.

"Eh, I don't know about that."

"Come on, Awen, give yourself some credit here."

"It seems like the Jujari already had it all figured out. They just used me as their messenger, that's all."

"Messenger or not, you were the one who did what they never chose to do. That's saying something, in my book."

"Oh?"

"Knowing the mountain is high is not enough. Anyone can see that. But it's those who risk everything to climb it who get to say just how tall it is. *They're* the ones with bragging rights. Unless you climb the mountain, you don't get to say. And you, Lady Awen, climbed the damn mountain."

"Lady Awen?"

Now it was his turn to feel heat in his face. Why had he even said that? "Sorry. It just kinda slipped out."

"Slipped out from where?"

"From…" He had *no* idea how to answer her.

"Don't answer that."

Thank the mystics, he thought.

"I liked it anyway. No one's ever called me that but my father."

"Great," he said. "Now I'm acting like your dad. That's not weird or anything."

"He is a good man. And so are you."

That was unexpected. "Thank you?" He made it sound like a question.

"I'm not paying you a compliment because I want something."

"Who said anything about wanting something?" he asked. "I didn't say I wanted anything either."

"So… let's drop that part, then," she said.

"Roger that."

"Don't even know what we were talking about."

"Me neither…" And what *were* they talking about again? "The Gladio Umbra," Magnus finally said.

"Right, the Gladio Umbra. You want me to talk to Rohoar?"

"Why don't we do it together?"

Awen smiled with a twinkle in her eye. "I'd like that."

"Let me finish this next training rotation, and then we'll connect with him. Copy?"

"Copy that, trooper." They held each other's stare before the door opened and bright light spilled into the space between them.

"Looks like it's time to get back to work," Magnus said.

"Have fun." Awen winked. "I know you will."

30

When Magnus saw Saasarr walking toward the OCSE—*open combat simulation environment*—his heart froze. He instinctively drew his Z from his chest plate and held it in low-ready position. *What in the hell is he doing here?*

He'd been so caught up in training over the last several days that he'd completely forgotten about the lizard. Now, as he prepped the arena for morning sparring, the last thing he expected to see was the archenemy of the Jujari striding out of the rows of tents.

"Stay where you are," Magnus ordered, ready to point and shoot without hesitation.

Saasarr looked at Magnus and raised his hands… talons… claws. *Whatever.*

"Don't shoot, Marine," Saasarr said with a hiss. "Saasarr is unarmed."

"That means nothing to me. Who let you out of your cage?"

"What means nothing to you?" Saasarr said, taking another step forward.

Magnus raised his Z, aiming down the sights at the lizard's center mass. "I swear to all the mystics, if you take another step, I'll drop you, no questions asked."

"Is Magnus afraid of Saasarr even when Saasarr is without a weapon?"

"I'm not afraid of you, but I am afraid of what will happen when you meet the rest of my team."

Saasarr let out a long hiss. Magnus could feel his muscles coiled up and ready to spring into action. He'd met Reptalons on several other occasions, and they were—without question—one of the vilest opponents he'd ever faced. Second maybe to the Jujari. "There's no need to worry," came a new voice, and a tall, dark-haired woman emerged from one of the tents.

"Sootriman," Magnus said, dropping the barrel of his pistol ever so slightly.

"Good to see you too, Magnus." She pointed to his pistol. "Mind putting that away?"

He hesitated. *Away?* "Sootriman, begging your pardon but—"

"I've got it all worked out."

He squinted at her and then at Saasarr. "You've got *what* worked out?"

Given the long list of grievances the Jujari and the Reptalons had with one another, he found it hard to believe that Sootriman had "worked it out." That said, she *was* a woman of significant power and resources. *Hell,* she'd managed to employ the lizards as members of her personal guard. Magnus figured that was equivalent to catching lightning in a bottle and using it as a nightlight on command.

"I figured out how to get the Reptalon and the Jujari to play nice." She skirted Saasarr, approached Magnus, and laid a palm on the top of his Z.

That rubbed him the wrong way—nobody touched his weapons but him. But Sootriman wasn't exactly your run-of-the-mill *nobody*. She had a way about her. Magnus had hardly known her more than a few hours all told, and he noted that she had a way of getting people to do what she wanted. *You don't become ruler over Ki Nar Four because you play by the rules.*

"Okay, I'll bite. What'd you do?"

"I reminded him of his blood oath to me and told him that if he didn't put his grievances aside, I'd offer him back to his overlord on Orin Five and tell his nest that he betrayed me."

Magnus glanced at Saasarr. The lizard flicked his tongue in the air but said nothing to contradict Sootriman's story.

"You just told him not to attack the Jujari after how many centuries of grudges…?"

"Just a couple," she replied with a smile.

"And how's that working out for you, lizard brain?" Magnus asked Saasarr, who licked the air again but said nothing. *That's not good enough.* "'Cause a bunch of Jujari are gonna walk out here in about five minutes, and they ain't gonna just let you waltz around here without taking a bite out of you."

"Magnus, please," Sootriman said.

"And you're telling me"—Magnus took several steps toward Saasarr—"that you're just going to *let them* do that? After all they did to your people? You're going to let them walk all over you?"

Magnus noticed the lizard's eye twitch. *There it is.*

"Imagine what your overlord is going to say to you when you had a prime opportunity to slaughter almost a dozen unarmed Jujari in cold blood. Imagine the shame."

Several blood vessels pulsed under the creature's scaly skin. Magnus could even smell the hormone sacs excreting their defensive scent across the scales behind his neck. That stuff was nasty.

"What's it gonna be, lizard breath?" Magnus took two more steps, his Z mere centimeters from the end of the Reptalon's snout. "Go ahead. I'm ready for you. *Do it.*"

"Magnus!" Sootriman scolded.

"No," Saasarr said at last. He lowered his head and took a step back.

That was new. Reptalons never retreated. *Ever.* Just like they never let go once their jaws clamped down on something. It was their fatal flaw but something that shouldn't be toyed with nonetheless.

"Damn, woman," Magnus said to Sootriman. "What'd you do? Work some voodoo magic on him or something?"

"I already told you—"

"The shame of failing a blood oath," interrupted Saasarr, "is greater than the shame of failing to kill a Jujari. Saasarr knows where his priorities are."

"Good," Magnus said, satisfied. He holstered his sidearm and nodded at Sootriman. "That's step one."

"What's step two?" she asked.

"What do you think?" No sooner had Magnus spoken than his three new platoons emerged from the mess hall. Sootriman turned with Saasarr and watched as the warriors filed out. It wasn't long before the Marines noticed their lieutenant and then spotted the Reptalon. Once that happened, the Jujari took notice.

Howls echoed through base camp as if a pack of wolves had just discovered a woodland kill in the dead of winter. Magnus felt the hair on the back of his neck go rigid, just as he was sure the Jujari's hackles were raised. Shouts went up from among the Marauders and the Marines as the Jujari started bounding straight for Saasarr.

"Dammit," Magnus yelled, ripping his MAR30 off the maglock on his back and drawing it on the incoming pack of hyenas. "Awww, spliiick! Stand down! I said, stand down!" But the beasts weren't even listening. Foam frothed from their jowls, claws scratched at the stone, and snarls filled the still morning air.

Magnus didn't want to shoot them. Rohoar and Abimbola had nearly died trying to secure these recruits. Mystics knew, Magnus would need everybody he could to have a fighting chance against Kane's operatives on Ithelia. Otherwise, this was going to be a bloodbath.

And so what? One less Reptalon to worry about isn't such a bad thing.

Suddenly, Sootriman stepped in front of Saasarr. The Reptalon said, "My lord, no!" But the woman wasn't going to budge. Magnus stared in wide-eyed wonder as eight Jujari warriors bounded toward the dark-haired beauty as she stood in front of the Reptalon. The moment was one of a kind... and someone was definitely going to die.

A loud roar went up from somewhere in the camp. Magnus ducked instinctively, swinging his MAR30 around in the direction of the sound. But the noise was so loud that he couldn't get a bearing on it. He covered an ear with a hand, trying to shield the other with his shoulder. "What the hell?" he asked no one in particular.

The effect on the Jujari, however, was more dramatic. The warriors slid to a halt, their claws scraping across the stones and dirt, creating furrows in the ground just three meters short of Sootriman, painting and sweating. But now their heads hung low, ears folded down in... *deference?*

Rohoar strode out from between the buildings leading up the temple road. He was on the far side of the open area, ambling toward Magnus.

"For crying out loud," Magnus yelled. "Think you could have done that a little sooner? I almost had to shoot some of your warriors to make a point!"

"I have made the only point that needs to be made," Rohoar said, now within a few meters.

"And what point is that?"

Rohoar looked at Sootriman and then the lizard. "Does Magnus wish this Reptalon to remain unharmed?"

Magnus eyed Rohoar then Saasarr then the Jujari. "Yeah, one hundred percent."

"And this Reptalon is a vital part of the mission's execution?"

"He is, Rohoar."

"Then he shall not be harmed."

Magnus looked again at the Jujari. Their heads were bowed in reverence—all but one of them…

"Would you like to say something, Grahban, son of Helnooth?"

Grahban's ears were erect. *That's different.* Rohoar didn't miss a thing, which was no surprise as he was these warriors' former mwadim.

Grahban raised his head. "Why have you become soft?" When Rohoar didn't respond, Grahban continued. "Why, after generations of bloodshed, would you let this drehglesh harcum breathe the same air as us?"

"And what would you do?" Rohoar said, stepping closer to Grahban.

Grahban stood up on his hind legs, raising himself as tall as Rohoar. "I would flay his hide from his body and feed it to the carrion atop the ramparts of the Great Gate."

"And can you see the Great Gate from here?" Rohoar asked.

Grahban sneered at Rohoar. "I do not need to see it to know that—"

"And tell me, what about Oorajee? Do you see it too?"

"Yes, in my heart, I see—"

Rohoar struck the other Jujari with a single paw, knocking him to the ground. The strike was so swift that Magnus never even saw it coming. He only heard the sound of fur rippling through the air and the deep *thud* of the blow against the side of Grahban's head.

"You are a fool, then, Grahban. Oorajee is too far to see. If we hold to our bitterness, it will only lead to death. But if we embrace honor, if we embrace the pledges we give to those whose lives we are sworn to protect, then we have a chance of living. Do you want to live, Grahban?"

The Jujari was recovering from the blow to his head. He licked his chops and winced as blood pooled from the corner of his mouth.

"Do you want to live, Grahban?" Rohoar said, his paw coming to rest on Grahban's shoulder. Magnus could see the long nails pressing into the soft flesh at the base of the hyena's neck.

"Yes, Mwadim. I want to live."

"I am not your mwadim anymore, Grahban. But I will kill you just the same if you bring harm to this Reptalon or anyone else whom my blood oath deems essential. Do I make myself clear?"

Grahban lowered his head and bared his neck. As soon as he did so, Rohoar removed his paw and stepped back. "They are yours to command," he said to Magnus. "You won't have any more problems from now on."

Magnus glanced at Sootriman, who looked as surprised as he felt. "Mystics, had I known it was going to be that easy, I would have done it days ago."

"Sure you would've." Sootriman patted him as she passed him, heading for the arena. When Magnus didn't turn to follow her, she added, "Are we doing morning PT or what, Marine?"

She was pushy. But Magnus liked pushy—it was a hell of a lot better than being a pushover. He glanced at Rohoar and then the rest of the teams. "You know what?" he said over his shoulder. "Why don't you get them started, Sootriman."

"Me? But—"

"Since you seem so enthusiastic, they're all yours. I've got something to discuss. I'll relieve you in a while."

"But—"

"They're all yours, warlord."

Magnus, Awen, and Rohoar stood in the shade of the temple tree, their feet not more than a meter from the edge of the fountain's cold, clear waters. Rohoar had followed Magnus and Awen, his brow furrowed in suspicion. The Jujari had every reason to be concerned. Neither Magnus nor Awen had taken the time to debrief with Rohoar after the virtual binary bomb he'd dropped on everyone two days prior.

"You are upset about our history," Rohoar said, breaking the silence.

Awen shook her head. "Rohoar, we—"

"I am sorry. I did not mean to unsettle you. I understand that everything I shared must have come as a shock."

"Well..." Awen conceded. "Yeah. Pretty much."

"It was not my intent to cause distress in any of you."

"Listen," Magnus said, "we're not here about that. Well, not exactly. But we're not mad about anything. We just want to run something by you."

Rohoar looked to his right and left. "This is a strange custom. What is achieved by running by someone?"

"Mystics..." whispered Magnus with a shake of his head.

"He doesn't mean it like that," Awen said. "What he means is we'd like to ask your opinion on something."

"My opinion?"

Awen nodded. "Yes. We'd like to ask your permission to call our new group of warriors the Gladio Umbra."

Rohoar looked confused. "I don't understand."

"We need a name for our team," Magnus said.

"And you want to call yourselves the Gladio Umbra?" Rohoar scratched the side of his neck. "I do not understand. You are a Marine, and you are a Luma. What reasons do you have to require redefinition?"

"That's the right question to ask." Magnus looked at Awen then back at Rohoar. "I can never go back to being a

Marine after what happened to my eyes. And even if I could, the Republic's out to arrest me. My career there is done."

"And I can never go back to being a Luma," Awen added. "After whatever So-Elku has done to it, there is no more Luma for me." Awen lowered her head, and her voice softened. "Sometimes, when old things die, something new has to be birthed… something that reminds us of the way things used to be. But since it's new, it must do things as they've never been done before."

Awen raised her head and looked Rohoar in the eye, not blinking. Interestingly, it was the Jujari who finally looked away, not the Elonian.

"We wish to use the name of your ancestors, Rohoar," Awen said at last. "But only if you allow it and only if you are a part of it. If you don't wish us to, we completely understand."

"I would be honored if you used the name—if *we* used the name."

Well, that was easy, Magnus thought.

Rohoar took a deep breath. "Being with you these last several days, I have seen some lights."

"Seen some lights?" Awen asked.

"Yes. Isn't that what you say? When you have ideas?"

Magnus did his best not to laugh, and he could see Awen was attempting to suppress her response too.

"There is more to life than fighting just to protect your own interests. This is the Jujari way, of course—to survive at the expense of others. But I know there is also fighting that puts others before yourself. You have demonstrated this well. Again, it is not the Jujari way, but I do believe it was the Novia way. Perhaps it was the Gladio Umbra way too.

"We—the Jujari—have strayed from the path, it seems. Further than I thought… further than any mwadim suspected. In wanting to distance themselves from the Novia, the Gladio inadvertently became the thing they despised: a self-righteous inward-looking tribe. They became Jujari. They became us."

Rohoar looked into the branches that shaded them. Magnus could see that he was having a real moment. He hadn't even known the beasts were capable of such deep thoughts. *So much for being all gnashing teeth and swiping claws.*

"It was Rawmut's greatest wish," Rohoar continued, "to see this place, Ni No, and to see Itheliana. He imagined that the Novia were good people. And he dreamed of what a reunion would look like. He dreamed so much that it often made me wonder if he'd lost his mind. At long last, however, I have arrived in the land of my ancestors. My only regret is that I cannot do for my mwadim what I wished to."

"And what's that?" asked Awen.

"To show Rawmut that he was right. That the Novia were real and that a peaceful reunion was possible."

Magnus wondered if Rohoar was talking about the same Rawmut whom he and Awen had met atop the skyscraper. That big-ass pooch definitely did *not* seem like the sentimental type. He'd seemed more like the type to bite someone's head off and chase it with a strong fermented drink. If all this was true, Magnus had just learned the preeminent lesson of *Don't let looks fool you.*

"I think," Rohoar continued, "that if our ancestors had survived, perhaps a peaceful reunion would have been possible after all."

Magnus and Awen shared a look—one that Rohoar noticed. *Splick.*

"What is it?" the Jujari asked.

"Well..." Awen said, rubbing her hands together. "A peaceful reunion still might be possible."

Rohoar looked from her to Magnus and back again. "I do not understand. Are you saying my people are still alive?"

"No," Awen answered. "Not that we know of."

The Jujari frowned. Magnus had to admit that Awen was being quite cryptic. The only problem was he couldn't do any better himself. *Hey, your ancestors are still alive, but they're a computer program, so... have fun with that.* But Magnus didn't think this was the time or the place to spring the news on Rohoar. It wasn't their story to tell anyway—wasn't that what TO-96 had told Awen? The way Magnus saw it, this needed to come from Azelon.

"Then how is a peaceful reunion possible?" Rohoar asked. "I don't understand."

"Because," Magnus interjected, "we think you'll be able to learn all about your people by spending time with Azelon. She is a wealth of information." He glanced over at Awen, who looked relieved. *Dodged that blaster round,* he thought.

"I will do as you say when our training is complete. Thank

you. If I am what is left of my ancestors, then it seems we must continue their work. We must inhabit this place and train to defend the galaxy. Therefore, I can think of no more fitting title than resurrecting that of the Gladio Umbra."

"Well," Magnus said, scratching his beard, "sounds good to me."

"Me too," Awen replied. "Thank you, Rohoar."

"It *sounds good* to me too," Rohoar said, but the words seem strained in his mouth.

Awen stared at the Jujari. "Are you okay, Rohoar?"

"No." He shook his head, brow furrowed as if in pain. "There is no sound that is good in my ears. I was just trying to agree with you."

31

MAGNUS SPENT the night creating a new urban landscape using the ECSE's creation interface. He'd never seen—let alone heard of—holo-projected hard-light before, but the possibilities astounded him. He was able to create buildings, vegetation, and particles that not only looked authentic but actually felt real to the touch as well. As soon as a simulation was terminated and the hard light dissipated, it was as if nothing had been there at all.

Learning how to use the creation interface had taken him several days. Truth be told, he was having a good time with it. Azelon's patient tutelage helped him create his first viable scenario. By his fourth, he was making them on his own. They were, however, far from flawless.

"LT?" Dutch asked, her hand raised.

"Just call me Magnus, Dutch."

"Right. Sorry, sir. *Magnus*." Dutch pointed at something overhead. "Is that supposed to be there?"

Magnus looked to where she indicated and saw half of a dune skiff, upside down and floating about ten meters off the ground.

"Definitely not." He cursed. Maybe he wasn't as good at this programming thing as he thought.

"I'm on it, sir," Cyril said, running over to the access panel on the wall near the door.

"Computer," Magnus said. "Share creative authority with Cyril."

"Request acknowledged," the AI replied.

"Okay, the rest of you, fall in."

Magnus waited as his unit gathered around him. In all, he was overseeing thirty-eight warriors including himself, nearly enough for a special-units company. So, following Awen's advice, he'd decided to do just that—make a small company and break everyone up into compact recon-style platoons according to species.

Alpha Platoon belonged to Dutch and included Valerie, Nolan, Haney, Gilder, Sootriman, and Ezo. He also put the Reptalon with them since he didn't trust Saasarr to get along with Jujari or Marauders. Magnus imagined that Flow and Cheeks would eventually join this platoon, but he still didn't have the heart to introduce them to any Jujari, let alone tell them that they were on a Jujari starship in orbit over the ancestral home planet of that species. The two Marines were still confined to sick bay, the mess hall, and a cargo hold that

Magnus had converted into a gym for them. He didn't expect their PTSD to go away anytime soon, and neither he nor Valerie felt they were ready for the full truth. They'd taken well to the half truths that he'd fed them so far—being en route to a planet to start training and prep for the next mission. But they were getting restless. It was only a matter of time before they demanded to know what was going on, and Magnus wasn't about to avoid the truth with them any more than he already had.

Bravo Platoon was led by Abimbola. It consisted of two of the surviving Marauders they'd taken to Worru—Rix and Silk—as well as some of the additions Abimbola had picked up on the return trip—Berouth, Cyril, Nubs, Dozer, "Doc" Campbell, and Reimer.

Magnus decided that Titus would make the best leader for Charlie Platoon. Charlie Platoon was Magnus's old unit designation, and he gave it to Titus with pride, knowing the man would lead it with distinction. Magnus assigned Zoll, Bliss, Robi, Jaffrey, Ricky, Shorty, Ford, Andocs, Bettger, and Baker to him. The team was well rounded and ready to send some blaster bolts downrange.

Last but not least, Magnus gave Delta Platoon to Rohoar. The roster consisted of Saladin, Arjae, Lugt, Redmarrow, Dihaze, Czyz, Longchomps, and Grahban. The nine Jujari were a veritable storm of destruction. Magnus just hoped he could manage to rein them in long enough to get them within proximity of their targets. Then he'd loosen the reins and let them do their thing.

Magnus raised a palm to get everyone to quiet down. "Over the last couple of days, I hope you've noticed a difference in our team dynamic."

The team shared nods and more than a few grunts.

"You're working better together as individuals and as platoons. And that's good. But we need to do better, and I expect more from you than you're giving me right now.

"The enemy we're going up against is highly trained. They're a fluid unit, able to adapt to sudden changes and still carry out the mission. That means that we need to hit them hard and fast and give them something they'll never be able to adapt to. The good news is that I think we have that covered. No one will know how to adapt to the likes of you."

A smattering of laughter and growls went up from among the group. Magnus let them have the moment.

"Go ahead, look around."

They eyed one another—some in disgust, some in fascination, and all in some semblance of wonder.

"That's right," Magnus said. "You're the craziest-looking bastards I've ever seen in one unit—no exceptions. Which means..." Magnus let the word hang in the air for a beat. "I expect you to fight like crazy sons of bitches too." He caught the eyes of several women in the group. "And daughters of bitches." *Damn.* It just didn't have the same ring to it.

"We get the point, Magnus." Valerie gestured for him to keep going.

"Right." Magnus cleared his throat. "Today, we're trying

an urban-warfare simulation, one that I don't expect you to survive."

"That's a little dark, isn't it, sir?" asked Cyril.

"No, it's not, Marauder. It's real. Because while each of you has fought in a context like this before, none of you have ever done it together. That means that you've got to talk more, call things out clearly, and move in a coordinated effort. Until that happens, every sim will end with you meeting the same fate. It's the same fate, mind you, that you'll meet in Itheliana if we try to take these Paragon troopers without you knowing what you're doing. And I'm not about to lose my first command in the Gladio Umbra because I didn't do my part in training your sorry asses. Copy?"

The response was a mess of people saying, "Copy," grunting, a hiss, and other words of assent not in the Marine lexicon. He'd need to fix that.

"Magnus?" Bliss said, looking between his other Marauders as he stepped forward. "Gladio Umbra?"

"That's right," Magnus replied, understanding the man's implied question. "That's our new name, our new allegiance. You may have fought for the Galactic Republic, and you might again one day, but not today. You may be Jujari, and you may always be Jujari because that's the blood that runs in your veins, but not today. And you might be a ragtag bunch of Marauders from all corners of the galaxy, pulled together by a giant Miblimbian, but not today."

A hand went up. It was Ezo. "What if you don't fight for any of those factions?"

"Yes," Saasarr echoed.

"Then that means you belong to me," Sootriman replied.

The entire team replied in longwinded *Oh!*s and snorts.

"And today," Sootriman added, "that means I fight with Magnus, and so do you."

"You fight with me." Magnus nodded, looking around the group. "But you also fight for one another. Because you're fighting for the future of the galaxy that you want to live in—that our children's children's children will inherit. And let me remind you, none of our children will want to inherit the galaxy that's coming if we don't get this right. So today, you check your particulars at the door. Today, you are Gladio Umbra. Today, you are fighting for a new future. Which means we've gotta train like we want it. You've gotta taste it."

"I can taste Paragon flesh," Arjae said, licking his chops.

"That's good," Magnus replied. "That's good. But now you've gotta be smart about how you get to that meal. Copy?"

The group started nodding and talking.

"Hold up." Magnus waved his hands. "When I say 'Copy,' I need one response back, not a dozen different ones. If I say 'Copy,' you say, 'Yes, sir.' And that's all. Copy?"

"Yes, sir," they said as one.

"Good. No more of that wishy-washy splick. Copy?"

"Yes, sir," they said more loudly than the first time.

Magnus's brain suddenly kicked into other points of nomenclature he hadn't yet taken to the time to cover. "And from now on, you're not Marines or Jujari or Marauders.

You're not soldiers or troopers or combatants. You're gladias. Copy?"

"Yes, sir," they said together.

"That's what the Gladio Umbra called themselves. *Gladias*. So that's what we're calling ourselves—I don't want to hear anything else from this point forward.

"And, while we're at it, we also need a rallying call. We need *our* word for making sure we're on the same page, breathing the same air…" Magnus knew the kind of words they used in the Corps, but none of those felt right, not anymore, now that they were gladias. With so much change, his vocabulary needed to change too.

"How about *la-raah*, sir?" Sootriman asked.

Magnus looked at her, his head upturned, inviting her to explain.

"I was doing some more research on the Gladio Umbra last night. Turns out that word, in their native tongue, means 'as one.'"

"La-raah," Magnus said, trying it out. If he could imagine shouting it with a loud voice in a firefight, then it worked. "I like it. *La-raah* it is."

He pointed to the team as if he were a conductor asking for a note from the orchestra. In one voice, they replied, "La-raah."

"I can't hear you," Magnus yelled then pushed a fist into the air.

"La-raah!" the team yelled.

"Again!" He punched the air.

"*La-raah!*"

The vibrations of over thirty warriors shouting the word shook the building's walls. *That'll work*, Magnus thought. He looked at Sootriman and dipped his head as if to thank her. She replied with the same gesture.

"One more thing," Magnus said, raising a finger. He hadn't planned on this, but it just felt right. "When I say dominate, you say liberate. Dominate."

"Liberate," replied the company in a loose fashion.

"I can't hear you! *Dominate!*"

"*Liberate!*" they yelled as one. The air was charged, and goose bumps appeared along Magnus's flesh. "That's our motto. When you're downrange, when you've run out of options, when you're thinking of giving up, you remember what we, the Gladio Umbra, are there for. We dominate the field—it's *ours*. It doesn't belong to them. The *whole* thing—*it's ours*. But we have a mission beyond mere destruction. We serve those who need rescue, who need our help, who need to be liberated. That's what drives you as a Gladio Umbra from now on. That's what's going to stir you to get up when you feel like staying down. That's what's going to make you step toward the enemy when you feel like turning back. And should you fall in the field of battle, that's what will be written on your tombstone—on *all* our tombstones. *Dominate!*"

"*Liberate!*"

"Now," Magnus said, a surge of emotion pumping through his veins and swirling in his head. "Who's coming with me to take this street?"

Gateway to War

Alpha Platoon was playing it safe, just as Magnus thought they would, taking turns moving between columns and buildings and laying down covering fire. It was methodical and textbook Marine doctrine. But it was also too slow for what this mission called for. Magnus had given enemy simulants a ninety-percent accuracy rate and a seventy-five-percent aggression rate. That was high by any Marine standards and certainly much more demonstrative than what Alpha Platoon was serving.

Within the first sixty seconds, Gilder had been lasered twice in the same leg, and Valerie was cussing like a sailor, laid out on her back in the middle of the street from enemy sniper fire. The warriors wore bracelets on their wrists that delivered small electrical charges when they'd been hit by a simulated blaster bolt, whether from enemy weapons or friendly ones.

Magnus had tried to construct this scenario based on what he'd gathered from those who'd actually fought in the city of Itheliana. Awen, Sootriman, Ezo, and TO-96 had been instrumental in making this street feel as authentic as possible, right down to the blades of grass growing between the massive stones.

Everywhere Magnus looked, there were vines and trees and the ruins of millennia-old buildings. Though technologically advanced, they still showed numerous signs of weathering and age. They lined both sides of the avenue leading to a Repub-style encampment that Magnus had developed from his own experiences in the Recon. It was spartan but highly defensible, made of several concrete berms, windowplex shields, and portable sensor towers for long-range data collection. He also included a mobile shield generator just in case the real Paragon had thought ahead—which, Magnus concluded, they probably had.

While the Marines were busy getting pinned down under heavy enemy fire, Bravo Company was advancing much more quickly. Their approach had the right idea—move fast, stay low—but they hadn't figured on the enemy using heavy weapons on the objects they used for cover. Despite their best efforts to advance up the street, Abimbola's platoon was taking heavy casualties. Even Abimbola himself took a head shot when he stepped from behind cover to help pull one of his men to safety. Magnus made a mental note to create some sort of protective throw bag like they used in the Corps—no need to come out from behind cover to retrieve a gladia.

For all his creative thinking, Titus's platoon was doing even worse. At first, Magnus was impressed that Titus had decided to use the building interiors as a means of advancement—which would have worked in a typical urban setting in almost any other known city in the protoverse. However, these were ruins, and just because one building joined another didn't mean any existing passages between them were usable. After disappearing for the first minute, Titus and his platoon were eventually spat out in the middle of an unprotected plaza, where they were raked with enemy fire.

Delta Company got the prize for making it the farthest

—*and* dying the most dramatically. Rohoar had led his warriors along the tops of the ruins to the right, their feet treading across the hard-light surface as if the buildings were real. They hopped between the gaps in structures as easily as if they were skipping along a trail in the countryside. The platoon made it as far as the enemy's encampment, save for the fact that they were ten meters up. That didn't matter much to a Jujari, of course, as that distance was easy to leap from, and they incurred little more than an ache in their joints.

So it wasn't the jump that killed them all—it was the automatic turret fire from the nearby rooftops. In their haste to storm the enemy position, Rohoar and his unit failed to take into account the defenses that they *couldn't* see. As the bodies fell safely to the padded ESCE floor, kill indicators popped up over their heads, floating above them as flags to signal their deaths. More than one Jujari batted at the red tag, trying in vain to swat it away. They spoke incessantly in their mother tongue, presumably cursing at the small apparitions.

"Computer, reset simulation," Magnus said.

"Acknowledged."

"Granther Company," Magnus bellowed, "form up on me." Magnus had decided several days ago to name his company after one of the most feared alpha predators on Abimbola's home world. The Limbian granthers, he was told, were quite nasty. He figured if Abimbola was afraid of one, it was safe to say they all would be. More than that, however, Magnus felt that naming their company after something from Abimbola's home might be meaningful to the Miblimbian. Sure enough, as Abimbola heard it for the first time, his eyebrows went up.

"Do you approve?" Magnus asked as the black giant fell in.

Abimbola nodded. "Granthers rip their prey apart before swallowing them in tiny pieces."

"So I've heard."

"If that's what we get to do to Kane's forces and So-Elku, then yes, I approve."

"Glad to hear it, because my next option was Sorlakk Company."

Abimbola winced. "The soft Paglothian sea creatures?"

Magnus smiled. "The same."

"Granther is much better, buckethead."

Magnus winked at him. "You see, Bimby? I've got you covered."

Once the rest of the company fell in, Magnus motioned them to stop talking. "After-action review. First, give me three things you got right."

"We killed some enemies," Jaffery said, smiling.

"Yeah, just not enough," Shorty replied. A few laughs went up.

"What else?" Magnus asked.

"We stuck together," Dutch said.

"And got killed together," Valerie noted, giving Dutch a slight nudge with her elbow.

"Give me one more positive," Magnus said.

"Abimbola tried to save me," Doc Campbell said.

"Only because you are a medic," Abimbola added. "Everyone wants to save a medic and never the big guy."

"That's 'cause you're too hard to drag," Nubs said. More laughs.

"Extra points to Bimby for saving the good doctor," Magnus said, nodding to Abimbola. "Now, what went wrong?"

One by one, each platoon leader relayed what had taken them and their respective platoons down. It was painful but absolutely necessary if they wanted to get better. And they *had* to get better.

"All right," Magnus said when they were through. "That's what took you out. But I want to know if you identified what you could have done to help one another out." No one responded. "Dutch, did you see the auto turrets at the end of the street?"

"Affirmative."

"And had you called them out…"

"Rohoar's team might have had a chance. Roger that."

"Abimbola," Magnus said, calling the Miblimbian by his full name in front of the company. "You left Dutch's platoon behind. Did you ever consider leapfrogging with them?"

"They are too slow," Abimbola said.

"I understand that, but maybe their discretion could have saved you some unnecessary losses. And Rohoar?"

"Yes, Magnus."

"Please tell me that you saw the RPGs *before* the enemy fired them at Abimbola's platoon?"

Rohoar gave a somewhat embarrassed nod.

"By my count, we could have mitigated several casualties by communicating what we saw on the battlefield. Use your comms, people." Magnus made a show of tapping his earpiece. "That's what they're there for. You're on an important date, and you don't know enough to sweep this lady off her feet by yourself…" Magnus paused to look at Valerie, Silk, Bettger, and Saladin. "Or *man*. That's why you have a wingman, someone to feed you the lines. Without them, you're screwed, and there is no second date—this was your only date. La-raah?"

"La-raah," replied the company in unison.

"And, Titus?"

"Yes, sir?"

"Next time you decide to go treasure hunting through some old buildings—which wasn't the worst idea, by the way…"

"Thank you, sir."

"Do a scan first."

"Yes, sir," Titus said with a crisp nod.

"Okay, Granther Company, let's run it again. Computer, reset simulation."

"Request acknowledged."

32

Awen could hardly believe that she'd been training Piper for just over a month. The time had gone by more quickly than she realized, probably due to the fact that she was enjoying her time with Piper immensely. In fact, she couldn't remember having as much fun with anyone in recent years.

Perhaps this is what Willowood felt like with me. Awen thought better of that idea when she considered just how gifted Piper was. The girl was a marvel, doing things Awen had never seen another Luma do, herself included. But she and Piper weren't Luma. *We're Gladio Umbra now*, Awen reminded herself. The rules would be different, and so would the results.

Ni No was quite small, so after the last six weeks, everyone had begun to get island fever. Most of the team split their time between the island and the *Spire*, taking advantage of the change of scenery. For her part, however, Awen preferred staying on Nieth Tearness as much as possible. She most enjoyed the strand on the west side of the island, walking along the sand in her bare feet during sunset. After a few weeks, Magnus had discovered her evening ritual and started joining her occasionally. Sure, she was more of a closed person, preferring to be alone whenever she wasn't training Piper or getting a history lesson from Azelon. But she never complained whenever Magnus showed up to join her.

"So, how'd things go today?" Awen asked Magnus. The two of them were halfway to a large set of rocks that blocked the northern reach of the strand. The purple-hued sun was just about to touch the far ocean horizon, and the temperature was dropping.

"Best day yet," Magnus replied. "I'm proud of them."

"Seems like they've really come a long way."

"They have. Further than I expected in this amount of time, truthfully."

"That's great, Magnus. But you shouldn't be surprised."

"Why's that?"

"You're a good leader."

Magnus didn't say anything right away, and the sounds of the ocean took center stage. The seabirds were flying to their nests to roost, sending out their final cries to the sky, while the salty waves crashed rhythmically against the shore. Awen wasn't sure if she'd embarrassed him or if he just didn't want to say anything in reply.

She was about to change the subject when Magnus said, "Thanks."

A man of few words, she thought, smiling to herself.

"What's so funny?" Magnus asked her.

"Oh, nothing."

"Nothing? 'Cause you're smiling."

"It's just that…" She wasn't sure how to say it. "You're a fairly understated person. But that's okay. I like it."

He paused again. "That's good."

And why's that good? She was all for men of few words, but this was a little over the top. "So," Awen said, changing the subject, "how soon before you think your company will be ready to see combat?"

"Combat?" Magnus said, scratching his beard. "I'm guessing another six months. But I'd prefer a year."

"A year?" *Is he crazy?*

"Yeah. Why? You think that's a lot?"

"Well, in protoverse time… that's two-and-a-half weeks at the most."

"But in metaverse time, it's a long time for Kane's recon unit to uncover stuff they could use against the galaxy," Magnus concluded.

"Exactly."

"I get it, Awen. Trust me when I say that they're making progress. I just don't want…"

Awen slowed and looked up at him. "Don't want what?"

"I just don't want anyone to get hurt."

Awen chuckled. "Is this happening right now?"

"What?"

"Me, the former emissary, is about to lecture the former Marine on the risks of combat and the greater good." She laughed some more. "What's happened to us, Magnus? You going soft on me?"

"And you're getting nasty to kill somebody?"

"Not exactly," Awen replied. "But I do want to stop bad people from hurting innocent ones."

"Careful." Magnus raised his hands. "You're starting to sound like a Marine."

"And you're starting to sound like a—"

"Don't say it."

"A Gladio Umbra?"

"That's better." Magnus smiled then looked down in the sand. He'd actually taken off his boots for the first time. Awen didn't recall ever seeing his bare feet before. *They're... kinda cute.*

"I guess the more people I lose, the more I tire of fighting. Not because I don't want to fight—that's not it at all." Magnus worked his jaw, thinking. "It's because I'm tired of bad people having access to power that they can use to harm others. I want everyone to have the ability to fight for themselves and stand up for what they believe in."

"Mystics, Magnus. I think you missed your calling."

Magnus looked at her with a half smile. "I told you," he said, holding a finger to her face. "Don't you say it…"

Awen batted his hand away and kept walking. The smell of the water and the late-blooming flowers above the dunes was intoxicating. She could spend all night out here... if she didn't have so much to do.

"How's Piper doing?"

"Wonderfully well," Awen replied.

"Yeah?"

"Yeah. I mean, she's exceeded all my expectations. She's doing stuff that I've never seen any other person do in the Unity."

"Not even you?"

"Not even close! But don't tell her that. She'll get a big head."

"Piper? A big head? Somehow I think her only downfall will come from wanting too many Jujari around to snuggle."

Awen nodded. "She's naive. But still powerful." Awen's thoughts drifted away like the ocean currents. This whole conversation bothered her in ways she couldn't express.

"Hey, what's gotten into you?"

"Huh?"

"Come on, Awen. I've known you long enough to know when you're preoccupied."

Awen shrugged. "Eh, I don't know…"

"Come on, Awen. Cough it up."

"Well, it's about Piper."

When she didn't say anything after a few seconds, Magnus said, "Do I need to interrogate you?"

"No," Awen said with a chuckle. "It's just that… well, she's naive, right?"

"You established that."

"And she's powerful too."

"Also previously established."

"What happens when she kills someone?"

Magnus looked at her—she could feel his eyes staring at her. "That went dark fast." He cleared his throat. "All things considered, she'll be at the back of the line, and we'll do all the killing—"

"Come on, Magnus. We both know it's just a matter of time before something happens. Either the enemy finds her, or her powers get away from her. There's only so much all this training can do. At some point, she's going to come face-to-face with…"

"With what?" Magnus placed a hand on her forearm, causing her to stop.

"With who she is and what she's capable of."

Magnus turned to face her. The sun was setting over his shoulder, hiding his face in shadow. "Awen, isn't that what we all have to face?"

"Yeah, but she's different."

"No, she's not."

"What?"

"She's *not* different from any other person. She's going to have to decide for herself who she is and what she's going to do with her powers. I know you don't want her in harm's way, and you certainly don't want her hurting anyone else. But, Awen, she was born for this hour. I mean, come on—what are the chances that someone of her ability is born in a time when people like Kane and So-Elku are trying to take over the galaxy? The universe… it *knows*. I don't know how, but it does. And we need her. We need everything she can do."

Magnus held Awen's biceps. His hands were warm and strong. The way he held her—it felt so good. But he needed to let go, didn't he? This wasn't right. There was something about him and Valerie… but she didn't want him to stop. If anything, she wanted him to hold her closer.

"And we need you," he said, pulling her closer.

"You need me?"

Magnus nodded.

"So do I," Awen replied. "You, I mean. I need you too."

Mystics, just shut up and kiss him.

But she didn't need to, because Magnus pulled her toward him and kissed her instead. It was the best kiss she'd ever had. *When was the last time you were properly kissed anyway, Awen?* She couldn't remember, but she didn't need her inner self ruining this moment.

When Magnus finally pulled away, Awen kept her eyes closed, not wanting it to end. But it needed to—of course it needed to. When she opened her eyes, Magnus was smiling at her, barely discernible in the fading light.

"That was nice," she said.

Nice, Awen? That was incredible!

"I've been wanting to do that since…"

"Since we were hanging in Abimbola's jail?" Awen asked, laughing in spite of herself.

Magnus nodded. "Pretty much."

"Wait." Awen brushed her hair out of her face. "You're serious?"

"Yup."

The truth was, she'd liked him the moment he saved her from the mwadim's skyscraper. And nothing would ever change that. It was a mix of admiration, respect, and desperation—a potent concoction she doubted would ever let go of her.

"Listen… about Piper," Magnus said. "Just let her be what she's gonna be. Earlier, you told me that I'm a great leader. Well, *you* are a great teacher, and you've got to trust what you've invested into her. But you're not responsible for who she becomes—you're only responsible for who you are to her. And I can assure you, you've done more for her and mean more to her than you can possibly know."

Awen lowered her head and took a deep breath. *Mystics, why does he always have to be so compelling? And charming. And handsome.*

"You good?" Magnus asked.

"Huh? What?"

"You *okay*?"

"Yeah, yeah. I'm fine." Awen squished her toes in the sand as Magnus let go of her. "Thanks. For what you just said."

"No problem."

Suddenly, a voice crackled over the comms device attached to Magnus's shoulder. Awen could barely make it out but was pretty sure it was TO-96.

"You gonna answer that?" Awen asked.

Magnus snapped the earpiece off its clip on his shoulder and placed it in his ear. He winked at her and then tapped the comm to open the channel. "Go for Magnus."

Magnus listened intently, turning away from her slightly. Whatever TO-96 was sharing with Magnus was important. If Awen had brought her own comm, she would have listened in, but she purposely left it back in her tent when she took these walks.

"What's your best estimate?" Magnus asked. There was a beat as he listened. "You're absolutely sure about that?" Another beat. "Okay, then. Bring both shuttles down here, and we'll get the team off the ground in twenty. Magnus out."

"What's going on?" Awen asked.

"Seems the recon unit is getting a little too close to something for Azelon's comfort."

"In Itheliana?"

Magnus nodded.

"Wait, wait—so you want us to…"

"We're moving out, Awen."

"But… no. I mean, we need more time. You just said—"

"I know we need more time. But we just lost that luxury. The first lesson in combat is that no plan survives contact with the enemy. So we move with what we have."

"And what if we have isn't enough?"

Magnus shrugged. "Then hopefully, the universes have some other heroes to do what we couldn't. But until then, we prove that no one else is needed." He reached down and grabbed her hand. "Come on. We've gotta go."

33

Magnus stood before the members of Granther Company inside a cavernous shuttle bay on the *Spire*. His team waited in a loose semicircle. He could tell they were nervous just by the expressions on some of their faces. Behind Magnus sat a series of vertical shipping containers, four across and eight deep, each dark gray and emblazoned with red and yellow Novia script. Two shuttles also rested on either side of Magnus, loading ramps extended, cockpits powered up.

"Everyone listen up," Magnus said. "I've got a lot of ground to cover, and quickly, so I need your full attention." He purposefully made eye contact with several members in the group before continuing. "As you've probably guessed, we just made the jump from Nieth Tearness to Ithnor Ithelia, and I can confirm that we will be landing in Itheliana to engage the enemy in approximately seventy-five minutes."

Murmurs went up from among the teams.

"Quiet down," Abimbola said, raising a hand but with little effect. "I said, quiet down!"

The bay went silent again.

"I know you probably don't feel ready yet," Magnus continued. "And while I, too, wish we had more time to train, the reality is that we cannot wait a moment longer to strike the enemy. Azelon and TO-96 have both assured me that the enemy recon unit is very close to discovering something that should not leave the planet—that should not fall into enemy hands. From what our intelligence tells me, if Admiral Kane or Luma Master So-Elku gain access to whatever this recon unit has discovered, it's game over for us. For everyone.

"Therefore, it is absolutely imperative that we stop them from stealing any Novia technology. Our mission is to kill or capture all enemy combatants and get them off the planet." Magnus let his words hang in the air before saying, "And to help us along, I brought some new toys…"

He turned to the nearest freight container and pressed his hand against an oversized bio-scanner—one better suited to a Jujari than a human. A sensor swept his handprint, and then the device chimed just as a solid white light changed to purple. An internal maglock deactivated, and Magnus pulled the doors apart. Inside were seven glossy-white assault blasters bathed in soft light.

"These," Magnus said, retrieving one of the weapons and holding it up for everyone to see, "are your new NOV1 assault blasters."

Quiet whistles and exclamations went up from the teams. Then everyone shushed one another, presumably in anticipation that Magnus would explain the weapon. He wouldn't disappoint them.

"The NOV1 is based on a Novia design with Repub mods. Call it a hybrid, if you will. Azelon and I designed this ourselves. It features a lattice-work stock, bio-linked operational access, dual inline mag ports, adaptive maglock technology, multidirectional sighting, and ultra-high-speed energy delivery, which means it's capable of delivering one megajoule of energy in point-zero-two-second pulse intervals."

Magnus was happy to see that they looked just as dumbstruck as he had been when Azelon first rattled off those stats to him.

"I want you to picture a one-megagram dune skiff traveling at about one hundred sixty kilometers per hour and slamming into your target. That's what your new NOV1 can deliver three thousand times per second on full auto."

"Great mystics," someone whispered.

"You got that right," Magnus replied as several other members laughed. "The weapon also features an AI-assisted single-pulse variable-frequency mode, which, using a gimbaled barrel, can identify and take out up to twenty targets at once. This, of course, is contingent upon your energy-mag capacity, fire rate, and target composition. However, until you're all outfitted with the proper biotech interface, this function will remain offline.

"Azelon needs more time to integrate each of us into the

Novia defense architecture, or NDA. But what you *can* use is the variable fire-rate function that we've given you—single-round, three-round burst, and full-auto mode. Under no circumstances do I want any of you using full auto unless you're assaulting an armored hover tank—is that clear?"

"Yes, sir," the company replied as one.

"Once the NOV1 encodes itself to your palm, the weapon is yours and can't be fired by anyone else."

"Unless Cyril gets ahold of it," Silk said from beside Abimbola. Several members of Bravo and Charlie companies chuckled.

"Quite true," Magnus replied, using the opportunity to lighten the mood. "Mystics know, Cyril's never met a system he can't slice."

When the laughs and nods of agreement dissipated, Magnus held the weapon aloft one last time. "The NOV1 also has one more feature you might find interesting." He touched the side sensor pad and swiped, activating the first skin on the weapon's stock menu. Suddenly, the weapon went from glossy white to matte black.

Gasps went up from among the Granthers. One Jujari even howled, perhaps in fear—Magnus couldn't tell. He touched the pad and swiped again. The second stock skin appeared, turning the weapon into a close-up of jungle foliage. The projection was picture perfect. More gasps came from the company.

Finally, Magnus swiped a third setting—one he'd specially preloaded on this particular weapon. It displayed a picture of

Abimbola, smiling broadly, wearing a hat that had an embroidered red heart between the words *I* and *Bucketheads*.

"Son of a bitch," Abimbola said from across the semicircle. Laughs went up all around—including from the Miblimbian, who mouthed to Magnus, "I'm gonna get you back."

Magnus winked back at him, knowing the Miblimbian would make good on his promise. Magnus powered off the weapon and placed it back in its container. When the laughter subsided, he said, "Each of you will receive six energy magazines located in the drawers below the blasters."

He pulled open a bin and withdrew a mag. It had the same connection as a Repub standard issue but was almost twice as long. It was also the same glossy white as the NOV1 and bore an illuminated capacity indicator on one side.

"Each mag will adopt whatever skin you've employed on the main weapon. And for those of you used to Repub issue, these mags will last almost three times as long as you're used to. Six will give you three full reloads and will be more than we'll need for this mission." He replaced the mag and closed the drawer.

"Next," Magnus said, walking to another vertical container and opening its secure maglock, "comes your sidearm." He spread the doors apart to display a row of pistols seven across. He removed one of the glossy-white pistols and held it aloft. It had a rectangular front receiver leading back to a grip molded into the body. The weapon was sleek and raked forward, like a single-seater racing skiff leaning into rapid acceleration. "This is the VD2. Yes, in case you were wondering, that stands for Very Deadly Too—a play on words lost on all you non-common speakers. Sorry."

Several laughs went up from around the teams.

"You can just call it the V for short. Like the NOV1, the V was co-created by Azelon and me. It features bio-linked operational access, smart-fire AI-assistance targeting, single-round and five-round burst modes. It sports a special visual emulation compound and can accept both the NOV1's extended mags and the smaller ones we've designed here."

Magnus opened a drawer below the pistol rack and withdrew an energy magazine almost a quarter the size of the NOV1's. "You also can expend an entire magazine in one squeeze if you want. I call it death-wish mode. Should you select it, know two things. One, your mag will drain to completion, and there's no way to stop the discharge once initiated. And two, you will need to wait for the mandatory cool-down period to cycle before attempting to reload. But I can promise you that whatever you were aiming at, it won't be there when you're done. Oh, and hold onto her hard on this setting—she bucks like a bitch."

Magnus replaced the weapon and walked to a third container, then unlocked it and opened its doors. "In here, we have a play on the Repub-issue variable-output detonator—or VOD." Magnus removed yet another glossy-white device, but this one was perfectly spherical, interrupted only by a small input screen on one side. "Those familiar with the devices, which I think would be all of us"—Magnus looked around the room for any dissenters—"know that it has options for

Gateway to War

emitting a flash bang, crowd-deterrent gas, or smoke. Well, this beauty also includes options for fragmentation, thermite, electromagnetic pulse, and a directional breach charge. Essentially, it's a one-stop-shop grenade that you won't find at your local stores, and you each get four."

More whistles and laughs went up. That was good—Magnus knew they needed as much levity as they could muster to break the tension that was mounting in the room. For as much fun as they were having at seeing their new toys, Magnus also knew an inverse emotion was at play: anxiety. He was talking about weapons, after all—killing tools that were about to be deployed in combat, where people were going to die. Talking about weapons always created a strange mix of unbridled enthusiasm and grim disbelief.

"And last but not least..." Magnus walked to a fourth and final container along the first row. It was much wider and deeper than the others. He unlocked the unit but held it shut for a moment. "May I present to you..." He flung the sliding doors apart. "The Gladio Umbra Mark I combat suit."

Granther Company came unglued, to put it mildly. Shouts, grunts, howls, and hollers went up from across the room.

Inside were two different suits of armor standing side by side. One was human shaped, consisting of a fully enclosed combat suit and helmet in the same glossy-white finish as the firearms. Its articulated joints and multilayered plate-armor appearance made it seem incredibly dexterous yet menacingly resilient. The all-white helmet tapered to a leading edge that swept vertically from the chin to the back of the head—it resembled two halves of a knife blade meeting in the center of the face. And Magnus had to admit, it looked badass.

"Humans and humanoid-sized equivalents, your Mark I armor features a high-density, low-weight composite-nanofiber weave that makes up the majority of the fabric and the armor plating. The material is not only able to mitigate the damage of most material strikes delivered in a range of velocities, but it also contains electrodes for a personal-shield emitter—PSE—capable of displacing blaster energy equivalent to about ten direct hits from a standard MC90 blaster. Observe."

Magnus touched a screen on the armor's wrist pad and activated the PSE. A soft blue glow emanated a centimeter off the suit's entire surface, almost indiscernible to the naked eye. It followed every contour and corner, fully encasing the armor in a shield. Magnus pulled his Z from his chest plate and fired three rounds into the suit at point-blank range. It happened so fast that many of the gladias winced at the Z's report. Each blast, however, was absorbed and displaced into the suit's shield, causing small waves to ripple around the body.

"This suit's shield is now depleted by thirty percent," Magnus said. "But don't worry—it has my name emblazoned on it, not any of yours." The acknowledgment was met with more laughter. He'd have wanted to know the same thing if his superior had just used armor for a demo that might potentially be assigned to him.

"All your weapons can maglock to any part of the suit

that you desire," Magnus continued, "allowing you to customize your loadout. The suit includes full life support, nano-bot triage, thermal-radiation suppression, and autorehydration—hell, this thing even lets you piss in it and won't throw a fit."

Magnus liked making them laugh. *This is the last you'll get to for a while.* When the room quieted down again, he continued.

"The vertical clamshell-style helmet has the very latest tech that I've ever seen—thanks entirely to Azelon and the Novia Minoosh—which includes a vast array of functionality. We're talking a full neural-sensor suite, tactical navigation, quantum squad communication, spatial-coherence extrapolation, and weapons-system interfacing, just to name a few. The rest, you're gonna need to read the manual when you have some downtime."

"What are those marks?" someone asked.

Magnus assumed the speaker meant the small icons on the side of the helmet and the shoulder plate. He pointed to the blue broken circle with an open-bottomed triangle touching the top. "That is the symbol for the Gladio Umbra." Then Magnus indicated the shoulder icon—four claw-like lines in dark gray. "And this is your new unit emblem for Granther Company."

Magnus looked about—several people nodded in approval.

"Then, over here…" Magnus indicated the next suit. "We have an armor line branded for our more robust warriors. I'm looking at you, Redmarrow."

"What?" the Jujari said. He was easily the most rotund of his platoon.

Where the human version of the Mark I was fully enclosed, the Jujari equivalent was not. The helmet, for example, left the entire snout uncovered while a white clamshell visor and helm covered the eyes and head. Likewise, while the chest, back, shoulders, pelvis, and thighs had limited armor plating and straps of nano-fiber to hold everything together, the forearms, hands, calves, and feet were exposed, leaving them free to tear into enemy targets. Magnus had figured that millennia of evolutionary development shouldn't be covered up by a shiny new suit—a conclusion that Azelon had praised.

"And, Saasarr," Magnus said.

The Reptalon's head perked up.

"We made a special one for you." Magnus opened a drawer and lifted a suit similar to the Jujari's but fashioned to fit the lizard's unique body shape.

"Thank you, sir," Saasarr said with a quick bow. "I am most grateful."

Resuming his address to the rest of the room, Magnus said, "The best part about the Mark I isn't how it protects you from being struck by enemy fire. No. It's how it protects you from being seen at all."

Magnus reached over to both suits and tapped the control panel, activating chameleon mode. Suddenly, the telecolos coating went live, and the two suits of armor disappeared.

The gladias gasped. Several took steps closer to the container, unable to resist their curiosity. They were like a class of schoolchildren seeing a Venetian mawslip for the first time during a trip to the zoo. If there had been windowplex separating the Gladio Umbra from the suits, their faces would have been pressed up against it for a better look.

"The only reason we have access to anything like this is because of Azelon passing along the Novia's advanced technology to us. Without it, well, you'd be stuck in Repub armor, and who wants that?" A few in the company clapped at that one. "Like your firearms, the telecolos compound on each suit can completely camouflage it into whatever the surrounding environment is. And yes, it can display standard colors and patterns too—but chameleon mode is by far the most impressive and my personal favorite.

"Lastly, each suit has your name on the right chest and has been custom tailored to your measurements. Make sure you take *your* suit and not someone else's. It could make for a long and painful day if you're not careful."

As Magnus concluded his showcase of the new armaments, resetting the suits to their normal visual states, he returned to the front, where he'd started. "Listen," he said more solemnly than he'd intended. "I know you're walking into all of this a little blind." Magnus gestured to the containers. "Hell, you should have had six months to a year to train with this kit before moving out. For that, I'm sorry. And if I didn't believe in the weapons systems so much, I wouldn't even spring it on you. Truthfully, I thought we were going to have more time—Azelon's printers only finished the last suit yesterday. But I don't get to tell the enemy how to set their clocks. However, with all this"—Magnus swept his arm to indicate the new tech behind him—"we *do* get to tell the enemy when to run."

The room erupted with a loud "La-raah!" which honestly surprised Magnus.

Hell, yeah. Now they're getting it.

"Azelon's sensors tell us that there are twenty-four Paragon recon troopers down there," Magnus continued. "They're good. *Real good.* One or two of them I probably trained myself at one point. The important thing, though, is to remember that what we lack in practice or skill, we're going to make up for in heart, determination, and pure overwhelming fire supremacy. 'Cause I can sure as hell promise you the enemy hasn't seen anything like this."

"La-raah!" the gladias shouted.

"Now, listen… listen," Magnus said, bringing the energy of the room down with his hands. "It's time to get you suited up and kitted out. If you have any questions, don't be afraid to ask. Help one another out too. You see someone struggling, lend a hand. And for the love of all the mystics, *do not* power up your blasters until we're on the shuttles headed for the LZ. Copy?"

THE ROW of containers had been thoroughly ravaged. Old armor, helmets, clothing, and firearms lay scattered across the shuttle bay floor. Magnus had even placed his MAR30 on a table, quietly thanking it for its service. It was the end of an era—one he never thought he'd say goodbye to. Now he couldn't imagine returning to it.

"Can you zip me up?" Valerie asked. Magnus had just finished helping Gilder squeeze into his suit when he turned around to see her bare back.

"Sure thing," he said, swallowing hard.

The suits required that each wearer be nude. Life-support functions, as well as rehydration and triage, all required direct contact with the skin. While everyone pretty well managed to be discreet, being so close to Valerie's unclothed back made Magnus uneasy—not in a bad way but not in the best way either. These kinds of thoughts clouded his judgment, and that was the last thing he needed at the moment. Magnus pulled the suit tight and drew the zipper up as Valerie gathered her hair and held it out of the way.

"There you go," he said.

"Thanks." Valerie turned and looked up at him, quite stunning in her suit. It was so form-fitting that he needed little imagination to—

"You know, we haven't had a lot of time to spend together over these last few weeks," Valerie said.

Magnus was about to mention all their training time but figured that wasn't what she meant.

"I just wanted you to know how much I appreciate you."

"I appreciate you too." It was all Magnus could think to say, and it sounded stupid even to him.

"And that no matter what happens down there today, I'm with you. Always."

Magnus was about to say something in reply but didn't know what. She was just too pretty, and his brain wasn't working right. Fortunately, he didn't have to say anything. Instead, Valerie went up on her toes and kissed him on the cheek.

"See you on the ground, Lieutenant."

It took almost forty-five minutes for everyone to get squared away—longer than Magnus had wanted. But damn if they didn't look sharp in their new armor. The members of Granther Company returned to their positions in the semicircle. Where before they'd looked like a ragtag bunch of miscreants and vagabonds, now they stood like a veritable shock troop—humans, humanoids, and Jujari, each arrayed for battle. Magnus couldn't help but notice that they stood a little taller too. He could have sworn that their chests were puffed out a little more as well.

When Magnus had their attention, he said, "I'd like to present two extraordinary people to you. Many of you have already met them, and I think most of you have already seen them around camp. For numerous reasons, we've needed to keep them apart from us. But they've been vital members of this mission from the very beginning. In fact, I'd wager they are more Gladio Umbra than any of us, myself included.

May I present Awen dau Lothlinium and Piper Stone, guardians of the Unity."

Awen held Piper's hand as they emerged from around one of the shuttles near Magnus. They were outfitted in their own power suits and carried helmets under their free arms. Awen made eye contact and smiled at the many faces among Granther Company, while Piper seemed only to have eyes for Rohoar. The former mwadim raised a single finger and waved at Piper. *Those two definitely have a connection*, Magnus had to admit, thinking back to when he'd found them on the bridge together. He'd never forget that moment.

"If you see them on the battlefield doing something you can't explain, something that messes with your head, don't stop, don't admire it—just keep on going. Because whatever they're doing, they're doing so you can get your job done. La-raah?"

"La-raah," the company replied.

"Now, you probably won't see Awen and Piper up front much, if ever. But that doesn't mean they're not there, fighting as hard as you are. And trust me when I say that they're in harm's way just as much as you, if not more. They deserve your respect and admiration. And more than that"—Magnus looked at Piper—"they deserve our *lives*.

"Hear me out," Magnus continued, raising his voice so that it echoed in the shuttle bay, "and I'll be as clear as I can. If either of these ladies die, there is no mission. Mission success includes the preservation of these two lives above all others. Awen and Piper must go downrange with us. There is no battle if they cannot fight with us, and there is no victory if they do not survive. Our existence is tied with their survival, and if you have the choice between saving yourself or saving one of them, you save them every time, no questions asked. Do I make myself clear, Granther Company?"

"La-raah!" cried the battle group in one voice.

"Good," Magnus replied, giving their shouts a chance to die down. He motioned for Awen and Piper to move into formation with the rest of the company. "From this point forward, we'll be outside the wire. It means we're committed. It means we're in harm's way. Unless you've fought a recon team before—and I know some of you have—you've never fought an enemy quite like this. They're fast, they're highly coordinated, and they never stop coming. But that's precisely what we've trained for. So remember the simulations—not the bad days but the good days. Remember your training, and remember how you got to those wins at the end of every street. Work together, call things out, and move with your team."

Magnus moved his helmet to his left hand. "I know you might be feeling a little nervous right now. Maybe even afraid. But I want you to remember something and hear me: I don't care if you feel afraid. Everyone feels afraid. Fear is there to remind you that you like being alive—that you have something worth fighting for. What I really care about is why you decide to stay and fight. Why you decide to clear one more room, why you decide to take one more step down a street

Gateway to War

filled with blaster fire. Everyone's afraid, but not everyone's a hero. That's why you're here."

Magnus straightened up, brought his feet together, and tucked his helmet in his left arm. "Granther Company?"

The team members stood up straight.

"It's time." Magnus brought his hand up in a salute, and the entire company followed his lead, returning the salute. "Dominate!" Magnus roared with his right fist held high.

"Liberate!" answered thirty-nine souls with their fists to the sky.

34

No one spoke as the shuttles entered Ithnor Ithelia's atmosphere. Flames flickered across the windowplex while the ships bounced and jolted. Nolan piloted *Red One*, carrying Alpha and Bravo Platoons, while Andocs piloted *Red Two*, taking Charlie and Delta Platoons.

Magnus sat beside Nolan, examining the holo-map, while the remaining two crash couches behind him held Awen and Piper. The two were extremely quiet, which made Magnus feel even more uneasy. While he loved silence, this mission was tense enough as it was, so anything to break up the constant hurry-up-and-wait aspect of prebattle anxiety would be welcome.

"So we're going to come in from far away, right, Mr. Lieutenant Magnus, sir?" Piper asked.

Mystics, favor her, Magnus thought, grateful that she'd had broken the bridge's constricting silence. *Even if she can't separate my old rank from my name.* "That's right, Piper. You ever see a shooting star?"

"Lots of times."

"Well, that's what we look like right now." Magnus pointed out the window as the flames began subsiding. "All that fire's from friction, and it makes us visible for hundreds of kilometers in every direction. So we need to make sure no one in Itheliana can see us." He enlarged the holo-map so she could see from behind him. "The navigation computer gives us an exact path to follow so we're out of view."

"Then we fly fast and low to Itheliana?"

Magnus chucked. "Have you been studying military tactics in your spare time, little one?"

She shook her head. "Uh-uh. Just makes sense is all."

"That it does," Magnus said, turning back to study their progress.

"So we're gonna land over there, Mr. Lieutenant Magnus, sir?"

Magnus followed her pointed finger toward the green dot that lay east of the city in a forest about one klick from the city's eastern border. "We sure are. Mr. Nolan here is going to drop us in the middle of a small clearing. We'll go the rest of the way on foot."

"Will I get to walk beside you?"

"I'm afraid not, Piper." Magnus turned in his chair to face her. The girl was such an enigma to him. On the one hand, she looked so childlike that she seemed younger than her nine years of age. But on the other, she was so mature, so confident, that most adults paled in comparison. He had trouble reconciling the two images he had of this young lady. "You'll need to stay back with Awen for this mission."

"But you'll rescue me when I get in trouble, right, Mr. Lieutenant Magnus, sir?"

"Right." Magnus leaned toward her. "I'll always be there to rescue you... but you need to make me a promise."

"Sure, anything."

"That you'll be there to rescue me when I need it too."

"Promise," she said. Then she did something incredibly spontaneous—she kissed her fingers, reached forward, and placed them on his cheek.

Somehow, he felt he was supposed to do the same to seal the mutual deal, as it were. So Magnus kissed his fingers—far larger and rougher than hers—and placed the imaginary kiss on her cheek. She closed her eyes and smiled, accepting the pat with a warmth he couldn't remember seeing elsewhere—at least not in a very long time. "Promise," he said.

THE SHUTTLES SKIMMED along the tops of the trees for another ten minutes before Nolan called out the time to landing. "Two minutes," he said, flipping several switches.

Magnus heard changes in the ship's drive core and noticed the craft start to decelerate. He unbuckled his harness and passed between Awen and Piper. "Stay here until I come and get you."

"Copy," Awen replied, smiling up at him. She was nervous—he could see it in her eyes.

"Hey," Magnus said, leaning down toward her ear. "You've got this."

Awen nodded but didn't say anything.

Magnus left the bridge and stepped down the alternating-tread staircase into the shuttle's extended cargo bay. "Heads up. We're less than two minutes to touchdown. Pre-combat check means helmets on, lock and load, and check the gladia beside you."

One by one, each gladia donned helmets, powered on and charged NOV1s, and examined the gladias to their right and left to make sure they were buttoned up and ready to move out.

"One minute," Nolan yelled from the bridge.

"One minute," Magnus echoed, holding up one finger. The gesture was mimicked throughout the cargo bay.

Magnus placed his own helmet over his head. His visor powered on, giving him a crystal-clear view of the cargo bay. Both platoons stood and turned toward the aft. He still couldn't believe how clear the view was in the Mark I helmet. It was as if he wasn't wearing a helmet at all—perfect peripheral vision—and the tech even interfaced with his bioteknia eyes, thanks to some custom coding by Azelon.

The advanced neural interface took only a second to boot up, calibrating to his brain waves via the embedded sensors pressed firmly against several points on his skull. As soon as they established a secure connection, the displays in his visor and his eyes synced, creating a multidimensional mesh of data that made Magnus feel like he was seeing the world from inside a hyper-intelligent AI.

'Cause that's exactly what you are doing, dummy. Gone were the days of having to use his eyes to navigate menus, let alone his hands. All he needed to do was *think* about doing something, and it happened.

From inside his helmet over comms, Magnus heard Nolan say, "Thirty seconds."

Magnus held his hand over his head in the shape of a C, denoting second and final call before loadout. A sliver of late-morning light appeared at the ceiling as the shuttle's rear door crept open. Within another two seconds, Magnus saw leaves rustling under the shuttle's thrusters.

"Activate ambient-environment skin," Magnus said over comms. Pings of acknowledgment lined his visor as each gladia acknowledged the command. Even Magnus's command was displayed in real-time text along a chat feed, supplying a time-stamped log for every mission order and action. *The Repub's got nothing on this*, Magnus thought.

To Magnus's astonishment—even though he *knew* it was coming—the gladias disappeared as they activated their telecolos system to replicate their immediate environment. "Splick," he said, looking around the room. The only evidence that anyone was there at all were dozens of minor *bumps* in the scene—places where the suit's infrastructure had a hard time projecting across the curvature of limbs and joints. Still, if Kane's troopers didn't know what they were looking at, they'd be hard-pressed to know there were almost two dozen armor-clad beings waiting to tear them apart. *Which is exactly what we want.*

"Ten seconds," Magnus said over the sound of the straining drive cores. The ramp was almost fully lowered, revealing a dense frost without.

"Hey, where'd everybody go?" Piper exclaimed from the bridge. Her tiny face peered down at Magnus, who still hadn't activated his telecolos system.

"Everyone's still there, Piper," Magnus replied, grabbing a strap of webbing to brace himself against the landing.

"Just use the Unity," Awen added.

"Oh," Piper said. "I see them now."

Just like that? Magnus thought. *Mystics, she is... incredible.*

Wait until you see her in action, came a second voice inside Magnus's head. He almost hit his helmet with his hand—a bad habit he'd picked up from bungling around inside old Mark IV armor—but realized the voice sounded exactly like Awen.

That's because it is me, she replied.

"Three..." Nolan said. "Two... one..." The shuttle bounced only slightly as Nolan executed a textbook landing. "Touchdown!"

"Did you just read my—are you in my head?" Magnus asked out loud. Hell, this was distracting. He had an op to run.

Only if you want me to be, Awen replied.

Me too! Piper added.

Magnus wasn't sure he could handle having either one of them in his head. "Shut up for just a second, okay? I'll be right back."

MAGNUS ORDERED everyone out of the shuttles. Both platoons exited and set up a perimeter around the ships. Amazingly, optical sensors hardly detected anything save the rustling of long grass and shifting shadows among the distant tree trunks. Even his thermal imaging had a hard time identifying the shapes. It wasn't until Magnus activated his atomic sensors that the shapes of his gladias filled his vision, echoed by his bioteknia's redundant imaging systems.

"All right, platoon leaders," Magnus said, singling out Dutch, Abimbola, Titus, and Rohoar over comms. "Let's secure the enemy shuttle and prep for entry into the city. Smooth is fast, and fast is deadly."

"La-raah," Rohoar said.

"La-raah," the other three echoed.

"I'll be right behind you with our mystics," Magnus added. Once the company was off and moving, Magnus walked back inside *Red One* to retrieve Awen and Piper. They'd already descended from the bridge and donned their helmets.

"Looking good," Magnus said to both of them over comms.

Thanks, Mr. Lieutenant Magnus, sir.

"Piper, can you please use comms with me for right now?" Magnus asked. "I'm… just not sure I'm ready for you being in my head yet."

"Sure. I didn't mean to freak you out."

Freak me out? This kid is something else. "Okay, you both ready to move out?" he asked.

They nodded.

"Stay close, and keep your eyes open for anything out of the ordinary, or however it is you track stuff in the Unity."

"Understood, Magnus," Awen replied. "We're with you."

"Yeah, we're totally with you," Piper added.

Half of Magnus felt really strange for purposefully escorting a child into a hostile environment. It was just something a person never *ever* did. Yet the other half of him wouldn't want to enter a battlefield without her.

"Here goes nothing." He turned and led them down the ramp, carrying his NOV1 in low-ready position, and activated his suit's chameleon mode.

Granther Company proceeded through the forest as planned, moving in two columns with scouts farther out. Their first objective was securing the enemy's transport shuttle, which was located adjacent to the ruins of Ezo's former command, the *Indomitable*. His ship, as he told it, had been scuttled by the departing Admiral Kane to prevent any later escape.

According to Azelon, the enemy's shuttle hadn't been used in several weeks, and therefore, it was unlikely to be occupied. Still, Magnus didn't want to take any chances—the craft needed to be cleared and disabled, or else the enemy might use it later on. It was best just to take the thing out of play.

Eight minutes had ticked by on the mission clock before the first scout announced, "Eyes on the *Hotel One*."

"Good work, Zoll," Titus said over comms.

Magnus watched as the blue dot in his projected topographical map changed to yellow, confirming the first waypoint but designating it as unsecured.

"Charlie and Delta Platoons," Magnus said, "set up a perimeter. Alpha and Bravo Platoons, initiate search and seizure."

Again, confirmation pings sounded as green icons lined the chat thread. Magnus watched the map as the white dots, signifying each member of each platoon, spread out into the target area. Small member designators also spread across his field of view, allowing him to call up exact coordinates and distances should he desire.

"Can we go look too?" Piper asked.

"Not yet," Magnus replied. "I want you staying here behind this tree. Since your suits don't change color like ours, it's important that you keep out of sight. I don't want you moving forward until we're sure where the enemy is."

"I understand, Mr. Lieutenant Magnus, sir."

Magnus patted her on the shoulder then looked to Awen. "Stay here for a sec?"

She nodded. "Will do."

Magnus turned and ran toward *Hotel One*. He could barely make out the shuttle's black hull through the trees with optical sensors, but the ship appeared clearly through the rest of his spectral sensors. He could even see members of Alpha and Bravo Platoons moving around inside it.

"Dutch, Abimbola, report," Magnus ordered.

"Looks to be abandoned, buckethead," Abimbola said. "And Cyril says there are no signs of remote detection or active relays either."

"They pulled the drive core right out of her too," Dutch added. "Whatever they found in the city, I'm guessing they needed the power there instead."

"Yeah, that can't be good," Magnus said. "Disable the flight systems. But don't do anything we can't fix later."

"Copy that," Dutch replied.

Magnus moved under the ship, heading for the far side of the clearing. The hulking mass that was the *Indomitable* lay to his right. How Ezo had ever managed to fly that piece of junk was beyond him. That Nimprith was either a damn good pilot or a damn crazy one. *Probably both*, Magnus thought.

Saladin crouched beside Rohoar at the edge of the clearing, looking through a stand of trees toward the eastern gate's ruins. While the Jujari's lack of telecolos-coated armor failed to blend all of their bodies into their environment's visual palette, their fur certainly went a long way toward adding to their unique version of camouflage.

Magnus approached the two cautiously, careful to make his presence known over comms—the last thing he wanted to do was startle a Jujari from behind. "On your six, Rohoar."

Rohoar and Saladin turned slowly, motioning Magnus to crouch beside them.

"Waddya got for me?" Magnus asked.

"Do you smell it?" Rohoar asked him.

"Smell it?"

"Humans," Saladin said, licking her chops. "Many humans. Upwind, nine hundred meters to the west."

"Anything closer than that?" Magnus asked.

Rohoar shook his head. "No. That is the only place where we smell humans."

"But you might not be able to smell all of them, right? We need to—"

"Jujari always smell all humans," Saladin said. "Jujari never miss any humans. All humans stink."

Magnus had both his eyebrows raised. "That's good to know." To Dutch and Abimbola, he asked, "How are you coming with the ship?"

"Good," Dutch replied.

"Cyril says he's almost done," Abimbola added. "Five more seconds and then—"

Pop! Pip–pip. Crack!

"I think it's done," Abimbola said. Magnus could practically smell the electrical smoke.

"Yup," Dutch replied. "Shuttle scuttled."

"Good." Magnus switched to the *Spire*'s dedicated channel. "Azie, do you read me?"

"I do," the AI said. "That is, if by *read* you mean detect your audio transmission with sufficient clarity. And if so, I believe I am starting to get the hang of your human idioms."

"Congratulations, Azie. Listen, the Jujari are picking up human scent nine hundred meters to the west. Can you confirm that?"

"Negative, sir. Whatever shielding the enemy is using has made me unable to pinpoint their exact location. The only thing I can tell you is that nine hundred meters from your present location is within acceptable margins of error for possible enemy presence. If I were you, I would *go with your gut on this one*."

"Well said," TO-96 added over comms.

Magnus rolled his eyes. "Thanks, you two. If anything pops up, I need to be the first to know."

"Affirmative, sir," TO-96 said. "We'll do our very best."

"Yes," Azelon confirmed, "we'll *put our backs into it* and *give it the old college try*."

Magnus chuckled. "I couldn't ask for more. Magnus out." Before they could demonstrate more of their idiomatic speech, he turned off the channel.

"All right, teams, listen up," Magnus said over company wide comms. "We're detecting a human presence nine hundred meters to the west. But I want that confirmed before we move in. Awen, are you able to *see* that far?"

"Stand by, Magnus, I'll—"

"Yup, I see them," Piper exclaimed. Magnus winced, as the audio compression wasn't fast enough to catch her sudden outburst. He could see several other gladias reacting to the loud sound too.

"Thanks, Piper. Try not to shout, okay?"

"Okay, Mr. Lieutenant Magnus, sir."

"Can you describe what you're seeing?"

"Uh-huh." Magnus heard her little voice counting under her breath. "I see twenty troopers dressed in black. They have… a base camp, like ours! But smaller. And no ESCEs or ISCEs, but they might have a temple. No, wait! Twenty-one troopers. No, wait! Twenty-two!"

"Piper, slow down," Magnus said. "Where is this base camp?"

"It's up the main street in front of us. You have to go under the gate. Then we have to jump two streets over, and then it's diagonal. It opens into a pretty-looking plaza. That's where they are."

"And why do more of them keep appearing? Something about a temple, you said?"

"Oh, that's easy. 'Cause they have a tunnel."

"A tunnel?"

"Uh-huh. They keep going in and coming out. Ooo! There's another one—twenty-three!"

"Magnus?" Titus said.

"Go, Titus."

"Bettger has marked the location on the holo-map using Piper's directions."

"Perfect," Magnus replied. In addition to the map icon, he'd also noticed a new waypoint in his field of view along with a distance-to-target indicator, both of which moved and updated in real time—much as his bioteknia eyes did. "Granther Company, we have our next objective. Your nav systems have been updated. This is it."

35

Amazingly, the street advance felt exactly like the simulations—the ruined stonework, vines, vegetation, smudged windows, and moss-covered buildings. It was almost uncanny how good the hard-light holo-projections had been. Magnus's gladias wouldn't feel surprised by a foreign environment, which was good. The downside, of course, was that they'd be too comfortable with it and forget that here, when they got shot, they were dead forever—no resetting the scene.

"Stay sharp," Magnus said. "Eyes peeled."

"Great mystics!" TO-96's voice erupted over comms. "They're peeling your eyes with sharp utensils? Of all the insane—"

"Ninety-Six, shut up!"

There was a brief pause. "Ah, I'm terribly sorry, sir. That was... my mistake."

"Yeah. It was. Now, don't interrupt like that again."

"As you wish, sir."

Magnus rolled his eyes, unsure how they were going to make it through the day. They were a nine-year-old wonder kid, two advanced but socially inept AI robots, and a barely trained company who were decked out in ultra-advanced tech that they'd never trained in. *What could go wrong?*

Magnus shook off the bad vibes. "Dutch and Abimbola, I want you entering that plaza from the south."

"Roger that, sir," Dutch said.

"Titus and Rohoar, you've got the east entry point."

"Shouldn't one of us take the other two points of entry?" someone asked.

Magnus looked at the speaker's title tag. It was Baker. He was new. "Negative. Too much friendly crossfire. Better to leave them an exit than risk getting our own killed—at least until we understand their position better."

"Hey, stick to the chain of command, Baker," Titus said. "Run those comments by me first, copy?"

"Copy. Sorry, sir. Sirs."

"Listen up," Magnus said, reining the conversation back in. "Platoon leaders, use your best judgment. Titus, don't be afraid to use those buildings as you did in training. Just remember—"

"To verify layouts and building junctions before committing."

"Good. Same for you, Rohoar. If you go high, look for

those turret emplacements. Call everything out, share the load, and cover down. Granther Company, move out."

THE NEXT SEVERAL minutes were tense. Magnus could feel himself trying to control his breathing. Even he was getting a bit nervous. He couldn't help feeling that the enemy had seen them land. Maybe they were tracking them at that very moment with advanced sensors, and all this was a trap. Maybe they had snipers trained on them, just having some laughs before squeezing the trigger.

Or… maybe the plan was going exactly as it should, and the gladias' suits were keeping the entire company hidden. Or maybe, given the hopeless scenario that Kane's unit found themselves in, they'd utterly given up hope of being discovered and saw no point in setting up—let alone defending—a perimeter.

Yeah, right. Magnus remembered the cardinal rule of what happened to plans when they met the enemy. Plus, Azelon had already detected a localized shield. They wouldn't use that unless they thought someone was watching.

Magnus advanced behind all four platoons, marveling at how well they moved—not to mention how ridiculously nonapparent they were. Azelon had truly outdone herself with all this new tech. If Kane's forces were watching, the Gladio Umbra sure were making it hard for them to spot anything.

For Magnus's part, he remained at the rear of Titus and Rohoar's columns, escorting Awen and Piper toward the enemy's suspected base camp. Awen held Piper's hand as the little girl looked around at all the ruins.

"Hey, Piper," Magnus asked over a restricted comms channel—Awen and the bots were the only other ones allowed in.

"Yes?"

"See anything new?"

"New?"

"Yeah, you know, like any change in how the bad guys are moving? Maybe something new they're fiddling with?"

"Hmm," she said. "Nah, they're still busy just going in and out of the tunnel."

"Let me know if that changes, okay? As soon as it does, I need you to tell me."

"No problem."

"And, Azie?"

"Yes, Magnus?"

"Is there a reason the Novia Minoosh felt their resources were in imminent danger but none of you can see exactly what the recon team is doing? I guess I'm not getting how your sensors in the city work."

"That is a valid question," Azelon replied. "The Novia's sensor network—while vast—is limited to certain sections of the city. Worse still, it seems that the enemy's shield is somehow disrupting the Novia's sensor array."

"Then, going back to my original question, how do they know Kane's team is knocking on an important door?"

"I'm afraid that is proprietary information, sir."

"No, no, it's definitely not proprietary. We're down here risking our asses for you and the rest of the galaxy. That's need-to-know intel, and right now, I need to know."

"Very well. The approximate location of the tunnel that Piper has identified happens to be directly over one of the main power centers for the entire city."

"Power centers?"

"That's correct. While the main access doors to the plant are highly secure—arguably impenetrable for the technology found in your protoverse—the recon team has discovered an alternate way into the center which bypasses the main entrance."

"And you guys didn't plan for something like this?"

"In short, no."

"Some super-intelligent alien species you are."

"I beg your pardon, sir?"

"Never mind. Listen, how would they have gotten plans for the city? I mean, how would they have even known where to dig?"

"I think I know," Awen said.

Magnus looked over at her. "And?"

"The temple library."

"That is one hypothesis, yes," Azelon replied.

"Okay," Magnus said, waving Awen off. "You can tell me

all about that later. Right now, I just want to make sure I'm putting all these pieces together."

"Contact!" someone whispered forcefully over the companywide channel. Magnus closed the restricted channel and joined in.

"What d'you see, Robi?" Titus asked.

"He's taking a piss, sir," Robi replied. "Damn!"

"A what?"

"Yeah. I'm up here behind some columns bordering the square, and this guy in black armor, three stripes painted on the shoulder, just steps out from behind their blue shield wall and starts relieving himself on a boulder—right in front of me. Damn!"

"Splick," Titus said. "You getting this, Magnus?"

Suddenly, a video window appeared in Magnus's field of view. He wasn't sure which surprised him more—the fact that the comms system had live video support that he hadn't known about or the view of a Paragon recon trooper taking a leak, up close and personal.

"Sure am," Magnus replied. Seeing the trooper and the shield wall that close to Robi gave Magnus an idea—a splicking crazy idea.

He started running and sent a text order out to the entire company: *Rush enemy location on my command.* Then he followed it with a second message: *Watch for auto-turret fire when the shield comes down.*

"What do you want me to do, sir?" Robi asked.

"How close is that shield wall to you?" Magnus asked, examining the blue dome.

"Can't be more than a meter, sir."

"Then I want you to stuff him, Robi."

There was a brief pause. "Stuff him, sir?"

Magnus couldn't believe he was saying this, but it was a tactical opportunity they couldn't afford to pass up. Charging the shield head-on without any real glimpse of what lay behind it would make for a long day. And he hated long days. People died on long days.

"You're giving him a third ball, Robi," Magnus said between breaths. "VOD, electromagnetic pulse, in the shorts."

"Mystics, are you serious?"

"Robi, this is a direct order."

"Splick, he's finishing up."

"Stuff him!"

"Dammit!"

Robi shoved the trooper back behind the protective wall moments before the EMP in the man's pants detonated. He survived, of course—EMPs were not fatal. Should the trooper last the day, however, it was doubtful he'd ever procreate.

The shield wall flickered. And then, just like that, it was gone.

Did we really just get the jump on an entire recon unit? They'd gone from atmospheric entry to securing a shuttle to advancement all the way to a hostile base of operations, and all completely undetected. *That's just impossible*, Magnus thought. But it was true nonetheless, and he'd take the point.

Standing like a bunch of guys with their pants down, the recon team looked around in abject confusion as they spotted Piss Boy rolling on the ground, trying to pull an expended VOD from his pants. They also looked for an approaching enemy.

But you ain't gonna see a thing.

The first shots came from Dutch's platoon as she called out enemy targets. There were too many to count. Magnus slid to a halt on the square's east entrance just in time to see all eight of Alpha Platoon's NOV1s open up on the unsuspecting troopers. The weapons belched torrents of high-pitched bright-blue light into the enemy encampment. One trooper's body was blown apart so forcefully that his limbs twirled away as if a giant animal had shaken him to shreds.

A second trooper managed to raise a personal wrist-mounted shield before a stream of high-joule energy slammed into him. The blast's intensity was so powerful that the trooper folded and flew backward, colliding with two others. Magnus could hear bones crack from his position on the east side.

A third trooper got several rounds off, aiming randomly in the direction of fire. Magnus couldn't remember ever seeing a recon team member miss so horribly. Apparently, the gladias' suits were doing their job. Unfortunately for the trooper, his last rounds downrange would all be misses. NOV1 fire tore through him, transforming his body into a puff of mist and meat.

"I—like—these—blasters!" Dutch yelled over comms.

She always did have a thing for firearms, Magnus thought as he raised his own weapon to join the action. But no sooner had his sights acquired a target than the blue dome reappeared over the enemy's camp.

"Splick," Magnus yelled. "Take cover!"

He knew what was coming next. He suspected auto turrets would be activated from inside the shielded area— maybe even from locations around the square if they'd brought enough with them. What Magnus hadn't anticipated, however, were auto turrets placed along the streets leading up to the encampment.

As soon as he gave the order to take cover, blaster rounds filled the street behind him. The rounds indiscriminately criss-crossed between buildings from somewhere above. Magnus lunged for the protection of a ruined doorway and hid in the shadow of a massive column. His eyes instinctively looked at the company roster and team map, waiting for casualty indicators to ping him. Instead, all he noticed were elevated heart rates, elevated blood pressures, and a frenzy of neural activity.

"Platoons, report in!" Magnus ordered as blaster fire peppered the street in front of the column. All the leads confirmed their positions and statuses. Amazingly, they were good to go. "Anyone have eyes on those turrets?"

"I can see one," Silk reported.

"Me too," Saasarr replied. "Just under an overhang."

"If you can get a shot off, take it." Magnus knew that the enemy was regrouping behind their shield, thanks in no small part to a backup generator that they'd kept offline—precisely in the event of a naturally occurring or hostile EMP blast. System redundancy was standard Repub procedure. Magnus just hadn't expected them to have a *second damn generator*.

"Got one," Rix said.

"Me too," Silk added.

Three more gladias reported taking out turrets, but still, the blaster rounds kept coming. *Damn*. This recon team was better supplied than he'd imagined. Even though the machines couldn't see the gladias' heat signatures—a testament to Azelon's suit design—they were still in blanket mode. The turrets laid down low-energy covering fire, which meant they could keep up their current rate of fire for several minutes while the recon team got their splick together behind the shield wall.

And they don't need minutes. They need about another thirty seconds before that wall comes down and they start advancing toward us.

Magnus had to get those turrets offline. "Awen," he said over comms.

"I'm here."

"Any chance you and Piper can do something about these auto turrets?"

"We're checking now."

By *checking*, Magnus hadn't expected the two women to step into view at the end of the street some one hundred meters away.

"What the hell?" Magnus's heart lodged itself somewhere in his esophagus. "Get back behind cover," he roared.

But Awen and Piper stood as calmly as if they'd been casual observers of a training exercise back on Ni No. The gladia mystics balled their hands into fists and closed their eyes as if concentrating, deep in thought. Then, at the same time, their eyes opened, and their suits glowed an even brighter yellow.

Up and down Magnus's street, the auto-turret fire was interrupted by mechanical whines and metallic shrieks. Gearboxes ground to a halt, groaning against a far superior force. Blaster barrels curved, causing unexpended bolts to back up into firing chambers. Chain reactions of unreleased energy exploded out of turret housings, ripping against seams and blowing off panels.

One by one, the auto turrets popped like giant firecrackers, billowing out sparks and smoke as Magnus looked down the street. He counted no fewer than fourteen emplacements—far exceeding his estimations. He imagined the other streets leading up to the enemy's base camp having just as many.

"You seeing this on your street?" Magnus asked Titus and Rohoar.

"If by *this* you mean spontaneously combusting turrets," Rohoar answered, "then yes. We are seeing lots of *this*."

"I can confirm that too," Titus added.

Within another few minutes, Magnus's street was clear. He looked across at Awen and Piper as burning debris fluttered down from above. Awen's helmet suddenly looked directly at Magnus even though he knew she couldn't see him. *Or can she?*

The woman gave him a small wave. "How's that?"

"That's..." Magnus's brain kicked back into high gear. "Good job, mystics. Platoons, direct all fire on that shield. Rohoar, I want you hanging back until I say."

"Affirmative, sir."

"You want us to hit it like we're taking down an armored tank?" Dutch asked, referring to Magnus's earlier stipulation about using full-auto mode.

"Like taking down a splicing armored tank, yes." Magnus selected Full-Auto on his own NOV1 and stepped into the street. "Let's introduce ourselves, gladias."

36

Awen watched in amazement from half a block away as the Gladio Umbra converged on the enemy position. Their new assault blasters produced a piercing scream that even her helmet had a hard time filtering out. The sound reminded her of Sqwillian forest banshees during mating season. But the blistering torrent of blaster fire was unlike anything she'd witnessed.

Steady streams of intense blue light poured from the weapon receivers, appearing in midair and racing toward the shield wall. The two energies collided in a dazzling display of color and sound, emitting red, yellow, and blue sparks, while the ultra-rapid strikes sounded like rivets popping from the trusses of a collapsing bridge.

On and on the assault went until Awen was sure either the weapons would fail or the shield would. Still, however, the

NOV1s rained hellfire on the fortification. Awen saw several streams cease while, in her second sight, she watched gladias pop out expended energy magazines and reload fresh ones. A few of the more seasoned fighters were able to swap out one energy mag while firing from the other—a feat made possible only because of the NOV1's dual-mag feeding system. Awen wasn't into guns, but that seemed pretty cool even to her.

When the shield finally came down, the enemy forces were nowhere to be seen—by the naked eye, at least. She felt herself starting to panic. Awen was sure Magnus's sensor suite was able to make out the same thing she was seeing, but just in case, she said, "They're in the building... and... behind the, the—"

"Behind the barriers," Piper interjected over comms. "And in the tunnel, and some are running down side streets and into some buildings!"

"Copy," Magnus yelled as his NOV1 started firing on a concrete barrier not ten meters away. The force of Magnus's semiautomatic fire blew chunks out of the berm and began sliding it along the ground. Finally, as it gave up under his assault, the barrier fell backward, pinning the trooper beneath it. Magnus moved forward and finished the combatant with a single round to the helmet. Awen watched in her second sight as the trooper's head ceased to exist.

"Piper, don't watch, okay?"

"Watch? That was *awesome!*"

"Piper! That was *not* awesome!"

"Yes, it was!"

"No, it wasn't," Awen insisted, stressing each word.

Piper glanced up at her, seeming to register Awen's tone. "*Not* awesome. Okay, shydoh."

"Good."

Apparently, the little girl had more of a stomach for war than Awen did. Somehow, that just seemed wrong. To Awen, people dying were people dying, and that should never be celebrated—certainly not by children. But if killing one life to save more lives was the only option, Awen could at least tolerate it. For the moment. That was the only real reason she was able to be a part of this entire mission. Bad people had to be stopped from doing bad things to good people. It was as simple as that.

When another two troopers had been cleared from the encampment, someone yelled over comms. "I'm hit!"

Awen checked her visor's overlay to confirm the name. It was Reimer in Bravo Platoon.

Magnus took a knee and looked toward Reimer's position. The former Marauder had stumbled backward and was taking cover within a doorway.

"You're fine," Magnus said. "Check your shield's percentage."

"Eighty—I'm at eighty percent," Reimer replied, his voice less shaky than before.

"Right. That was just…" Magnus paused to send a stream of blaster fire into a second-story window. "That was just the kinetic energy dissipating around your suit. Keep your blaster downrange, and bring the pain."

"Copy that, sir."

No sooner had Reimer finished speaking than someone else mentioned being hit. It was Dozer. "I'm at fifty percent," he said. Awen could see him clutching his chest. Apparently the wind had been knocked out of him.

"Sixty percent!" yelled another voice—this time, it was Jaffrey.

Why are the gladias taking so many hits all of a sudden?

"They're tracking the blaster rounds," Piper replied over their dedicated channel.

Awen ignored the fact that Piper was openly reading her thoughts. "You sure?"

"Yup. I can see the recon guys looking down the blue streams. Magnus's super suits are really neat, but the NOV1s are still giving them away."

"Magnus," Awen said over a direct link.

"Go ahead!"

"Piper says they're tracking you by your blaster rounds."

"Copy that."

"You think that helped him?" Piper asked.

Awen shrugged. "Don't know. But let's hope so."

The fighting continued as Magnus and Alpha, Bravo, and Charlie Platoons forced the enemy troops out of the plaza and into hiding. At least three more troopers met their ends in the encampment. One combatant's torso exploded from a single round to the gut. His shoulders and head dropped onto his collapsed legs. Awen closed her eyes and turned her second sight elsewhere. This was horrible.

"Find cover, gladias! They're tracking our blaster fire, and now they're holed up in those buildings." Magnus sat against a large container in the middle of the enemy encampment. Several members of Alpha Platoon rested near him, catching their breath. "Rohoar?"

"I am ready, scrumruk graulap," the Jujari replied.

"I want you taking your platoon in through the side door of that center building. I've marked the entrance on your map. You should see a new waypoint vector too."

"Affirmative."

"Good. Wait for my command. And, Titus?"

"Go ahead."

"I want you entering the second building here."

Awen watched in her map as Magnus placed a second entry icon on another building's perimeter adjacent to the first.

"You clear those two buildings, we have ourselves the beginnings of a victory."

"Copy that, sir," Titus said.

"Consider it done," Rohoar added.

No sooner had Magnus finished speaking than a massive explosion erupted five meters in front of his crate. The force of the blast sent the gladias in the encampment flying. Every window in the plaza must have shattered at once, filling Awen's head with a deafening cacophony that made her stumble.

"Magnus!" Awen watched his suit's telecolos system blink out. He slammed into a nearby building and fell to the ground in a heap. "Stay here," Awen ordered Piper. She forced the girl to stand just inside what once might have been an office building's entrance. Then Awen took off, covering the remaining half block in only a few seconds.

Blaster rounds crisscrossed the open square, which was now covered in thick black smoke. Awen used her second sight to find Magnus's body just to her left. He was struggling to get up but moved very slowly.

"Magnus!" she yelled, kneeling down to examine him in the smoke. "Are you okay?"

"Damn remote bomb," Magnus said, shaking his helmet. "Yeah, I think I'm fine."

The glossy-white surface of his armored suit was stained black and had several pockmarks in the plating. She assumed that whatever personal shield the suit had left was now depleted. Its chameleon mode seemed out of commission too.

Magnus swore and let out a pained groan.

"What?" Awen asked, tensing. "What is it?"

"Damn suit just stuck me!"

"What?"

"It stuck me! But…" His voice seemed to relax a little. "It feels… good."

Awen guessed it was the medical nano-bots doing their thing. "Come on. Let's get you to cover." She moved to the top of his head and placed her hands under his shoulders. Magnus was heavier than she'd expected, but she was able to pull him around a corner and out of harm's way. Then she squatted next to him and placed a hand on his chest. "How are you doing, Adonis?"

He coughed over comms and started to sit up. "Yeah, yeah. I'm good. Feeling better. I shoulda seen that coming."

"It certainly would have been nice to avoid, yes."

"What about the others…?"

Awen could tell Magnus was reviewing the company roster. She did the same. "Looks good. Couple bumps and bruises but no casualties. You all just survived a bomb blast. These suits are *incredible*."

"Remind me to kiss Azelon on the mouth when we get back to the *Spire*," Magnus said, struggling to get up.

"I feel no need to experience or reciprocate human osculation," Azelon said over comms.

Awen laughed as she helped Magnus stand up.

"Don't care, Azie. You're getting a smooch." Magnus groaned as he stretched his back and rotated a shoulder.

Awen was so relieved that Magnus was okay. But there was something beyond relief too. She remembered how So-Elku had tried to take Piper, how he tried to hurt Magnus, and how Kane had tried to hurt Sootriman. She felt indignation. And raw anger.

"You sure you're all right?" Awen asked.

"I am. Now, where's my blaster?"

"Sir," TO-96 said, "there should be a directional vector marking the location of your—"

"Got it, 'Six. Thanks." Magnus stole a look down the street then ran several meters toward a pile of burning rubble.

He slid to one knee and retrieved his NOV1, which—despite several burn marks and the absence of its color-changing skin—seemed operational as far as Awen could tell.

"It's good?" she asked.

Magnus tilted the weapon left and right as he ran back to cover. "Yup. I think she'll still shoot straight."

"Well, what are you waiting around here for?" Awen asked. "Get back out there and *kill* something!" She swatted him on the butt.

Magnus took a step forward and turned to look at her. "Yes, ma'am."

AFTER LOOKING to make sure that her mother was okay from the bomb blast, Piper used her second sight to track Rohoar down one of the side streets. It led right to the building that Magnus had indicated for the giant doggy. He stood just outside an entryway that led to a stairwell, presumably waiting for Magnus to give the order to enter, like he'd said he was going to.

Magnus left Awen after she touched his butt—*gross*—and moved back into the smoking plaza. Most of the enemy's equipment had been blown to itty bits, and there was a big crater in the middle of the open space.

"Rohoar, Titus, you both still good to go?" Magnus asked. As soon as the two platoon leaders responded positively, he gave the order to move in.

Piper watched as Rohoar stormed up the stairwell, taking five or six steps at a time on all fours. The rest of his warriors followed closely behind. When they got to the first landing, half of Rohoar's platoon broke off to search the floor while the other half doubled back and bounded up a second flight of stairs.

From within her second sight, Piper could see five Paragon troopers taking cover beside windows that looked down into the square.

"Do you smell them?" Piper said over comms to Rohoar.

The Jujari seemed to hesitate. "Piper?" he whispered.

"It's me, yup. I just wanted to make sure you sniffed them."

"Yes, I smell them."

"And there are five more on the floor above you too."

"Thank you, Piper."

"You're welcome. Get 'em good, okay?"

"I shall endeavor to."

"'Kay, bye." Then she added in a whisper, "I'm watching in case you need my help."

Rohoar didn't respond to that, but she figured he was busy thinking about how to eat the bad guys. Plus, she knew he would be appreciative of the help if she gave it.

Rohoar and his first four Jujari stalked toward the rooms that each trooper was holed up in. At the same time, the other four Jujari did likewise on the floor above. Piper could feel herself tense up, anticipating the clash. The enemy troopers were so busy firing down into the plaza that they forgot to check their... *What did Magnus call it again?* Piper got stuck on the word. *Their six,* she suddenly remembered.

Rohoar seemed like he was about to strike when an alarm suddenly sounded. The Jujari in the rear—a doggy named Lugt, Piper thought—looked down to see he'd triggered some sort of warning device.

Only it wasn't a warning device.

Piper screamed as the grenade detonated.

Awen was beside her in an instant. "Piper! What's the matter? Are you hurt?"

"Poor Lugt!" she cried. "Poor, poor, Lugt..."

"Piper, talk to me! What's Lugt?"

Piper could hardly feel Awen patting her body down, checking for injuries. She was thinking about the Jujari who'd just died. The poor doggy's legs had been—

Piper noticed the troopers in the rooms spin around and charge into the hallway. But Rohoar was there. Saladin too. Arjae seemed like he'd been hurt by the blast but was still on his feet.

The trooper in the room ahead of Rohoar turned into the hallway and fired his blaster. Several shots hit Rohoar but were absorbed by his personal shield. The man stared in disbelief as the Jujari just kept coming.

"Good doggy!" Piper screamed. "Get him!"

The next instant, Rohoar clamped down on the man's raised forearm, splitting the bone in two places. The trooper cried out, but Piper guessed only those on his comms system could hear him. She could hear him, too, of course, but that was different.

The man fired a few more rounds into Rohoar's midsection, but the Jujari batted the weapon away. Rohoar swiped at the trooper's chest, neck, and groin. Within a matter of seconds, the man lay still on the floor, bleeding out.

Rohoar looked up at a second trooper, who came from farther down the hall. The man was a good shooter, taking smooth steps and aiming directly at the center of Rohoar's chest. But it didn't matter. Piper smiled as Rohoar reached down, grabbed the first trooper's body, and flung it at the advancing man. The force knocked him over, and the two bodies tumbled down the corridor. By the time the second trooper reached for his blaster, Rohoar was on him, slitting his throat and kicking his weapon away.

Behind Rohoar, Saladin had clasped a third trooper's helmet in her jaws. Still, the trooper fired his blaster, bolts ricocheting off windows and walls. Saladin continued biting down until her teeth penetrated weak points in the helmet. The man screamed. His punctured skull sent him into convulsions until, finally, his arms and body went limp and he fell to the floor.

Arjae took on a fourth bad guy, pushing him back into the room he tried to emerge from. The two warriors struggled. Piper was surprised at just how big this trooper was. She'd never met a person as strong as a Jujari, except maybe Abimbola and sometimes Magnus. This trooper was like that—big and strong. Arjae had managed to knock the man's weapon from his one hand, but the trooper held a knife in his other. The two struggled to hold each other's wrists, exchanging swipes with claws and blade and blocking with their arms.

As the pair neared the open window, Piper thought to warn Arjae of the danger. But just as she was about to speak, a single blaster round struck the trooper in the back from the outside. It was Magnus who'd fired it. The round went through the trooper's body and slammed into Arjae's shield, causing the pair to fly backwards and land on the floor. Piper watched as Arjae's shield flickered and died out. The Jujari raised his head and shoved the trooper's body off him in disgust.

It was the fifth and final Paragon trooper on this floor that worried Piper the most. He emerged from the opposite end of the hall *behind* Lugt's dead body. For some reason, Rohoar hadn't noticed him, and neither had Saladin.

Piper could see the trooper smile as he brought his weapon up and aimed at Saladin. Somehow, Piper knew the rounds would go straight through the female Jujari and strike Rohoar too. She wanted to blurt something out over comms, but there was no time. This was happening much too fast. She had to do something herself.

Several thoughts went through Piper's mind at that instant. They ranged from creative things, like pushing down a wall or opening up the floor, to more direct things like…

Like crushing the man's heart.

Perhaps it was fear for Rohoar. Or maybe it was just nervous excitement about everything she'd witnessed. Piper didn't know. But in that instant, she envisioned the trooper's heart being squeezed like a tomato under a Boresian taursar's foot.

The trooper never fired a shot. Instead, he clutched his chest and gave a soundless scream. He was dead before he hit the floor.

"Piper!" Awen screamed. She ripped her own helmet off and grabbed the girl. "What have you done?"

Awen pushed the girl farther behind cover and pulled the small helmet off her head. Awen knew the act would help snap the girl out of the Unity.

Piper squinted against the bright light and started coughing as smoke filled her nose.

"Piper!" Awen yelled again. "Did you just kill a man?" Awen didn't need to ask, of course. She'd seen the last few seconds of the battle in the building for herself. To her dismay, Piper had just ended another human life. *On purpose. She just killed a man—at nine years old.*

Awen was so mad she could... "Piper! Answer me!"

"Yes, yes," Piper said, coughing into her arm. "Of course I killed him!"

"But—no! You're not allowed to do that!"

"Why?" Piper coughed more. "We're—we're fighting, aren't we?"

"But that's not our job here. That's not *your* job."

"But he was going to kill Saladin and Rohoar, shydoh! I thought you said—" Piper coughed more. "I thought you said we have to protect everyone."

"I did, but—"

"So I was protecting them!" Tears formed in the little girl's eyes, and her lower lip started to quiver. "I was just protecting them…" Piper repeated, hands trembling.

"Oh, Piper." Awen knelt and embraced the girl.

Piper rested her head on Awen's shoulder and began to sob. "I was just trying to protect them."

"I know." Awen stroked the girl's hair. "I know you were. And I'm sorry too. I…"

You're what, Awen? Being too protective? Not letting her choose for herself? Not letting her be the answer that the universe is providing?

But the girl was still too young. Children shouldn't be doing this. Yet… Piper *was* doing this. *Could* do this. In the deepest part of her heart, Awen knew Piper could probably save everyone's lives if given a chance.

But that would mean so much death.

Only the alternative wasn't any better.

Awen held Piper as the girl cried. As much as Awen had looked forward to a day like this, when the girl's gift would be let loose for the galaxy to see, she'd also dreaded it, knowing it would bring… well, precisely what it had brought. Pain.

There was no *right* way to war. The best thing was just to keep going until they got through the other side. And that was what Awen decided to do. *Keep going. Just get through.*

"You saved them," Awen said finally. "You saved them well."

Piper pulled her head back, smearing snot and carbon across her cheek. "You really think so?"

"Yes, doma." Awen brushed some of Piper's stray blond hairs behind her ear as blaster fire echoed off the buildings around the block. "I do. And I know Rohoar and Saladin will thank you when today is through. Good job."

"Thank you, shydoh." Piper leaned back in and squeezed Awen's neck hard. "I just don't want them to die."

"Neither do I, doma. Neither do I."

37

Enemy fire subsided after Rohoar and Titus had finished clearing their respective buildings. Thus far, only Charlie and Delta Platoons had taken casualties, if Magnus's roster was accurate.

"Report!" Magnus said from his position across the plaza.

"Building One secure," Rohoar replied. "Two injured, and I have lost Lugt."

Magnus noticed that the Jujari emphasized the personal pronoun.

"Building Two secure," Titus added. "But Baker is down. And we have three injured."

Magnus wasn't sure if he should be happy or disgusted with the day's results. On the one hand, his unit had just survived their first brush with the enemy—and it was a damn fine enemy at that. But had it not been for their superior firepower and stealth technology, this battle would have gone a lot differently.

"I want the wounded and the dead out of there ASAP," Magnus ordered. "Fall back to the meeting point."

Both platoon leaders acknowledged the order.

"Doc Campbell, Haney—you all green?"

"Affirmative, sir," the two medics replied.

"Give Titus and Rohoar a hand."

The medics acknowledged the order.

"But what about you, sir?" Rohoar asked.

"I still have plenty of gladias, and the enemy has lost their fight. We've got them holed up in the tunnel. They're not going anywhere. The best thing you can do is prep for exfil. Now, get to work."

"Understood, sir," replied Rohoar.

Magnus figured there were only one or two recon troopers left in the tunnel. Sure, it had taken four platoons of gladias to do it—equipped with superior weaponry and armor—but a win was a win, and losers didn't argue about semantics. *They're too dead for that.*

"Easy there," Magnus said to Dutch and Abimbola's platoons as the remainder of the company neared the opening in the ground. A single ladder led down into the darkness. Everyone was itching for a look into the chute. "I don't need anyone getting their heads popped off, copy?"

Gateway to War

"Yes, sir," everyone replied.

Magnus noticed that Rix and Silk were closest. "Rix, pop an EMP. Silk, pop smoke. Let's fumigate these critters."

The two gladias nodded. They pulled VODs from their suits, dialed in the desired settings, and tossed the devices down the tunnel.

"Fire in the hole," Rix said as he stepped away from the chute. Silk did the same, and the platoons waited for the detonations.

The EMP went off first. A subsonic tremor moved through the ground and emanated straight out of the shaft. Magnus suspected all his units would be fine since the blast was contained by the ground. He was right.

Next came the smoke. Silk's VOD popped. Within ten seconds, white wisps of smoke emerged from the tunnel. With the troopers' life-support systems offline, their rebreathers would be little use. Any survivors would be forced to remove their helmets and seek fresh air.

Any second now...

"Don't shoot," came a gruff voice from near the cave's mouth. The man coughed, tossing his helmet out ahead of him. Magnus knew it was a test to see how trigger-happy the capturing force was—if it was more *kill* than *capture*, the helmet would get riddled with blaster rounds before it hit the ground. But Magnus held a hand up, wanting his gladias to keep their weapons checked.

A hand appeared on the ladder's top rung, then another.

"Slowly," Silk said, pointing her NOV1 at the trooper's head. "No sudden moves, buckethead."

A trooper climbed from the pit, clad in all-black Mark VII armor with three white lines painted across his chest and shoulders. The man looked to be in his early thirties. He'd also seen a lot of action—Magnus could tell that simply by the way he moved on all fours, because it wasn't a *crawl*. It was a *stalk*.

"That's far enough. What's your name, Marine?" Magnus squatted to look the man in the face. But the trooper refused to look up. Magnus withdrew his V and placed it under the man's chin. "Hey, I'm talking to you. What's your name?"

The man moved his chin away from the pistol's barrel, avoiding Magnus's attempts to get a good look at him.

"Hey!" Rix yelled, suddenly pressing his NOV1 into the trooper's side. "He's talking to you, bucket brain!"

"I've got this." Magnus lowered his V, removed his helmet, and placed it under his arm. "Listen, I don't know who you are or what you think you're doing here, but—"

"You don't know who I am?" The man let out a low snort. "Now, that's rich."

"Listen, pal. I'm gonna give you—"

"Give me what? The same amount of time you gave me to walk away from those whores on Caledonia?"

The trooper looked up, and Magnus froze.

"Hi there, Adonis. Remember me?" The trooper started to laugh, a trickle of blood spilling from the corner of his mouth—from some old chipped teeth. "That's right. It's been a while, hasn't it?"

"Get him up and outta here," Magnus ordered.

"What's the matter, Adonis? You don't want to catch up, for old time's sake?"

"Shut up, buckethead," Silk said, putting her boot into the man's side.

"Whoa! We've got a feisty one here," the trooper seethed.

"No, Silk," Magnus said, waving her off. "Not you."

"Wah-ho-ho! Adonis Olin Magnus, still the defender of the weak and the betrayer of his brother."

"That's enough," Magnus ordered. "Rix, Dozer, get this man secured."

"And just like that, you're done with me, Magnus?" The trooper coughed up phlegm and blood that landed on Magnus's white armor. "I guess things haven't changed a bit, have they?"

Rix and Dozer grabbed the trooper around the biceps and hauled him to his feet. The trooper winced. "Do they know, Magnus?"

Magnus was already turning away to address the rest of his gladias.

"'Cause I know. I know it *all*. And you *know* I do."

Magnus could feel his blood pressure rising and his face beginning to burn.

"That's right, *betrayer*. I know everything you—"

Magnus spun on his heel and cracked his fist against the

man's face. Blood flew into the dirt as Rix and Dozer struggled to hold the man upright.

"I have nothing to say to you, Nos Kil. You died on Caledonia, and that's where you should have stayed." Magnus looked at Rix and Dozer. "Get him out of here."

As the two men dragged Nos Kil away, Magnus could hear him saying, "Wait until they find out… just wait until they all find out…"

"Sir?" Dutch said, tapping the side of her helmet. "It's for you."

Magnus reached down to retrieve his helmet and placed it over his head. Right away, he saw an urgent incoming transmission request on a private channel from TO-96. Magnus accepted the invitation, and a channel opened, this time with video.

"Sir, it is good to see you *in one piece*, as it were," TO-96 said. Azelon stood over his right shoulder, and the *Spire*'s main window filled the background.

"What's up, 'Six? Got a lot going on down here, so—"

"Sir, I am sorry to cut you off, but we have a developing issue of concern here."

"Go on."

"There seem to be several ships entering the system."

"Several ships? That's *way* more than a developing issue of concern."

"I agree, sir."

"What *kind* of ships, Ninety-Six?"

"They appear to be Galactic Republic vessels from third fleet. One battle cruiser and a squadron of FAF-28 Talons, sir."

"A squadron of—are you kidding me right now, Ninety-Six?"

"As you are well aware, my attempts to *kid* are lackluster at best." Suddenly, a sensor image appeared in Magnus's visor, displaying a massive battle cruiser and fourteen smaller starfighters. "Their current trajectories indicate that they are headed directly for Ithnor Ithelia. And, sir, while I cannot confirm this hypothesis, the data would seem to indicate that these ships are connected to Admiral Kane. Given the time dilation, I suspect that they followed Abimbola and Rohoar from Oorajee."

"Ya think?"

"Yes, sir, I very much—"

"How much time we got?"

"Approximately one hour before the ships reach geosynchronous orbit and another ten minutes before the fighters could be at our location."

Son of a bitch. Magnus threw a hand in the air and moved it in several quick circles. "Gladio Umbra, it's time to roll out. We've got a ship to catch."

MAGNUS and ARWEN will return in VOID HORIZON, coming Oct. 2019.

For more updates on this series, be sure to join the Facebook Group, "J.N. Chaney's Renegade Readers."

LIST OF MAIN CHARACTERS

List of Main Characters

Abimbola: Miblimbian. Age: 41. Planet of origin: Limbia Centrella. Giant warlord of the Dregs, outskirts of Oosafar, Oorajee. Bright-blue eyes, black skin, tribal tattoos, scar running from neck to temple. Wears a bandolier of frag grenades across his chest and an old bowie knife strapped to his thigh. Assigned as commander of Bravo Platoon, Granther Company.

Adonis Olin Magnus: Human. Age: 34. Planet of origin: Capriana Prime. Lieutenant, Charlie Platoon, 79th Reconnaissance Battalion, "Midnight Hunters," Galactic Republic Space Marines. Baby face, short beard, green eyes. Preferred weapon: MAR30.

List of Main Characters

Allan "Mouth" Franklin: Human. Age 32. Planet of origin: Juna Major. Corporal, heavy-weapons operator, Charlie Platoon, 79th Reconnaissance Battalion, "Midnight Hunters," Galactic Republic Space Marines. One of the "Fearsome Four."

Aubrey Dutch: Human. Age: 25. Planet of origin: Deltaurus Three. Corporal, weapons specialist, Galactic Republic Space Marines. Small in stature, close-cut dark hair, intelligent brown eyes. Loves her firearms. Assigned as commander of Alpha Platoon, Granther Company.

Awen dau Lothlinium: Elonian. Age: 26. Planet of origin: Elonia. Order of the Luma, Special Emissary to the Jujari. Pointed ears, purple eyes. Wears red-and-black robes and has a Luma medallion around her neck. Won't back down from anyone.

Azelon: AI and robot. Age: unknown. Planet of origin: Ithnor Ithelia. Artificial intelligence of the Novia Minoosh ship *Azelon Spire*.

Cyril: Human. Age: 24. Planet of origin: Ki Nar Four. Marauder, code slicer, bomb technician. Leads Magnus' mine removal fire team. Twitchy; sounds like a Quinzellian miter squirrel if it could talk.

Darin Stone: Human. Age: 34. Planet of origin: Capriana

List of Main Characters

Prime. Senator in the Galactic Republic. Husband to Valerie Stone, father to Piper. Impossibly white smile, well-groomed blond hair, radiant-blue eyes. Luxuriantly tan.

David Seaman: Human. Age: 31. Planet of origin: Capriana Prime. Captain in the Republic Navy, commander of the *Black Labyrinth's* two Talon squadrons, Viper and Raptor, and the head of SFC—strategic fighter command.

Dozer: Human. Age: Unknown. Planet of origin: Verv Ko. Marauder, infantry. A veritable human earth-mover.

Gerald Bosworth III: Human. Age: 54. Planet of origin: Capriana Prime. Republic Ambassador, special envoy to the Jujari. Fat jowls, bushy monobrow. Massively obese and obscenely repugnant.

Hal Brighton: Human. Age: 41. Planet of origin: Capriana Prime. Newly appointed fleet admiral, First Fleet, the Paragon; former executive officer, Republic Navy.

Idris Ezo: Nimprith. Age: 30. Planet of origin: Caledonia. Bounty hunter, trader, suspected fence and smuggler. Captain of *Geronimo Nine*. Wears a long gray leather coat, white knit turtleneck, black pants, glossy black boots. Preferred sidearm: SUPRA 945 blaster pistol.

Josiah Wainright: Human. Age: 39. Planet of origin:

Capriana Prime. Captain, Alpha Platoon, 79th Reconnaissance Battalion, "Midnight Hunters," Galactic Republic Space Marines. A legend in his own time.

Michael "Flow" Deeks: Human. Age: 31. Planet of origin: Vega. Sergeant, sniper, Charlie Platoon, 79th Reconnaissance Battalion, "Midnight Hunters," Galactic Republic Space Marines. One of the "Fearsome Four."

Miguel "Cheeks" Chico: Human. Age 30. Planet of origin: Trida Minor. Corporal, breacher, Charlie Platoon, 79th Reconnaissance Battalion, "Midnight Hunters," Galactic Republic Space Marines. One of the "Fearsome Four."

Moldark (formerly Wendell Kane): Human. Age: 52. Planet of origin: Capriana Prime. Former fleet admiral of the Galactic Republic's Third Fleet; captain of the *Black Labyrinth*. Dark Lord of the Paragon, a rogue black-operations special Marine unit. Bald, with heavily scared skin. One eye pale pink, the other dark brown.

Mauricio "Ricio" Longo: Human. Age: 29. Planet of origin: Capriana Prime. Republic Navy, squadron commander of Viper Squadron, assigned to the *Black Labyrinth*.

Nubs: Human. Age: Unknown. Planet of origin: Verv Ko. Marauder, infantry. Has several missing fingers.

List of Main Characters

Piper Stone: Human. Age: 9. Planet of origin: Capriana Prime. Daughter of Senator Darin and Valerie Stone. Wispy blond hair, freckle-faced. Wears a puffy winter coat, tights, and oversized snow boots. Carries a holo-pad and her stuffed corgachirp, Talisman.

Rawmut: Tawnhack, Jujari. Age: Unknown. Planet of origin: Orrajee. Jujari Mwadim of Oosafar on Oorajee. Chief of the massive hyena-like warrior species.

"Rix" Galliogernomarix: Human. Age: Unknown. Planet of origin: Undoria. Leads Magnus' infantry fire team. Wanted in three systems, sleeve tattoos, a monster on the battlefield.

Robert Malcom Blackwell: Human. Age: 54. Planet of origin: Capriana Prime. Senator in the Galactic Republic. A stocky man with thick shoulders and well-groomed gray hair.

Rohoar: Tawnhack, Jujari. Age: Unknown. Planet of origin: Oorajee. Former Jujari Mwadim; former blood wolf for Mwadim Rawmut; formerly nicknamed "Chief" by Magnus. Assigned as commander of Delta Platoon, Granther Company.

Saasarr: Reptalon. Age: unknown. Planet of origin: Gangil. Lizard humanoid. Former general of Sootriman's Reptalon guard.

List of Main Characters

Shane Nolan: Human. Age: 25. Planet of origin: Sol Sella. Chief Warrant Officer, Republic Navy, pilot in command of light armored transport Sparrow 271. Auburn hair, pale skin.

Silk: Human. Age: 30. Planet of origin: Salmenka. Marauder, infantry. Slender, bald, tats covering her face and head.

Simone: Human. Age: 27. Planet of origin: Undoria. Marauder, sniper. Team leader for Magnus's sniper fire team. Smooth as ice.

So-Elku: Human. Age: 51. Planet of origin: Worru. Luma Master, Order of the Luma. Baldpate, thin beard, dark penetrating eyes. Wears green-and-black robes.

Sootriman: Caledonian. Age: 33. Planet of origin: Caledonia. Warlord of Ki Nar Four, "Tamer of the Four Tempests," alleged ex-wife of Idris Ezo. Tall, with dark almond eyes, tanned olive skin, dark-brown hair.

Titus: Human. Age: 34. Planet of origin: unknown. Marauder, rescued by Magnus. Known for being cool under pressure and a good leader. Assigned as commander of Charlie Platoon, Granther Company.

TO-96: Robot; navigation class, heavily modified. Manufacturer: Advanced Galactic Solutions (AGS), Capriana Prime.

List of Main Characters

Suspected modifier: Idris Ezo. Round head and oversized eyes, transparent blaster visor, matte dark-gray armor plating, and exposed metallic articulated joints. Forearm micro-rocket pod, forearm XM31 Type-R blaster, dual shoulder-mounted gauss cannons.

Tony Haney: Human. Age: 24. Planet of origin: Fitfi Isole. Private First Class, medic, Galactic Republic Space Marines.

Valerie Stone: Human. Age: 31. Planet of origin: Worru. Wife of Senator Darin Stone, mother of Piper. Blond hair, light-blue eyes.

Victorio: Tawnhack, Jujari. Age: Unknown. Planet of origin: Oorajee. Son of Rohoar, blood wolf to the Jujari Mwadim. Life saved by Magnus.

Volf Nos Kil: Human. Age: 32. Planet of origin: Haradia. Captain, the Paragon. Personal guard and chief enforcer for Admiral Kane.

Waldorph Gilder: Human. Age: 23. Planet of origin: Haradia. Private First Class, flight engineer, Galactic Republic Space Marines. Barrel-chested. Can fix anything.

William Samuel Caldwell: Human. Age 60. Planet of origin: Capriana Prime. Colonel, 79th Reconnaissance Battalion, Galactic Republic Space Marines. Cigar eternally

List of Main Characters

wedged in the corner of his mouth. Gray hair cut high and tight.

Willowood: Human. Age: 61. Planet of origin: Kindarah. Luma Elder, Order of the Luma. Wears dozens of bangles and necklaces. Aging but radiant blue eyes and a mass of wiry gray hair. Friend and mentor to Awen.

GLADIO UMBRA, GRANTHER COMPANY

Alpha Platoon (Marines snd Navy)

- Dutch
- Sootriman
- Ezo
- Valerie
- Nolan
- Haney
- Gilder
- (Flow)
- (Cheeks)

Bravo Platoon (Original Marauders)

- Abimbola
- Berouth

List of Main Characters

- Silk
- Rix
- Cyril
- Nubs
- Dozer

Charlie Platoon (New Marauders)

- Titus
- Zoll
- Bliss
- Robillard
- Jaffrey
- Ricky
- Handley
- "Doc" Campbell
- Reimer
- Ford
- Andocs
- Bettger
- Baker

Delta Platoon (Jujari)

- Rohoar
- Saladin
- Arjae
- Dihazen

List of Main Characters

- Redmarrow
- Lugt
- Czyz
- Longchomps
- Grahban, son of Helnooth

Echo Platoon (Unassigned)

- Awen
- Piper
- Saasarr

JOIN THE RUINS TRIBE

Visit **ruinsofthegalaxy.com** today and join the tribe.

Once there, you can sign up for our reader group, join our Facebook community, and find us on Twitter and Instagram.

If you'd like to email us with comments or questions, we respond to all emails sent to ruinsofthegalaxy@gmail.com, and love to hear from our readers.

See you in the Ruins!

GET A FREE BOOK

J.N. Chaney posts updates, official art, previews, and other awesome stuff on his website. You can also follow him on **Instagram**, **Facebook**, and **Twitter**.

He also created a special **Facebook group** called "JN Chaney's Renegade Readers" specifically for readers to come together and share their lives and interests, discuss the series, and speak directly to me. Please check it out and join whenever you get the chance!

For updates about new releases, as well as exclusive promotions, visit his website, jnchaney.com and sign up for the VIP mailing list. Head there now to receive a free copy of *The Other Side of Nowhere*.

https://www.subscribepage.com/organic

Get a Free Book

Enjoying the series? Help others discover the Ruins of the Galaxy series by leaving a review on Amazon.

ABOUT THE AUTHORS

J. N. Chaney has a Master of Fine Arts in creative writing and fancies himself quite the Super Mario Bros. fan. When he isn't writing or gaming, you can find him online at **www.jn-chaney.com**.

He migrates often but was last seen in Avon Park, Florida. Any sightings should be reported, as they are rare.

Christopher Hopper's novels include the Resonant Son series, The Sky Riders, The Berinfell Prophecies, and the White Lion Chronicles. He blogs at **christopherhopper.com** and loves flying RC planes. He resides in the 1000 islands of northern New York with his musical wife and four ridiculously good-looking clones.